Forsaken

Book Five of The Gwen St. James Affair

Nicole McKeon

Tower Room Publishing

Content Notice

MAY CONTAIN MILD SPOILERS

This book was written for adults and contains mature themes and content that may not be suitable for every reader, including but not limited to the following:

- Violence including gun violence

- Death and death of a loved one

- Grief

- Dismemberment

- Gun-related injuries

- Explicit sexual content

- Strong language

- Post traumatic stress

- Family-related trauma

- Fire-related destruction

I've dedicated books to my beloved husband, my precious kids, my parents, my brother and sister, my teachers, friends, and even my readers.

But this one...this one's for me.

Book Five of The Gwen St. James Affair

FORSAKEN

Magic. Mystery. Malice.

NICOLE MCKEON

TOWER ROOM
publishing

1
Welcome to New London

LIA

Lady Ophelia hated New London. The great chimneys belched multi-colored smoke into a sky the color of tobacco spit. Rust-stained buildings blurred past the windows of the speeding auto in a dirty smear, and the constant stink of rot and refuse scratched the back of her throat with every breath.

After spending the last twelve years living inside a sentient oak tree, New London felt like a dead alien planet. Instead of moss carpets, wildflowers, and spreading branches, a stone knife of pavement severed the earth from the sky, choking out anything that dared grow in this wasteland.

Lia *hated* New London, and the Guild District was the worst.

How could such beautiful, useful works of art and artifice come from such an austere place?

She pressed a handkerchief over her nose and glared at the offending buildings as she and Tony motored down the avenue in Gwen's auto. "How does anyone breathe here?"

"Badly," Tony said and stomped on the gas.

The engine growled, and the auto lunged forward, racing down the tightly packed street too fast for such poor visibility. Tony's worry for Gwen was making him reckless. Lia was worried, too. The gnawing fear hadn't left her even after they knew Gwen would survive the bullet wound. But *Lia* wasn't driving thousands of pounds of speeding metal.

Tony was, and he needed a distraction.

"Will Delilah know what the symbol means?" Lia asked above the clamor of the engine. Her gaze strayed toward his pocket, where the torn piece of embroidered jacket waited to be examined.

Tony replied through his teeth while whipping the auto around a blind corner. "If she doesn't, there's no one else to ask. We'll have no clue who the bastard was working for or why he shot Gwen."

"Are you certain he was working for someone? Isn't it just as likely he held a grudge? Gwen has been rather busy over the past few years."

Tony's cheek twitched beneath his right eye, and the engine roared louder, as if picking up on its driver's mood. He didn't like the reminder that Gwen had made several enemies. "The bastard tried to kill her before a very public trial, *knowing* Aris would come for him. No one would do something so stupid over a personal grudge, not without insurance of some kind." He swerved around

2

a discarded box and jerked the auto back into the center of the narrow lane. "No, the two are related, and if I am going to protect this city and your damned sister, I need to know how."

Speeding *and* swearing. The man was more on edge than she'd seen him since they'd gotten the news Gwen had been shot. He whipped around a tight corner, rolling the auto hard onto its outside wheels. Lia clung to the seat as the force of the turn pulled her toward Tony, only for her stomach to drop as he stomped on the brake.

A line of artificers and apprentices blocked the road as they wrestled a massive sheet of brass from a delivery wagon. Tony shoved the shifter down a gear, making the auto rumble un-happily as it lurched to a stop.

Lia pushed her hair out of her eyes. Apron-clad apprentices wrestled the enormous piece of metal across the road, swearing and cursing, under the watchful eye of the master artificer.

"Watch your pace!" the dwarven man growled around his cigar. "You damage that stock, and I'll take it out of yer wages!"

If the apprentices hadn't already been sweating, that threat would have done it. Their shoulders hunched up around their ears as they maneuvered the sheet across the road. Lia took ad-vantage of the distracting opportunity to study her employer.

Tony Hardwicke, former Inspector of Scotland Yard and current owner of Supernatural and Paranormal Investigations, frowned at the delay. The muscles in his broad shoulders looked tense enough to snap, and his knuckles were white on the steering wheel.

Silent evidence of sleepless nights was written in the shadows beneath his brown eyes and the deep frown lines around his mouth. Lia hadn't slept much, either, and was equally worried, but her expression was serene. Hiding her emotions had become second nature, a requirement of surviving the Faerie Court. If no one knew what she was thinking or feeling, they could not use that knowledge against her.

Of course, Tony was too honest for such a disguise. Outside of questioning suspects, he had likely never needed one, so his emotions boiled around him like a thundercloud. Perhaps it was time for a bit of teasing. If he was busy being dismayed by her lack of morals, he wasn't thinking about Gwen and...well, everything else they had to worry about.

Lia flicked her fingers suggestively. Green sparks sputtered from her fingertips. "I could hurry them along if you like. The steel toes in their boots should conduct heat quite nicely."

Tony's scandalized expression was delightful.

He narrowed his eyes and said in a warning tone, "Lady St. James..."

Lia squashed the temptation to smile, keeping her expression cool as the last apprentice hefted the brass sheet through the loading doors. If her outrageous suggestions distracted him from worrying over Gwen, she was content to let him question her character. Gwen needed him to be a functional investigator, not

4

a distracted former lover. Her sister could not afford liabilities, not with potential assassins still lurking in the city.

Not with the threat of faerie invasion hanging over their heads like a guillotine.

They couldn't keep Gwen or this rotten-damned city safe without Tony. So she let the sparks fizzle and shrugged. "As you say, guv."

Tony cleared his throat in something that sounded suspiciously like a laugh, shifted the auto into gear, and accelerated at a reasonable rate. Lia turned her face away to hide a smile.

Iron Rose Industries sat at the corner of the next cross street, distinguished only by the rose and anvil sign hanging above the door.

As Tony parked, Lia took a few calming breaths. She was not precisely scared of Delilah Irons, but the dwarven woman had no regard for station or the polite niceties of social interaction, rules which had kept Lia alive for years in the Sunset Lands.

Because they could not lie, faeries were exacting in social etiquette, turning every action and conversation into a political chess match. But Delilah did not play games. She was more likely to swipe the pieces from the board than decide whether to sacrifice a pawn.

Dealing with Delilah forced Lia to dig up parts of herself long buried, parts she did not want to think about, let alone bring back from the dead. Unfortunately, she had little choice in the matter.

And she refused to be a coward. Lia squared her shoulders as Tony opened the door for her.

Smoke, sulfur, grease, and chemicals made the air nearly impossible to breathe. Half a dozen apprentices worked forges, hammered metal, and stood over tables covered in instruments Lia would not have been able to name at the threat of her life.

Delilah marched toward them like a bulldog ready for a fight. She was average height for a dwarf, somewhere near five feet, but carried herself as if she were twice that size. Her tanned skin was flushed from the forge, making her round cheeks red and smudged with soot.

A pair of brass goggles engraved with runic sentences sat nestled in the dark curls above her forehead. Pale scars criss-crossed her forearms, and one broad, capable hand rested on the handle of the hammer in her tool belt. She should not have been so intimidating, but apprentices scurried out of her way.

Delilah didn't seem to notice. She gave them a once over with dark, inscrutable eyes, then waved them toward the back room. "Come on."

As soon as Delilah turned, Lia held the cloth to her nose and edged between work benches, stepping over slags of glowing metal left ignored on the floor. Why were pleasant scents so hard to find in this town, but every godawful smell rose to choke one?

The back room was blessedly free of sulfur and smoke. Rows of tables and mannequins lined every wall but one. Gouges and pockmarks scored that wall, and the only spot not sooty with burns was a vaguely humanoid shape.

Delilah turned to face them, hands on her hips. "Alright, Tony, tell me about this embroidery that's so important."

Tony dug in his pocket. "It was on Bowler Hat's lapel. You know, Lord Rutledge's driver, the one who blew himself up. We thought he died in the subsequent fire, but Aris claims he was the one who shot Gwen."

"And what happened to this Bowler Hat?"

The corner of Tony's lips turned down as if the words didn't sit well in his mouth. "Aris tore him to pieces."

"Good. Any chance you can investigate the body?"

"From what I understand...there wasn't much left."

"Shame."

Lia understood the discomfort in Tony's voice. Aris had always frightened her, even when she held his loyalty—and his life—in her hands. Sending him to mortal lands to protect her sister had been an act of desperation, and one she secured with a geis that would have killed him if he hurt Gwen.

But Delilah behaved as if tearing a man's head off was the least Aris could have done. The woman was as pragmatic as Lia pretended to be.

Delilah made a flapping motion with one hand and said, "Show me the embroidery."

Tony handed over the scrap of cloth, and Delilah flattened it on one of the low tables, leaning over to examine it. Lia gave the two of them plenty of space as she could not tell a rune from any other shape.

After staring at the embroidery for a few moments, Delilah grunted and left.

The door slammed. Lia flinched. "That was rather abrupt."

"Trust the process," Tony said. "She's as good as they come."

"I can see she's very skilled, but her manner leaves a bit to be desired."

"She's as good as they come," he repeated. "Not only in her artifice but as a person. You'll see with time."

If she doesn't kill me before that, Lia thought.

With Delilah gone, Lia wandered the room and peered at the gadgets. Some appeared to be no more than bracelets or watches, but others were much harder to distinguish. The mannequins wore long, elegant coats, dresses, and even the ugly overalls Lia had been forced to wear during the battle at Trafalgar Square.

That night, she lit a dozen vampires on fire, expending so much energy she promptly fainted. The enchanted cloth hadn't so much as smoked. In the Sunset Lands, Lia's fire burned only what and how she willed it to. But the mortal world changed the nature of her magic and did not care what it burned. The only fire she was safe from here was the fire that trickled across her skin.

The door banged open, Lia flinched again, and Delilah strode through the room to drop a heavy leather book on the table. She ran one blunt finger across the arcane markings.

"Whatever it is," she said, "it's obscure. These symbols are runic but nothing contemporary. I don't have Gwen's magic book, but I would bet they were blended with—wait..." She flipped to another page, traced the markings, and stopped.

Lia edged closer to peer at the book. Neat runes and alchemical symbols had been printed in reddish ink next to banks of text running right to left, as dwarfish script did in antiquity.

"Here," Delilah said, tapping a symbol.

Lia frowned at it. The embroidery they brought was a kind of elaborate *S* with a line through it flanked by ornate flourishes. This mark was more angular and sparse. "That does not match the embroidery."

"No, it does not, *your ladyship*," Delilah replied.

Lia frowned at the emphasis on her title but wasn't stupid enough to reply.

"But the foundation of the runic sentence is the same. Which means this is likely the base of whatever spell craft they used to create that rune. This or something damn close."

Tony turned the book and tilted his head. "I thought blending magic and artifice was impossible outside of the experiments you and Gwen were doing."

"So did I," Delilah said, running one finger across the bridge of her nose. "If this embroidery granted Bowler Hat some kind of protection, then we were wrong. It may take me a while to get to the bottom of this. Give me a few days. I'll have to experiment a bit."

"A few days?" Lia asked. Her voice was cool, but her insides twisted at the thought that Bowler Hat may have accomplices in the city, others who wanted Gwen dead.

Delilah closed the book with a thump, giving Lia a look that meant *you shouldn't bother with things you don't understand.* "Artifice is not a safe profession, your ladyship, and it takes time. If I blow myself up, your chance to learn anything about this symbol will be as dead as I am." With that, she dismissed Lia and turned to Tony. "How is Gwen? Aris says she is recovering?"

"That is as much as we know. She looked...well"—he swallowed—"it was frightening to see her that way."

"Someone doesn't want this trial to be so public. If she lives, they'll try again."

"Yes, they will."

"How are we going to keep her safe? If all this goes as deep as assassination, those slagging bastards won't stop until she's no longer a threat."

"Well, Aris won't hear of moving her, not until she's awake and can make decisions for herself."

"That man is too smitten for his own good," Delilah said, pointing a finger at Tony as if he could do something about it. "Gwen is the cleverest person I know, but she's not infallible. She isn't always right."

"Don't try to tell Aris that."

"He'll learn it in time, but I worry it will be too late when he does."

10

"The Raven is no fool," Lia said, her cheeks warm with indignation on her sister's behalf. She never thought to find herself defending the Raven, but the words poured out anyway. "He respects Gwen's choices and cares enough to see that they are honored, even if he disagrees."

"Even if those choices get her killed?" Delilah demanded, turning on Lia with her hands on her hips and her chin thrust pugnaciously forward.

Lia drew herself to her full height, clamped down on her thundering heart and unruly emotions until only the cold General of Obyrron's armies looked out of her eyes. "How would you like to have your free will stolen because someone disagrees with your choices or does not like the possible outcome? Freedom requires danger, Miss Irons. To steal that from someone makes them less of who they are and more of who you would like them to be. Would you truly do that to Gwen? Rob her of what makes her who she is?"

Delilah didn't answer. Memories crept into Lia's voice, traces of who she once was, bits that clung like the scent of lavender that lingers long after the flowers are gone. "Do not try to change someone for your comfort. You may find the version that makes you the most comfortable erases the person you once loved."

Delilah's eyes widened, and Lia thought the dwarven woman might hurl more than insults at her. But after a moment, she replied in a much more civil—though still disgruntled—tone, "I don't say Aris should make Gwen's decisions for her. But he might fight a bit harder to help her see the danger. When Gwen doesn't want to accept something, she's damned stubborn about it."

"I suppose that could be said of most of us," Lia retorted, letting her eyes wander back to the scorch marks on the wall.

Delilah regarded the scars of old fires, then laughed. "You are right enough. Well"—she clapped her hands—"time to unravel this mystery. I'll ring you once I've got an answer. In the meantime"—she glanced between them with an almost apologetic expression and held up the torn fabric—"I think you should take a copy of this to the Cutthroat King."

Tony leaned back as if dodging a blow. "What? The man is a lunatic."

"But a resourceful one," Lia heard herself say with some surprise. How had she found herself defending two scoundrels in one day? "He has a veritable army of potential spies. If he unleashes them upon New London, we may gather more information in a night than the two of us could find in weeks."

Tony's jaw muscle worked as he considered the two of them, finally agreed on one thing, at least. Before he responded, Delilah cocked her head, said, "It's about time," and turned a gimlet eye on the door.

Percy sashayed into the room elegantly disheveled from the rush and carrying a bulging carpet bag as if it weighed a hundred pounds. The sky blue jacket and gold embroidery made his dark skin glow but couldn't distract from the harried expression on his handsome face.

"So sorry I'm late, D," he panted as he dropped the bag to the floor with a thump and kissed Delilah on both cheeks, a greeting she allowed but did not reciprocate. "There was an overturned cart that backed up traffic for blocks, and my driver was incompetent. Tony, Lady Ophelia, it is a pleasure. How is my Gwen?"

Lia raised a brow. *My Gwen?*

"Healing," Tony said, noting the offended color in her cheeks and giving her a slight shake of his head. "She was asleep when we left her."

"I nearly fainted when Sally rang me. Ringed me?" Percy glanced at his silver ring and scowled as he struggled to conjugate the past tense of the strange verb they'd begun using to describe the mind-to-mind conversations granted by their rings. After a moment, he waved the thought away. "Never mind. But I must know: does everyone's voice sound particularly loud, or is that only my ring? Is there a way to quiet them? Because I've stabbed myself with too many needles to count over the past week. My shop won't survive continued trauma to my digits." He held up one hand in evidence.

"Get to the point, Percy," Delilah said, the hint of a smile making her round cheeks bunch up beneath her eyes. "Time is money in my shop."

"Of course."

He unzipped the bag, pulled out garments, and laid them on the table under Delilah's direction. The pair was a study in contrasts: a dwarf with the forearms of a blacksmith and the face of a cherub and an elf as thin as a sapling with eyes the color of the sky. And yet, for all their differences, they worked together as if the two of them shared one mind.

"We will have to alter this one to fit Sally," Percy said, turning the hem of a long coat inside out and peeling back the lining to expose a row of beautifully embroidered runes. "Where can I make the cuts without damaging the sentence?"

"Not in the hem," Delilah said, "or this is likely to burst into flame as soon as it takes a bit of damage. It will simply be too wide for her at the bottom, that's all."

"What about creating pleats at the waist, will that—"

"That *might* work, just don't—"

"Of course not. Have a bit of faith."

"Sam will be the real problem if—"

"I've already started on that, my dear; have no fear. What about my new gizmo?"

"Nearly done."

Following their conversation was like running through a labyrinth in the dark. Lia's head began to pound.

"Forgive me," she said, making them both stop and turn to face her, "But, might there be anything I can wear while Tony and I investigate? A bit of armor would be welcome if we visit the Cutthroat King."

Percy stood to his full height and placed one finger on his shapely lips. The glamour he used to appear as an elf made him a startlingly lovely person, with cornflower blue eyes and dark skin, wearing garments of rich jewel-toned velvet—perfectly be-spoke, of course—from head to foot. Being stared at by him in his professional capacity was like being pulled apart at the seams and measured for tailoring.

Lia found herself raising her chin and squaring her shoulders.

"Hmm. You are about the same size as Gwen, but the coloring is all wrong. Those blues would make your delicate complexion look pale. You are going to the Undercroft, you said?"

"Yes."

Percy advanced, taking in every detail of her face and form. "How do you plan to approach this?"

"What do you mean?"

"Are you going to skulk in the shadows, power your way in, and demand answers while you use your station as a sledge-hammer, or are you going to use that gorgeous face to charm the King into giving you information?"

"What does it matter?" Tony asked.

Percy rolled his eyes. "It matters, Hardwicke. If she plans to use a sweet and innocent act, but I dress her in red, no one will believe it. If she plans to demand answers and I dress her in rose, no one will be intimidated. If she is going to sneak, well. That is a different sort of ensemble, entirely."

"We don't have time for a fashion consultation," Tony said. "She needs the clothes to protect her from violence, not charm herself a husband."

"No." Lia held up a hand. "I know something about using one's appearance as a kind of shield, and Percy has a point."

"Of course he does," Delilah said. "He's a genius."

Percy winked at her.

Lia held up one finger, forestalling them. "But Tony has a point, as well. What can be done with the most speed?"

"I do have a jacket nearly made up for Sally, and I can finish that quickly, but it will be a bit snug through the waist and..." He gave her an apologetic smile. "It is a champagne rose gold. You will be stuck playing either an ingénue or the coquette if you wear it."

He said the last as if that possibility were beyond her. Of course, he did not know her. No one did; she made quite sure of that, so she could not blame him. But perhaps she had better make an example of him. If she were going to use the skills she'd spent years perfecting to protect Gwen and help save the city, the people Gwen loved and trusted needed to know what she was capable of.

While living in the Sunset Lands and fighting her way up the political ladder, she had used every means of survival at her disposal: her wits, her body, and even outright violence. Of all the skills she acquired in her bid for power, subterfuge was the easiest.

Lia softened her expression, widened her eyes, and glided across the room with the liquid grace she had studied at the feet of the most seductive fae creatures in the court. When she stopped scant feet away and spoke, the iciness she was accustomed to using had melted, and her voice was warm and rich. "You are an expert in your field, Mr. Bywater. I know you will make the right decision for us both."

Then she put a hand on his chest and leaned close. "Just tell me what to wear, and I will wear it for you."

Percy blinked, stunned, his eyes fixed on her face. "Ah..." He cleared his throat and tore his gaze away to brush non-existent wrinkles from his jacket, "The rose—the rose gold will work beautifully."

Lia retreated to give him space to recover, ignoring Delilah's derisive snort. Tony's hard swallow, on the other hand, was harder to brush off.

The act fell away, as easy as shedding an uncomfortable garment, but no one in the room was likely to forget how well it fit. That should have reassured her. Faeries would have seen the mask as impressive, making her a more valuable ally and a more dangerous opponent. But the ease with which she donned the mask only made Gwen's friends avoid meeting her eyes.

Suddenly, the workshop felt more lonely than it had when they walked in. Lia pretended to examine the gadgets on display while Percy hunched over the coat with single-minded determination.

Delilah packed clothing for Sally, Samuel, and Tony, then tossed the other garments over the head of an unused mannequin. "Aris heals fast enough on his own, so he will have to wait while we focus on more delicate members of this bunch. Here." She grabbed a bracelet off a table and tossed it to Lia. "Keep this. It's called a Sightscreen. Just press the button, and you'll be effectively invisible for about five minutes. Once it's done, it's dead till you replace the diamond inside."

"Diamond?"

"That's what I said. The gem is a sort of conductor for magical energy, and it's slagging expensive, so use it wisely."

"It will also make you dizzy," Percy warned through the side of his mouth not pinched around a dozen pins. "Especially the first time. So be careful, Lady Ophelia."

"Lia will do."

Percy offered her a crooked smile and nodded in acceptance. She sensed the capacity for a great friendship between them if she could bring herself to foster it. There may be time for such things if they managed to save the city.

Having a friend would be rather nice.

Once the coat was finished and the fit altered to Percy's exacting standards, there was nothing left to do but risk their luck by asking the king of the criminal underground for his help. The thought of walking into the dark beneath the city made Lia's stomach somersault, but Gwen was lying unconscious on a cold cot. Lia wouldn't feel easy until they'd made certain no one else would try to hurt her. If that meant asking a monster for help, so be it.

She gave Tony a meaningful glance.

He cleared his throat and shook Percy's hand. "We'll leave you to your work then."

"Good luck, Hardwicke. And take care of that one," Delilah said, jerking her chin at Lia. "I have a feeling she's going to be as much trouble as her sister."

Tony sent her a quick, sideways glance but said, "I'm certain she can take care of herself."

He didn't look at her while he held the auto door open or when he climbed in and turned over the ignition. His expression was stiff and troubled: brows drawn low over his eyes as he squeezed the steering wheel in his big hands.

"Is everything all right?" she asked, knowing it was not.

Tony took a deep breath and ran one hand through his hair. "You gave a rather convincing performance in there."

"That doesn't sound like a compliment."

He passed one hand over his face, palm scraping across the stubble on his jaw. "It isn't."

A small, cold shard of pain dislodged itself from the inside of her ribcage and dropped like an icicle into her gut. She folded her arms and leaned back, unwilling to question him further. If he had something to say, he could bloody well say it.

"Which is the act?" he asked at last.

"What do you mean?"

He turned toward her, his honest, handsome face creased in lines of frustration. "A talent for acting is a powerful tool. It's also a dangerous one. I have now seen at least three different versions of Lady Ophelia St. James. If we are to work together in situations as dangerous as this one, then I must be able to trust you. To trust you, I need to know which is the real Ophelia."

She tore her eyes away and faced steadily forward, but the weight of his gaze was hard to ignore. It felt as if he were prying beneath her skin and bones to dig out the creature inside.

Which was the real Ophelia? Lia had been asking herself that question since she learned she was a changeling: half human, half faerie. And he was right. If they were to work together and successfully ferret out the conspiracy putting the city—and Gwen—in danger, there must be some trust between them.

But life in the faerie court taught harsh lessons, the most important being the danger of trust. When pushed to their limits, people would always bow to self-interest, no matter the cost to those whose trust they violated. Trust was a vulnerability, one she—and Gwen—could not afford.

Lia shivered despite the oppressive late summer heat. Which was the real Ophelia? "If you happen to figure it out, Mr. Hardwicke," she said, "please let me know."

They drove for some time in silence, and when they left the Guild District, Lia took a deep breath of horse-manure-scented air. It was better than sulfur, though not by much. Tony turned into a rundown neighborhood and dug Gwen's coin from his pocket. The silver *smiling man*, a coin embossed with a man's head with its throat cut, glowed on his palm—a symbol of someone in the King's service.

"I know it's hot, but keep your coat buttoned tight," he said grimly and shifted gears. "We are going to see the bloody Cutthroat King, and it's cold in the Undercroft."

2

Poetry

GWEN

During my illustrious career as a lady of adventure, I have been injured dozens of times: burned, struck, cut, bitten by both werewolves and vampires, and suffered countless other scrapes and scratches. But nothing compared to the pain of the bullet wound in my chest.

Perhaps it would have been more bearable if a surgeon had not spent a glorious hour digging about in my torso, but I suppose I will never know. And, truthfully, I hope never to find out. The pain enveloped and overwhelmed everything.

My only escape pain was morphine. It carried me into realms of oblivion where my consciousness floated on a crystalline sea of nothingness. Now and then, I would swim back toward shore long enough to catch a blurry glimpse of someone's face or feel the lurking shadow of pain waiting to catch me with sharp teeth.

I am certain I spoke at some point, but have no memory of what I said. The only thing I can recall with clarity is the shape of Aris's face. Whenever I came close enough to consciousness to feel or see, he was there, leaning over me.

Eventually, the pain dulled enough that the first bite did not send me fleeing for oblivion or moaning for morphine. I swam to the shore and paddled around a bit, then ventured to set foot on land.

Pain waited for me, bit it was dull and achy rather than sharp.

"How long?" I asked. The words scratched up my throat and sounded more like a croak than human speech.

Chair legs scraped on the floor, and someone took my hand. "Gwen? Can you hear me?"

"How long?"

Another set of footsteps echoed through the room, and a voice said, "It has been three days, Gigi."

Prying my eyelids open was a task of herculean proportions because my eyeballs were dry as sandpaper, but I managed it. Lia's face swam into focus, her blond hair tousled, and her eyes red from lack of sleep.

"I'm thirsty."

Someone pressed the rim of a glass against my lips, and though the water was tepid, it felt like the first gulp from a cool mountain stream. That bit of effort was enough to send me back out to sea.

"Who wrote it?" I asked, my voice still weak and scratchy from disuse.

"An Irish fellow named Yates. It is relatively new, I think, as mortals judge such things. Would you like me to read it to you?"

"Please."

Aris cleared his throat, followed by the dry fluttering of pages and the hiss of his fingertip sliding down the paper. God's breath, his voice was beautiful, deep, resonant, and soft. When he spoke, he did not just read the words but caressed them, bringing them to vivid life in my mind.

"I went out to the hazel wood,
Because a fire was in my head,
And cut and peeled a hazel wand,
And hooked a berry to a thread;
And when white moths were on the wing,
And moth-like stars were flickering out,
I dropped the berry in a stream
And caught a little silver trout.
When I had laid it on the floor

I went to blow the fire a-flame,
But something rustled on the floor,
And someone called me by my name:
It had become a glimmering girl
With apple blossom in her hair
Who called me by my name and ran
And faded through the brightening air.
Though I am old with wandering
Through hollow lands and hilly lands,
I will find out where she has gone,
And kiss her lips and take her hands;
And walk among long dappled grass,
And pluck till time and times are done,
The silver apples of the moon,
The golden apples of the sun."

On the edge of sleep, I had visions of golden hair flickering between trees as Lia disappeared into the forest. A tear streamed hot down my cheek. "That was beautiful."

3
The Mad King

LIA

The subterranean passageway to the Cutthroat King's domain opened before them like a yawning mouth. Tony followed their guide without hesitation, leaving the dim but visible interior of the warehouse for the utter blackness of the passage. Lia froze as her stomach crawled into her chest, and cold sweat beaded her upper lip.

It was so impossibly dark.

A rough hand pushed her forward. Her feet acted on instinct, taking one unsure step after another as they left the lighted world behind. For a moment, she considered using magic, but the memory of green light and shadows on the walls of her first prison made the magic fizzle and die.

Their guide, a heavy-shouldered man with sagging earlobes and hands the size of hams, strode into the darkness with a dwarven lantern held high. Shadows played across the ancient, lichen-covered stone that lined the walls and ceiling, and the light of the warehouse behind them dimmed until there was no way back.

It took every ounce of her self-control not to turn and run. Lia gasped in a deep breath and released it slowly. She had been through worse. She would survive this, as she'd survived everything else.

Tony said over his shoulder in a low voice, "Are you alright?"

"Mmm," was the only sound she could force past a throat tight with suppressed terror.

"Stay behind me."

Her palms ran across the wool of her coat from her throat to her breast, abdomen, and back, trying to let the texture pull her mind away from the fear. She was no longer trapped in the dark earth. She never would be again. She was here, now. And with Tony. She was safe.

But her trembling hands proved her body did not believe the litany, so she clenched her fists and stuffed them in her pockets.

Before the Sunset Lands, darkness had never bothered her. But now? Dread, ice cold and tingling, ran down her spine, sunk its claws into her guts, and held on. With a simple thought, she could kindle a light that chased away the shadows reaching for her, shadows desperate to pull her back, lock her away, leave her alone in

27

the cold darkness where small, slimy, unseen terrors could slither across her fingers, inch up her ankles...

Lia's mouth went dry. Her heart hammered against her breastbone. Everyone would hear the pounding of it. They'd scent her fear and descend on her like foxes on a rabbit, her terror becoming their pleasure. Without consciously approving the idea, she clasped Tony's hand. His skin was warm, blessedly warm. After a moment of surprise, his fingers tightened around hers.

A pair of worried brown eyes glanced at her over his shoulder, barely visible in the shifting lamplight. He opened his mouth as if he would speak, but she only shook her head. *Not now.* She might have a problem with dark, confined spaces, but if she revealed her weakness, she would break. That was a mistake they could not afford.

One did not show weakness in the den of a predator.

Besides, the reassuring pressure of Tony's fingers tied her to his calm presence like an anchor to a ship in a storm. She would be fine. She could do this. For Gwen, she could.

She'd done worse, after all.

When warm light and echoing voices finally rescued them from the darkness, Lia had to swallow back a cry of relief. It didn't matter that the voices were rough and raucous and punctuated with words that would have made her mother blush. She could have kissed every foul mouth in the bunch.

Of course, she reassessed that thought once they stepped into what amounted to a great hall. Had the room been built five hundred years ago and excavated, or was it built by a shoddy work-man recently? The vaulted ceiling and crooked pillars looked as if they were waiting impatiently for the opportunity to col-lapse. And, from the look of the company gathered beneath the rafters—and the ripe scent of them—it would have been no great loss.

Don't be cruel, she told herself. Nothing made her more cross than fear, but that was no reason to judge these people. After all, if King Obyrron had discovered her betrayal, she would have been considered more treacherous than anyone in this room.

Tony's grip on her hand tightened in a silent warning as they approached the edge of the crowd milling about a dais at the front of the room. A man stood in the open center of the floor before a throne, crushing his tatty hat against his chest in a white-knuckled grip. He had one of those moderately handsome faces with dull but regular features that could have made him any one of a thousand men in the city.

The man who stared down at him from the throne, on the other hand, was anything but forgettable. Not because he was handsome, although he was. But because violence hung in the air around him like a cloak of shadows. He had sharp features and the bright, dark eyes of a snake ready to strike.

Lia's body reacted to his presence before her mind did, her instincts screaming *danger*. She straightened her shoulders. An expression of cold, haughty pride froze itself onto her features. It was the mien of the General of the Fae Army, someone who had faced down the deadliest faeries in the Sunset Lands and lived to tell the tale.

The Cutthroat King lounged on his throne, leaning an elbow on one armrest with the opposite leg thrown casually over the other. His crown, hammered of silver spoons, sat negligently on his brow. One corner of his mouth curled into a derisive smile.

"Let me be sure I understand the situation, Mr. Cunningham. Instead of paying your tithe, you *reinvested* the money in a gambling scheme. In a tavern owned by a rival gang. Is this correct?"

The man—was he on trial?—hunched in on himself until his shoulders almost reached his ears. "Aye, Your Majesty. But it was rigged! I fixed the odds! When I won, I would have put ten times my tithe into—"

"But you did not, in fact, win, did you? No, Mr. Cunningham," the King said, raising one finger. "You gambled away *my* money. Had you won, the story might have ended very differently. But you lost. And now you owe the court. Would you rather pay your debt with a finger or an ear?"

Blood drained from the man's face in a rush, leaving him white and trembling. "N-n-no, please, Your Majesty! I can pay, I—"

"Shall I leave the choice to the crowd, then? It is your peers who have been wronged, after all."

A lusty roar rose from the assembly as Mr. Cunningham blurted, "B-but Majesty!"

The Cutthroat King stood, uncoiling from his chair with the sinuous grace of a cobra staring down a mouse. Silence engulfed the room. "You knew the price of my protection, Cunningham. You chose not to pay it. There are consequences for such actions." He raised his arms to the side. "You may walk away from the court at any time. But my protection ends at the surface, and your peers may not take your treachery as kindly as I have."

Judging by the sea of hard faces and harder eyes leveled at the accused man, Lia guessed that, if Cunningham left, he would not live out the night.

"Ear," the King asked again, "or finger?"

Cunningham's face crumbled, and his arms fell limp to his sides. His hat lay disregarded on the ground at his feet. "E-ear, sir. The left one, please."

A hungry murmur made the room buzz, and the King waved to a set of guards behind Cunningham. "See it done."

Cunningham was dragged from the room as the King regained his seat and held out one hand. An extraordinary woman stepped from the shadows and placed a full goblet against his fingertips.

She was tall but as delicately built and graceful as a willow. Long, fine, nearly white hair hung down to her hips, and her bare arms were pale in the candlelight. She was a moonbeam made flesh.

Something passed between the two of them, something as intensely personal as hatred or passion, though they never so much as brushed fingers. And when the King took his drink, the woman melted back into the shadows behind the throne.

"It appears the good Inspector has graced us with his presence once more," the King announced to a chuckling crowd. "Come forward, sir, but allow me to caution you." He leaned forward and lowered his voice as Tony and Lia took the recently vacated place of Cunningham. "Use Lady Gwen's coin too freely, and I will begin to think you and I have dealings beyond those stipulated in the alliance."

Lia had not been present for the negotiations Gwen held with this snake of a man, but she did not like to wonder what Gwen had done to secure it. She stood behind Tony and to one side, hands hanging loose and ready, chin high and defiant.

"My business concerns your people as well," Tony said. Unlike the King, his voice was flat and emotionless. He held out the folded drawing and waited for one of the King's men to deliver it.

"That drawing," Tony said, "represents the symbol embroidered on the lapel of the man who shot Lady Gwen. Your ally."

The King glanced at the drawing. "Indeed. My scouts were responsible for searching for a man wearing such a symbol before the Battle of Trafalgar Square, after all. I remember it well. Did you have a point or merely desire my stimulating company?"

Tony's jaw muscle worked, but no other sign of irritation showed on his face or in his posture. "We need to learn more about what the symbol represents and who it might be tied to. The man wearing it survived the asylum explosion, so it is likely some form of protection. If others have access to the same symbols—"

"You refer to the style of embroidery on the inside of your new coat, Inspector? The embroidery that makes you, and the lovely General behind you, brave enough to berate me in my own court?"

A spear of surprise pinned Lia's heart to her ribcage. The King leaned to the side and leered at her around Tony's shoulder. "Yes, Lady Ophelia, I know who and what you are. Your outstanding display in the square made it obvious to anyone who knew what to look for. Though one does wonder why the Inspector would bring you here, knowing what he knows."

Ah, yes. If she were still in the service of Obyrron, it would be her duty to capture the Cutthroat King and turn him over to be executed for treason. If he was not useful to the war effort, that is. And to be imprisoned by a geis, if he was. Every faerie refugee living in the mortal world was considered a traitor.

If she were a spy, bringing her here would have been a very dangerous move.

She heard herself say in the General's voice, "If Mr. Hardwicke wanted to insult or intimidate you, he certainly has better weapons to use than me."

Her disdain didn't make the King angry. Instead, his eyes glittered with something like pleased malice. "You enter my court to ask for help and tow along a faerie spy who insults me before my subjects without so much as guest rights? That is either stupidity of the highest order or commendable arrogance. Only one of those traits will let you leave this hall alive."

Metal hissed across leather as the gathered crowd drew assorted weapons and readied themselves to remove the threat to their king. Should they attack, she and Tony would never see daylight again.

The idea of Tony's death, the mere possibility of it, made her chest tight.

Her mind offered a gory vision of what his body would look like after the Unseen Court was through with him. His mother would be inconsolable. Anger burned away Lia's surprise and fear, leaving cold resolve in its place.

Climbing the ladder of power in the faerie court required Lia to learn and do things she never imagined as a naive sixteen-year-old. And while she'd never withdrawn from a challenge, she didn't rush thoughtlessly into them, either. Better to bide her time and deal with threats from a place of power when they least expected it.

The Cutthroat King, however, had no intention of allowing her to do that. This was a game, a subtle and deadly game he was inviting her to play at the risk of their lives. All of their lives. So she stepped calmly out from behind Tony, raised both hands, and snapped. Every candle in the room died without so much as a flicker, plunging the hall into absolute darkness. The acrid stink of smoke hung in the air for a few silent moments.

"I believe you are mistaken, petty king," Lia said, and her voice rang off the stone walls, echoing through the dark like a curse. "I am here of my own free will and under my own power. You"—a single candle sprang to life with green fire—"only continue to rule at my pleasure. And your subjects"—another candle—"live because I have no desire to do them harm. In fact"—a dozen lights, then a hundred, flamed brilliantly, drowning the room in light so bright the members of the court squinted and shielded their eyes—"visiting your court today with this warning was a kindness, not a service." She brought her hands down, and the flames dimmed, giving off just enough light to see the dark smudges of humans, elves, and dwarves cowering against the walls.

Lurid green flames rose from her fingertips, no doubt painting her face in monstrous light that would make her cold expression all the more ghastly. When she tilted her head to the side, a tongue of fire snapped to life and licked up the King's dark pant leg.

"Threaten me again, and you will not live to do so a second time. I have more dangerous enemies than you. And they are coming. I would rather fight them with your knife at my side, not at my back."

Common yellow flames replaced her magic, returning the room to normal, but fire still climbed the King's leg and filled the air with the sulfurous bite of singed hair and burning cotton. The malicious amusement on his face had vanished, leaving his features cold and immovable as granite.

If the flame bothered him, he showed no signs of it.

"The rumors about you were true, then," he said in a deadly quiet voice. "I am pleased to see it. If you don't mind?"

Heart in her throat, Lia willed the flame away, leaving his pant leg burned in a long strip and the skin beneath red and blistered. He tossed the paper to the closest subject and said, "Make copies and circulate them. Learn all you can about anyone who carries this mark and report back to me. Do not engage them. Do not be seen."

The dwarven man who caught the paper ran from the room without looking back.

The King raised his voice and said, "Lower your weapons. It would be a shame to shoot an ally in the head now that we have evidence of how useful she is."

Clinking followed the order, and a thrill of fear scraped down Lia's spine. Those sounds did not come from the room but from the walls. Small, nearly invisible slits had been carved in the mortar between stones, and she caught the almost invisible glint of candlelight on the bolt of a crossbow as the weapon was lowered.

The King had prepared unexpected weapons, and those wielding them, elves most likely, had trained them on the single weak point in her armor. The King saw the moment she realized the danger they'd been in and smiled. He had also publicly named her an ally, though she made no vows or agreements. He was daring her to contradict him and make an enemy of herself—a neat little trap.

"You do not think me such a fool as to allow the General of Obyrron's armies into my court without certain precautions, do you? Oh, a man likes to have capable allies...once they know where things stand."

"Agreed," Lia said. "Particularly when a man lives in enclosed spaces with such delightfully flammable fuel so close at hand. Strewn everywhere, really. Have you ever seen farmers use fire to drive rabbits from their warrens? It is quite a sight, I assure you.

One can only imagine what it must be like in those cramped tunnels when the smoke appears."

For a stomach-clenching moment, the King said nothing. He stared at her with dark, unreadable eyes. A grin stretched his lips. "Indeed. When the rabbits run out, the farmer picks them off one by one with a single, carefully placed bullet. Poor creatures never see it coming."

Her heart did a painful flip-flop. When she'd conspired against Obyrron with Queen Titania, she'd only had herself to worry about. But now? Gwen, Tony, and the children... The King commanded enough people that, if he chose, he could station gunmen on rooftops throughout the city. Not even her fire could protect them from that.

Very well. A threat for a threat. She would not murder his family, and he would not murder hers.

"I'm glad we understand one another," she said.

"As am I."

The King regained his seat and adopted a negligent pose, leaving the painful burn on display while sipping his wine with apparent relish. "Should my Ratcatchers return with information relating to this symbol, I will contact you. It was a pleasure to see you, Inspector, as always. Lady General. I hope I never see your beautiful face again."

"The feeling is mutual, Your Majesty."

The guards muscled them out of the crowd and through a sea of glaring eyes as the next complainant was ushered into the King's presence. Lia had never been more willing to be manhandled in her life.

It was dusk by the time they surfaced. Tony spun on her as soon as they exited what appeared to be a sewer drain and backed her toward the concealment of an alley. When they were safely out of the sight of passing eyes, he grabbed her shoulders in both big hands and demanded, "What happened to staying behind me? Were you trying to get yourself killed?"

Tony was generally so considerate that it was easy to overlook his sheer size, which was much more difficult to ignore when his face was only inches from hers. Were it not for the clear worry in his eyes and the relieved frustration in his voice, she might have been intimidated by his nearness. But having someone concerned for her wellbeing, someone who was not obligated to do so by blood, was still a novel experience.

So she said, in as reasonable a tone as she could muster, "I did not have much choice."

He ran a hand through his hair and blew a frustrated breath through his nose. "I know this man, Ophelia. He is useful, yes, but he is also mad as a rabid dog and twice—no, three times—as dangerous. He was baiting you. I thought you were too smart to be tempted to reply."

A cold little smile touched her lips. "I guess you were wrong, then."

"I have been wrong about many things, but I'm not wrong about this. Why did you let him bait you? Why put yourself in such danger? To prove a point?"

"Yes," she growled, stepping forward and poking him in the chest with one finger. "Yes, to prove a point. To make certain he knew with whom he was dealing. I want there to be no questions about exactly what I will do to him and every criminal in those tunnels if he so much as breathes a threat against someone I love."

Tony opened his mouth to reply, closed it, then stared at his feet for a long time. A lock of blonde hair slipped loose and hung over his forehead. The absurd desire to brush it back made her fists clench.

Lia sighed and relented. "It wasn't *just* to prove a point. The King is mad, yes, but not in the way you think. He's a faerie, one twisted by the worst parts of both of our worlds, and he rules people neglected by society. If he intends to maintain his rule, it cannot be mere trust that governs those people. They learned a long time ago not to trust those in power. He must also rule through fear." She folded her arms and shivered. "If he bends to the will of another power, especially in front of those he rules—"

"It must be through strength," Tony finished, raising his head.

"It must be through strength," she agreed. "We are strong enough to become useful allies. He needed me to demonstrate that. And he needed his people to see what to prepare themselves for if I become an enemy."

"That was a hell of a way to do it."

"Well. He *is* mad."

Tony's expression softened into amusement, almost making him look boyish, before his eyes flicked to the shadows, and he tensed. A thrill of fear raced up her spine. Tony spun her by the shoulders to place his body in front of hers and raised a pistol in the same instant that green flame sparked to life along the blade of her left hand.

"Show yourself," Tony ordered, pointing the barrel into the gloomy alley.

A pale smudge grew closer in the growing dark, a nebulous form that condensed into a graceful figure with long, pale hair. The woman paused just inside the mouth of the alley and raised both arms. Blue energy crackled from her hands, spreading like a spiderweb made of electricity up her arms and across her torso. White hair rose from her head as if on a ghost wind, and her pale dress almost seemed to float.

"*White Lady*," Tony whispered.

Despite the superstitious thrill that made goosebumps run up her arms, Lia knew the vision was no specter. And whatever caused the energy to ripple across the woman's body, it wasn't magic.

"Peace," the woman said. "I only protect myself. I mean you no harm."

The crackling energy lit the woman's face from below, throwing blue light on delicate elfin features a wide, silver-green eyes.

Lia let her fire die and put one hand on Tony's shoulder, but spoke to the woman. "I saw you in the Unseen Court. Promise us safety and we will grant you the same."

The White Lady lowered her arms. Her hair fell down her back, and the blue energy subsided. "Promised," she said.

Tony lowered the pistol and Lia released a breath. "And promised."

The magic of their promise sharpened the air for a moment. When it disappeared, the woman nodded and stepped closer the light. Her brows and lashes were such a pale blonde they were nearly white. She would not have been considered beautiful by the fashionable set who valued pink cheeks and round bosoms. But Lia had never seen anyone more compelling or otherworldly, not even in the faerie court.

The woman glanced over her shoulder once, then said, "I don't have much time, but I must speak with you. I know the symbol you showed the King."

4
Reunion

GWEN

A week after being shot, I sat in bed trying to eat a bowl of soup while arguing with Tony inside my mind.

I still think we should smuggle you out of town, he thought. *It would keep you safe while we try to stop the city from falling apart.*

Let's say you discover who Rutledge's co-conspirators are. How do you plan to distribute your findings? I thought while slurping down a spoonful of pea soup under Aris's watchful eye.

We go to the Times.

Have you proof they are not part of the conspiracy?

A hesitation. *Not yet.*

Then the answer is no, Tony. I am not keen on— The swallow of soup stuck halfway down, which sent me into a coughing fit that hurt like the very dickens. Aris rubbed my back until the worst of it passed. *The only way we can protect this city is to share the truth with as many people as possible.*

And you think a trial for treason, while someone is actively trying to kill you, is the right way to go about that? he demanded.

My mental voice sounded tired, even to me. *It is our best, most visible chance. Besides, the man who shot me is...more than dead.* Aris had explained to me, in stomach-turning detail, exactly how safe I was from Bowler Hat. And while I appreciated his enthusiasm for securing my safety, I preferred not to imagine the outcome. *Speaking of people who want to kill me, any news on the embroidered symbol?*

Yes. And it is almost as disturbing as it sounds.

I set my soup aside. *Do tell.*

As Tony explained his trip to the Undercroft, my fists curled so tightly in my lap that my knuckles threatened to pop through my skin. The Cutthroat King had naturally expected a visit and positioned sharpshooters in the walls of the Undercroft to kill my sister. Rage heated my cheeks until they burned.

You would have been proud, Tony offered. *Ophelia established herself as both an ally and a threat, if it is any consolation.*

No, it is not. How could you bring her there? You know how unstable that man is!

Tony's mental voice was both tired and amused. *You mean the way you brought me there?*

That's different.

Why?

*Because...*but it wasn't different. Lia was capable and dangerous in her own right. She was used to being in positions that would make the average person break out in a cold sweat. And she had chosen to work with Tony. My wanting her safety didn't make his decision to bring her reckless.

But I did not have to like it.

We can finish that part of our conversation another time, I thought, rubbing a hand across my brow and trying to release the simmering anger. *How did that visit end with information on Bowler Hat's embroidery?*

The following explanation was quicker, if not less interesting.

My brows rose. *A White Lady? You are referring to a real person, I presume, and not the specter of folklore?*

Are you trying to be insulting?

It can be difficult to tell the difference between a more powerful specter and a corporeal being.

Do you mean to tell me there are actually—he paused and a vague sense of frustrated resignation seeped through our mental connection—*never mind. She was real enough and I believed her.*

That is fair, I suppose. Though I do not see what we can do with the information until we've located more members of this Covenant.

The Ratcatchers are searching the city. And Alix and Cyrus are on their way back from their meeting with Doctor Hesselius. They can join the search when they arrive.

I closed my eyes and nodded. God's breath, my chest hurt. *Very well. We are doing all we can do. If you get the chance, check on*

Samuel, will you? I know he's taking terrible advantage of Mrs. Chapman and Mr. Yates while I'm away. You are the only one who can save them. Aris is more likely to commend the boy's bad behavior than curtail him.

Tony's mental voice softened. *No one takes advantage of Mrs. Chapman if she does not allow it.*

No one but the children. She has a child-shaped soft spot she refuses to acknowledge. And Tony?

Hmm?

Thank you.

I cut off the magical connection and leaned back against my pillows with a sigh, shifting until the healing wound didn't throb with every heartbeat. When I planned to get myself arrested after the Battle of Trafalgar Square, I had, of course, anticipated a certain level of physical discomfort. I had not prepared myself for how much healing from a near-fatal wound would drain my physical and mental resources.

Aris knelt in front of me and brushed escaped tendrils of hair out of my face, his eyes searching mine like they were the pages of a book. "You're going to wear yourself out."

Of my various family and acquaintances, Aris was the only one who managed to stay with me in my convalescence. Once they determined I would survive with minimal care, my jailers returned me to solitary confinement. I was a criminal, according to the upstanding law enforcement of New London, and therefore did not deserve the succor of companionship. They allowed my nurse to check and change my dressings and the surgeon to assess me periodically but used the battering ram of the law to keep everyone else out.

Fortunately for me, laws did not always apply to faeries.

Aris was able to either charm anyone who entered the room or make them forget he was there, and so he stayed.

I yawned. "If I do wear myself out, I will simply nap. There is nothing else productive for me to do in any case."

"Don't whine, darling. Your life is not defined by productivity."

"You try lying on your back for days with nothing to keep your mind or body occupied while all of the people you care about put themselves in danger trying to keep you safe and tell me how inclined you are to whine."

"Your body is occupied," he said. "It's busy healing."

"Well, if it could heal a bit faster—"

"You have already pushed yourself well past the limit of your mortal body. Let it rest a while you catch me up. It sounds as if Tony had a few revelations."

I levered myself upright. "Normally, I caution against assumptions, but yours are so often correct."

"While flattery is the key to my heart, I'd prefer you save the teasing for when I can properly punish you for it." The mischievous grin he gave me made it clear that flattery wasn't only the key to his heart but also to other, more interesting parts of him.

That thought conjured up all kinds of exciting possibilities that I was in no shape to explore. "Apparently," I began, somewhat less enthusiastic than before, "there is a White Lady in the Unseen Court, and she has previous experience with people who wear that symbol."

"A White Lady? You mean a ghost?"

"A mortal woman, but pale of skin and hair and eye. Tony says she is elven, but I wonder about her lineage, given such unique physical traits."

"Albinism?"

"No, not from his description."

"Interesting. How does an elf woman in the Undercroft know so much about our mysterious symbol?"

"According to Tony, her father had dealings with them in the past. She said they call themselves The Covenant of the Silver Dawn."

Aris barked out a laugh. "It is a fantastically pretentious title. They must think rather highly of themselves."

"Given what Bowler Hat survived, they may have some reason for confidence. I do not know if they have access to the kind of robust runic magic Delilah and Percy are using, but if they do..." I let the thought hang in the air.

The gadgets that had kept me alive over the past few years were only possible because we had discovered a way to combine artifice and old fae magic. If the Covenant had similar technology, we could be in far more danger than we realized. "I cannot pinpoint why, but something about this Covenant makes my brain itch."

"Did Tony happen to know what they want?" Aris asked.

"Besides my demise?"

Aris scowled at the reminder, but I could not be contrite. Between the Covenant and the conspiracy, New London was in what my father would have referred to as *a tight spot*. And stuck here in confinement, I was in no position to help. It was profoundly infuriating.

But I manfully—or rather *woman*fully—controlled my impulse toward self pity and sighed. "They hired the White Lady's father to help engineer something, but she would not say what the device was. The man was an inventor of some renown, apparently."

"If she was willing to share so much, why not name the device as well?"

"Tony thinks she approached them without the King's permission. He said she seemed nervous and left as soon as she warned them of how dangerous the Covenant are. Her story corroborates their ability to withstand damage that would kill normal mortals. She told Tony to aim for the head."

Aris considered that, watching me carefully for some time before sighing and shaking his head. "Another enemy to add to the ever-growing list. Well, there is nothing to be done about them right now." He ran the pad of his thumb across my bottom lip. "And you are tired. Shall I bring you more of Mrs. Chapman's tea?"

I grimaced. "If I drink another cup of that stuff, I will explode. But," I sighed, "you are probably right. Nothing will get me back on my feet faster."

Aris kissed my forehead, said he would return with all possible haste, and opened the window to leap into the air. He dropped, transformed into a raven, and shot into the sky in a blur of black feathers, leaving me alone in the small office that had been converted into a temporary convalescent room.

I promised myself I would never take my freedom for granted again and promptly fell asleep.

When you button the shirtwaist, Percy thought to me, *be certain the seams are straight. The runic sentences will work either way, but they are most effective if they meet.*

I shoved the last button through the hole and pulled the hem down to ensure every seam lay straight and even. *That's a bit shoddy. If a twisted seam puts me at risk, I'm guaranteed to end up in trouble at some point.*

Percy's mental voice was disgruntled when he thought back, *You design a magical shirtwaist, and tell me how well you handle the lighter fabric. The wool in your jacket is heavy and takes the embroidery without twisting. I've sewn backing material into the seams but—*

You are the professional, I thought, wincing as Aris helped me into my waistcoat and jacket.

I trust your judgment.

As you should. His tone softened. *Be careful today, Gwen. If they were willing to shoot you in front of a crowd, they won't stop just because you are on public trial.*

So everyone keeps reminding me, I thought back, knowing I was about to be as exposed as a proverbial fish in a barrel.

Promise?

I sighed. *Promise.*

Percy and I said goodbye, and I collapsed onto the bed, breathing hard. It was still difficult to fully get my breath, and bending or stretching made my entire torso hurt.

"This has been the longest two weeks of my life," I grumbled as Aris sat next to me and gathered me against his side. "And yet, my body still feels as if it has only been a few days."

"Mortals," he said, rolling his eyes. "Such fragile creatures."

"Thank you so much for the reminder, oh blessed immortal being."

He cupped my cheek with one hand. I closed my eyes and leaned into the touch as a warm, fluttery feeling replaced the burning ache in my chest.

"What can I give you for the pain?" he asked.

I pictured the locked drawer in my study: the comforting little brown bottle; felt, in memory, the way it would burn; how the warmth would slide through my limbs, making my pain and worries disappear. For a moment, I even felt the cool, hard weight of the glass against my palm.

"Nothing," I said, swallowing hard and opening my eyes as I shook my head. "I need my faculties about me. If I am fuzzy-headed or lose my wits and let them get the best of me, all of this will have been in vain. If a girl is going to get shot proving a point, she had better make it worth the effort, hadn't she?"

The last was said with as much breezy unconcern as I could muster, but it didn't convince either of us. I was going to stand trial, and I would do it in pain because that was the only way to be certain I could make the most of the opportunity.

Aris searched my face, brows pinched in concern. After a moment of hesitation, he cleared his throat and dropped his gaze. "I could...if you'd like me to, I could—convince you that you feel fine. At least, for a while."

A lump formed in my throat. I had to push the words past it. "You mean, without your glamour?"

"I wouldn't offer except"—he risked meeting my eyes—"I hate seeing you in pain. And you won't accept another analgesic. So."

Aris once told me never to ask him to use his influence as a weapon. He, more than anyone, knew the helpless resentment of having his will dominated, of being subject to the whims of another. That he was offering it now made my chest ache.

I cleared my throat and tried to ignore the compelling memory of his influence. He could convince me I felt no pain with little effort. I did not doubt it. But if I accepted his offer to cross this boundary, how long would it be before I was tempted, even for some noble reason, to ask him to cross it again?

I took his hands and pressed his palms against my chest, where my heart beat hard enough to feel even through layers of fabric. "I can live with pain," I said. "I cannot live with knowing what taking it from me would cost you."

"It's a small thing, Gwen." He seemed confident, but something below the surface made his voice sound like that of a man standing on ice, hearing the cracks while assuring the drowning victim that nothing was wrong and they should take his hand.

Without breaking eye contact, I said, "It isn't a small thing. Not to me."

Relief warred with frustration for control of his expression, so I saved him from being forced to choose and kissed him instead. His lips were tender, his brow furrowed as his fingers curled into the lapels of my jacket to hold me close. A tingling rush of pleasure washed from my breastbone to my knees.

Aris broke the kiss and rested his forehead against mine, letting our breath mingle for a moment in silence. "You are still certain this is the right path?"

"No?" I sighed and shook my head. "Yes, dammit. Rutledge hid his tracks well. Our gambit in the square gave people enough information to question their government, but if this conspiracy succeeds in pinning the last few years on me, no one will bother protecting themselves. They will write everything off as the results of my deviant behavior and go on about their business as if the world isn't about to crash around their ears. If the authorities are colluding with the conspirators, or if they will not protect the common people, this is the only way I can see to warn them at scale."

Aris nodded thoughtfully. "I know this is what you wish, so I will not try to stop you. But I must warn you, Gwen: if they condemn you for treason, I will tear this place apart, all the way down to its foundations, and carry you out of the rubble tossed over my shoulder. You will *not* see the inside of another prison."

I blushed. How could a lady not blush in the face of such devotion?

Three knocks on the door interrupted whatever response I might have given and provided Aris enough time to shift into a raven and leap onto the windowsill. When the door swung open, he spread his wings and croaked a warning at the constable.

"Cor blimey," the man said from beneath his mustache. "That's a big'un. You ought to be careful leaving that window open, Your Grace. Omens of bad tidings, ravens are. That's what my grandad always said. Go on!" He made a wide shooing motion with both hands. "Get out of 'ere."

Aris croaked one last warning—aimed at me, I thought—then took flight. The constable gave me an apologetic look and held out the manacles I was to wear to trial. At least he wasn't pleased to be chaining me. But the iron snapped into place around my wrists all the same.

When he was done, he offered me his hand and helped me to my feet. He and the other constable, a pale dwarven man with shoulders like an ox, escorted me out of my room and down the long, echoing corridor toward Westminster Hall.

"You know," the chatty constable said, "this is the first trial they've held in the Hall in decades. They've got it all fitted up with wooden stands and everything. It's quite a sight. You're famous, Your Grace."

His use of my proper title, one I had always reserved for Mama, made a shiver of discomfort run down my arms. "How lucky for me."

When we arrived at last, and my jailers ushered me through the great doors, I saw that the constable had not been lying: Westminster Hall was transformed. Temporary terraced seating had been constructed on either side of the hall, rising from the stone floor up to the bottom of the ornate wooden vaults. People filled every available seat, and ogled me as we passed down the center aisle toward the defendant's box.

Opposite my plain wooden chair, raised upon a dais below the great stained glass window, was the bench where the Lord Chief Justice sat in robed and bewigged glory. Rainbow-stained sunlight shone upon his head, making him the bright point of justice in the darkened room.

The glowing wig made it hard to see the man's face, so I focused on climbing to my seat without falling and tried not to look up into the faces glaring down at me. Anticipation made the air in the great space thick and volatile, and the sound of muttering and creaking wood was like the sound a spring makes when it is fully depressed and humming with energy.

These people had gathered to see whether I would be condemned for treason. After spending the last month trying to keep them safe from vampires and werewolves, it was difficult not to feel a little—or a lot—angry about that.

But they could hate me if they wished, so long as they were alive to do it. Because if Obyrron invaded New London unchecked, I had the feeling that none of us would live long enough to regret this trial. And if we did live, we wouldn't be grateful for it.

"This is a farce!" someone shouted from high in the benches to my right.

"Your face is the farce!" a very clever respondent jeered to the amused chuckles of the other spectators.

"She saved our lives from the monsters!"

"Only because she was the one brought 'em 'ere."

"She's a witch!"

With that comment, the stands erupted in shoving and shouting that made the scaffolding squeak and sway dangerously. Three sharp raps of the gavel echoed off the vaulted ceiling like gunshots, and the crowd stilled into uneasy muttering.

"This trial is public by the grace of our king for the benefit of the people," the Judge said in a ringing voice aided by dwarven amplifiers sitting on either side of the bench. His voice was vaguely familiar. "If the people cannot conduct themselves in a manner befitting a trial of this magnitude and seriousness, the stands shall be cleared."

That quieted the crowd even further, and their complaints died in sullen silence. They had opinions, but whether they believed me guilty of treason or innocent, they wanted to stay for the show.

Along the bottom row, the journalists sat with pens scratching, their eyes keenly suspicious. After a moment of searching, I spotted them: Tony and Lia, with Aris next to them, watching me with concern.

My heart rate slowed, and I breathed easier. I could do this. With them at my back, I could weather this storm and tell everyone the truth about what was happening to New London. The papers would run the day's events, and the city would know that members of our government were conspiring with enemy faeries to destroy the empire.

I just had to make it through the prosecution first.

"The trial will come to order!" the bailiff shouted. "The Supreme Court of Unified England is presiding over the case of The Crown versus Lady Gwenevere Violet St. James, Duchess of Wainwright, on the charge of high treason by adhering to the King's enemies while in the King's realm, contrary to the Treason Act. The Right Honorable Rufus Melville, presiding."

My stomach curled into a painful little knot and tried to climb up my throat. Rufus Melville was the Lord Chief Justice? I'd never cared to stay abreast of things like political appointments but if I had known my former future father-in-law would decide my fate, I would never have allowed myself to be caught.

I could still see his eyes when he walked into the drawing room to find my handprint red on his son's bloody face, several pieces of broken furniture at my feet.

I had been too furious to care then. After all, my fiancé had just told me that no man would ever want me for myself, not with such a juicy title available, so there was no point in denying him a taste of what he would buy in our marriage before the vows were said.

Whatever illusions I had cherished of love and constancy had been shattered, and my youthful fury was too great to keep in check. Young Lord Melville had been lucky I had not broken something of more significance than his nose and a few pieces of furniture.

But his father was incensed and insulted, and it was only Mama's admirable command of every situation that let us leave the ruined celebration without bringing a lawsuit down upon us.

My reputation had been destroyed—the Melvilles had seen to that—but my young ex-fiancé did not have an easy time of it, either. No young lady of acceptable pedigree wanted to marry him after that. It seemed a suitable punishment to my disillusioned heart.

Lord Melville disagreed. His son had been the prospective Duke of Wainwright, but the dissolution of our alliance left him no more than a petty lordling with a small estate, a slim pocketbook, and no social prospects.

As the sun slipped behind a bank of clouds, the room darkened enough for me to see the face of judgment staring down at me: a pair of satisfied blue eyes that promised retribution for the loss of his family's prospects.

He smiled at me, and my stomach revolted. The hope I cherished of winning over the court, slim as it was, evaporated.

I was doomed.

5

The Trial of Gwenevere Violet St. James

GWEN

As I stared up at my former future father-in-law, all I could think was *dratted, double-damned, son-of-a-weasel!*

To make my current situation even more enjoyable, the throbbing pain in my chest made concentration nearly impossible. I tried not to show it because there was nothing to be done but endure. That, and I did not want to give the man the pleasure of knowing he disconcerted me. Childish, perhaps, but there it was.

"Here begins the proceedings of the trial of Gwenevere Violet St. James, charged with Conspiracy to commit Treason before His Majesty the King. These charges encompass the kidnapping and murder of His Majesty's citizens, the practice of witchcraft within city limits, and conspiring with enemies of the Crown to throw

New London into chaos and facilitate the murder of King Edwin, Second of His Name. Do you understand these charges as I have read them to you?"

I took a careful breath and wrestled my mind into order. "If I may ask for a point of clarification, Your Honor? Exactly who am I supposed to have conspired alongside?"

The crowd muttered, but the Lord Chief Justice only glared at me in disgust. "According to the charges, with werewolves and vampires."

I clenched my jaw. *Don't laugh. Don't. Laugh. Now is definitely not the time.* "Do the charges specify who leads these monstrous forces, or am I suspected of canoodling with every individual, violent, and highly solitary creature?"

Justice Melville drew himself up. "Before impudently interrogating duly appointed members of this body and making your tenuous situation more dire, you would do well to remember that the justice system is not on trial."

"Perhaps it should be."

Gasps and titters rose from the crowd.

"You will watch your tone, madame, and remain silent till you are addressed by this Court," he sputtered, barely controlling the anger that flamed in his cheeks.

Shut up, Gwen, Tony warned in my mind. *He can hold you in contempt, and we would be far worse off.*

He was right, and yet every fiber of my being burned with righteous indignation. I thought I had prepared myself for this. I knew it was coming. And yet to have such flagrantly false charges flung in my face before the city I had been fighting to protect made my throat close with rage.

So I gave Justice Melville the only thing I could manage: a small, cold bow of the head.

The barrister, a young man with more bravado than sense, who was preceded by an impressive nose, held up a piece of paper and said, "If it pleases the court, I will begin by establishing the defendant's character. According to these records, you have helped to fund several so-called charities for years. Many of those charities"—he turned to the audience—"have been directly responsible for disturbing the peace of our fair city, causing riots that damaged countless businesses, and callously overturning the natural established order. Madame, tell the court whether you have, in fact, financially supported the Suffragettes."

"Your *Grace*."

He paused and stared at me. The young barrister clearly had every word and action planned in an attempt at theatre, and my impolite intrusion unsettled him. "Pardon me?"

"My honorific," I said, though I had deferred to Mama and not used the damn thing once since my father died, "is Your Grace."

I may be obliged to let the Chief Justice scold me, but I would be damned before I'd let this wet-behind-the-ears boy try to deny me the honor of my station when he was so intent on humbling me.

He frowned, and his eyes cut toward the Chief Justice, but he didn't dare look for approval with so many spectators. *If they were determined to sully my good name before the people, I might as well remind them exactly who they were addressing. It was a petty revenge, but I needed every advantage I could get. And if it threw the boy off his stride, so much the better.*

The barrister cleared his throat and continued with a little less volume, "Your Grace, have you financially supported the Suffragettes?"

"Yes, I have."

"Andrew's Home for Destitute Children?"

"Yes."

He appeared to be on more confident footing now, and nodded. "The League for Equal Representation, a fringe group responsible for months of rioting?"

"No."

He stopped pacing and turned to face me. "Pardon?"

"No, the League for Equal Representation is not a fringe group, nor did they riot. Agitators were responsible for the riots."

A chorus of "Hear, hear!" rose from the crowd, only to be answered by hissing from dissenters.

The barrister worked his mouth like he'd just tasted something sour and said in clipped tones, "You financially supported the League for Equal Representation, Your Grace?"

"Yes."

He resumed pacing with his hands clasped behind his back in a dignified manner as he considered my many misdeeds. "These acts of financial support do not, in and of themselves, constitute treason, of course. Other noble and upstanding members of our society hold views and support causes with which many of us disagree. However"—he raised one finger—"it is the first in a long line of character-defining actions that will prove the defendant is an enemy of the kingdom we have so painstakingly unified and protected."

The rest of the morning went on in much the same manner, with the prosecution detailing my heinous crimes in lurid detail: how I had kidnapped and sacrificed orphan children to gain my dark powers and used them to compel monsters to attack the city. The list of my faults dragged on until the court adjourned for lunch, where I was escorted to the privy and then locked again in my small room to await the rest of the trial.

I stared down at the cold fish soup for a solid minute before pushing the dish away.

That was not promising.

The last thing I needed was Tony explaining to me how badly the morning had progressed, but I thought back, *I noticed, thank you.* But the overall tone of the event had given me a sense of dread that expanded beyond simply using me as a scapegoat. *You and Aris removed my sensitive books and notes from the townhouse?*

Yes, ages ago. They're in the safe house.

During the monster invasion of New London that had caused this whole affair, we hid a group of faerie refugees in a nondescript house I purchased months before. Now that the city was safe for them again, they went back to their homes and jobs, but the house sat empty.

Not out in plain sight, I assume? I asked.

Are you insulting me on purpose?

No. I'm sorry. I'm tired and irritated.

I can imagine. That was the longest you have kept your mouth closed in years, I'd wager. It must have been trying.

I snorted and then thought back, *Are you teasing me, Inspector?*

Is it helping?

A bit.

Then yes. Fair warning: I have been corralling the Dowager with great difficulty since she arrived after your injury, but I don't know how much longer Lia and I will be able to keep her from inserting herself into the situation.

A tapping at the window made me turn to see Aris standing on the sill, clicking his beak at me. As I crossed the room to open the window, I thought, *It was an inevitability, I suppose.*

Can you convince her to abstain from throwing around the weight of the Duchy?

I sent back the equivalent of a mental eye-roll. *What do you think? No one has ever been able to convince Mama to do anything she did not want to. I may have publicly claimed my title at last, but everyone knows who wields the power of Wainwright.*

Noted. Be careful out there. I have a feeling this is going to get worse. Sam intercepted a note from the barrister, and from the sound of it, they plan to lay your personal life bare.

Aris hopped off the sill and into the room, shifting to his human form in midair and kissing my head as we walked back to the bench.

I expected no less, I thought.

My sense of Tony's presence faded, and Aris pulled me carefully into his lap. "I was proud of you this morning."

I snorted. "Were you?"

"Indeed, I was. You kept your mouth shut for a long—"

I turned to pinch him, but twisting my body that way sent a spear of pain through my chest. I sucked in a breath through my teeth and waited for the stabbing to fade.

When it was gone, I said, "Tony said much the same thing."

"He beat me to it, eh? That is unfortunate. Spending time with humans is making me dull." His voice softened. "This is going to get much worse, you know."

"I know. MacSweeney watched me for months, at the very least long enough to warn Tony off before he was fired from Scotland Yard. Perhaps even before that. They have more than enough information to blacken my name."

"Are you ashamed of anything they might have seen?"

"No. Well...no. I suppose not. But I never expected to share it all with an entire city."

He turned me on his lap until we faced one another, our noses inches apart. "Say the word, Darling."

And he would take me out of here, away, somewhere none of this mattered. It was easy to imagine getting lost with Aris, disappearing into the folds and fabric of the world like two small threads, unnoticed and unimportant. Free.

But the guilt would follow me no matter where we went, and I knew it. Besides, if the fae successfully invaded New London, who knew how far their reach would spread? So, instead, I said, "I love you."

Before he could respond, something happened. The sensation was akin to when an electric light unexpectedly flickers, and you stare at the steadily glowing bulb and wonder whether you imagined it.

But when Aris said, "What was that?" I knew it had not been merely my imagination.

Goosebumps ran down my arms, and I shifted carefully until I stood between his knees. "You noticed it, too?"

"I certainly noticed...something."

"Can you describe it?"

He rubbed the fingers of his right hand over his forehead, brow furrowed. "It could have been the shadow of a cloud passing the sun. Or a moment of—what did you call it? When you feel as if you have experienced something before?"

"Déjà vu?"

"That. But both things at the same time, and far stronger."

I nodded as I tried to reconcile his experience with mine. They were similar in the fleeting nature of it, but—"I thought it was like seeing a person pass in a reflection through a window or noticing a bulb flicker."

The metallic sound of the key scraping into the lock signaled that we were no longer alone, so Aris bent and kissed me, then disappeared out the window once more. We would have to examine the strange experience some other time.

The constables entered my room with shackles in hand to escort me back to trial, leaving me far more confused than I had been when I entered. But I did not have time to puzzle over the phenomenon because Aris's voice buzzed in my mind less than thirty seconds later. *Gwen, be careful. The crowds are pushing inside. I'm on my way to you.*

This morning, the halls leading to the public sections of Westminster were empty and echoing, letting every footfall signal how alone I was, how much closer to facing judgment. Now, people filled the halls, gathering in doorways and alcoves to watch us pass, stretching their necks to get a glimpse of me like I was an exotic bird only spoken of in stories. Some expressions were merely curious, but others were outright hostile.

More constables joined us, forming around me as if I were a visiting head of state. Being jostled between them as they struggled to keep me away from the growing crowds was rather claustrophobic.

"How did so many people get in?" I asked the guard ahead of me. "Don't they lock the gates for trials? Are there not security protocols?"

"Aye, there are. Someone must be sleepin' on the job."

"Yeah, or someone opened the door," another guard muttered beneath his breath, so low I barely heard him over the clamoring crowd.

The guard behind me took my upper arm in a steadying hand and said, "Stay close to me, Your Grace."

That was a directive I didn't mind following. In a one-on-one confrontation with a spectator, my odds were better than fair, particularly with Percy's blouse keeping my vital organs safe. But if the crowd decided to rush the guards, none of us would live to laugh about it.

The only thing keeping them away from us was the unconscious respect for authority baked into most New Londoners. That, and the pistols my guards kept holstered on their hips. I tried to take comfort in that fact as they rushed me down the corridor under shouts and censuring eyes.

"Witch!" a feminine voice shouted.

A stone the size of my fist flew through the air and cracked against the wall near my head with the report of a gunshot. Rock splinters bounced off my back and shoulder like stinging hailstones. Everyone froze. The flying rock had put a crack in the metaphorical dam. The manic energy of the crowd burst through their restraint, and they surged toward us like a flood.

"Get the duchess to safety!"

Before my guards could act on that very sensible command, the ground began to shake, but not from anything as mundane as the rushing crowd.

It felt as if the earth was tired of our tickling feet and decided to knock us off of them. I threw my arms wide, trying to maintain my balance as everyone around me stumbled into the person next to them, grabbing at anything they could reach for stability.

In their fear, the people forgot all about me. They huddled against the walls as mortar dust rained from the ceiling. I glanced up, hoping the massive stones above us wouldn't fall, and curled my arms over my head as I shoved through the crowd toward the nearby arch. As the strongest architectural point in the hallway, it was least likely to collapse.

One of the guards threw himself at me, wrapping his arms around my shoulders and protecting my head as dust and broken bits of stone rained down. I squeezed my eyes shut and prayed that no one I loved was inside the building.

The shaking stopped, and for a moment, no one moved. People had been flung about like a discarded deck of cards; they lay on the ground, crouched in groups, or sat in shock. When no further catastrophes followed, they peeked through their fingers and opened dust-caked eyes to make certain the world was still in place.

"Let's go!" shouted the protective guard. "Get Her Grace out of here!"

The constables, covered in grey mortar dust and looking shaken, reformed and hustled me down the hall at double time while the spectators struggled to regain their feet.

The constable who'd protected me leaned in and said in my ear, "Stay close to me."

His familiar voice made my heart jump into my throat. He stood behind me so I could not see his face, but I would know that voice anywhere.

"What under heaven do you think you are doing?" I demanded.

"Protecting you, my lady. As I always have done."

We rounded a corner, the lead guard pushed a door open, and the rest of us followed him into the unoccupied room. They locked the door behind us.

The protective constable guided me to a bench, letting his hand rest on my shoulder as he sat next to me, turning his face so it wasn't properly visible to the rest of the room. "You've been quite shaken," he whispered. "You need a moment."

The chief of my guards, a grizzled old sergeant with a salt-and-pepper mustache, dusted the powdered mortar from his hair and said, "Collins, LeGross, go get backup and clear these halls. Get us when it's safe. Henry, watch the door. Lady St. James?"

"I'm here," I said. "Just...a bit shaken. I need a moment."

He nodded and began issuing other orders while the rest of my retinue asked one another, "Was that an earthquake?"

Which left me free to whisper to Mr. Yates, "How did you get here and what—"

"Did you assume I would stay safely in the townhouse and take in the mail while you were in danger, ma'am? I do hope you give me more credit than that."

I was entirely unable to articulate my surprise, so I simply said, "How?"

"Master Samuel secured me a uniform, and Mr. Aris spirited me onto the grounds last night during the shift change. He thought whoever wanted to hurt you might try something, and it appears they have. I doubt a security gate was left open by mere accident."

"Given that someone threw a rock at my head with significantly more than mortal strength, I think we can safely assume you are right."

"I generally am, ma'am."

That made me smile and drained some of the tension from my body. I curled my shoulders, took an exaggerated breath, so my guards assumed I was still recovering, and said in a low voice, "Just so. I appreciate your efforts, Mr. Yates. I cannot tell you how much. But I must ask you to return to the house. I cannot stomach the idea of you putting yourself in danger this way."

"I must respectfully decline."

Dismay stiffened my expression. He could have been crushed by falling stones or attacked by angry spectators if the earthquake hadn't saved us. Yates was a capable man but this was danger of an entirely different sort.

My voice sounded stiff when I said, "Then consider it an order from your employer."

He squeezed my shoulder once, his mouth flat in an apologetic smile. "In that case, I am afraid I shall have to resign."

It took every ounce of willpower not to turn on him in shock. "What? You would leave me for asking you to protect yourself?"

"No, my lady. But I will leave you for asking me not to protect you, even in this small way. It is clear there is far more afoot than someone merely wishing to use you as a scapegoat to defer blame for what happened in Trafalgar Square."

I glared at him over my shoulder. Mr. Yates had helped me solve more than one riddle over the years, and I did not doubt the state of his intellect or his empathy. Bringing him on as my butler was one of the wiser decisions I ever made.

But he'd never involved himself in my shenanigans to quite this degree. No matter what I struggled with, part of me had always felt relieved knowing Mr. Yates and Mrs. Chapman, at least, were relatively safe from the backlash. Was I not to have even that small comfort now?

"The hall is clear," the chief said in a no-nonsense tone. "Time to move. Your Grace, if you please."

With no more time to either question or caution my butler—god's breath, my former butler—I was hauled to my feet and into Westminster Hall. Before they could separate us, I growled beneath my breath, "I refuse to accept your resignation, Mr. Yates."

The man did not so much as look in my direction but turned to join the ranks forming up along either side of the hall as if he'd done it a hundred times. His absence left me with a pit of unease in my stomach.

No one in my household was safe from the consequences of this trial, save poor Charlotte, the upstairs maid, who had taken my offer to relocate her family to a place in the country where they might be safe from the tide rushing toward the city.

That, at least, had been well done.

"Your Grace!"

I blinked, pulling myself back out of my head and staring up at Lord Melville. Red stained his cheeks and neck, all the way down into the tightly fitting collar of his robe, and his eyes looked as if they might bulge out of his head. He was clearly in no mood to be trifled with. And was that sweat on his brow?

"Forgive me," I said. "I was overwhelmed."

The crowd murmured in assent, likely still on edge from the rare earthquake.

Justice Melville said, "Must I repeat the question?"

I sighed, straightened, and lied. "No. I am ready to stand trial."

So long as no one killed me in the meantime.

6

Sneaking, Supper, and Suppositions

GWEN

"That did not go very well for you, Your Grace, if you don't mind me saying," the chatty, mustachioed constable—whose name I had never bothered to learn—said to me as his contingent led me back to my room.

The second half of the trial had somehow managed to be worse than the first, and I was painfully out of temper, so my response was loaded with tired sarcasm. "Truly, Constable, I cannot tell you how much I value your input."

Instead of being embarrassed, the man perked up and said, "Kind of you to say so, ma'am. I have always been an observant sort, or so my mum says."

He conscientiously guided me past the cleaners removing the last bits of earthquake rubble, and around the corner into an empty corridor. A woman stood alone in the center, her hands folded primly. My heart gave a little stutter, and I stopped, dragging my guards to a halt with me.

"I don't suppose your mum told you how to handle problems like that?" Since my hands were still bound, I jerked my chin to the person standing halfway down the hall, blocking our path.

Chatty Mustache turned with a start, hand on the butt of his pistol, until he realized it was only a small, beautiful blonde woman.

"Don't need advice to deal with that," he chuckled and led our small contingent forward with all the misplaced confidence of a schoolboy. I shook my head and followed him. He was about to get a very interesting lesson.

"Stand aside, please, ma'am," he ordered.

"Your Grace," she corrected, using the magnanimous yet authoritative voice only those born to it seemed able to command.

He froze with one hand extended. "Pardon me?"

"You may address me as Your Grace, Dowager Duchess of Wainwright."

Ah. So Mama was following my lead and accepting the role of Dowager. Something about that made a little icicle of regret freeze my heart. I could never think of her as anything other than the Duchess. But Chatty Mustache didn't see the way her words affected me. His eyes were locked on Mama, wide and staring as his confidence deflated like a two-day-old balloon. But his shoulders straightened and he recovered admirably.

"Ah, yes. Please stand aside, your Grace. We are moving a prisoner, as you can see."

Mama raised her chin. "I would be happy to oblige you, constable...?"

"Er, Hayes, my la—Your Grace."

"Constable Hayes," she repeated, offering him a kind smile that lit her face with warmth. No one could resist that smile. It did not hurt that she was lovelier at fifty than she had been at twenty-five and that she wore her rank with as much elegance as the finely embroidered dress and expensive but understated jewels. "I will happily oblige you as soon as I speak to my daughter."

"But—"

"I will not move from this spot, Inspector, and neither will she. You have my word."

He blushed. "It's, ah, constable, Your Grace."

"Of course. Forgive my mistake. It's only that you have just the air one might expect of an inspector. If you will but give me a moment, Constable, I would deeply appreciate it."

That last clever compliment did the trick. Constable Hayes did not know it, but Mama now owned him as thoroughly as she did the rest of us.

He puffed out his chest and waved at his compatriots. "Stand to the side, gents. Give Her Grace a bit of space. Horowitz, Ladybird, watch the corridor."

"Gentlemen, you have my thanks."

The men obeyed with bemused expressions, leaving Mama and I standing alone with about twenty feet of space around us.

I wanted to throw myself into her arms, but she was Her Grace at the moment, and not Mama, so I took her hand and pressed it between both of mine. "You should not be here, Mama."

"Gwenevere?"

"Yes?"

"Hush. The only reason I have not been at your bedside is that you kept your injury from me."

"I did not want you to worry needlessly when there was nothing to be done."

"Worrying about you is my job, dear heart. Now." She edged in closer under the pretense of kissing my cheek and said, "If Tony does not explain this entire situation to me, and quickly, I will begin pulling roofs down on people's heads."

"Why not ask your daughter?"

Mama twisted her hands in chagrin. "Lia appears to be even more stubborn than you are and harder to intimidate."

"Finally met your match, have you?"

"It was bound to happen. And I suppose I cannot regret having strong daughters. But I expect you to tell Tony. He has a misplaced sense of honor, believing that keeping me in the dark is what you wish."

"He believes that because it is true."

"Gwen—"

"I do not want you in harm's way, Mama. I have enough to think about without trying to protect you, too."

She stood to her full height, still two or three inches shorter than me, and said, "That is not your job, darling. Now do as I say, or you will not like the consequences."

That was a dismissal. I leaned down to kiss her cheek, and she pulled me into a hug that nearly crushed my ribs. It hurt, but I bit my lips and bore it. She was far stronger than she looked.

"Thank you very much, Inspect—Constable Hayes," Mama said after releasing me. "You have been the absolute soul of gentility."

The poor man actually saluted her before finishing his escort duty and leaving me in my makeshift cell. Perhaps I should've asked Tony to tell Mama everything. After all, she was here now and dangerously determined. She was also clever and resourceful and could be of great help. But I wanted her safe, and whatever this business was, it certainly wasn't safe.

Wrenching myself out of my jacket without searing pain was a long and arduous process that required contortion of the highest order. As soon as I was done, I opened the window for Aris's eventual arrival and sat on the bed to rub my aching shoulders and think.

Hayes had not been wrong in his assessment. The trial was not going my way. The investigators had been thorough in their research, and they were about to lay a mountain of proof at the foot of the judge to show that I, and not Lord Rutledge or his governmental co-conspirators, was to blame for the recent calamities that befell the city.

And, as much as I hated to admit it, they would find quite a lot to support their claims. I had been involved in the affair in ways no outsider would understand. If the prosecution succeeded, every listening ear would be forced to conclude that I had, at best, engaged in suspicious activity and, at worst, been actively plotting against the realm.

I could only hope that, when it was time for my defense, the truth would be clear enough to convince the citizens of New London to protect themselves, not only from the invading faeries but from their own corrupt officials.

I took a deep breath, paused at a familiar scent in the air, and said, "Sally?"

"Lady Gwen?"

Though I knew she was there, I still gasped and jerked backward so violently that white-hot pain shot from one side of my torso to the other. One does not get used to a whole person appearing out of nowhere. My right hand flew to my chest while the left steadied me on the bed.

Sally stood in the center of the room with a Sightscreen on her wrist and a shame-faced expression turning her cheeks pink. She had to have been in the room when I arrived, but I had not seen or sensed her at all. If it had not been for the faint hint of violets in the air, I wouldn't have guessed she was near.

I put one finger to my lips and motioned for her to sit by me as I caught my breath.

"Sarah Elizabeth Dawes," I said in a low voice, "how on earth did you get in here?"

She wrinkled her nose. "The Sightscreen, of course, and...Lady Evelyn."

"You and Mama were working together? Of course. She distracts the guards, and you slip inside?"

"Something like that."

"Don't look so proud of yourself," I groused. Sally smiled. Not only did she smell of violets, a scent she'd taken to wearing over the last year, but she was pretty as a flower, with light gold freckles, blonde curls, and the glowing skin of youth. And there was now a strength in her features that had not been there when she was younger. Was she seventeen already?

In her eyes, though... "Sally? What's wrong?"

Her expression stiffened, and she clasped her hands in her lap. She looked at her entwined fingers for a long time before she said quietly, "I have a problem, and I don't know who else to turn to."

"You can always come to me, darling. I hope you know that."

She nodded. "I do. It's just that...you warned me, and I should have known, and I don't want to put you or anyone else in danger; I just feel so—so stupid!"

Her balled fists hit the bed with impotent fury and embarrassment, and for a moment, she was wound tight as a spring. A few deep breaths later, she calmed enough to say, "Madame Matilda left the coven."

I froze. "What?"

"During practice for a rather dangerous casting, one of the apprentices broke the circle. She shouldn't have done it; it was stupid and careless. We all know the dangers of breaking a circle. It's the first thing we learn! I don't know what drove the girl to do it, but the magical rebound—" Her face took on a sickly green pallor, and she swallowed hard. "Well, there wasn't much left of her."

The need to put my arm around Sally was so great I had to clasp my hands together in my lap. I knew what it was to carry guilt heavy enough that comfort only made the shame more crushing. So I waited as she gathered the strength to finish.

"Deborah—you remember her?— said it was Madame's fault. That she had grown careless and distant. Madame has been busy in town lately, doing something she chose not to share. Deborah said that's why the apprentice died, because Madame's priorities had slipped, and she didn't prepare the girl as she ought. The next day, Madame was gone. We have not seen her since."

I could not have been more bowled over if someone had hit me with a club. Madame Matilda had seemed to be in absolute control of the Triumphant Sisterhood. And despite my personal feelings, she had always appeared to have the best interests of the city and her coven at heart. Then again, I had never been privy to what happened behind closed doors, and the Sisterhood was nothing if not secretive. Perhaps Madame was not so altruistic as she led me—led *us*—to believe.

Placing one's trust in someone unworthy of it is a painful experience, and this wasn't the first time Sally suffered from such an open-hearted mistake. And no matter how much I wanted to protect her from the consequences, it wasn't a mistake she would easily recover from.

Just last month, Sally had pledged herself as an apprentice to the coven for the required period of six years. She would learn all they could teach and be required to give service in return. And that oath bound her whether Madame Matilda led the coven or not.

She took my hands in cold, trembling fingers. Her distress sliced me to the core. "I was wrong, Lady Gwen. Everything changed when Madame left. It's nothing like I thought it would be. I'm so sorry."

"Oh, my darling." I pulled her into a hug as my heart broke for her. Was anything as painful as disappointed hopes, the kind that made you question whether you could trust your own judgment? I should have been more present, more aware that Sally was walking this path. I might have warned her, might have seen the signs if only I hadn't been so damned distracted by the monsters and my own pain. I held her by the upper arms and forced her to look at me so I could say slowly and with as much conviction as possible, "It is not your fault."

"It is," she said, wiping her cheeks and shaking her head. "I wanted power. I wanted...moon and stars. I wanted to know that no matter what happened, I would never be forced to be Sally Dawes from the Narrows again, stealing to live and trying...I wanted some agency over my life and to—to..."

Realization hit me like a cresting wave and made my heart turn to ice in my chest. When I spoke, my voice came out weak. "God's breath. You wanted to be like me."

"I could never be a duchess, so I could not have the power to chart my own course that way, but—"

"There was magic," I finished.

She nodded her head, ashamed, but I caught her up in another hug, letting the pain in my chest throb as it would. I deserved worse, so I would take it as a penance. That Sally would see my chaotic life as something to emulate had never occurred to me. But it should have. It should have.

"Alright," I said, trying to pull my thoughts into some coherent shape. "It will be okay. All will be well. We'll sort this out."

"That's just it. There is nothing we can do. If Madame does not want to be found, no one will find her. And that's not the worst of it."

Dread slid like ice down my spine. "Explain."

"They want the grimoire back. And they expect me to return it to them. They can no longer trust Madame, and if she tries to recover it, who knows what she might do?"

The Mordegant Grimoire. God's breath. I had taken the ancient tome as payment for services rendered to the Sisterhood. Madame appeared to want it out of the hands of her coven, which was understandable given what Cassandra Monmouth had done with it. If she wanted it back now, that did not bode well for the coven, the city, or me.

"Deborah said that Madame gave it to you without consulting the coven, and they are the only ones who can protect it from her. Lady Gwen"—she locked gazes with me, her blue eyes earnest—"What do I do? I've made an oath I cannot break."

I thought for a moment. "Why did they not ask you to request it from me? We have had a cordial relationship despite our differences."

Her lashes fluttered, and her lips thinned into a hard line. Which likely meant she'd been ordered not to reveal something related to the answer of that question. So they either expected me to give the grimoire to Sally or for her to steal it from me. "What exactly did they order you to do?"

"To find the grimoire and return it," she said promptly, relieved.

"Well, I suppose if you cannot find it, you cannot return it."

"But I know where it is."

"Not for long," I said with a wink. "I'll have it moved. All you must do is walk slowly. You've continued wearing your amber amulet? To keep them out of your head?"

She nodded, though she looked sick.

"We will figure this out, my darling. In the meantime, learn all you can and remember: you are bound to the letter of your oath, not the spirit of it. Do you understand me?"

"Yes, ma'am." Something flickered in her expression, crossing her features so fast I barely had time to register the look and could not interpret it. She sighed and repeated, "The letter, not the spirit. Just like the fae."

"Exactly."

The lock scraped. It must have been time for the evening meal. I stood, pulled Sally to her feet, and whispered, "Next time, use your ring to contact me. I don't want you putting yourself in more danger. Keep yourself safe, and be smart."

Sally hugged me hard, crushing her slender frame against me, her fingers curling into the back of my shirt as if we dangled from a cliff and I was a rope. She looked me once in the eye, whispered, "Just like the fae," and then pressed the button on her Sightscreen. The door opened.

Sally was not exactly invisible, only so uninteresting that it was impossible to actively notice her. Should one try to over-power the spell the Sightscreen emitted, dizziness and nausea struck so hard that looking anywhere in that direction was torture.

The guard stepped inside and ignored Sally as if she were no more interesting than a lamp or chair. He placed a dinner plate on my small table, and Sally slipped out while his back was turned. I waited, listening, but no sound of discovery followed.

I let my head fall into my hands and thought, *Ophelia Magnolia St. James.*

Gwen? Is everything alright?

Not entirely, no. There is some infighting amongst the witches and Matilda is missing, according to Sally, who took it upon herself to sneak into my room with the help of our Mama.

I suppose some part of that that should surprise me, but strangely it does not.

It had certainly surprised me. *Will you retrieve the grimoire from the safehouse and hide it?*

A moment of shocked silence followed as my clever sister processed the implications of that request. *The witches want it back? That does not seem like a good sign.*

Will you?

Of course.

Thank you. Be careful?

Lia projected a mental eye-roll that felt like a wave of exasperation. *Being careful is all I ever do, Gwen.* And she was gone.

I allowed myself a moment to settle my nerves, decided a bit of food might help, and sat down to regard my supper: cold mutton in watery gravy, a stale roll, soupy beans, and something that had possibly been potatoes once upon a time. A sprig of wilted rosemary poked valiantly out of one soggy lump.

"This must be a war of attrition," I muttered, snapping open the napkin and laying it in my lap. If my captors could not argue me into an admission of guilt, they would starve me into it. But I had eaten worse. I would persevere.

Perhaps you'd like richer fare?

I turned to see Aris standing on the window sill in his raven form with a large cloth bag clasped in his beak.

I leaped to my feet and caught the bag as he dropped it. "You absolute angel."

The savory, rich scent of meat pie filled the air when I untied the knot.

"Courtesy of Monsieur," Aris said after he shifted. "There should be enough in there for two if you don't devour it all."

"I will make no promises," I said around a mouthful. The pastry crust was flaky and buttery, and the venison, potatoes, carrots, and onions swam in a delicate broth that made my mouth water.

Aris retrieved his pie and held it against his chest as if I might steal it, but I was too busy devouring my own. We sat to finish our meal, enjoying the hard cheese, berries, and chocolate trifles Monsieur had carefully packed.

"Thank him for me," I said, wiping the corner of my mouth with the napkin.

Aris leaned his elbow on the table, rested his chin on his palm, and watched me with amused affection. "Of course. I will describe for him, in loving detail, the way you stuffed your face with his delicious confections like the cutest and most delicate of piglets."

He caught the napkin I threw before it hit him in the face, chuckling at my indignation. I leaned back to give my stomach plenty of room to take up extra space in my abdomen and sighed.

"Call me whatever you like," I said, rubbing my belly. "So long as you feed me delicious food and read me poetry."

Aris lifted the book from the table and wiggled it. "This poetry? What are you willing to trade me for it?"

"My eternal gratitude."

"I'll take that as a start. But"—his gaze flicked to my lips, and one corner of his mouth quirked in a suggestive smile—"I have a few additional requests."

I grabbed his chin and kissed him quickly but leaned back before he could make my knees weak. "Your requests must wait. We have a problem."

One dark eyebrow rose. "Another? The mind boggles."

I explained everything Sally told me about the witches. His eyes narrowed as I spoke, and when I was done, he said, "We should find her."

"I agree. But we must also keep the grimoire away from the Sisterhood. If the witches are willing to fight over it, I do not want any of them to have it. I've asked Lia to retrieve it and keep it safe."

Aris leaned back and folded his arms behind his head. It stretched his shirt across his chest in a rather enticing way and pulled the collar open enough to reveal several inches of skin.

"Stop that," I said.

"What?"

"You know what."

He rolled his shoulders. "I am merely ensuring you know what you're missing. You have the right to make an educated decision about how to spend your time, after all."

"Aris, focus."

"Yes, ma'am."

I tapped the table with one finger as I thought aloud. "What Sally did not say was who had the Eye, and that is nearly as concerning. I was content to abide with the Sisterhood while Matilda was in charge, because while I do not entirely trust her, I believe her intentions concerning the city were pure. But something has clearly changed."

"Whoever has the eye and the grimoire would be dangerous."

"Extremely so."

He thought about that for a moment, then raised one finger. "I could—"

"No. Does your answer to every problem include homicide?"

Aris placed his fingertips on his chest and looked at me as if I were dense. "Assassin."

"We cannot simply murder people because they may become threats someday. Despite this debacle, the Sisterhood has kept the peace and protected the city for years. They deserve the benefit of the doubt. But," I added when Aris raised a brow, "it cannot hurt to keep our eyes on them. And, in the meantime"—I reached beneath my shirt and pulled out the amber talisman I always wore—"I have this. Sally and Sam have one as well, and so does Tony. We need to make certain you, Lia, Mama, and the rest get them as well."

"Human magic does not work on faeries that way. They cannot enter our minds. And amber is not foolproof, Gwen. Not if the magic is strong enough."

"True," I agreed. "But it is the best protection we have."

"Very well," he said. "I will avoid killing witches unless they become truly irritating."

"Thank you. Besides, we have other matters to concern ourselves with."

"Truly? I hadn't noticed."

I took a deep breath and rolled my shoulders, loosening the tension gathering in my muscles. "It's nothing much, you know; trying to puzzle out who is collaborating with the faeries so we can expose them and protect the city—worrying about the Covenant of the Silver Dawn and what other methods they might employ to assassinate me. Considering how we might stop the powers that be from hanging me for treason. Nothing out of the ordinary."

"Is that all?"

I shrugged. "All in a day's work."

Aris stood and lifted me into his arms as if I weighed nothing. "Since Lia is securing the grimoire and we have nothing at all to worry about otherwise"—he carried me across the room toward the cot—"you and I will negotiate my price for reading you poetry."

7

Surprise

LIA

Of all the mundane torments she'd faced returning to the mortal world, shoes were the worst. The tightly laced boots pinched with every step, and Lia longed for a carriage, an auto, a horse, anything that would save her feet from further torment.

Of course, when one is used to walking on moss in bare feet, any restriction feels like torture, but walking several blocks in heeled boots, even boots made to fit one's feet was particularly heinous.

Tony would pay for this.

He had insisted she walk at least a few blocks before hiring a hansom despite the urgency of her mission. "No one will notice a housekeeper walking through the city, no matter how beautiful she is. Establish that disguise before you hire a hansom. You're more likely to throw off interested eyes that way."

He was right, of course, but that did not stop her bloody feet from hurting. She indulged in several imaginary scenarios in which she threw said boots at his head. At least until she finally climbed into the hansom. The relief was so great that she groaned, unlaced the boots, and wiggled her toes. It was rapturous.

To savor the moment, she unbuttoned her jacket and blouse. In the summer, New London sulked in its own stagnant, soggy heat. The cobbles and brick buildings radiated like an oven. Thanks to the horse's brisk pace, the air that was stifling while walking now cooled her neck and chest. Lia flung her arms across the bench seat.

She tried to take a deep breath, but the stink of dung and boiled cabbage made the air stick in her throat. The carriage stopped at an intersection next to a gentleman on horseback. He glanced at her with casual interest, then his gaze locked on her exposed chest with outrage, his cheeks flaming with offense. If he could have scolded her for indecency, he would have.

Despite time and progress, the puritanical views of Christianity persisted long after the religion declined, like rats clinging to the detritus of a sunken ship. The man's outraged reaction to a few scant inches of skin was so exaggerated it made her want to slap him. But his face was too far away to reach, so she made a rude gesture as the hansom pulled away, leaving him gobsmacked at the intersection. If he'd seen faeries dancing naked during celebrations she was used to, he likely would have died on the spot—and good riddance.

When the carriage reached the first house on the block, she asked the driver to wait and circled the row from the opposite direction. The garden door was guarded by a tall hedge, making it invisible from the street, especially in the dark. No one would see her enter that way.

Lia paused in an out-of-the-way place, checked for interested eyes, then squeezed through the hedge and let herself in the back door.

Sneaking about the city in disguise and then breaking into her sister's home made her wonder if she wasn't carrying this espionage game a bit too far. But, from what she was given to understand, Madame Matilda was a capable witch, and the Mordegant Grimoire was exceptionally dangerous. Worse, it was not the only dangerous artifact inside. The fewer people who knew about the safe house, the better.

She listened at the back door a while to be certain no one was inside but heard nothing of note. Enhanced senses were a benefit of being a changeling, though she did not have the increased strength and speed Gwen seemed to possess. But she did have fire, so when she eased the door open and slipped into the house, her left hand was raised and glowing.

The hall was silent. Empty of danger. Why was she so intent on making herself nervous by seeing threats around every corner?

With a deep breath to settle her nerves, Lia passed the closed doors to the dining and drawing rooms on her way to the front staircase. Just last month, the house was filled with faerie refugees hiding from the vampires who infested the city. Now it was empty and so quiet the hairs on her forearms stood up. It was hard not to picture someone waiting just around the corner with a raised knife or pistol. Or perhaps a spell?

She fought back a shiver of irrational fear, told herself to stop imagining things, reached the bottom of the staircase, and froze. Directly across the foyer, the door of the sitting room hung half off of its hinges. It had been struck dead-center with something large that splintered the wood and left the room exposed to view.

Broken furniture lay tumbled on the floor. Books were scattered about like dead birds with broken spines. Cushions had been disemboweled. Even the drapes hung in shreds from their hooks. Her stomach somersaulted at the damage.

Someone had punched holes through the plaster and wood of every wall, perhaps searching for hidden compartments. Fine debris settled on flat surfaces, leaving the room stinking of dust and a smell she could not place: musky and wild. Luckily, there was nothing of particular value in this room, but—

Oh, moon and stars.

She bolted up the stairs with a dry mouth and an upset stomach, only to find more of the same. Every room was turned inside out and upside down. This was not the result of a mere search but a masterpiece created by someone who enjoyed destruction, someone with a vendetta.

Lia gaped at the wreckage, trying to swallow as her heart fluttered against her breastbone. Who had done this? As she stared, something happened.

When Lia was young, she would steal any pair of spectacles she could find and try to navigate Wainwright while wearing them. The familiar halls and rooms of her family home changed subtly when looking through a pair of spectacles, as if there were a secret world hiding just beneath the one she usually saw. She loved taking them off and putting them back on, watching objects change places or become softer.

That was the exact feeling she had, like the world had shifted in some indefinable way that changed everything just enough to become unfamiliar. But then, in a startling second, it snapped back into place, as ordinary and frightening as it had been before.

Sweating and shaking, she sank onto the corner of the bed and tried to catch her breath.

The house has been compromised, she thought to Tony. *And Gwen's books have been destroyed.*

After a beat of startled silence, Tony's voice filled her mind. *Are you safe?*

Yes. Whoever was here is now long gone.

You sound shaken.

She took a deep breath and tried to calm herself using the techniques she had learned while her life was in daily danger in the court of the faerie king. *I am, but not because of the burglary.*

Something just happened, but I cannot put my finger on what. I only know it was not something physical.

You had better come back to the office.

No, she thought, pushing herself off the bed and squaring her shoulders. *I need to catalog what is missing. Then we can decide what to do about it and what to tell Gwen.*

She got the impression through their joined minds that Tony was thinking, so she wandered to the hidden trap door. It had been smashed open by something blunt, the splintered wood making the hole look like a hungry mouth.

Very well. I suppose there is nothing she can do about it in the meantime, anyway. Then, after a moment, he asked, *Do you need me? I can be there in a quarter of an hour.*

A warm little ember of affection sprang to life in her chest. Tony was a truly good person, and earning his concern felt like winning a prize, even if he still did not fully trust her.

No, thank you. I would finish my search well before you arrived. I shall meet you at the office.

Keep yourself safe.

Lia looked down at her hands, which had been glowing with the promise of fire for several minutes, and thought, *If anyone finds me here, I will not be the one in danger.*

Tony was in his office when she arrived hours later, his face already buried in a pile of notes, collar open, shirtsleeves rolled up. His blonde hair was lit by morning window light and ruffled, likely from running his hands through it so many times. His jaw muscle clenched and unclenched as he read. Had he slept?

When Lia entered, he dropped the sheaf of papers, blinking in confusion as his eyes roamed over her costume. She must have been nearly unrecognizable in the black, high-collared blouse and long skirt. And likely looked dreadfully pale, as well.

"Come in," he said after a moment and gestured to the chair across from his desk as he hurriedly cleaned up.

She pulled the door shut behind herself, separating the two of them from the rest of the office, and sat. Before Tony could ask any questions, she unlaced her boots, slid her feet out, and wiggled her toes gratefully. Her white cotton cap landed unceremoniously on the floor.

Pins followed suit until her heavy curtain of hair hung loose down her back. Lia massaged her sore scalp and groaned as prickles ran from the crown of her head to the base of her neck. Moon and stars, it felt good not to have her hair bound to her scalp.

She squinted at Tony through pleasure-heavy eyelids. "Forgive me. Being imprisoned in all that nonsense since last night has made everything sore. I have not had the chance to harden to such restrictive clothing."

Tony's gaze flicked up and down her frame once. "You're not, ah...going to remove any other garments, are you?"

"You are safe with me, sir," she said lightly. "I promise to compromise your virtue no farther than unbound hair and stocking feet."

Tony sighed and sank onto his chair, muttering something about St. James girls. She ignored that and pulled her notes from her black reticule. It had taken her hours to search the entire house and record what had been stolen. And the news was not good.

As she described the house, Tony's eyes narrowed, and his heavy blond brows drew low in thought. He ran the tip of one finger back and forth across his lower lip. Now and then, he stopped her to clarify details and compare her story to the notes she had taken.

When she finished, Tony leaned back and ran a hand through his hair. "The grimoire is gone."

"Yes."

"But you do not believe Matilda stole it?"

"No."

"Why not?"

"I don't pretend to know nearly as much about human magic as Gwen," she said, "but I do know that most practitioners are subtle rather than frank, especially when their very existence is outlawed in the city. They would have been more likely to search with spells of their own or to leave the place as untouched as possible to avoid casting suspicion on themselves. Whoever broke into Gwen's safe house was as subtle as a club to the head and just as brutal."

"It sounds as if the destruction was as much a message as a method of discovery. Which certainly does not match my impression of the witches I have met thus far."

She narrowed her eyes at him. "If you had already come to the same conclusion, why ask for my thoughts?"

"Because you were there, and you are clever and observant. If your conclusion differed from mine, I would want to know why."

Such a small compliment should not make her heart beat faster. She had been regaled and beguiled with silver-tongued homages and heartbreaking poetry dedicated to her beauty, written and sung by the highest members of the faerie court. They had been looking for favor with the king, but it made their compliments no less powerful.

And yet this humble man, with his tousled hair and workaday clothing, embarrassed her with a bit of thoughtless praise. She shook her head and smiled to herself at the pure ridiculousness of it.

"What?" Tony asked.

"Nothing. I was just thinking about the underrated power of a good man."

"What does that mean?"

She laughed. "Nothing for you to worry about, employer of mine. Speaking of which: if not the witches, who would have broken into the safe house looking for the grimoire?"

"We have no proof they were looking for the grimoire," he said, raising one finger. "That's the first thing to keep in mind. They stole several valuable artifacts, according to your list. Any of those things might have been their goal. A second, and perhaps more important, question is this: who knew that Gwen kept a safe house?"

He had the manner of a professor trying to lead his student toward a conclusion, which meant he had already formulated one of his own, so she said, "Who?"

Tony flicked a glance at a newspaper on the corner of his desk. The headline read, *Eccentric Heiress Tried for Treason*. Below that, a summary of yesterday's hearing was printed in what Lia could only assume was the breathless rapture of sensationalized tragedy that would vilify her sister for the delight of the public.

He made a disgusted noise and dropped a stack of notes atop the offensive paper before turning his attention back to her. "We know Mac Sweeney had Gwen followed for months, so Scotland Yard is high on the list, particularly now that Gwen is on trial. And the Cutthroat King helped us guard the faeries, so he knows as well."

Lia grimaced. The Cutthroat King was Gwen's sworn ally, but he was also fae, so if betraying her benefitted him and could be done while upholding the letter of his oath rather than the spirit of it, he would. Both Scotland Yard and the Unseen Court made dangerous enemies.

"We were not precisely careful about hiding the place," Tony continued, "so there is a more than fair chance that the witches also knew. But, if so, and if they wanted the grimoire, why wait till now, and why leave such a mess? They know how dangerous Gwen can be."

Neither of them said it. They both seemed to be carefully ignoring it. For her part, Lia had been avoiding the mere thought that the only person who openly stated they were looking for the grimoire was Sally, because the possibility that Sally might have done such a thing was unthinkable.

They stared at one another, the words hanging unclaimed in the air between them, neither willing to speak them into existence. The doorbell jangled, breaking the moment. Lia's muscles tensed, and Tony's hands flattened on the desktop as if he would spring over it in an instant.

"Who is it, Olive?" he called, his voice carefully neutral.

The office door opened, and Olive stuck her head inside. "A client here to see you, sir. I asked her to wait, but she insisted."

"Very well," Tony said. "See her in."

Olive backed out of the doorway, and a woman in a drab brown dress took her place. The fabric hung off of her frame like oversized drapes, and the slouching brim of her tattered hat drooped so far down that it hid her eyes and nose.

What was visible of her mouth must have been identifiable enough, for Tony shot to his feet, sending the chair tumbling backward to crash to the floor. Lia's hands leaped into flame in response.

"There is no need for the fire, Lady St. James. And your caution is unnecessary, Inspector. I mean neither of you any harm." The woman's voice was rich and perfectly modulated, her tone cultured. That was not the voice of a middle or even upper-class woman. Hers was the speech of the truly, abominably wealthy.

But a barely detectable current of wariness in the air told Lia that something about the woman was not right. She did not dispel her flames but retreated just enough to give herself room to work, if necessary.

"Truly, you are a suspicious lot," the woman said. "What can I do to make the two of you more comfortable?"

Tony replied, in a stern voice, "You can explain what the hell you're doing here, Madame Matilda."

The woman raised both hands in a placating gesture, and her long fingers, callous-free palms, and carefully manicured nails spoke volumes about class and privilege. "I have every intention of explaining. Though, I had hoped to do so without the threat of violence from your changeling."

Lia's expression did not alter. She had assumed the mantle of General as soon as Tony leaped to his feet, and she stood cold, proud, and unmoving as she stared down the former leader of the Triumphant Sisterhood.

"Lady Ophelia belongs to no one," Tony replied in an equally cold voice. "If you wish for any goodwill from me, you will not insult her. You will also find a way to assure me that you are not a danger to my staff, and you will do it quickly."

Madame Matilda sighed and dropped her hands. "Forgive me. As you can imagine, the last few days have been rather stressful. Please, I meant no insult, and I mean no harm to you or your staff. I give my word."

The air came to life with a crackle of energy that Tony seemed not to notice but which Lia felt like static electricity on her skin. She let the fire die and said, "She is telling the truth."

Tony raised an eyebrow but nodded and gestured to the chair. Madame Matilda inclined her head and sat. Lia took up position behind Tony, where she could see everything and react quickly.

Gwenevere Violet St. James, she thought.

Her ring gave a little jolt as if she had just woken her sister unexpectedly, and Gwen's voice came back, *Lia? Is everything all right?*

Are you somewhere safe where you can pay attention?

In my lovely makeshift cell, breaking my fast with watery porridge. Why?

Madame Matilda is here. Don't scream.

With an act of will, Lia activated the full power of the ring. Hers was made by a fae artificer and imbued with magic from the Sunset Lands. The copies Delilah made using Gwen's ring as an example were impressive but limited; they conveyed thought as if it were speech, but that was the end of Delilah's understanding. Fae artifice drew on magic as well as natural forces, and this ring would do much more.

Lia and Gwen were more deeply connected than any average two people, and their shared blood and bond made extraordinary things possible; extraordinary but tiring. She hoped the effort would be worthwhile.

As soon as the ring activated, she had the sense of getting jerked backward out of her body, though she never moved. Her eyes stung as Gwen gasped and thought *God's breath!*

Can you see her? Lia asked inside her mind.

Yes! Yes. Is that Madame Matilda?

Obviously.

You have your amber talisman on?

Of course.

Do not take your eyes or your fire off of her for an instant, Lia, Gwen commanded. *That woman is incredibly dangerous, even as an ally.*

This is nowhere near my first dangerous encounter, so please do not patronize me.

"Given your reserved welcome," Matilda began, "I assume you have spoken with my former sisters?"

I can hear her, too? Gwen said, wonder replacing her caution.

Yes, if you would hush and listen.

"Something like that." Tony's voice and posture were stiff.

Matilda read his body language accurately and gave a tired nod. "I see."

"Why are you here?"

Madame Matilda lowered her gaze and picked at the ill-fitting sleeve of her coat, her fingers trembling. "My knowledge of your character leads me to believe you are a good man. We have worked together in the past through Lady St. James. I had hoped...you might help me."

Ha! Gwen thought with relish.

Gwen—

What? She has always been so confident and condescending. She is finally being brought down a peg.

That is beneath you.

Gwen gave a mental sigh and said, *You might have let me enjoy the moment. I am in prison. I deserve some small bit of happiness.*

You are in a comfortable room in Westminster where your fae paramour can reach you. Stop complaining.

Complaining stops me from worrying.

Shush.

Spoilsport.

"Madame, you manipulated Lady St. James into destroying Cassandra Monmouth and put her in additional danger by giving her the grimoire that nearly got her killed. I am also given to believe you have abandoned your sisters. Explain to me why I ought to be concerned about your plight."

He is laying it on a bit thick, Gwen thought.

Perhaps her sister did not realize how deeply Tony held grudges where people he loved were concerned, Lia thought, but kept that insight to herself.

"I used the tools available to me, yes. But I assure you, my actions were necessary. If my word is not enough—" She took a deep breath, and her shoulders slumped. She clasped her hands in her lap. "I am happy to create protective wards around your building as a show of gratitude."

Something isn't right, Gwen thought.

Lia wobbled and gripped the back of Tony's chair for support as a trickle of sweat ran from her temple down to the corner of her jaw. The ring was pulling on her physical resources to maintain the connection between her senses and Gwen, and her body strained under the weight. But Gwen was right: something about Madame Matilda was off.

Tony thought a moment. "If I accept your offer, I expect honest answers to my questions."

Matilda looked up at last, though most of her face was still shadowed, and her voice sounded weak. "I am certainly open to negotiations, though I must warn you: I will share no information that will endanger my family."

"Then answer one question in good faith: where is the Mordegant Grimoire?"

My shop! The anguished words crashed through Gwen's mind and into Lia's like a wrecking ball, echoing off the inside of her skull and making her knees wobble.

Delilah? Gwen's internal voice floated back, but it seemed far away. Lia threw her arms out to catch herself.

"Ophelia?" Tony asked, frowning at her over his shoulder.

Cold sweat stood out on Lia's forehead, and chills ran down her arms. She'd held the binding too long, and her knees quaked, but she wanted to give Gwen as much usable information as possible.

Madame Matilda sighed like air rushing from a balloon and listed to the side.

"Tony!" Lia rasped with the last of her strength.

He followed the direction of her gaze and lunged across the desk, catching the witch before she hit her head on the corner. Lia gasped, and the connection to Gwen ripped away. She caught herself on the back of the chair and panted until the little white stars at the edge of her vision faded.

"Shit." Tony eased Matilda back in the chair. Her hat slipped off, revealing a split upper lip and a bruise the size of Lia's fist high on her cheekbone. Purple smudged her under-eyes, and her normally vibrant olive skin was pale. "Someone beat the hell out of her."

Lia doubted it was merely physical injury that brought the woman low. Matilda must have expended quite a bit of magical energy to spend several days in the city without being detected by the other witches. "We need to get her somewhere safe."

"Upstairs," Tony said and hoisted Matilda into his arms. "We can use the room the faeries sheltered in. Hilder said something about their combined magic protecting the place? It's the best we've got until she wakes."

"I'll ask Olive to watch over her until we return," Lia said, watching Tony climb the stairs.

He paused and glanced at her over his shoulder. "Return? From where?"

"The Iron Rose. Delilah is in trouble."

8
The Last Straw

GWEN

Delilah's voice crashed into my mind like a runaway train, and the force of it ripped Lia's consciousness away, making me tip drunkenly to the side as I regained the use of my own eyes and ears. The room spun in a nauseating blur of color.

I caught myself on the edge of the bed before I toppled off, fingers curled in the sheets as I panted.

Lia? I thought, blinking away the afterimages of Tony's office.

An impatient voice came back. *No, it's me. Gwen, they're taking everything!*

D? What do you mean, who is taking what?

Men in black frock coats. They claim to be from the Ministry of Defense, but why would they be here? They're ransacking my shop! They've taken my notes, and my—

Her voice cut off.

I sprang to my feet as if I could turn and run out the door, only to be brought up short as Constable Hayes unlocked it and held out the manacles. It was time for the second day of my trial, and I had not even properly broken my fast. Had I been in Lia's head so long?

"Time to go, my lady," Hayes said, shaking the chains till they clinked.

I held out both hands, trying to project outward calm while yelling in my mind, *D? Delilah, are you there? What's happening?*

No response.

Constable Hayes led me from the room and down the long hall, but every bit of my concentration was focused on trying to connect with my friend.

Delilah? I thought as we turned a corner. *What is happening?*

No response.

Why were ministry goons ransacking her shop? Likely, they were looking for more evidence against me. Which meant every close contact of mine was also in danger of having their business or property confiscated.

Percival Bywater, I thought.

Gwen? Aren't you at trial? Is everything alright?

No, and no. Percy, get to your shop and remove whatever you cannot stand to lose.

What?

The Ministry of Defense has just ransacked the Iron Rose. It must have something to do with my trial. Whatever is most important in your shop and most sensitive must be moved to a safe location as quickly as possible.

Are you serious?

As the plague. I haven't the emotional wherewithal to tease you right now, and I hope my jokes would be in better taste. Go, and hurry.

The sensation of his mind dropped away, giving me a moment to recover before we entered the Great Hall. Only we were not in the right part of the building. In fact, we were walking further from the Great Hall. A sliver of unease pricked the back of my neck.

"Where are we going?" I asked.

"The Chief Justice has asked for an audience in his chambers," Hayes said as if I should be both honored and flattered by such attentions.

I most certainly was not. First, too much was happening too fast for me to puzzle it out with anything like my usual focus. My head spun with a thousand possibilities I had no time to piece together. And second, Rufus Melville could have nothing to say to me in confidence that I wanted to hear. Which meant it was likely something painful, cruel, or bad news I would prefer to avoid. But the constables dragged me along anyway until I stood before the man himself.

Lord Melville sat enthroned behind an enormous oak desk in all his florid glory, cheeks stretched in a self-satisfied grin. Without his wig of office, his scalp was covered in a fuzz of iron-grey hair, like a blown dandelion puff atop a slowly melting ball of wax—fuzzy and round at the top, falling into heavy draping folds at the bottom. If he had ever possessed a jawline, it abandoned him long ago.

He dismissed the guards, then folded his hands over his narrow chest and glared at me down the bridge of his nose, which was far too small and sharp for his face.

Such features on a pleasanter man might have been engaging marks of character. My dislike made them all distasteful, and I did not care.

"Lady Gwenevere St. James," he said with some relish. "I thought never to see your face again, not after you shamed my boy so many years ago. And now here we are. It is unfortunate, really. If your mother had raised a daughter with any manners, we might have met under different and much happier circumstances."

"Lord Justice Melville. What a relief to see that you have not changed at all. Should I ever regret not marrying your dog's ass of a son, simply looking at you would remove all doubt."

I heard myself say the words, even recognized the folly in them as they slipped out of my mouth, and yet was powerless to stop them. I could excuse my cruelty by saying that I was distracted and worried about Delilah and Percy, but the truth of the matter was that I had spent the last day and half squirming under his smug, rheumy gaze, and I *wanted* to be unkind, petty as that may be.

My insult had the desired effect: his already flushed cheeks went up in flames, followed by the tip of his nose and sagging earlobes.

His chins fluttered as he fought for something to say, eventually settling on calming himself before he replied.

"Your clever mouth will chase away your last chance at salvation and have you in a hangman's noose before the end of the week, Lady. Have you ever seen a man hanged?"

I swallowed. "I have not."

"It is quite a sight, if the neck does not break straight away. The victim fights as they strangle, trying to claw their way free. Legs kicking in the air, you know, like this." He raised one hand and waggled two fingers frantically back and forth. "They foam at the mouth and piss themselves and eventually nearly bite their own tongues off. I saw one man let go of his bowels in front of hundreds of people."

He watched my reaction, but I kept my face absolutely still, even though my hands clenched painfully around the chain.

"When they are cut down," he continued, "family members hardly recognize them. Blood in their eyes, face swollen, and all that. I suggest you think long and hard about whether that is the way you would like to leave this world. Because I can make it happen."

Through clenched teeth, I said, "What do you want, Lord Melville?"

He smiled and picked up a dagger-like letter opener from the corner of his desk. As he spun the blade, light from the window reflected off the surface, making white spots dance across the wood paneling. "What, indeed. You know, I am risking quite a bit by telling you this, but some very powerful people have offered me a great deal of money to rule against you."

A shock of electric fear tightened my muscles. "Who?"

"I cannot divulge such information, of course, but...money is only money, after all; you have it one moment, and it is gone the next. And it cannot buy the things that truly matter in this life. But title and legacy"—he raised the blade as if making a point—"that is something that can be passed down. Something that will stand the test of time."

A little laugh of surprise escaped my lips before I said, "You cannot be serious."

He scowled at me. "Consider this your chance to address the wrong you did my son all those years ago. He will be elevated to the station he deserves, and you will be safe from the hangman's noose."

"And you are willing to anger the powerful people who would like me dead to secure a duchy for your son? Do you think yourself powerful enough not to fear their retribution if you cross them?"

"I am the Lord Chief Justice of His Majesty's court, Lady." He tossed the letter opener on his desk. "And my son will be the Duke of Wainwright. Together, we will be nigh untouchable. And you will be protected, of course, as soon as you deliver a son to secure the title."

"Of course."

"After all," he said, eying me head to toe. "You are not such a loss that my grandsons will suffer. And since Hugh and I will have the raising of them, they are certain to turn into fine young men."

The fury building in my chest mingled with my fear for Delilah and Percy, my worry over Lia, resentment at this farce of a trial, and every other insult, degrading look, and wrong done me by those of my class over the years, resulting in something dangerous I had never felt. It was not a fire or even an explosion but a tsunami, churning and inexorable.

When the Cutthroat King had manipulated Samuel into service, my rage was cold, like the blade of a knife, freezing every emotion until there was nothing left but the drive to remove the threat by any means necessary.

Whatever this anger was, it did not make me simply wish to remove a threat but to hurt people. Not to save someone, achieve justice, or even stop a wrong, but to cause pain and enjoy doing it. I stood staring at the pleased look on Melville's face, and for the first time, I wanted to see fear and pain in someone's eyes and know that I caused it. I wanted to hear him plead for mercy, to say my name, and beg forgiveness that I would not give.

Every muscle in my body tensed and swelled until the chains binding my hands looked like no more of an obstacle than a bit of twine.

With the last threads of my sanity, I hurled the desperate thought into the space between his mind and my own. *Aris?*

Gwen? What is it? Where are you?

I am going to kill Lord Melville.

A moment of shocked silence passed like a skipped heartbeat before he thought, *Don't move. I'm coming.*

"Of course," Melville continued, absorbed in his vision of the future, "you shall be free to practice whatever hobbies you enjoy, so long as they are appropriate. You must play the proper hostess, support my son, and submit to your wifely duties, but you will be alive. It is a much better offer than the hangman's noose, you must admit."

His words began to run together, sounding like buzzing nonsense as he asked me to buy my life with my title so he could imprison me behind it. My ears started ringing. Any desire for Aris's help fizzled and disappeared as my mind went gloriously blank.

I glanced down at the chain binding my wrists and pulled. The links held for a moment, then screeched. The center ring snapped and flew through the air with enough force to shatter the bottom pane of window glass.

So, I thought with a vague sense of interest. *That is what they meant by coming into my strength as a changeling.* That would come in handy when I killed the Lord Chief Justice. The letter opener on the table wasn't quite sharp enough for a clean disembowelment, but with enough strength, I could still spill his guts on the floor.

Then, I could pull out a bit at a time and make him watch.

Melville stared down at me with wide eyes that flashed from the broken chain to my face and back. His mouth popped open in shock. I judged the space between his desk and my position—short enough for a leap. With little effort, I sprang across the room and landed on the desk. Melville gasped and flung himself from his chair. I swiped the discarded letter opener from the desk and dropped to the floor in front of him.

A quick slash between his hip bones ought to do the job.

My fingers flexed on the handle.

A black missile tore through the broken window pane, shimmered in midair, and hit the marble floor in a roll. Aris lunged to his feet and doubled my leap, placing himself directly between Melville and me.

"Get out of my way," I said.

His eyes, dark and wide with worry, locked on my face. "Gwen?"

"Move, Aris."

"What is the meaning of this?" Melville roared.

I made to lunge around him, but Aris wrapped both arms around my torso. I twisted, driving us both to the ground behind the desk. He rolled as we fell, taking the impact on his back, and held me tight against him.

The next few moments—seconds or hours?—passed in a swirling, red-black haze. When the world reemerged, my chest hurt, and my arms were locked against my sides. Someone banged on the door behind me.

"There is nothing amiss, Constable," Aris said. He sounded so much like Lord Melville that my stomach tightened in revulsion, but it seemed to work on the constable. The knocking stopped.

Aris turned me in his arms, dark eyes boring into mine. "Are you alright?"

That question encompassed half a dozen concerns, but the central ones were: *are you in your right mind,* and *are you hurt?*

I tried to swallow but failed, then nodded.

"Bolt the door," he said.

The lock snicked quietly into place.

Lord Melville sputtered with a mixture of fear and outrage as he brandished the letter opener I had intended to use—when had I dropped it?—and backed away from Aris, who stalked toward him with inhuman grace.

"You were going to kill this man, Gwen?" Aris asked.

I swallowed back bile, remembering the hot desire for violence that had swamped my body and burned away all emotion. I'd never experienced anything like it. A shiver of disgust at my own monstrous desire ran up my spine. "Yes."

"Would you like *me* to kill him?"

I nearly choked. "No. Don't."

As soon as Aris was close enough, Melville took a clumsy swipe with the letter opener. Aris caught his wrist and plucked the weapon from his fingers. The old man whimpered and flattened himself against the wall, turning his face away and squeezing his eyes shut. His body shook so forcefully that all three chins wobbled at once.

Did he hurt you?

Only with words, I thought back. *Don't kill him. He has information we need.*

Aris stopped mere inches from the trembling judge and inhaled through his nose as if smelling the bouquet of a fine wine.

A low, purring rumble of pleasure, a sound one might make when smelling dinner in the next room, vibrated in the air before Aris said with particular relish, "He is *terrified*."

Melville whimpered in response, and I added, "He said powerful people had offered to bribe him for a guilty verdict."

"Did he, indeed? Well, then." Aris placed one hand on the side of Melville's face, turning it until the man had no choice but to make eye contact. "Who offered to bribe you to condemn this woman?" He did not use the honeyed voice that made my knees weak or even the force of his glamour. He didn't need to.

The desire for unrestrained violence was in his eyes, and it had an impressive effect on Justice Melville because the man blurted, "I lied! There was only one. One man. Lord Pennyfeather."

The ground dropped from beneath me. I might have asked the question aloud, but revealing anything to Melville was too big a risk, so I activated my ring. *Lord Pennyfeather is the Lord True. And a member of the Privy Council.*

Yes, Aris thought. *We've met.*

What? When?

He is the one who decided to keep you in Westminster after your surgery.

A hundred thoughts rushed through my brain like uncoupled train cars, and I was powerless to stop any of them. If he wanted me dead, why not just instruct the surgeon to let me die? Was the conspiracy truly so deep? Was the King also involved? What hope did we have of saving the city now?

It is not safe for you to stay here, Aris thought, giving Melville one last contemptuous look before leaving him shaking against the wall behind his desk.

The man was about to preside over the second day of my trial, and we had just intimidated and coerced him. *Will he forget you?*

Yes. And you. And everything that happened in approximately the last several minutes. Shall we go?

I thought furiously for a moment while coupling cars in my mind. *No,* I decided. *No, not yet. If I leave now, it will be tantamount to pleading guilty. And the entire city will be on high alert. Everyone who knows me will be in more danger.*

I don't care about everyone else. Aris held my chin between his thumb and forefinger. *I care about what happens to you.*

How could the man make my knees weaken now, in the middle of all this? *But I care.*

He sighed. *I know. If you are determined, then I will not leave your side. If the Lord True wants you dead, he will find a way to make it happen. Especially if the verdict is not guilty.*

There is no chance of that now. Melville offered me clemency...if I agreed to marry his son.

I caught Aris's arm before he could turn back toward the dazed judge. Our eyes locked, and I thought, *That doesn't matter. I would hang first, anyway. What matters is finding out how far this conspiracy goes and protecting who we can. The Ministry of Defense is raiding Delilah's shop. I warned Percy to clear out. And the witches have overthrown Madame Matilda. She is unconscious at SPI—or she was a quarter of an hour ago.*

Aris cast a glance at the clock. Mental communication happened much faster than spoken words, but we could only delay so long. *This cannot all be a coincidence.*

No, it cannot. And if Lord Pennyfeather is involved. I swallowed. *The conspiracy to invade may go all the way to the King. If it does not, he and the royal family are in as much danger as the rest of us.*

What is our next step, then?

I considered Aris, then Lord Melville, who had stopped shaking and was now frowning in confusion. *Could you follow the Lord True and get into the palace?*

"No."

"Aris—"

"No, Gwen." *I said I would not leave your side, and I meant it. But if the faeries invade and we are not ready—*

"Listen to me. I will do almost anything you wish of me. I will respect your decisions and your boundaries. But I have boundaries of my own, and your life is one of them. I nearly lost you once to a small piece of metal—" His lips twisted around the word as if it tasted sour. "I won't leave you in danger again, not at any cost. Not even if you hate me for it. Please do not ask it."

For years, Aris was bound by a geis, and he could not do or say the things he wished. He had watched me put myself in danger time and time again, only able to render what aid a raven could give.

Now the geis was broken.

For the first time, Aris had the right to choose what his life should become. And by some miracle, he had still chosen me. A cruel voice whispered that he chose me before he knew what a monster I could become, that I was capable of killing an old man in cold blood, but I stuffed that voice into a deep void to be dealt with later, and focused instead on the man I loved.

He was free after years of mental slavery. Could I blame him for protecting his free will? Then again, the fate of the city, maybe even the world, rested on us. I should try to convince him that spying on the Lord True was more important than my safety. But looking into those dark eyes, both determined and vulnerable, melted my heart.

"Damn you." I sighed, dropping my head and tapping my forehead with my fingers. I had to focus. It was one thing to expose a marquis and his co-conspirators, but casting public aspersions on the Lord True? We would need much more significant evidence than Lord Melville's panicked confession.

"Your Honor?" a male voice called through the door. "We cannot extend this delay. The crowd grows restless."

Melville blinked, shook his head like a dog shedding water, then shouted, "Constable!"

Aris rolled his eyes and unlocked the door. Hayes hurried in, only for Melville to growl, "What is the prisoner doing out of her chains? Remedy this situation immediately."

Hayes flinched as if he had been struck, looked down at the broken chains hanging limp from my manacles, and said, "Yes, sir. Right away, sir!"

As he replaced my bonds, I thought to Aris, *I'm sorry. I'm sorry I put you in a position to influence their minds.*

This isn't quite the same, darling. I haven't overridden their will. They'll simply forget, just as they would have if they drank too much wine. I can only influence so many people at once, or I would have forced the whole damn city to forget your name so I could steal you away. Alas, I can only affect the memory of three or four people in close proximity, so I cannot stay by your side in the Great Hall. But I'll be close.

That was some small comfort as they clasped new manacles around my wrists. None of them seemed to see anything strange about the presence of a tall dark-haired man striding at my side.

Melville followed close behind, muttering to himself as he fixed his white wig. "You will regret this soon, girl," he said as he pushed past me to enter the hall.

I rolled my shoulders and prepared for another few hours of torture as the man made his slow, stately way toward the bench. He would need to be properly seated before they hauled me in, so I thought, *Ophelia Marigold St. James?*

I'm here. Sorry. That was rather tiring.

Are you well?

Enough. Just tired. Tony is caring for me.

Good.

Gwen?

Yes?

A moment of silence, a shiver of foreboding. *Someone ransacked the safe house. The grimoire is gone. And Matilda—*

"Bring in the accused!" A voice bellowed.

9

When One Door Closes...

LIA

Men in dark coats and bowler hats left the Iron Rose in a steady stream, carrying boxes of gadgets, bags, sacks, and stacks of papers. It was like watching ants carry waste out of an anthill.

Lia followed Tony toward the shop, unbuttoning the top two buttons on the rose-colored jacket. The protection was nice, but it was too bloody hot to be trussed up like a turkey. And her muscles felt like lead weights after the encounter with Matilda.

The witch was still unconscious. Someone wanted Matilda gone permanently. Before they left SPI, Lia bullied one of the Cutthroat King's Ratcatchers into watching the door. The man had been more than surprised when Lia approached him for help.

"You did not truly think I was unaware of your presence, sir," she'd said, amused at his stupefied expression. "You've been loitering here for nearly a week. You may as well come and make yourself useful while you spy."

He'd followed her to the office door like a bemused ox. She was certain he'd guard the door but less certain Matilda would be conscious—and alive—by the time they returned. If she was right, the witch had used more magic than was good for her.

Tony must have had the same worry because he strode across the street like a man itching for a fight, stopped the first frock-coated agent he could reach, and made a wall of himself by folding his arms across his impressive chest. "What is the meaning of this?"

"Government business, sir," the man replied without meeting Tony's eye.

Delilah barreled out the front door, chest puffed, and fists clenched, her small white teeth bared as she shouted some of the most impressive curses Lia had ever heard.

"You have no right!" She threw herself at the last man in the row and wrestled the box from his arms. "These are mine, my work!"

The ministry agent may have been taller than Delilah by nearly a foot, but she was stronger. He lost his grip on the box and tripped over his own feet, landing hard on the asphalt with an "Oof."

Fleur, Delilah's delicate elven wife, rushed out of the Rose and grabbed Delilah by the elbow. "Do you want to end up in jail?" she demanded, her red brows drawn low as she pulled Delilah away from the frock coat, who climbed unsteadily to his feet.

Delilah freed her arm with a jerk and raised a foot to kick the wobbly man. "If that's what it takes!"

Tony gave Delilah a warning glance, but she would not be intimidated. "They're stealing my property, Tony. It's unlawful!"

"And you won't be able to remedy it if you're in a jail cell," Tony said. "Give me the box."

"No."

"Then give *me* the damned box," Fleur said and snatched the burden out of Delilah's hands so fast that she looked at her empty palms in shock.

The Frock Coat set his jaw and reached for the box. "That is no longer personal property. It is evidence."

"Says who?" Tony asked.

"Says me."

Another Frock Coat entered the fray, but this one was not a nameless agent of the government. He wore a fine linen suit and silk waistcoat beneath his formal coat, and his blue eyes were hard as agates. "Hello, Mr. Hardwicke."

Tony's expression did not change, but his posture did. He tensed as if preparing to take a blow or strike one. That meant this man was an enemy. Lia flexed her fingers and positioned herself with a clear line of fire.

"Mr. Grey," Tony said in a neutral tone. "Where is your warrant?"

Mr. Grey pulled a folded piece of paper from his pocket.

Tony took it and scanned the words, his nostrils flaring. "This is fabricated bullshit."

"Tell that to the judge. Our search and seizure is legal, Inspector—wait, forgive me, *Investigator* Hardwicke. And if you don't want to add an arrest to the reason for our visit today, I suggest you control your client."

"Arrest?" Delilah said, sticking out her chin and elbowing past Fleur. "What for? *You're* the criminals!"

"Assault on a duly appointed government official, for one," Mr. Grey said as he tucked the paper away, his voice coldly amused. "Interference, obstruction...the list goes on."

"I didn't—" Delilah began, but Lia stepped between them and glared down at her with cool authority, a blend of her mother's training and years in the faerie court. Delilah opened her mouth, her face flushed with righteous indignation. But Lia would not be moved. With a growl, Delilah stormed back into the shop, followed by her redheaded wife.

Mr. Grey tipped his hat and closed the back door of the cart with a *click*. "Thank you for your cooperation."

The carts loaded with Delilah's tools, papers, and experiments rumbled down the street and turned off of Artificer's Row. Decades of work were gone. Lia's stomach twisted at the thought, but she pushed her discomfort away and turned to Tony.

"Mr. Grey was particularly unpleasant. How are the two of you acquainted?"

"I had a few run-ins with him when I worked for Scotland Yard. He's a cleaner."

"Which means?"

"The ministry sends him in to clean up messes and keep things quiet."

"Was he a self-satisfied prig, then, too?"

Tony rolled his shoulders and pushed a hand through his hair. "He was always a bully, but he's been worse since I was sacked. Now that I'm a civilian, I apparently deserve less respect."

"You should have punched him."

The shock in Tony's brown eyes was surprisingly adorable. "What?"

"You should have punched him. I know you wanted to."

One corner of his mouth twitched. "One does not simply punch government officials, Lady St. James."

"Only if one is too uptight for one's own good."

"Only if one wants to go to jail for assault and battery."

"Fine," she said, noting that her attempt at humor had released some of the tension in his hands and shoulders. "Next time, *I* will punch him."

He snorted. "I'll hold him for you."

"There's a good lad."

Tony turned toward the Iron Rose with the air of a man facing a pit of lions. "Delilah runs a clean shop, and she's as thorough with her paperwork as any bureaucrat. If this has nothing to do with Gwen's trial, I'll eat my hat."

"You've left your hat in the auto."

"Guess I'm off the hook then."

Lia flexed her fingers, letting the energy tingling at her fingertips dissipate. She was tired of failing. She hadn't been able to protect Gwen. Even sending the Raven, the most dangerous faerie she knew, to the mortal world hadn't been enough. Gwen had still been shot. Rutledge's co-conspirators were still in hiding, they knew next to nothing about the Covenant and why they'd tried to kill her sister, someone had raided the safe house, the Sisterhood had gone rogue, and now *this*.

She hadn't even been able to update Gwen because the trial had begun before she'd fully recovered from nearly fainting. It was too much to bear. Where was all her strategic genius now?

Lia chewed her lower lip. "All of this is connected; it must be. Too much is happening for everything to be a coincidence."

The ground bucked, rolling almost like a wave, pulling them both off balance before Tony could reply. He caught her arm to steady her and bent his knees to absorb the motion. "Aftershock. Hang on!"

Mortar dust showered from the sides of the buildings as they tried to maintain their footing, holding one another while the world shook. A deep rumble from their right made Tony leap to the side, dragging her with him. He hit the ground on his side with his arms around her as a block the size of her chest slammed into the ground where they'd been standing. Little splinters of paving stone burst from the impact, spraying them with stinging cuts.

They lay panting for several moments after the shaking stopped, waiting for their hearts to calm enough to climb to their feet. Tony rolled them so she lay atop him, one hand pressed against her side, the other cradled the back of her head against his chest. His heartbeat slowed beneath her cheek, and hers followed suit as if drinking his calm energy like wine.

"That was exciting," he said, his voice rumbling in her ear.

"I could have done very well without it."

"Can you stand?"

Lia hesitated. She could stand, but she did not really want to. It had been a long time since she'd allowed anyone but Gwen and Mama to hold her with tender concern, and the sensation was nicer than she wanted to admit. Faerie men were intoxicating, skilled lovers, but they only saw her as a novelty or a path to greater influence with the King.

She'd played their game and beat them at it, even enjoyed herself a few times, but she was never foolish enough to believe their professions of love. Of course, Tony did not love her, either. Gwen held his heart despite the overwhelming bond she formed with Aris. But he cared enough to protect Lia with his body, and that was far more potent than faerie beauty.

She wanted to hold onto that feeling for a moment. Just a moment. She braced her hands on the pavement and began to push herself up but froze when their eyes met. Mortar dust powdered his hair and stuck in his brows, but his eyes were clear and warm, the exact brown of the chestnuts she and Gwen used to roast on long winter nights.

His brow furrowed, and his fingertips grazed her cheekbone just below a stinging cut. "You're injured. Are you alright?"

Another moment, she told herself, but when her eyes dropped to his mouth, she flinched and rolled away from him. Stupid. Stupid even to be tempted by someone who loved another. It was the adrenaline and her loneliness, nothing more. She was simply unused to having someone to look to for comfort when the fear rose to strangle her. That was all.

Lia dusted mortar from her clothes with a few fierce swipes of her fingers. "I'm fine." Then, to change the subject, she said, "It's lucky there wasn't more damage."

A few broken windows and tumbled stones marred the street, but it could have been much worse. Artificers gathered in small groups outside their shops, gazing at the architecture, pointing and exclaiming.

Her eyes drifted to the fallen block that would have crushed her. "What is that?"

"What?" Tony climbed to his feet and batted dust and rock chips from his trousers.

"Those markings?"

He followed the direction of her gaze and narrowed his eyes at the complex symbol that appeared burned into the stone. It was nowhere near as neat and clean as the magic circles Gwen and

Delilah discovered, but it had the same sense of purpose and a familiar set of lines she felt she should recognize.

"A maker's mark, perhaps?" Tony asked. "It was one of the capstones of the building. If something like this fell, I hate to guess what the interior looks like. We had better see if Delilah and Fleur are safe."

She nodded and followed him into the shop, glancing over her shoulder once.

As it turned out, Delilah wasn't entirely safe. A cabinet door swung open when the shaking started and cut her forehead just above her right eye. Blood smeared the side of her face, disappearing beneath the rag pressed to her head.

Fleur strode out of the back with a bowl of water, her delicate lips pinched unhappily, eyes narrowed.

"I warned you to put latches on those blasted things," she said as she bent and pried the rag away from Delilah's head to assess the damage. A fresh stream of blood immediately oozed down her cheek. "Damn. You'll have to hold that a while longer before I clean you up."

Delilah replaced the rag and sat quietly on her stool, eyes dull, face slack, but Lia did not think that was from the wound. Her expression resembled the faces of fae soldiers returning from failed skirmishes in the Wylderlands. Some had been angry or defiant, but others looked as if they could not process their experiences and shut down so they would not go mad.

"How is she?" Tony asked in a low voice.

Fleur put the bowl down on an empty table and rubbed her forehead. "Shocked. When she could still fight them, that was one thing. But..." She glanced at Delilah, and her eyes filled with tears. "She built this place. Her blood and sweat are in the mortar. They took her prototypes, her books, her notes. Everything."

Tony's eyes strayed toward the back of the shop and the inconspicuous door in the wall. "What about the boom room?"

"That, too."

"Not everything," Delilah said. Her voice was ragged from yelling. She dug into her overalls and pulled out a small book bound in black leather, ragged and scarred with use. "Not this."

"Is that—" Fleur began.

Delilah nodded. Fleur sighed and pressed one hand to her chest.

"What?" Lia asked, looking between them. "What is it?"

"That's the notes for the new artifice, isn't it?" Tony asked.

"I'm not a fool," Delilah said, replacing the book and patting it once. "I wouldn't leave this out for just anyone to find. It's too slagging dangerous. I would have thrown it in the forge before letting them have it."

"Thank the moon and stars," Fleur breathed.

"My workshop is still as good as dead." Delilah sounded as if she wanted to be angry but hadn't enough coals left to stoke the fire.

Lia's stomach, already tight with worry, turned over in sympathy. She, too, knew what it was like to lose a life's work. She folded her hands and let her guard down enough to say, "I am sorry."

Delilah raised her head and held Lia's gaze for a long moment, making her feel as if she were being weighed and measured on some scale she could not see. Finally, Delilah nodded and went back to staring listlessly at the floor.

"Here," Fleur said as she bent to recheck the wound. "Let me see that."

Tony canvassed the empty shop as Fleur cleaned and bandaged Delilah's head. Lia stood frozen, unsure of what to do next. The shop, which had always been full of purpose, voices, clinking hammers, and scratching awls, now felt like a cemetery. Every sound made hollow echoes, and snooping for clues felt like desecrating a grave.

But there was nothing helpful to say or do, so she wandered across the room to examine the dirty bootprints, discarded papers, and rubbish left scattered on the floor and trampled underfoot. It *was* a desecration, and a very purposeful one, as violent as the sacking of Gwen's safe house in its way.

The door to the Boom Room was still closed but dented near the handle. Had it been kicked? If Delilah reopened the shop, the door would have to be replaced. A damaged door would not protect the artificers from explosions.

A wave of giddiness hit Lia, making her wobble and throw her arms out for balance. Another earthquake?

"What the—" Tony gasped somewhere from her right.

Delilah moaned, and Fleur squeaked in surprise.

A shimmering, translucent wave washed across the room, warping her perception and coloring every surface in refracted rainbow light. A second image was superimposed over the stone wall and damaged door, but it was so faint it was hard to decipher. Or, it would have been hard for anyone who hadn't seen it before.

But Lia had seen it nearly every day for more than twelve years. Her knees gave out, someone vomited, and the mirage shimmered, then vanished. She was left sitting on the floor, staring at the wall and shaking.

"Are you alright?"

The only thought that Lia seemed capable of was *the door is broken. The door is broken.*

"Ophelia?" A warm hand on her cheek.

She blinked and looked up into a pair of concerned brown eyes. "The door is broken," she said. "Not the wall, the *door.*"

Tony knelt by her side and searched her face, his hands settling on her forehead as if she were feverish. "Are you alright?"

Gears ground into place in the back of her mind, picking up speed as the wheels turned. Of course. How could she have missed it? They weren't just looking for the door.

"Ophelia, are you well?"

"Yes," she snapped, waving him off and pressing her fingertips to her temples. "Let me think." Gwen was the solver of riddles, not she, but Gwen had not lived in the Sunset Lands long enough to recognize what was happening.

"What was that?" Tony asked the room.

Fleur said, "I don't know, but it was the strangest thing I've ever felt. Like being drunk."

"Alchemical poison can do something like that," Delilah said. "We'd better make certain those sparking idiots didn't spill any of my tincture when they stole everything. If you find a wet spot, stay away from it and tell me."

Lia stood and rested both hands on the stone wall, mind racing. "It's not alchemy."

"What?" Delilah asked.

"It's not alchemy," she repeated, closing her eyes and trying to block out everything but her swirling thoughts. The events of the last few months tumbled through her mind, crashing into one another with such force it was almost painful. She grasped at the edges of a unified picture only for it to slip away.

"Shall I make her a cup of tea, or—?" Fleur asked.

"No," Tony said, though concern was evident in his voice. "Give her a moment."

Lia heard the words as background buzz while her temples throbbed.

"Alright," Fleur said. "If there's nothing else to do, I'll just ...hang the closed sign and shut the door, I suppose."

Lia's eyes snapped open as the picture solidified, and she gasped. "Yes! The wall! The door!"

Fleur and Delilah joined them by the back wall and glanced at one another with worried eyes.

Fleur whispered to Tony, "Are you certain she did not hit her head?"

"I am not concussed," Lia snapped. "Don't you understand? We have been searching for conspirators to expose so the citizens would take our warnings seriously and prepare for the invasion. We have been treating it as a certainty.

"But we never asked ourselves the single most important question: how are the faeries going to get through the wall with a large enough force to threaten the city? If we know *that*, we can stop them, not just defend against them."

Delilah narrowed her eyes. "I thought you worked for the faerie king. You don't know how they plan to get through?"

"No. I was the general, but Obyrron is too wary to share everything with anyone. I knew as much as he thought safe, as much as I needed to know to carry out my role to his satisfaction. But I was conspiring with Queen Titania to stop the invasion from the inside before his forces breached the wall, so I wasn't concerned with what would happen if I failed. Because that would mean I was dead."

The tips of Fleur's ears glowed red with excitement, and she flapped her hands. "Wait, wait. So, what does that mean?"

Lia tried to calm herself enough to make them understand. "The wall was created by magic to keep mortals and faeries separated, but magic is a living thing. It draws on the power of both realms to sustain itself. Or"—she tilted her hand back and forth—"the magic creates both realms. It is difficult to distinguish which. In any case, it isn't a perfect wall. It moves and flows like water, like life. Sometimes, breaks or rifts form. But those rifts only allow one or two people through, and half of the refugees who try to get through are killed."

"But you made it," Delilah pointed out. "You and Aris."

Lia snorted. "If one were to create a scale of faerie magic, Aris and I would be near the bottom of it. My fire is certainly effective, but it is only a single skill, and I have honed it like a blade. Aris's presence is one of the most powerful I've ever seen, but his magic is mostly inward-facing. It doesn't affect the outside world like other magic does. And we only made it through because he used his body as a kind of shield or bridge for Gwen and me." The memory of Aris's still form made Lia shudder. "And the second crossing killed him. I restarted his heart with what was left of my magic, but only just."

She still didn't understand how she'd managed that. The crossing left her drained, disoriented, and empty, but Gwen's cries had wrenched at her soul. Lia had tried to stop her sister's grief despite the fatigue, but using what was left of the potent magic had drained her. It had taken weeks to access even the weakest parts of her magic.

She doubted she could pull off another such feat.

"So," Tony said, as if continuing her thought, "the stronger the magic one carries, the more damage the wall does?"

Lia pulled her mind away from the snowy clearing and back to the hollow shell of the Iron Rose. "Yes. There are only two paths through the wall: a spell or artifact that diverts the magic—and most of those were lost when the wall was formed—or a weak spot in the magic." She slapped her hand against the dented door to illustrate. "*Doors in a wall.* And you cannot fit an *army* through a *door.*"

Understanding flashed in Tony's eyes. He turned a sickly green, his voice weak. "You must breach the wall."

"Exactly. Even if there were an artifact in the Sunset Lands that would hold the door open, and I'm certain Obyrron would have found it by now, it wouldn't be large enough to allow an army through. So we don't need to know *who* is conspiring; we need to know—"

"Who has enough explosives to blow the wall to pieces," Tony finished, sounding sick.

The four of them stared at one another in a silence tight as a drawn bowstring.

At last, Delilah swore. "Great slagging hell."

Tony rolled an old silver franc over his knuckles, back and over again, as his eyes unfocused. "So it must be someone on *this* side of the wall," he said slowly. "Someone strong enough to punch an army-sized hole in it. Just a moment, I'm going to catch Gwen up. Perhaps she'll have some insight."

A little twinge of pain shivered through Lia's chest. This had been *her* discovery, not Gwen's. The sudden jealousy was both sharp *and* stupid. Gwen was brilliant, and they needed every answer they could muster to save this ungrateful city. So, if her sister had insight, they couldn't do without it simply to coddle Lia's pride.

A moment later, Tony said, "Gwen said she knows of no one strong enough to bring down the wall unless every bit of magic on the continent were gathered in one place."

Lia leaned against the door and closed her eyes as her stomach sank into her toes. "No," she said, "But Gwen made it through the wall using the Grimoire, which is now gone."

Tony's jaw flexed as he slid the franc back into his pocket. "We must speak to Matilda."

"Who is Matilda?" Fleur asked.

"I'll tell you later," Delilah muttered, then turned to Lia with her jaw thrust forward. "How'd you come to this notion, and why now?"

Lia glared down at the shorter woman. "I do not appreciate the suspicion in your voice."

"I don't give a bloody damn what you appreciate," Delilah said, her fists curling at her sides. "I want answers, and I mean to have them."

Light flickered to life at Lia's fingertips. She'd been committing heinous acts that sullied her soul for a dozen years to protect this damnable realm from invasion. Being suspected of the very act she'd nearly sold her soul to stop made her throat tighten with fury. Lia refused to roll over and plead innocence to a woman who'd enjoyed both safety and Gwen's love while she'd been denied it. Her voice came out as cold and hard as ringing steel. "Or what?"

Delilah seemed to expand, as if her anger made her grow a whole foot, the muscles of her shoulders and forearms flexing. She was undoubtedly stronger, but Lia fought dirty.

Tony slid his considerable bulk between them. "We are not enemies," he said, his voice hard as he glared at them in turn. "We cannot afford this nonsense, not now. New London needs us united. Put your petty dislike aside."

Delilah ground her teeth, and Lia folded her arms, forcefully extinguishing the fire that had begun to build, and her anger with it. Tony was right. If her suspicions proved true, the city would need every bit of help it could muster. And despite her antagonism, Delilah was the most capable artificer Lia had ever heard of. What was coming would require all her skill.

The fear she'd been keeping at bay wormed its way between her ribs and curled up in her chest, heavy and slimy. "The phenomenon we just experienced, the one that made us dizzy...it showed me a reflection of the Wylderwood, a forest that stretches many hundreds of miles across the Sunset Lands between the domains of Obyrron and Titania."

"You saw that in the shimmering?" Fleur asked.

"Yes."

"But, what does that mean?"

Lia swallowed, took a deep breath, and forced herself to speak her fears aloud. "I think it means someone is already attacking the wall."

10

In Which Everything Goes to Hell

GWEN

Tony's catastrophic predictions rolled into my head, dumping doom and gloom like an angry rain cloud. The bad news sloshed around, making it impossible to pay attention as the prosecution called another witness to tell everyone what a horrible scoundrel I was—which, I will admit, did not seem terribly important when weighed against the fact that I had been wrong; dangerously, awfully wrong.

I failed to account for the single most important piece of common sense information: if the faeries were going to invade, how would they get through the wall en masse?

God's breath, I should have seen such a gaping hole in my plans, but I'd been too concerned with the trial. Now we were beset on all sides; the Sisterhood had the eye, the grimoire was gone—no one knew for certain who had stolen that—Matilda was unconscious, faeries were planning to invade, some secretive covenant with enough power to create runic wards on their clothing was creeping through the landscape and periodically trying to kill me, and the Lord True himself wanted me dead, which may or may not be connected to everything else.

Our battlefield positioning did not look promising. And here I was, trapped while my butcher impugned my reputation.

You must wake Madame Matilda. We must know whatever she knows; whether she wishes to share or not, I thought to Tony as the butcher in question left the stand.

Already on it, he thought back. *Be careful, and don't forget your amulets.*

Aris is hovering like a hen. I will be alright. Then... *Protect my sister.*

With my life.

Tony's presence in my mind faded, leaving me mere seconds to recover before the bailiff announced, "The prosecution calls Charlotte Tollbridge to the stand."

If my heart were not already sitting firmly in my bowels, it would have done a swan dive into my stomach. A familiar round face and dark curls peered back at me from the stand. Her cheeks were pale, and her hands shook as she gripped the lectern. They had tracked down my former upstairs maid, who had been moved to the country with her family for her safety, and dragged her to the city where she would be in infinitely more danger. And they'd done it merely to hurt me.

"State your name for the court," the bailiff said.

"Charlotte Ellen Tollbridge," she replied in a quavering voice.

The barrister peered at Charlotte down the bridge of his nose, his self-important expression reflected in his voice. "How do you know the defendant, Lady Gwenevere St. James?"

"I—I was her upstairs maid, sir."

"Was?"

"Yes, sir."

"You no longer work for Lady St. James?"

"No, sir."

"Interesting," he said, turning toward the stands, which were packed and groaning beneath the weight of spectators. "Why did your employment end?"

Charlotte's brown eyes were wide with fright and regret. I swallowed back my own fear and gave her a nod and a tight smile.

She licked her lips. "She said the city was going to be dangerous, and it might not be safe for us to stay with her. So, if we wanted, she would move us to the country."

"And when was this, Miss Tollbridge?"

Charlotte looked down at her feet and whispered her answer.

"What was that? Louder, please."

When she looked up, Charlotte's chin was trembling. The sight of her fear made a hot spark of rage catch fire in my chest. "Early this summer, sir."

"Before the monsters attacked Trafalgar Square?" the barrister clarified. Silence filled the Great Hall like the breath before a leap.

Charlotte nodded and dropped her eyes.

The barrister folded his hands behind his back and began pacing. "I see. So Lady St. James knew the city was in danger and took steps to protect her own household without warning a soul in the world to protect the city."

"I—I don't know, sir. I believe she tried to warn—"

"You told our investigators something else, Miss Tollbridge," he interrupted, raising one finger. "Something that may further elucidate the defendant's character."

Charlotte's eyes went wide and flashed between the barrister and me like a hare cornered by two foxes.

"Is it true, Miss Tollbridge, that Lady St. James, an unmarried woman, regularly invited strange men to her bed?"

A gasp rose behind me like a breaking wave as the prudish citizens of New London heard what they believed to be the worst allegation that had yet been leveled at me, and Charlotte's cheeks burned bright red.

"I don't know if she—if they—sir, I don't—"

"That's alright, Miss. Tollbridge, I realize this is a matter that may offend your proper sensibilities. I will not ask you to embarrass yourself further."

But he did ask Charlotte more condemning questions about my habits, training, experiments, the strange books I kept, and my late-night rendezvous. When she finally left the stand, her shoulders were slumped, and her head hung on her neck like it was too heavy to carry. Tears stood bright on her cheeks.

Whispers of shock and outrage filled the stands, and Lord Melville grinned down at me from beneath his white wig. My name was as thoroughly smeared as it was possible to be. Even Percy, who had become the ultimate name in fashion since our visit to Lady Chatsworth in the country, would not be safe associating with me.

Mama, with all her power and influence, would either have to publicly disown me or weather the storm and lose her social influence. And an innocent girl would now be unemployable because they'd dragged her into this farce of a trial against her will.

I clenched my fists and strained against my chains, letting the pain of the metal pressing into my skin stop me from doing something stupid.

"The court will take a brief recess before the defense pleads their case," Melville said before striking the sound block with his gavel. The sound echoed through the room like a gunshot.

What happened during the recess, I cannot say. It passed in a red blur of impotent rage so strong that I could not remember anything with clarity. In fact, I did not fully regain my composure until the guards escorted me into the hallway outside my room, and a familiar face shocked me into lucidity: Edith, Lady Ashcroft, stood among the illegal spectators, her pretty face twisted with worry.

I had not seen her since the monsters began invading the city, but we'd kept up a correspondence when time permitted, and her expression said no affection was lost between us. I wished that eased the tightness in my chest, but it only worried me more. Westminster was anything but safe for a delicate lady like Edith.

She clutched the rope meant to keep spectators out and shouted, "Lady Gwen!"

"Lady Ashcroft?" I blurted, trying to see past the shoulders of my guards as they hurried me away. "What are you doing here?"

Edith pushed through the crowd, edging sideways along the rope to keep pace. "I wanted to apologize. We've seen the headlines, and Edgar simply could not stand what they reported. After everything you have done, this"—she gestured with one hand as she pushed past a scowling older man—"is a travesty of the worst kind. But we will make it right, I swear it!"

Other spectators jostled and shouted, making it difficult to hear my friend. They cursed at her as she passed them, and it was too easy to imagine one of them hurting her.

"Edith," I called, trying to pitch my voice over the general hubbub, "you must get your family out of the city. Take your boys back to the country tonight if you can."

Edith's face scrunched up in confusion as if she were having trouble hearing my words over the rumbling crowd. "Don't worry!" she shouted back before being brought up short by another rope and a glaring guard. He held her at arm's length, and she leaned around him to maintain eye contact.

Mr. Yates, still in disguise, took my upper arm in a firm but gentle grip to pull me away.

"Don't worry!" Edith called again, standing on her tiptoes and raising one hand as the crowd swallowed her. "We will make everything right!"

We took a sharp right turn toward the grand double doors of the Hall, and I lost sight of her. The guards began their stately march toward the front of the room, dragging me behind them.

Furious eyes bore down from every angle. Flashes of lips curled in disdain and faces twisted with hate, appeared in a collage of frozen moments as I hurried past the stands. Anyone who supported me before had either fled or firmly entered the opposition. The weight of their hatred settled on me in a smothering blanket, leaving no time to wonder what Edith meant by making things right. I could only hope she heeded my advice to flee the city.

Anger made the room feel like a pot of water on the edge of boiling. As much as I tried, I could not separate myself from the energy electrifying the air. It was too much to bear, so heavy that I could breathe only in quick gasps.

I scanned the crowd, hoping not to see Mama. She did not need to witness her daughter's downfall. Nothing could be worse than seeing disappointment and hurt in her eyes. Luckily, her beautiful face was absent from the disapproving crowd. But Aris was there, standing near the edge of the stands, nearly invisible in his black attire. Calmness radiated from him. He winked at me.

I wasn't alone.

The weight lifted, and a full, calming breath filled my lungs, sending tingles of oxygen to my almost numb fingers. With Aris here, I could do this, no matter how it turned out. He would never abandon me. Never judge me.

I flexed my hands, firmed my chin, climbed into the defendant's box, and waited. A hush of anticipation fell over the crowd.

"We will begin the closing remarks of the prosecution in the trial of Gwenevere Violet St. James for treason against His Majesty and the realm," the bailiff shouted. "All stand for the Lord High Justice Melville."

The stands creaked as spectators rose, and my be-wigged doom took the place of judgment at the head of the room. His fingers curled around the gavel.

"As the prosecution has clearly shown over the last two days of testimony," the barrister began, "Lady St. James may have started her life as an innocent girl, but after the loss of her sister, she began a decade-long search for power that led her from our hallowed shores across multiple continents.

"The dark occult magic she found on her travels twisted and warped her mind so that she returned to England a witch, ready to sacrifice our city, ready even to turn traitor, for the power her dark heart desires."

"God's breath, put down the dime store horror novels before you torture your audience with such melodramatic prattle," I said. "This is not the Globe." And then realized, too late, that I did not mutter the complaint under my breath. I said it aloud. In fact, my voice echoed off the stone walls like a slap.

Reluctant laughter rippled through the room.

Well done, Aris thought.

I bit my lips together, against a smile or a grimace, I could not tell.

Lord Melville, however, did not find my comment humorous and threatened me with contempt if I did not keep my mouth shut. I studiously picked at my nails while the barrister finished his speech condemning me for witchcraft, treachery, and 'loose morals.' He stepped down to thunderous applause, which Melville silenced with more gavel smashing.

Once the judge was satisfied the crowd was under control, he said, "That concludes the prosecution's case against this woman. Are there now any witnesses who will speak for her?"

His tone said he expected no one to stand.

Of course, no one did. I would not allow anyone I cared about to take their lives in their hands or risk their reputations merely for my sake. Besides, the nightmare was nearly over. All I had to do now was wait for my opportunity to speak on my own behalf so I could tell the gathered crowd everything we learned from—

"I will speak for her."

The spectators gasped, I spun, and all of us watched a dark figure approach the bench. Slanting window light highlighted the stark cheekbones and salt-and-pepper hair of Lord Ashcroft. He was still too thin, though not as haggard as the last time I'd seen him.

But his eyes were hard, his expression resolute though he wasn't entirely free of the cravings, according to my correspondence with Edith.

One did not live as a vampire thrall for any amount of time without becoming addicted to the vampire's kiss. I'd only been bitten once, and still, the memory haunted me with dark yearnings that made my stomach sick. Coming here must have required more fortitude than I cared to guess at.

"Lord Ashcroft?" Melville asked, scowling down the hall. "What is the meaning of this?"

"I thought that much was clear, Your Honor. I am here to testify on behalf of Lady St. James."

Melville and the barrister exchanged a worried glance, but they couldn't very well silence him now, not with so many hungry eyes upon us. So he nodded his permission, and Lord Ashcroft cleared his throat.

"Lady St. James saved this city," he began, and the crowd booed and hissed so loudly it took eight strikes of the gavel to shut them up.

"I will have order or these proceedings will become private!" Melville threatened. The crowd quieted to an angry buzz.

"Lady St. James saved this city," Lord Ashcroft repeated, "and she is still trying to save this city. In fact, she saved both my life and the life of my wife when I..." His voice trailed off, and his face paled. He rubbed both hands on his jacket as if rubbing away sweat and cleared his throat. "When I was under the thrall of a vampire."

The silence that accompanied that statement was as profound as the hissing had been.

"Yes," Lord Ashcroft continued, "I was under the thrall of a vampire, and so were several other members of Parliament. We sold him secrets, we pushed his legislation, and argued in favor of bills the vampire arranged."

Melville's mouth hung open in mute astonishment, and the crowd did not even have the good sense to whisper their surprise to one another. Lord Ashcroft had just thrown what was left of his reputation into the trash with mine. God's breath, he would drag Edith and their sons down with him.

"Do not lie on my behalf, Lord Ashcroft," I began, but the barrister came to his senses and said, "Silence, lady. Lord Ashcroft, why have you disrespected this court with such nonsense?"

Muttered agreement from the crowd.

"Truly, sir," Ashcroft said. "I did not know of my predicament until Lady St. James broke the bond the vampire created by forcing me to see the truth." He loosened his tie and pulled his shirt open to reveal the scar of teeth marks on his chest. They shone silvery in the window light. "I have been recovering my mind and my memories for the last year," he yelled to the crowd. "I remember every meeting with the vampire and every—" His voice broke, and he swallowed. "Every time the vampire fed on me."

We shivered at the same time.

The barrister's eyes flicked back and forth as if looking for an escape, and Judge Melville may as well have been poleaxed. This was quite obviously not where they had expected the end of my trial to take us. Even I could think of nothing to say.

"This man just admitted to mental instability," the barrister said at last, flinging a panicked but accusing gesture at Ashcroft. "I move to strike his testimony from the record and have him removed from the court."

Melville shook himself as if waking up from a deep sleep. He silenced the muttering crowd with the crack of the gavel. "The motion shall be sustained. Guards, remove Lord Ashcroft."

Before the guards took so much as a step, Ashcroft shouted, "You may remove me, but you cannot silence the truth! Monsters have infiltrated the government!"

Melville's face went red. Everything was falling apart around him, and his eyes bulged as he screamed, "Take him! Arrest him!"

The guards rushed in.

Ashcroft bellowed, "Lord Rutledge invited them in! And he's not the only one!"

The stands erupted, the guards threw themselves at Ashcroft, and before they clapped him in irons, he shouted, "Our government has betrayed us! They are facilitating invasion!"

A shoe flew through the air and hit the wooden railing next to my hand with a crack. I flinched into the arms of Constable Hayes, who wrapped himself around me as the great hall went mad with shouting and struggling bodies.

"Order!" Melville screamed, but no one was listening.

Gwen! Aris's voice called in my mind.

I'm fine, I thought back as more guards surrounded me. Mr. Yates blocked me with his body as the constables forced through the press of spectators rushing the floor. The air was thick, electric with anger and body heat, shouts and curses. I gasped as the crush of bodies smashed Mr. Yates and Constable Hayes against me, squeezing until I could barely pull in enough air to keep myself from growing dizzy.

Fingers curled into the fabric of my waistcoat and yanked, hauling me off balance. I beat the grasping hands away as Mr. Yates wrapped his arms around my waist and jerked me off my feet with surprising strength.

"Get her!" someone shouted. "Get the witch!"

The doors were still a dozen feet away and thick with churning bodies and flailing limbs. Constables locked arms, using their bodies like a shield wall to force the people back, but it was a tide they couldn't stand against for long. Angry spectators had been whipped up into a mob. And they would kill me if they could.

My heart slammed against my ribs as Mr. Yates plowed through people with cold determination. A burning sting erupted from the back of my scalp, and my head rocked backward. Someone had curled their fingers into my hair. I couldn't fight back a cry of pain and shock as I turned and slammed a forearm over the offending wrist.

Gwen!

We're almost out, I thought back, fighting alongside Mr. Yates to beat a path toward the door.

I'll keep them off you, Aris thought.

Someone screamed as the knot of guards around me broke free and surged toward the doors.

Get Mama out of the city! I flung the thought at Lia as we burst through the crowd into the hallway. The guards pressed so tightly around me that it was hard to breathe, hard to see. They pinned me between them, hefted me by my upper arms until my toes dragged across the floor, and broke into a run.

Gwen? Lia thought. *What's happening? Are you alright?*

Put her on a train, I thought as we turned a corner and the din behind us faded. *Send Sam to protect her. Just get them out of town and back to Wainwright. Now!*

Lia's presence lingered in my mind for a startled second, then disappeared, leaving behind a sense of panicked resolve.

No one is following you, Aris thought. *There are too many guards, and it will take me a moment to catch up. Stay close to Mr. Yates and keep yourself safe by whatever means necessary. Do you hear me?*

It would be impossible not to, I thought back, infusing as much lighthearted sarcasm into my mental tone as possible despite the danger. The sound of his mental voice, cold and deadly serious, made fear run from the base of my skull to my lower back. Aris maintained a level of irreverence even in the worst situations. If he was serious now, he was worried. And if Aris was worried, I was in more trouble than I thought.

That's my girl.

We rounded a corner and ran smack into another mob. My guards formed a wedge, dropped their shoulders, and raised their truncheons. The fight was quick and brutal.

"Get the lady to safety!" Mr. Yates yelled and shoved me into Constable Hayes's arms before turning to smash his truncheon against the forearm of a man reaching for me.

I didn't even have time to scream, and the quarters were so close, body against body, that I barely had room to raise my manacled arms and reach for Mr. Yates as they dragged me away. He tried to follow, but the crowd closed in around him, a flood of bodies filling in the gap left by the guards' retreat.

For several moments, it was all I could do to keep myself on my feet. We squeezed into a room in a chaotic rush, leaving four guards inside with me and two standing outside as the door slammed shut. Constable Hayes released me and turned to secure the rest of the office, which appeared to be a conference room of some kind.

But the guard on my right tightened his grip on my arm, making my hand tingle with pins and needles.

"Kindly release me, sir," I ordered.

He only smiled and jerked me closer, close enough to smell his breath and see the unnatural sheen of his waxy skin. Just like Bowler Hat. I took in every detail of him in a single, terrified heartbeat.

"Your uniform fits rather poorly, you know," I said. "It isn't as convincing as it could be."

His smile widened to reveal a gold tooth. "It was convincing enough to let us get this close to you."

Us?

Oh, hell in a hand basket. A quick glance told me that of the four guards in the room, only Constable Hayes was familiar. In terms of sheer strength, we were outnumbered, and my hands were bound.

I was in trouble.

11

Quite the Criminal

GWEN

Time slowed as my strategic mind woke up and leaped into motion. There were three enemies, with only Hayes on my side. Hayes may not have been much of a fighter, and he was too far away for direct assistance, but he did have a truncheon and a pistol.

So did the smirking Gold-Tooth next to me, but his weapon was on the opposite hip, and my hands were bound. I needed my hands free. Gritting my teeth, I locked my shoulders against the manacles, as I had done in Melville's office, and *pulled*.

Apparently, fear for my life did not unlock the extraordinary strength that fury did because nothing happened. The guard near the door smiled, drew his service pistol, and leveled it at Constable Hayes.

"What is—" Hayes began, but the lightning crack of gunfire made my ears ring.

Constable Hayes staggered, his honest, affable face slack with shock as he stared down at the blood blooming across his uniform. The gun turned on me, and this time, it wasn't aimed at my protected chest. The bastard was going to shoot me in the head.

I dug my fingers into Gold-Tooth's uniform and spun, dragging his body between the pistol and me as the thunder of gunfire shook the room. The pain burned across my temple as a mighty crash rocked the double doors.

Gwen!

I ignored Aris's voice and the pain in my head as Gold-Tooth growled and plowed into me, tangling our feet. He plowed forward, and the soles of my boots lost traction on the marble floor. I twisted my body as we fell, scissoring my legs to wrap around his right arm, shoulder, and head. Luckily, my skirts were wide enough to accommodate the maneuver.

A choke wasn't the ideal way to end the threat, but with my wrists bound, I had to control his body and hands. Air rushed out of my lungs as we hit, but I managed to lock my right shin beneath my left knee, securing the choke. A chair sailed across my field of view, followed by a fleshy *thwack* and gasp of surprise.

I hoped that was Hayes in one last effort to protect himself, but I couldn't risk looking. Gold-Tooth jerked at his arm, trying to free the limb I had trapped across my stomach. I increased the pressure of my thighs on his neck and shoulder, squeezing hard enough to cut off blood flow to his brain. His face turned bright red.

With a grunt, he twisted us to the side, leaving my ribs open. The angle wasn't good for striking, but he was strong, and a solid kidney punch shot a fiery arrow of pain sizzling through my back. Too many more of those, and the pain would force me to release my hold. If I did, I was dead.

Two seconds. Three. Another vicious punch. I couldn't withstand many more.

With both hands, I grabbed the back of his head and pulled his chin down against my lower abdomen, squeezing my legs until stars burst at the edges of my vision.

The dull thump of fists striking flesh in a staccato rhythm sounded somewhere near the door, but I could not spare attention to find out if it was Aris, the gunman, the other guard, or someone else.

Gold-Tooth's face was turning purple. Just a few more seconds, and I would have him. But the Bowler Hats were far more resilient than mortals should be. With a grimace, he set his feet near my hips, spittle leaking from his lips onto the stomach of my blouse, and lifted his upper body. I was curled around his head and shoulder like a large parasite, but my body weight wasn't enough to stop him.

God's breath, he was going to crush me. I curled my back, hoping the angle would stop my head from bouncing off the marble floor just as he slammed us forward and down. My back hit the ground with a force that echoed through my whole body. The back of my head snapped off the floor.

White stars burst inside behind my eyes, and weakness stole through my limbs. But I was *not* letting this bastard go, not if the other guard shot me, not if the whole damned city begged me on their knees. I wasn't feeling particularly inclined to the city at the moment, in any case. A red haze covered my vision—ungrateful, spiteful traitors.

I squeezed.

I clenched every muscle in my body and bore down until I nearly passed out. Gold-Tooth's sweaty hair slid between my fingers as I forced his head downward. If he didn't pass out soon, I would break his bloody neck instead.

"Gwen!"

He would never threaten me again.

"Get her off of him, Raven. We have no time."

Hands pulled at me.

"If you'd deign to help me, *Your Highness*—"

I growled and squeezed tighter.

"Gods be damned, the woman is strong."

"Gwen. Gwenevere. Let him go."

I blinked, and the red haze slowly faded. Two dark-eyed faces stared down at me.

Gentle fingertips brushed away the curls matted to my forehead. "He's gone, darling. You're safe. We've got to get you out of here."

"She strangled him to death using a damned blood choke," the other voice said, awed.

"Check their clothes," I said. At least, I thought I said it. But the words came out in a slur of sibilance. I blinked and thought, *I sound like a drunk snake.*

"What?"

"Clothes." I fumbled a hand toward my collar. "The Silver Covenant." Was that the correct title?

A limp weight was dragged off of me, and I gasped as air flooded my lungs and the blood that had been in my legs surged up to my brain, making me dizzy. The world spun in a kaleidoscope, and the toes of my boots skidded against the floor. Light and color rushed by in a blur, like gazing through a carriage window after an enthusiastic night of drinking.

"Hayes?" I mumbled.

"Gone, I'm afraid."

That was really too bad. He had been a good sort. And he'd tried to protect me. Someone else had tried, as well. A hazy impression of a familiar face made my stomach flipflop, and a knife of worry stabbed my brain. "Mr. Yates?"

"Safe."

I sighed. That was good. The relief made blackness swirl at the edge of my vision. "Aris?"

"Hush, darling. We are getting you out of here."

"Oh, good. I'm dreadfully tired."

"You had better stay awake, lady," another colder voice said. "Or you will sleep permanently."

"That doesn't sound so bad."

"Hush."

The world came back together slowly, shapes and colors sliding into place like pieces of a stained glass window, forming a picture: frowning buildings looming in the dark, symbols scratched into the brick, blinding street lights, the cold bite of night air on my cheeks, and the rotten stench of trash left too long in the sun. We were fleeing through the city.

The normal evening symphony of muted voices, horse hooves, and closing doors had been replaced by a constant, doleful ringing. Aris carried me easily, his chest solid beneath my cheek, the warmth of his body keeping the evening chill at bay.

"I think," I groaned as an invisible knife stabbed me in the eye from inside my head. "I have a concussion."

"I would never have guessed," came the laconic reply. "What makes you think so?"

I pressed the heel of my hand against my throbbing eye socket to blunt the knife-edge of pain. "My ears are ringing."

"That isn't your head, darling. Those are the watch bells. The entire damned city is out looking for you."

Of course they were. At least we made it out of Westminster, though I did not want to know how much carnage that feat required. "Aris?"

"Hmm?"

"I need a vacation."

A dark chuckle vibrated against my cheek.

"If you don't keep your woman quiet, Raven," the other voice said, "The watch will find us, and we shall all end up vacationing somewhere much less comfortable than where I'm taking you."

I stopped breathing, then closed my eyes, and released a sigh of defeat. That was the voice of the Cutthroat King. He must have been the other guard, the one who threw the chair at the gunman. The bastard had been protecting me. Which could mean only one thing: he knew more than he let on, and we were going underground.

Aris and the King ghosted down alleys and side streets like stray cats, their feet soundless on pavement and cobbles alike. Now and then, the rhythmic thud of boots running in formation echoed off the buildings like the forerunners of doom, and we would melt into the shadows, still and silent, our hearts thrumming with anticipation.

The King has entrances to the Undercroft all over the city, I thought to Aris after one such encounter. *Why is it taking so long to find one?*

We crossed an intersection and ghosted into the shadow of a factory, which put us on the edge of the east side. Aris tightened his arms. *Too many open entrances present a security hazard. Imagine how many guards would be required to protect each one. We need one that is protected to stop anyone from following us.*

"Don't. Move."

The King's low, hard voice sliced through my thoughts. Aris went utterly still. I stopped breathing. The King edged toward the corner of the building and turned his head, arching his neck like a dog raising an ear. He turned back toward us and mouthed, *Werewolf.*

It was dark, and my vision wasn't as clear as it should have been, especially through the haze of my pounding headache. But I could have sworn his canines had grown.

Aris spoke in such a low whisper that I barely heard the words mere inches from his mouth. "Can you handle it?"

The King raised a brow and ran the pad of his thumb along his fingertips in the universal sign for money.

I rolled my eyes and said, in an equally low voice, "Go on, then."

His answering smile was predatory and confirmed my suspicion about his canines. A pair of hooked knives appeared in his hands as if by magic. Aris set me down slowly enough that my skirts did not rustle, and I leaned against the wall for support, head pounding hard enough to make my vision swim.

Aris positioned himself between the mouth of the alley and me. Something big snuffled at the air, growing closer. The King leaped ten feet straight up into the air. He caught the bottom sill of the second-story window and swarmed up it with the grace of a hunting mink. After a quick glance, he leaped out of the mouth of the alley and into the dark.

A wet, meaty sound of impact was followed by a surprised cry of pain that cut off in a gurgle. I swallowed the lump in my throat.

Seconds later, the King strolled back into the alley and casually flicked the blood from his knives. Drops spattered the brick wall before he slid the blades back up his sleeves.

"That was exhilarating," he said. "Shall we continue? The way is clear."

Aris scooped me up and followed the King past the mutilated body of the werewolf. It had already returned to human form. My eyes snapped shut, but not before I witnessed several disconnected body parts.

I rested my head on Aris's shoulder and released a breath. *That man is terrifying.*

Yes, and he knows it. Perhaps we would be better off if I killed him.

Could you? I wondered, imagining just how much strength and speed were required to kill a werewolf that fast and that thoroughly without silver.

Are you trying to insult me?

He does seem rather capable.

If he weren't, I wouldn't trust him with your safety.

Do you? Trust him, I mean.

No.

But you don't fear him? Those knives are...disconcerting.

I fear his mind, not his knives.

No matter what Aris said, the King had just killed a werewolf with far less effort than I had ever seen. Granted, he dropped onto one from above, but even Alix and Cyrus encountered more resistance than that, and they were professionals.

I fear his knives, I thought and shivered. The King may not be as physically threatening as Aris, but he was dangerous—an ally perhaps more dangerous than the enemies I faced. And if we followed him to the Undercroft, we would be at his mercy.

Shall I take you out of the city? Aris asked, sensing my unease.

You know the answer.

Yes, he thought with a mental sigh, *but it was worth asking.*

The world had begun to darken around the edges again, and buildings, boxes, and lamps became no more than fuzzy abstract shapes. We passed a bit of Thieves' Cant scrawled on the side of a building—only it did not look like any symbol I had ever seen—and slipped through the cracks in a badly patched-up door. Everything faded to blackness. Thoughts became harder to grasp. My limbs grew heavy.

Gwen? Are you about to faint?

Mhmm.

You are a terribly inconvenient creature.

I shall endeavor...to be worth the challenge, I thought fuzzily.

Aris pressed a kiss against my forehead. *You always have been.*

A warm hand settled on my cheek, and the scent of lavender and lemons filled the air. I turned toward that comforting smell with the instinctive hunger of a child, not needing to open my eyes to know who was next to me. Still, I wanted to see her face.

The invisible knife jabbed me in the brain, but the throbbing died away moments later and left me vaguely lightheaded. Mama sat in a tattered but comfortable-looking chair next to my bed, limned by candlelight. There was more grey scattered through her blonde hair. How had I not noticed before?

"Hello, Mama."

She brushed the hair off my forehead, her cool fingertips feather-light. "How are you, dear heart?"

"I am concussed," I said, trying to lever myself into a sitting position without my head exploding. "You?"

She propped more pillows beneath my upper back. "Worried. And rather tired of being forced to sit by your bedside while you recover from avoidable injuries."

"Someone attacked me. That wasn't my fault."

One blonde brow raised. "Wasn't it? If you would not have forced a trial—"

"It was the only way to—"

"Ladies," Aris said, his voice coming from somewhere behind me and cutting through our budding argument. "While I am certain you are both right—despite the contradiction in that phrase—a fight will not help Gwen heal any faster."

Mama did not have the grace to look abashed because she was never wrong, but her expression did soften, and she brushed the wrinkles from the coverlet. "How is your head?"

"There is a little man inside my skull wielding a large knife."

"I'll see if I can find Mrs. Chapman, shall I? She is certain to have a recipe that will ease the pain. If she did not smuggle herbs out of the townhouse, I miss my guess."

"Wait. Mr. Yates was with me. What of Monsieur? James?"

She touched my cheek in a comforting gesture, one that suggested when she looked at me she wasn't seeing a woman full-grown but the little girl whose bedside she sat by through fevers and nightmares. "Mr. Yates is here and safe. Monsieur and James are hidden in the city. Do not fret."

With one last glance, Mama disappeared into the hall. The comforting bite of lavender and lemon faded, and the dull mustiness of old stone took its place. Lia replaced Mama, her hair in a neat braid over one shoulder. But her skin was almost translucent, and her under eyes were bruised from lack of sleep.

Despite how tired she looked, I gave my sister a baleful stare and folded my arms. "You were supposed to put her on a train."

"Please," she said as she took Mama's seat, "regale me with the tales of how often *you* persuaded Mama to do something she did not want to do."

Since my record of winning arguments with our mother was embarrassingly small, I leaned back and gestured at the chamber with a circling motion of one finger. "How did this come about?"

Lia glanced around my room, which was less like a room and more like a bricked-over cave with curving walls and an uneven floor. "Aris. He made an arrangement with the King for our entry. I organized everyone, and here we are."

My blood ran cold. Taking shelter in the Undercroft was one thing, and bad enough after an earthquake. But making agreements with the Cutthroat King was a more dangerous proposition. I tried to turn so I could freeze Aris with an icy glare for taking such a risk, but the little man in my skull decided to punish me for assuming such liberties with my own head.

I squeezed my eyes shut until the stabbing disappeared. "Aris?"

"Hmm?"

"When Lia said you made an arrangement, what *exactly* did she mean?"

Aris appeared on my left and knelt by my bed. His hair was disheveled, which I had to admit was rather appealing, but he looked no more well-rested than my sister.

"Lady Ophelia spoke out of turn," he said in a mollifying tone. "I agreed not to tear the man limb from limb if he allowed your household sanctuary. In return for my laudable self-control, and in consideration of our current situation, he agreed to give your subjects a reprieve from unnecessary violence."

My eyebrows shot up into my hairline. "My *what*?"

"Your subjects, darling," Aris said, annunciating each syllable.

"I don't have subjects," I shot back.

Lia snorted. "Don't be tiresome, Gwen. You and the CTK are allies. You both protect the people of this city in different ways. Just because you do not rule part of it doesn't mean the people of New London—at least the people on the surface—aren't under your protection."

"That does not make them my subjects!"

"For our negotiations," Aris said, taking my hand, "it does. And a good thing, too. Delilah and Percy are not direct members of your household, so they would not normally qualify for guest rights under your authority. But since they are subjects of yours, he must offer them sanctuary if they ask it."

The pounding in my head worsened. "Are you telling me the—what did you call him? The CTK? That he only allied with me under the presumption that I am some putative ruler?"

"A man with as much power as the CTK does not make weak allies, Gwen," Lia said as if I should have realized this ages ago.

Perhaps I should have. I assumed his agreeing to our alliance was due to my competence and capacity for mayhem, not because I had staked a claim on the city by protecting it. Had I known doing so meant announcing myself a de facto monarch of sorts...well, I still would have done it. Not because I had any designs on a crown, putative or not, but because there hadn't been better options at the time.

The point was moot now, in any case. "Who is down here?"

"Sam and Mama," Lia said, "Mrs. Chapman and Mr. Yates, Aris, Tony and I, Delilah and Fleur, and Percy."

I swallowed the thickening lump in my throat. "Sally?"

Lia looked away, but Aris's thumb slid in a comforting circle across the back of my knuckles. The gentleness in his voice made his words hurt more. "She is sworn to the Sisterhood, Gwen. By her given word. We could not bring her even if we tried."

"Did anyone try?"

"Of course we did," Lia said. "She told us she would contact us by ring when she could, then cut off the connection. We have not been able to reach her since."

I forced my lips to stop trembling. I could do nothing to help Sally at the moment, but I could learn more about our circumstances and chart a way forward. "I assume I am now considered a traitor to the realm?"

"Oh yes, you are quite the criminal, my lady."

Every head in the room turned toward the open door where the King stood, leaning casually against the crooked frame. He wore leather britches and a loose black shirt and held the bent crown of spoons carelessly in one hand.

"In fact," he continued as he strolled into the room, "I believe you are now a more popular topic of conversation than I am. Well done."

I decided to ignore that. "I suppose I was destined for infamy one way or another. Very well." I released Aris's hand to push myself up straight. "Where do we stand?"

Tony, Lia, and Aris exchanged glances as if daring one another to be the first to speak.

"I'm not broken," I snapped. "Just sore."

Lia bent down and took my face between her hands, her eyes hard. "Stop being a child. You do not have the right to make the people who care about you feel guilty for not jumping when you order them to."

Those words were as potent as a slap across the face, and my cheeks burned just as hot as if it had been her hand chastising me and not her voice. My jaw clenched, and I blew out a furious breath through my nose. She was right, but that didn't make the words any easier to say.

"I'm sorry. You are right, of course. Perhaps I shall start. I know who Lord Rutledge has been conspiring with."

Tony rocked to his feet and approached my bed, standing just behind Ophelia, his expression hard. "Who?"

"Lord Pennyfeather."

The color drained from his face. Perhaps it was cruel to spring the news upon them in such a manner, but my patience seemed to fail in proportion to the amount of stabbing the little man perpetrated upon my brain. And he was most enthusiastic.

"The Lord True?" Tony choked. "When did you learn this?"

"Just before my hearing. Aris persuaded Judge Melville to share that with us after he offered to sell me to his son in exchange for the hangman's noose."

Color bloomed in Lia's cheeks, but Tony was still terribly pale. He swallowed and demanded, "Why didn't you tell me?"

"I did not have time to ring you. They dragged me into court shortly afterward, where Lord Ashcroft revealed that the vampire we killed was also taking orders from Lord Rutledge, and he was not the only thrall."

"It appears I have been left quite in the dark in regards to my children." Mama's voice rang through the chamber like a struck bell, and both Lia and I flinched. The little man stabbed with glee.

"Mama," Lia began, but the Dowager Duchess strode into the room in all her authority, and not even the Cutthroat King dared stand in her way.

"I will not hear it, Ophelia. Not now." She pointed one elegant finger at me. "Look at her."

Four pairs of eyes fixed on my face and widened as if seeing me for the first time. Did I truly look so terrible?

"Mama," I began, "I will be fi—"

"Quiet, Gwenevere. I do not care what monsters need slaying—and we will speak of *that* later, I assure you—or what evil deeds the Lord True has involved himself in. You will rest. This conversation can wait."

"Lady Evelyn," Tony began, but she turned on him with hard eyes and a regal bearing. I would swear that even the King shrank away from her.

"I have spoken, sir. Mrs. Chapman?"

My spindly housekeeper hurried into the room with a pot of tea and a steaming cup. Her face was set in stony lines, and she stared at us like a falcon stares at pigeons. "All of you, out. Yes, even you, Mistress Lia. Lady Gwen needs her rest. Go on, shoo, or I'll turn my broom on you. Lady Gwen, you'll drink this, and I'll hear no complaints. Every drop, if you please."

Everyone, including the King, left the room with Mrs. Chapman hot on their heels: everyone but Aris. Mama stared him down as if he were a bit of metal, and she was a furnace waiting for him to soften under the heat of her will. But he didn't budge.

"I respect you greatly, Lady," Aris said. "And I would happily be guided by you in almost any matter. But I will not be moved from Gwen's side, not even under the threat of your displeasure."

She stared at him in silence for a long time. "As you feel you have the right to make so free with my daughter, I assume you intend to marry her?"

Even the little man and his knife froze at that comment. My heart stopped. In fact, the entire world, the universe, gravity, and entropy slowed. I expected Aris to choke or stutter, but he seemed to be the only thing capable of motion.

He never took his eyes from Mamas, and when he spoke, it was with calm conviction. "The instant she promises to have me, madame."

The world jumped back into motion, and Mama nodded as if that magically settled everything. Apparently, I had no say in the matter.

"Sleep, Gwen," Mama said. "And rest well. Because I expect you to tell me everything when you wake up."

"Mama—" I began, intending to make my thoughts on marriage abundantly clear, but I did not have Aris's strength. I wilted beneath the command in her voice and the maternal authority in her eyes. This marriage debacle would have to wait.

After swallowing the rest of my tea, I fell asleep with Aris's hand clutched against my cheek.

12

No Bedbugs

LIA

"This is the closest exit," the elvin man said as the three of them reached the top of a dilapidated set of wood stairs. The familiar hazy glow of a night lit by stars and street lamps replaced the oppressive dark of the Undercroft, and Lia's body relaxed in a grateful rush. "You have an hour," he continued, turning to stop them before they reached the crooked front door. "Come back later than that, and I'll lock you out. Come back with anyone other than the woman, and I'll lock you out. Try to force your way in, and I'll shoot you from cover. Understand?"

Tony raised an eyebrow at her as if to say, *Do you still want to do this?* It echoed his earlier sentiments as he'd tried to convince her to let the Ratcatchers give her a room so she could rest. He was perfectly capable of retrieving Matilda, and the streets were not safe.

Lia raised her chin. The truth was that, no, she wanted no part of this. She desperately wanted to be safe in a bed with a full belly and an empty mind. But she refused to let Tony brave the streets without backup, and she certainly didn't trust the King's Ratcatchers to have his back.

Tony shook his head at her stubborn expression and gestured resignedly at the door.

Alarm bells rang from every quarter of the city, bearing down on them as much as the darkness and the heavy, humid air that coated her exposed skin. Lia brushed her cheek against her shoulder, dabbing at the sweat trickling from her hairline, but she could do nothing about the drop that tickled down her spine.

As they rushed across the street between pools of lamplight, Lia decided to commission Percy to design clothing fit for sneaking. And preferably made of something other than wool and not a rose gold that made her too easy to spot in the dark.

They crept into the shadow of a three-story building just as distant footfalls echoed up the street. Another patrol, likely armed with truncheons and torches. They'd avoided every patrol so far, thanks to her sensitive hearing, but they were already too far into the alley to turn back for better cover.

Lia pinched Tony's arm in warning.

He looked back over his shoulder once to assess their options, then hurried her further into the dark. The patrol was too close for them to retreat, but the alley was narrow, with no boxes or carts to hide behind. A single torch would show the two of them clearly. Heat tingled in her fingertips in an instinctive rush, but she did not allow the flames to escape.

Tony grabbed her shoulders and pressed her backward into a recessed doorway before covering her body with his. One leg slid between hers, and his hips and chest flattened her against the door as he tried to fit them both within the shallow shelter of the threshold.

Her face pressed tightly against his neck, the salty musk of his skin almost sweet. Lia closed her eyes and took small, short breaths as the echoing footfalls grew louder.

Tony squeezed her forearm and breathed, "Don't move."

His warm breath tickled her ear as it stirred loose strands of hair against her neck. She tried not to shiver. Muttering voices joined the thump of leather boots on cobbles. The patrol was at the mouth of the alley. Tony's body radiated leashed energy, the same way Lia's magic ached to escape as if it was fighting to pry through her skin. Subtle tremors ran through his body and vibrated into hers.

Though he blocked her view, she still saw the blade of light slice through the darkness over his shoulder. Her breath stuck in her throat. They'd have to fight. She'd have to push the Lia side of herself back into a corner of her mind so *the General* could take her place, crush her better nature, and summon fire that would kill and maim her enemies.

Her stomach wrenched at the thought.

Shh. Tony's voice floated through her mind, soft and low, as he squeezed her upper arm in a comforting grip. *It's alright. Don't move. If they see me, I'll lead them away from you.*

The touch grounded her, pulled her back into herself, and suddenly Tony's presence—the steadfast bulwark of his body—seemed more important, more immediate, than the danger of the patrolling guards. The rhythmic sound of his controlled breathing more significant than the danger mere feet away.

What's more, she believed him. He would jeopardize his safety to ensure her escape. Had anyone other than Gwen or Mama ever been willing to take such risks on her behalf? And he wouldn't do it because she was dear to him. No, he would do it because he was a good man. If the guards advanced, Tony *would* put himself in danger to protect her. She couldn't allow that.

Was letting the colder, crueler side of herself out worth keeping him safe? Yes, she thought without hesitation. *Yes.* Her fire could create a barricade long enough for him to run. Lia closed her eyes and pictured a wall of green flame between them and the guards. It would alert them, and their shouts would draw every other patrol in the vicinity, but—but the sound of footfalls faded. They moved on to another street, another alley. And the General slowly retreated.

Tony breathed a sigh of relief that tingled down her neck. "Are you alright? Your heart is racing."

Fear was certainly enough to make her heart gallop, but it had been a long time since anyone had pressed her against a wall, and that had been more about passion than safety. Tony was only protecting her, yet the position—and her response to it—felt embarrassingly intimate.

Lia gave a jerky nod. "Fine."

Tony eased away from her and brushed out his coat, his eyes downcast. "Let's hurry then. I don't want to be forced to kill honest constables just doing their jobs."

With a shaky breath, rattled at how close she had been to doing just that, Lia stepped out of the threshold and joined Tony at a jog.

Madame Matilda was still unconscious. She lay on the spare bed, her dark hair fanned on the rumpled pillowcase. Her normally vibrant skin was ashen in the moonlight and seemed stretched too tightly across the bones of her face.

"She's overused her magic," Lia said, noting the woman's pale lips and fluttering pulse. "I've seen faeries do this, use their magic to exhaustion."

Tony's brows furrowed. "I did not realize magic use had limits."

"I cannot say for certain how it works in mortal witches," Lia admitted as she wrapped Matilda in the blanket, "but for faeries"—and *myself*, she thought wryly—"it is like using any other muscle. Do too much, and you will exhaust yourself. At some point, the muscle simply fails when you call on it."

Tony scooped the sleeping woman into his arms and shifted until she was tucked against his chest. "I've experienced the same after a strenuous boxing match. At times where I could barely lift my arms after."

It was difficult for Lia to imagine someone as strong as Tony being unable to lift his arms, especially not when he held an entire person so easily. Then again, she'd seen mighty fae warriors collapse on the battlefield, their magic spent, only to be cut down by a simple blade. "Perhaps Mrs. Chapman can give her a draft of some kind once she is safe in the Undercroft."

Tony gave a half-hearted grin as he followed her out of the spare room and down the stairs. "I have no doubt. Mrs. Chapman has a foul-tasting concoction for nearly every condition."

Lia imagined the formidable housekeeper bullying tea down Madame Matilda's throat and smiled. The expression must have unnerved the Ratcatcher waiting at the door because he jerked his eyes away as soon as they met hers. It was pure pragmatism that forced Lia to take advantage of his discomfort to order him about, but they didn't have much time, and Tony's hands were literally tied.

She could handle one werewolf if they were still prowling the street as the King claimed, but two or three? A whole detachment of constables? That would be loud and bright enough to draw the attention of everyone within a block of their location. The more hands—and options—she had access to, the better.

She faced the burly fellow and leveled a cool gaze at him. "You will accompany us to the closest entrance to the Undercroft, the one in the abandoned shop with the red door. You know of it?"

"Aye, lady," he said, eyes cast aside.

"You have weapons on your person?"

He snorted, and a hint of a smile touched his face. "Always."

"Good," she said, closing and locking the door behind Tony. "Then lead the way."

Mrs. Chapman and a mousy little doctor with gold-rimmed spectacles were staring daggers at one another by the time Lia, Tony, and the burly Ratcatcher entered the room set aside for Madame Matilda. The housekeeper towered over the doctor, who glared up at her with his jaw set and his black surgeon's bag clutched protectively against his chest.

Whoever the man was, Lia wished him the best. It was a fight he could not win. Though her eyes were blurry with exhaustion, she was surprised to see that a thick line of salt encircled the bed. Would such a thing truly contain Matilda's magic when she woke? Lia did not know, but the King clearly wasn't taking any chances.

Tony lay Matilda on the bed, careful not to disturb the salt, and edged out of the circle just as Mrs. Chapman placed herself solidly between Matilda and the doctor.

"Now see here, madame," the man began, but Mrs. Chapman only loomed harder, leaning over him in her black blouse and skirt like a hungry vulture.

A rough-looking dwarf with a thick brown beard and a scar across one eyebrow entered the room without knocking, noted the looming argument, and quirked a thumb at the door. "You two want to sleep?"

Lia exchanged a relieved glance with Tony. His expression said he would be as glad to escape as she was. Deep lines were carved beneath his eyes, and his lips were thin, but he smiled tiredly and repeated Lia's earlier words.

"Lead the way."

The ripe stink of stale sweat and beer that wafted off the dwarven man's body stuck in Lia's nose and throat. It was almost worse than the stagnant, mildew scent of damp stone. Almost, but not quite. The smell was a small price to pay for staying within the comforting circle of light cast by his lantern.

Scuttling through the tunnels made her feel like an ant or a mole, the weight of the earth balanced precariously above and shoving in from all sides. Familiar fear pressed against her skin, cold and clammy, and wormed through her muscles to settle in her bones.

"It's not as far as it seems," Tony said and reached out to give her hand a reassuring squeeze. "Gwen is close. And she'll be fine, especially now that both your mother and Mrs. Chapman are caring for her. Your mother will bully Gwen back to health, and Mrs. Chapman will fill her belly with healing tea as soon as she's done doctoring Madame Matilda. I'd swear that woman is a miracle worker."

Shame made Lia's face hot. Thank the moon and stars it was too dark for him to see the guilty color in her cheeks. If only she could blame her body's reaction on her sister's injury and not a childish fear of the dark. She should be afraid for Gwen's well-being, not trembling in a cold sweat over the enclosed space and lack of light.

"I've always thought she had witch's blood," Lia said to distract herself. "Mrs. Chapman, I mean. When we were children, it seemed as if she could read our thoughts, and she always appeared where and when we least expected her, no matter how cleverly we hid. I hated her for that. All I wanted was to be free of Mama's watchful gaze, but Mrs. Chapman was almost as bad, always there squashing every bit of fun and freedom."

She shook her head, smiling at the memories she hadn't thought of in years. Mrs. Chapman, as a nurse, had been quite a tyrant, though no one else could have kept Gwen and herself from so much mischief. "I twisted my ankle terribly one summer, racing down a hill. I bet the farrier's boy a bag of sweets against a kiss I could beat him. I was thirteen, and he was fifteen, and he had dimples when he smiled."

"You wanted to kiss the farrier's boy?"

"He had *dimples*."

Tony cleared his throat. "Of course. And did you win?"

"Naturally. He might not have run as fast as he was capable of, but that didn't matter to me. I was so nervous about what would happen when I won that I tripped on a hummock. My ankle made a crunching noise when I landed. It was too swollen to walk on, and my toes throbbed with every heartbeat.

"Gigi wasn't strong enough to lean on. Besides, she was crying too hard to get help. So, Carlton carried me inside. That part was like something out of a novel. Of course, Mrs. Chapman ruined it as soon as she saw him holding me."

"You didn't get your kiss?" Tony asked. His hand was warm and solid, and his thumb ran back and forth across her knuckles. It was absurdly comforting.

Lia sighed as they turned yet another corner. "Not that day. Mrs. Chapman was furious. She mixed up a tea, and it tasted awful, of course, like someone poured it through the gardener's boots. I was naturally frustrated about being stuck in bed, but I think I was angrier about being denied my hard-won kiss."

Tony chuckled, and the warmth of the sound filled the small space. "I'll bet she had you back on your feet in no time."

"She caught me in the barn a week later," Lia confirmed. "With the farrier's boy. I was confined to the house for a month for that one."

The dwarven man stopped and nudged a makeshift wood door open with the toe of his boot. "Here you are. Only room with a bed big enough for two."

Tony froze. "Oh. We aren't—that is, Lady Ophelia is not my...ah, my paramour." He slid his hand out of hers. "She requires a room of her own."

Their guide's face twisted with irritation. "Fine. There ain't no other rooms close by so I hope you don't mind walking. We'll need more tapers and firewood."

Lia didn't hear whatever Tony said when he responded. The corridor in either direction was swallowed in darkness, and the single candle that burned in the room wasn't nearly enough to keep the shadows at bay. The idea of seeing green flame shadows on the wall while closeted alone stopped her breath. In fact, she'd been so caught up in memories during the walk she forgot how to get back to the lighted stretches of tunnels where the other chambers were.

Stomach sinking, throat closing, Lia grabbed Tony's wrist like a lifeline and blurted, "One room will do," through the crushing pressure in her chest.

Tony stiffened, but the guide took that as a dismissal and hurried down the passage, taking the light with him.

"Ophelia," Tony began, but she interrupted by dragging him inside.

A small dwarven heater rumbled happily where a hearth should have been, but she ignored that and headed straight for the candle. Her fingers trembled as she used it to light the other tapers one by one until light chased the shadows back into corners and under furniture, where they belonged.

Tony stood near the open door with his arms folded over his chest. His stiff posture made guilt uncurl in her belly, but she could not bring herself to regret forcing him to stay. She did, however, owe him an apology.

"I'm sorry. I know being afraid of the dark is childish, particularly for someone with the ability to create fire, but"—she wrung her hands—"the thought of staying here alone so far from the light made me want to crawl out of my skin. You are welcome to sleep in the bed. This chair will suit me if you do not mind lending me the coverlet."

"You are not sleeping in a chair."

"I don't mind. Truly. I know I've put you out, and I am sorry for it, I just—"

He crossed the space between them in two strides and pressed her lips closed with the pad of his thumb. Discomfort was evident in every line of his big body, but his voice was gentle and resigned. "I know what it is to be afraid. Don't apologize. And you are not sleeping in that chair." He eyed it, mouth curled into a grimace that resembled a smile. "Something might crawl out of it and bite you."

She stifled a relieved laugh but had to admit the possibility. The tufted wingback chair had been the height of luxury at some point in its life, but the threadbare brocade was faded and torn, and the stuffing leaked from a tear on one side of the cushion. "Did they steal this from an abandoned home?"

"Given the nature of our hosts, I would guess so. The mattress is marginally better, so long as we check it for bedbugs."

She shuddered. "Don't say that."

By unspoken agreement, they canvassed the room. The single bed, a chair, a rickety trunk, a table, and a bowl and pitcher were the only other furniture. But they were clean, if dusty, and blessedly free of spiders.

"No bedbugs," Tony announced as he resettled the blankets.

"That's a relief."

"They probably cannot get enough to eat down here." He ran a finger across the tabletop. "Judging by the amount of dust, no one has stayed in this room for a long time."

Lia yawned and sat on the bed. The exhaustion she'd been keeping at bay overwhelmed her in a wave, making her want to melt into the mattress. "I don't blame them."

"Get some sleep. I have a feeling there will be hell to pay when Gwen wakes up and your mother takes us all to task for keeping secrets."

She watched him settle into the chair and angle himself so the heater warmed his feet, turning away from her and letting his head fall back against the headrest. Guilt she hadn't been able to feel in her panic reared its head. After everything Tony had done today, he'd earned a restful night. But he was going to sleep uncomfortably because she was a coward. If he could sleep at all in that thing. And he'd done it without making her feel guilty simply because she did not want to be alone in the dark.

"This bed *is* rather large," she offered, turning her face away. "Certainly big enough that we'd never touch one another if you—"

"Sleep," he interrupted, turning away from her. "I'll keep the candles burning."

13

The Council

LIA

An assortment of breakfast foods filled the table once occupied by criminals. Lia, Tony, and everyone else sat in rumpled clothing and stared at one another in bleary-eyed surprise over the trays, bowls, platters, and pitchers.

Were they truly about to breakfast in the throne room of New London's most notorious criminal while he lounged on his throne and watched them with amused derision? It did not foster trust in the wholesomeness of the food. In fact, no one touched anything for so long that Lia thought they might go hungry by mutual agreement.

"Oh, for heaven's sake," Mama—who sat imperiously at the head of the table—huffed before piling her plate with whatever was within reach.

With the Dowager leading the way, the rest of them followed suit, and they ate without speaking. At least, until Gwen and Aris looked up, their dark eyes locked on the opposite side of the room like guard dogs alerting to a noise. A few seconds later, the White Lady entered in a flowing gown, and Lia caught her breath.

Watching her approach was like watching a white hind ghost through a moonlit forest; her grace and gentleness were so at odds with their surroundings that she seemed unreal. It was no wonder she inspired comparisons to the mythic spirit who forewarned of impending death. And she could not have been a greater contrast to the guests who followed.

Alix and Cyrus strode behind her with the confident ease of predators, their eyes alert. Alix's straight black hair hung over her shoulder in a simple braid, and her amber eyes stared out from her olive-skinned face like the eyes of a hawk. Her beauty was as arresting and otherworldly as that of the White Lady but more dangerous and hard-edged. Like looking at her for too long might cut your mind to ribbons.

Cyrus was ruggedly handsome, taller than Aris, brawnier than Tony, and his blonde hair hung to his shoulders in golden waves. The combination of beard and hair suggested a lion more than a wolf. His expression was friendly and open, but Lia had seen him fight and knew how savage he could be.

A deer, a hawk, and a wolf walk into a tavern, she thought with some amusement. But her humor was smothered at the metallic clink of metal claws. A construct dog followed the White Lady, his broad bronze head and body covered in delicately etched runes. He resembled a mastiff, if about half the size, and moved with a grace and articulation as organic as any living animal. His black glass eyes should have been flat and emotionless, but there was something of a sparkle to them, personality and life in the tilt of his head that Lia had never seen in another construct. The beast stayed close to the White Lady's flank as if protecting her.

"Alix, Cyrus," Gwen said, standing and drawing Lia's attention from the mechanical wonder. Her sister winced as she moved, but lingering pain didn't stop her from accepting a kiss on both cheeks from Alix and a bear hug from her husband.

"Don't break her," Aris warned. "Her head is rather delicate at the moment."

Cyrus set Gwen gently back on her feet and gave her cheek a smacking kiss. "Take better care of yourself, lady," he said. "Alix wouldn't let me rest if something happened to you."

"For the sake of your sleep," Gwen laughed, "I promise to do what I can."

A round of welcomes followed, and for a moment, it felt like the meeting of old friends.

Until Mama stood and said in her formal voice, "I do not believe we have been introduced."

Everyone froze, but Lia had eyes only for her sister. Gwen's face went through a series of lightning-fast expressions: consternation, apprehension, and finally, resolve. Her jaw clenched once before relaxing, and she rolled her shoulders. "Of course, Mama. If every-one would sit? Cyrus, you are hungry if I do not miss my guess."

"I always knew you were clever, hen," he agreed, reaching for a plate of sausages.

Alix gave her husband a lopsided grin. "He is *always* hungry."

"Aye," he said around a mouthful. "I am, that." But the look he gave Alix said his hunger wasn't confined to food. It was so blatantly sensual that Lia blushed all the way at the other end of the table.

Gwen remained standing as if preparing to turn and run. Lia was tempted to stand so Gwen could retreat, but her sister wasn't a shy fifteen-year-old girl anymore. She didn't need Lia to protect her that way. An unexpected shard of grief lodged itself in her chest.

"Mama, may I introduce you to Alix and Cyrus? They are mon-ster hunters from France and Scotland, respectively. I met them on my journey through the continent. You know Delilah and her wife, Fleur. You have met Percy."

He tried to give Mama a polite seated bow, but his natural grace was stilted. When he'd arrived in the Undercroft late last night with only the belongings he could carry, all the color and life had drained out of him like the plug being pulled from a sink. Perhaps he hated the dark as much as she did.

"I believe everyone else knows one another," Gwen continued. "Lia, Tony, Mrs. Chapman, Mr. Yates. And Samuel, of course."

Sam sat quietly on Gwen's left, his expression sober. He was very different from the boy she'd met when they'd come back from the

Sunset Lands. Age made his features leaner, and he had grown at least a foot. He was beginning to put on muscle thanks to training with Aris and had the promise of being a handsome young man. But beneath the fringe of light brown hair on his forehead, his eyes were haunted.

Lia knew that look. She'd worn it for years beneath the calm, calculating mask of the General. He missed his sister, and he was afraid for her, but he could not change anything about their current situation. The helplessness of it was the worst part, she knew.

"I wish I could say it was a pleasure to meet you all," Mama said. "But I would have preferred a less...unhappy gathering."

"As would we all." The King's voice floated through the room, smooth and resonant. His position had not changed, but the White Lady stood at his shoulder with her hands folded in front of her, her expression serene. A black king and a white queen, like rivals on a chessboard, the brass dog at their feet.

"Mama," Gwen said, a note of irritation coloring her voice as she sent a sharp glare at the man. "May I present the Cutthroat King? Your Majesty, this is Lady Evelyn St. James, the Dowager Duchess of Wainwright."

The King stood and bowed. "Your Grace, my humble halls are honored by your presence."

Mama gave an elegant nod of the head that managed to accept the compliment without putting her at a disadvantage. She had not thanked him for his hospitality, either, which would have acknowledged a debt. That was a mistake one should never make when dealing with faeries.

Something her mother knew well.

The King recognized her caution, and his eyes sparkled. "Now that we are all introduced, shall we begin the council? Let us have everything on the table. The sooner we can solve this problem, the sooner my fine, upstanding guests can rejoin the world above where they belong and leave mine in peace."

"Nothing would make me happier," Tony muttered. Mr. Yates gave him a solemn nod of agreement.

Gwen cleared her throat and summarized the history of current events, beginning with the missing children and Cassandra Monmouth, and ending with the betrayal of the Lord True during her trial.

Mama's pale skin turned white, and though her features remained placid, it was a strained expression. Her throat bobbed, and she folded her hands in her lap. "The Lord True tried to have you found guilty of treason?"

"So it would seem," Gwen said.

"Why would he do such a thing?"

"To shift the blame for Trafalgar," Tony said. "Rutledge and whoever he was conspiring with involved the government in an invasion plot, and the people saw it. They want justice. So, Pennyfeather pins the affair on Gwen, the people have their sacrifice, and the conspirators can continue conspiring."

Mama placed an elegant hand on her chest as if the pressure might calm her heart and asked breathlessly, "Then why try to have her killed before the trial?"

The memory of Gwen's lifeless body in a pool of blood made Lia shudder. She still heard Aris's voice in her head, his anguished cry of, *they shot her!* ringing in her very bones.

"That is one more question we have no answer for," Tony said, sounding tired.

Sam shook his head, his gaze flicking between Tony and Aris for confirmation. "Bowler Hat was Lord Rutledge's driver. Ain't it likely he tried to kill Lady Gwen for what happened to his boss?"

"It's possible," Tony admitted, "but we have no proof. The symbol that ties him to the Covenant suggests he might have had more than one reason to want Gwen dead."

"What symbol?" Alix asked, leaning forward on her elbows, eyes narrowed.

Tony dug the embroidered bit of fabric from his pocket and tossed it to her. "A rune or magical symbol of some kind. Delilah looked into it," he said as Alix plucked the fabric from the table, "but she couldn't find—Alix? Are you alright?"

The half-vampire woman stared at her palm as if it might explode. "Gwen," she breathed. "Why didn't you tell me about this?"

"You were busy, and I did get arrested rather quickly after the battle."

"But you know what this means!" Alix's fingers curled into a fist, and her eyes seemed to glow with orange light.

Gwen blinked. "If I knew I would have—"

"You do not recognize it?"

Her sister's brows pinched together above the bridge of her nose as Alix dug through the pack Cyrus had carried in. She produced a pendant tied to a leather thong and tossed it onto the table, where it bounced to a stop.

A silver symbol, something like an S with a line through it, gleamed in the lamplight. Gwen gasped. She grabbed the necklace, her lips pale, and held it up. "How did I miss this? It seems to have been altered, but...God's breath, Alix."

"Would anyone care to explain?" Fleur asked, her gentle voice cutting through the tension that filled the room.

"When I met Gwen," Alix said, "Cyrus and I were hunting werewolves in France. The beasts had been altered to resist silver and retain more of their conscious minds. It made them several times more dangerous than the average creature. The altered werewolves wore this talisman, one created by my father, as a symbol of their commitment to his vision." She took a deep breath and clenched her jaw as if biting back something she did not want to say.

Cyrus wrapped his arm around his wife as she took a steadying breath, his expression pained.

"The point is," Alix said at last, "my father experimented on monsters as a way to rid them of their weaknesses and make them strong enough to take control of the mortal world. And this"—she pointed to the necklace—"was the symbol they wore to signify their allegiance. And you say that bit of embroidery belongs to this Covenant?"

"The Covenant of the Silver Dawn, yes."

They turned to gaze in surprise at the White Lady, who stepped out of the shadows and paused out of arm's reach of the table.

"Dove," the King said, half coming out of his chair.

The White Lady—Dove, it seemed—turned on him, her pale green eyes flashing. "Our folk cannot survive without the Upstairs, no matter how much you wish it."

The muscle in the King's jaw flexed, but he did not gainsay her. Dove swallowed and folded her hands together. The motion was elegant, but her knuckles pressed white against her already pale skin. "A group calling themselves by that name abducted my father and stole his invention. They used that symbol."

Delilah held out her hand, and Gwen passed down the evidence. With both symbols positioned on the table, it was easy for even Lia to see the similarities.

"This is the base shape," Delilah said, tracing one blunt finger along the S curve of the pendant. "And it maintains its general form in both iterations. But the strike and these flourishes here have changed. It's not unlike the way I translate spells into runic sentences to marry artifice and magic. This one"—she flicked the embroidered symbol—"is cleaner, more efficient. If it did protect Bowler Hat from that explosion and an entire secret organization has access to it, an organization that wants Gwen dead..."

Lia's blood ran cold at the insinuation.

"The symbol did not protect my father or the wolves who wore it," Alix pointed out.

"No," Gwen said slowly, "but it has been altered. And Bowler Hat did not have only the symbol. He was injecting himself with vampire blood, as well."

Alix went preternaturally still. Cyrus growled deep in his chest, and the basso rumble made instinctive fear prickle the back of Lia's neck, the sort of fear felt by mortals hiding in caves before discovering fire.

The brass dog rolled to its feet in a watchful move, eyes locked on Cyrus. Dove motioned the dog down with an elegant gesture and said, "Lady Gwen is correct. They have a sort of serum created with vampire blood. I have seen them use it. It speeds healing and gives some of them enough power to enthrall mortals. For a time, at least. So it seems the Covenant is not only trying to rid monsters of their weaknesses, as Lady Alix says, but to give the strength of monsters to humans."

Gwen focused on Dove for the first time. "You said they stole your father's invention?"

"Yes."

"What did they want with it? What is its function?"

"*Was*," Dove corrected, raising her chin. "I destroyed it."

"Very well, what *was* its function?"

Dove considered a moment, her eyes downcast as she fiddled with the copper bracelets on her wrists. Something about the invention made her nervous and defensive. "The Aetheric Charger was meant to help people. My father designed it to recharge batteries for household use so people would not be exploited by the electric companies. So they could heat and light their homes without filling their lungs with coal dust."

"A worthy goal. I assume the Covenant did not want it for that purpose?" Gwen asked.

Dove shook her head, sending light shimmering across her white hair. "The Covenant altered it to drain faerie refugees of their magic and store it in a crystal. Under the right circumstances, the energy could be released. I believe they intended to use it to help faeries infiltrate New London, but I cannot guess at how."

Gwen's gaze flicked between Dove and the King. "And you chose to keep this information to yourself?"

The King raised his chin, an amused glint in his dark eyes as he leaned forward, a slight motion that seemed to close the distance between them as effectively as if he'd walked across the room. "As I recall, you were in prison at the time. And you have not seen fit to trust me with one of those clever little rings."

"Your Majesty, you are the last person I would willingly grant access to my mind."

"What we must understand now," Lia interrupted, feeling something like a school teacher calling two rival students back to order, "is how this relates to whoever is attacking the wall."

Delilah sat back and folded her arms. "Why don't you enlighten us since you know so much."

Every eye in the room turned expectantly on Lia. She'd been in this position before, standing before strategy tables under the eyes of those who would have happily stabbed her in the back to take her place. Surviving had required her to be cold. Calculating.

The General stood, ready to be summoned, but Lia suppressed the instinct and schooled her voice. "Obyrron plans to invade. So what does he do? He weakens his target. He finds allies who will subvert the government, sow distrust and fear, and make it impossible for mortals to mount a unified resistance. But he must give his allies something in exchange. In the case of Rutledge and his ilk, that is likely political and economic power. Whether he truly intends to grant them such boons is another matter, but it explains their motivations. As for the monsters—"

"Hunting rights," Alix interrupted. "According to my father, they believe they will rule over mortals once again with the right to feed at will, as they did before mortals gained the power of technology."

Lia nodded, accepting Alix's answer as the most likely. "So, with Obyrron's help, they make allies of the monsters through the Covenant and the government through Rutledge." Lia did not say what part she had in strategizing these moves. No one would understand that they were a cover for her treachery, that they never meant to succeed because, if everything had gone according to plan, Obyrron would have been too dead to carry them out. But that didn't matter now.

"Did he order Rutledge to give the grimoire to Lady Monmouth?" Gwen asked, her gaze dangerously intent, as if she knew what Lia hadn't said.

This she could answer with a clear conscience. "No. Rutledge took that upon himself. But it did offer Obyrron a tactical advantage. He liked the idea of sending an advance party of powerful fae to the mortal world en masse. Until then, he'd had to force them through the wall in ones and twos, which resulted in losing most of his agents. Had Rutledge's plan worked, Obyrron would have gained a foothold in the government"—she raised one finger for each point—"allies prepared to ease the transition and forestall the military, Aes Sìdhe to ensure no one was capable of backing out of their agreement, and a deadly force of monsters to carry out his will."

"Until Gwen showed up," Aris said jovially, "and ruined the entire affair by closing the door."

Lia's throat tightened at the memory. She'd fought Obyrron against that decision, argued with false logic and lies about the mortal world until he'd grown bored and struck her. *Then you will join the party to guide them through such difficulties,* he'd said as she looked up at him from the flat of her back. The full force of his presence bore down on her until she could feel nothing but joy at the prospect of serving him.

But then she'd stood before the magic portal, desperately planning some way to destroy the mission—even if it meant ending her life—when she'd seen Gwen. First, her sister was merely a dark smudge against the firelight, wavering like a reflection on water. But as the magic solidified, Gwen became a fierce-faced woman, bruised and burned, hair tangled, with her familiar brown eyes locked on Lia's face.

There she'd been, the girl Lia dreamed about almost every night, the one she'd been fighting for years to save. Only she was a woman now. Lia had wanted to bolt through the portal, Obyrron and the invasion be damned. In that moment, nothing had mattered but the family she'd lost and the possibility that she could join them at last.

But Gwen turned away from her with tears magnifying her brown eyes and destroyed the magic. The portal had shivered and faded, leaving Lia alone in the Sunset Lands.

"That would explain why the monsters want Gwen dead," Alix said. "I doubt they would merely roll over and accept the leadership of a stranger, not if they believe they can make themselves strong enough to become a threat, strong enough to renegotiate terms. The mortal conspirators may want someone to take the fall and draw attention away from them, but it serves the monsters best to be rid of Gwen."

"Especially after what she did to them in Trafalgar," Fleur said, holding Delilah's hand for support. Lia couldn't blame her. The scene had been more than mildly horrific.

"It bodes well for us that there may be division in the ranks of our enemies," Tony agreed. "Perhaps their goals do not align as closely as we suspected."

Aris tapped one finger on the table. "But we are not in a position to exploit that knowledge, not yet. And they are still dangerous. Bowler Hat was faster and stronger than any human, and so were the two men who tried to kill Gwen last night. They had the symbol embroidered on their shirtwaists. That protection coupled with their speed and strength?"

"Makes them a danger to all but the most powerful fae," Percy answered the rhetorical question, speaking for the first time and sounding as if he might be sick. As a selkie, Percy was clever, quick, and dexterous but not as strong and fast as Aris or as impervious to damage. He knew intimately the danger his folk might face if monsters without weaknesses were waiting on this side of the wall.

Alix pitched her voice to catch everyone's attention. "This changes the power dynamics entirely. Monsters without weaknesses would do more than hold their own against the fae. And mortals would not stand a chance."

"Mortals aren't helpless," Delilah cut in, her eyes hard. "We have artifice, iron, silver, and gunpowder. We have nitroglycerin and other explosives. We won't simply roll over."

"No," Gwen agreed with a steely note in her voice. "We won't. But do not think that automatically grants us a winning advantage. Even without the monsters to face, I cannot overstate the power the Àes Sìdhe wield."

"What kind of power?" Fleur asked, sending an unconscious sidelong glance at Aris, who did not embarrass her by meeting her gaze.

"Àes Sìdhe are the least common of the fae, as they reproduce the most slowly, so there will be far fewer of them when the invasion happens," Lia said. "But they have the most weapons at their disposal. Not only magic unique to each individual, not only strength and speed and increased healing, but a weapon far more dangerous to mortals: *influence*. It is difficult to kill something you love and want to obey."

Delilah snorted, pulled the broad-headed hammer from her belt, and plunked it onto the table. "If they invade my home, it won't be hard at all."

Gwen sent Aris a questioning glance, and Lia broke out in a cold sweat. She'd spent years hardening herself to withstand the influence of the Sìdhe, cultivating her pain and trauma like a shield against the bone-deep need to please them. And Aris was particularly influential, though he hid it well.

His jaw muscle flexed a few times, but he nodded. Lia wanted to order him to stop, to tell Gwen not to ask him to display himself, but she knew better. This was a lesson their companions had to learn, or they would have no chance of fighting back.

Aris's chest expanded in a preparatory breath. "I ask your forgiveness in advance," he said to the table as he slid his chair back to stand. "But this is necessary."

He dropped his glamour.

It was like falling into warm water, being wrapped in a soft blanket, staring at a beautiful sunrise, and tasting fresh strawberries all at once. By the moon and stars, he was beautiful. The symmetry of him, the grace and elegance of his form made her want to cry or kneel or both.

Someone so glorious could only be divine, must be adored, obeyed, pleased. A wave of dizzy euphoria made her mind fuzzy, and her muscles tensed as if to stand and make her way to the other side of the table.

But one did not become a mortal General of the fae army under a ruthless king if one could not control themselves. Her hard-won defenses slammed into place, iron walls that held the power of his influence at bay long enough for her mind to reassert itself.

Their companions, unfortunately, had no such protection.

They gazed at him in wide-eyed adoration, even Tony and Cyrus, their breathing labored, lips parted. Fleur wept openly, Delilah's tawny brown skin was ashen, and Alix's hands shook. Gwen's eyes had softened, but she appeared less overcome than the rest of them. Even Mama's lips trembled, and tears stood in her eyes.

Dove seemed to liquefy into molten silver. Her body swayed forward, pale hair shimmering and parting to reveal delicately pointed elfin ears that had gone red at the tips. The King caught her about the waist and pulled her against his chest to whisper in her ear. She blinked, her green eyes swinging back into focus before she turned and buried her face in his neck.

The tenderness with which he held her made Lia reassess her opinion of him, though not necessarily for the better. If the King valued Dove at all, he would protect her from Aris. Not even the

Sìdhe were entirely immune to him. That glorious sight was the last thing dozens of eyes had seen before he snuffed out their lives.

"You are a terrifying creature, Raven," the King said, his voice tight. Lia agreed. She had always agreed.

Gwen's lips were thin and strained, but she said, "Thank you, Aris."

Aris pulled his invisible glamour back into place until he appeared to be no more than a wildly attractive man with dark hair and sinful eyes. Everyone blinked, Fleur threw up in a bowl, and Alix shot to her feet to stride to the other side of the room, her chest heaving, silver knives in her hands.

"Please forgive me," Aris said to the room at large, lowering his head and stuffing his hands in his pockets. "I would never have subjected you to such an experience if it were not necessary. But if Obyrron and his armies make it through the wall, the Lords of Faerie will wield that power with abandon, the King most of all. Unless you train your minds well, they will order you to put down your arms and serve them, and you will do it. Worse, you will be happy to do so."

"What can we do?" Sam asked, breaking the silence. His eyes were still wide, his lips white.

"We must stop them before they break through the wall," Lia said. She did not add the *or else* that echoed in her mind. She didn't need to. It was on every face in the room.

Cyrus cleared his throat and pulled the room back to order. "Stop who? We still don't have a clear picture of who might attack the wall or how. And, strong as we are, our numbers are limited. The Sisters of St. Christoph could not marshal the hunters in time, and it appears the government won't help us."

Lia stood and flattened her hands on the table. "We don't need *help*. We need to stop the wall from collapsing."

"That is assuming we should be involved in any of this in the first place," Mama said.

Mrs. Chapman pounded the table with the flat of her hand. "That's right. Lady Gwen has suffered enough for this city, and I've treated more injuries that I can shake a fist at on half of the people in this room. Perhaps it is time to let someone else do the fighting."

"If we do not fight," Alix said, "who will stand up for the people of this city?"

Mama's eyes were cold. "My daughters have suffered more than enough for the people of this city."

"It isn't only New London that will be affected if—"

"Can you not see how foolish—"

The conversation devolved into an angry buzzing that made Lia's head spin. They were wasting time, had wasted enough already with introductions and conjectures, and none of it got them any closer to figuring out who was attacking the only barrier that kept the faeries out of the mortal world. Flashes of memory, of her dark cave, the bodies of dying fae, lashes, laughter, Obyrron's cruel smile—the one she knew he would use when staring down his nose at subjugated mortals—made every muscle in her body tighten.

"Stop!"

Heads swiveled. Lia found herself beneath a dozen intent gazes with her hands pressed flat on the table and her chest heaving. "Imagine what you felt under Aris's influence, but the being controlling you wants your service, your suffering. He does not care about your free will or your soul. *That* is your future if we do not stop fighting and discover who is attacking the wall."

Gwen stared, her eyes distant. It was the look her sister got when she began weaving loose threads together like an industrial loom.

"You told me the safe house was ransacked," Gwen began slowly, "but you do not believe it was the witches despite their desire to retrieve the grimoire?"

"Yes. There was too much wanton destruction. Whoever looted the house was neither subtle nor crafty. They wanted to hurt you, and they wanted you to know it was done on purpose."

"And yet the witches do want the grimoire. In fact, they charged Sally to return it. And they ousted Madame Matilda to retain the Eye. The timing is too much a coincidence. Matilda came to you for sanctuary, so she has reason to fear the coven."

"Given the bruises on her face," Tony said, "I'd say her fear is warranted. Assuming it was the coven who did it."

Gwen began to pace, her fingers twitching as if turning pages and her eyes flicking back and forth as she thought aloud in starts and fits, her brilliant mind making connections in acute angles and turns Lia could not follow. "I was so focused on the trial...but of course, they knew I would be. And the damned Sisterhood must have suspected I would not take the obvious bait, not while I was so distracted. *Assassins indeed*. Alive or dead, I served a purpose. Matilda would have known and tried to prevent it by giving me the grimoire. If they are all in league, why not send a member of the Covenant or a faerie to retrieve it for them? In fact..."

She stopped, eyes flashing. "I would bet my right arm that is precisely what they did. And I believe Sally tried to warn me of it. She could not say anything outwardly, of course, due to her oath, but I did not recognize it. *Damn*. Clever, brave girl.

"She did what she could, but they'd already been experimenting, and we all felt it. No wonder she was frightened. She told me they were after the grimoire and hinted at what she could. But I may be misinterpreting it. She is not exactly an experienced conspirator. Best to make certain, if we have the time. They'll need quite a bit of power and space so they can form a circle, but when? And where?"

"Back up, Gigi," Lia said, at last, dizzy from Gwen's frenetic energy. "You're thinking aloud too fast again."

"We must wake Matilda. And"—Gwen raised one finger—"I think we'll need a spy."

14

We Both Love Her

GWEN

"Absolutely not," Mama said, folding her arms and glaring at us.

Once we were alone in the room the King had set aside for me, she was free to drop her title and simply be a mother worried over her children. "I will not see him put at so much risk, not again."

"I'm not a child, my lady," Sam said. His fists were clenched as if he were holding onto his self-control by the fingertips. "I am a better sneak than anyone here, and Percy already made me a coat. I'll be safe as houses."

I turned on the boy. "Can we retire that particular idiom? I think we have proved that houses are categorically unsafe in this environment."

"You think of a better one, my lady, and I'll use it," Sam promised.

I smiled at him, and he winked.

"Your humor will not soften me, child," Mama said. "I do not like my daughters taking part in such dangerous affairs. It has already resulted in too much heartbreak. But I will be damned if I will allow my grandson to be placed in...in..."

Lia and I exchanged surprised glances, and my eyes stung quite suddenly. But it was Samuel's face that made a lump form in my throat. His brown eyes were wide, his lips parted, and his chest heaved. He stared at Mama as if she were the sun and he'd never seen a sunrise.

Mama blinked several times as she realized what she'd said. "Well"—her chin trembled—"What of it? Perhaps you are a bit old for the title, but that doesn't make it less true."

Sam's face and build looked more like a man's than a boy's. Gone were the upturned button nose and round cheeks. He was already taller than Mama and half-again as wide. But he threw himself into her arms like a bewildered child.

Lia and I backed out of the room, leaving the two of them crying on the old chaise. Sam would not like more witnesses to his tears, and Mama deserved a moment to come to terms with what she'd just revealed to herself.

The corridor outside my chamber was dark, so I pilfered a candle on the way out.

"I won't tease you if you cry," Lia said. There was a little catch in her voice.

I raised a brow at her. "You are far nobler than I. Let one tear slip, and the game is on."

She snorted but edged closer to me. "Mama is right, you know. Sam would be in far too much danger. I should go, and you know it. I may not sneak as well as the boy, but no one else has as much experience at espionage or the ability to protect themselves from both witches and monsters."

Green firelight kindled at her fingertip, a reminder of the devastation she could unleash if the need called for it. And a sign that she did not use it now for a reason, one that needed to be addressed before we made any plans regarding who would spy on the witches.

"When were you going to tell me?" I asked.

Her brows drew together. "Tell you what?"

"That the faeries tortured you in the dark."

Lia's skin was usually pale, like Mama's, but never sickly. At my mention of her past, she looked almost green, and her lips parted in a silent gasp. Her flame sputtered and died, and her arm dropped limp at her side. "I don't—it's not...it isn't any of your business."

That confirmed my observations, though I hadn't needed it after her speech in the hall. I wondered why she hadn't used her fire as a light in the Undercroft until I realized what might make her hesitate. "Your fire was the only light you had in the darkness, wasn't it?"

Lia shuddered and wrapped her arms around herself.

"I understand if you do not wish to speak of it, Lia. And I'm sorry to bring it up now. But I cannot ask you to put yourself in positions that may force you to relive your trauma."

"You are not asking. I am deciding. It is my choice."

"Lia—"

"They kept me in a dungeon," she whispered. Her voice was rough, her face blank. "Stone and dirt under the ground, not the lovely mossy room I made them give you. Roots dug through the cracks and tickled when I moved. It was utterly silent aside from moles and worms and other creeping things that scuttled in the dark. I spent the first week without light. That was how I discovered my magic. Desperation."

The tears that had not fallen for Samuel and Mama ran hot down my cheeks. I wanted to pull Lia into my arms, but I did not think she would welcome such a gesture, not after I forced her into these memories.

"Dark places and green light were my entire world for a long time. Now and then, they took me out to...play with me. It wasn't malicious, not as faeries go. I was a novelty. A pet kept in a cage. It simply did not occur to them I should want for things like light or space. For a while, I could not decide if it was worse to stay or to go." She squared her shoulders, and a dangerous spark entered her eyes. "But I survived it. I survive it now. And I will not let you turn my trauma into a weakness you must protect me from. *I* decide what I will do, and I am telling you that I am the person most suited to discovering the witches' plans."

I swallowed hard, tasting the bitterness of what I was about to say sharp on my tongue. "God's breath, Lia, I know how strong you are. I'm not worried about you, not in that way. I am worried about what happens if you fail."

Anger twisted her features, but I had to make her understand. Trauma had frozen me more than once, stopped me from taking action when staying still might have meant death. My sister suffered horrors I could not even fathom. What if those memories froze her at the wrong time? Why force her to confront them under the threat of death when she could help in so many other ways? When people like Aris and the King or Alix and Cyrus—with their physical advantages—might do our hunting for us?

I took her by the shoulder and tried to force her to hear the truth in my words. "I have lived in a world without you. I know how cold and empty it is, and I do not want to go back. If something happens to you, I don't...I don't think I could bear it. I don't think Mama could bear it."

She froze, her green hazel eyes glowing in the candlelight, eyes so different from when we were girls and yet still fundamentally the same. The old familiar spark was there between us, the one that marked our souls as two pieces of a whole and infused my entire body with the warmth of connection.

But her voice was cold. "And yet I am to sit back and keep quiet every time you put yourself in danger despite what it might do to *me* if *you* are killed?"

I wanted to say *that's not the same at all,* but it was, and I knew it.

"Do not forget that I know what it is to live in a world without you, too. And worse, to see you hurt by my order because it was the only way I could save your life. I watched you lie on a table near death with some clumsy surgeon digging about in your chest, knowing I could do nothing to save you. If I am strong enough to endure that, I am strong enough for anything else I choose to do. And if I respect your wishes enough to keep silent while you put yourself in one dangerous situation after another, you are bloody-damned-well strong enough to do the same for me."

She spun and stalked down the darkened passage without another word, green light blooming at her fingertips like a torch to lead her into the dark. I watched until the light disappeared around a corner. Lia was angry enough with me that she would rather face her memories in the dark than stand near me. And I could not blame her.

I didn't feel like spending time in my own company or forcing it on Mama and Sam while they shared such a tender moment. So, I rolled my shoulders and strode down the hall in search of Madame Matilda.

Mrs. Chapman held the vial gingerly and frowned down at her new patient, who lay pale-faced and still on the bed. "I cannot promise she'll wake, my lady. And if she does, she may not be lucid. It looks to me like she's reached the end of her rope."

"If I knew how much time we had, I would be content to wait for her to recover. But given the state of things"—a glance at missing mortar and cracked stone told me the last earthquake hadn't left the Undercroft untouched—"time is a luxury we cannot afford."

My housekeeper nodded solemnly, then pried the cork out with delicate precision. The bitter burn of Mrs. Chapman's strongest smelling salts stung the inside of my nostrils even from this distance. I did not envy Madame Matilda the experience she was about to have, but nodded to Mrs. Chapman.

With a quick swipe of her wrist, she passed the vial beneath the woman's nose. Matilda bolted upright. Her dark curls flew forward into her face as she gasped and coughed, pressing the back of one wrist against her nose while protecting her ribs with the opposite hand.

Mrs. Chapman corked the vial, dropped it into her apron, and bent to pat the woman's back. "There you are, ma'am, you'll be alright. Take a deep breath now."

Matilda wiped her eyes and sent Mrs. Chapman a questioning, bleary-eyed glance before spotting me. She went utterly still and stopped breathing, her dark eyes locking on the pistol I had pointed at her face.

"Oh, don't look so shocked," I said, rolling my eyes. "It is only in case of an emergency. I didn't want to presume that your offer to Mr. Hardwicke and my sister extended to me or that the admittedly cool goodwill between us survived your exit from the Sisterhood."

She sat up very slowly and pushed her hair out of her face before setting her clothing and blankets aright; no doubt an effort to calm herself and appear more confident than she felt before addressing me.

"So you threaten my life?" she asked with aristocratic disdain. "Of course. That is an entirely sensible solution to your uncertainty."

"No need for the sarcasm, Madame. The last two weeks have made this"—I waggled the pistol pointed at her chest—"the least questionable of all my solutions. However, I wish you no personal ill-will. You are in no danger from me unless you give me reason to distrust you."

She sighed. "Given our past, I hoped you would have known me well enough to assume empty threats would not move me."

"And I expected you to know me well enough to know that I do not make empty threats. You are exhausted and, unless I miss my guess, in much more danger than this mundane pistol can manage. If you are willing to discuss our situation frankly, then I will do what I can to protect you. If you will not, then you are a danger I cannot excuse."

We stared at one another for a long time, each waiting to see if the other would break, but I had more stamina than she did, and we both knew it. Her gaze flitted about the room, noting Mrs. Chapman and the black bag of medicaments to her right and Aris leaning casually on the doorjamb behind me.

Finally, she sighed and lay back on the pillows. Her voice was every bit as tired as she looked. "Very well. You are welcome to ask what you will, so long as you realize that I may not be able to answer to your satisfaction."

A little shiver of awareness ran across my skin like electricity. She said, *'May not be able,'* not, *'may not,'* or *'will not.'* Matilda may be tired, but she was never careless with words. I tucked that away and got down to business. "Let us begin with something easy. Do you intend to harm anyone I care about?"

"No," she said, her answer quick and confident. That was a good baseline.

"Was your intent as the leader of the Triumphant Sisterhood always to make use of me as a tool?"

One corner of her mouth curled. "In as far as you were useful to my goals, yes."

"Was that your only goal in our partnership?"

She hesitated, then said at last, "No."

I decided not to push her on that answer. After all, I wasn't interested in her sentiments about me, personally, only in how she would answer so I could judge her truthfulness. So I asked, "Are your former sisters trying to destroy the wall of magic that separates the mortal world from the Sunset Lands?"

Her jaw firmed. She swallowed and did not make eye contact.

"How can I stop them from carrying out this plan?"

No answer.

"Is Sally safe?"

"Yes," she blurted, sounding almost grateful to answer. "So far as I last knew."

I fought not to reveal how much that answer meant to me, the way it made every tense muscle in my body relax in sudden, almost painful relief. Then again, perhaps... "Thank you," I answered softly.

She nodded but did not look at me.

Ask her about tracking them, Aris thought, his mental voice intent. *The building on Tromwell has been empty for weeks, and the King claims his Ratcatchers have seen nothing of any of the witches despite constant searching.*

You mean you've failed in your attempts to track them down, and it wounds your pride? I thought back, amused.

How dare you suggest such a thing.

"Is there a way to locate your sisters?" I asked. It was not difficult to keep the amusement from my voice when so much rode on this answer. "We have failed to find any of them."

Nothing.

"Shall I assume, then, that they have shielding spells of some kind?"

No answer.

In most cases, I would have claimed that what someone did not say was as telling as what they chose to share. However, in this case, the information I needed was highly specific, and only the taciturn woman in the bed could provide it. I gritted my teeth and rubbed my palm across my face.

"Sally came to you because she wanted the power to protect her brother from poverty," I said. "She saw the Sisterhood, and *you*, as the answer to her helplessness. Did you know that?"

Very quiet. "I did."

"But more than that"—I chewed the inside of my lip and admitted—"she admired *me*, and I was not there to give her another option, one that did not require pledging years of her life to serve someone who did not have her best interests at heart. And now she is in danger, and I am the helpless one. I find myself facing down forces I do not have the resources to overcome, and the only person I can ask for help is the one who imprisoned my daughter."

The words burned in my throat and soured in my mouth. "I failed her. And so did you. But we don't have to let that failure stand. There must be something we can do to stop them and save the girl we both care for."

Because I did not doubt Matilda cared. Sally was a singularly lovable person, and the tear that trailed down Matilda's cheek told me she had been just as helpless against the girl as I had been.

But still, she did not answer.

Could a faerie convince her? I thought to Aris.

*I cannot say, darling. I don't know enough about the rules of mortal magic. I suppose you could ask the King to try but...*his mental voice faded, but I knew what he was thinking. Likely, the King would use his ability to influence the will of others. It might not be as potent as Aris's, but I doubted he had the same personal boundaries.

But asking another felt just as wrong as doing it himself. Yet neither of us could stomach not doing everything within our power to save Sally and protect the city. How far were we willing to go? What were we willing to become to save the girl? I had answered that question in the past. I had risked everything to save Lia.

And, in part, that was what brought us here today; what made Sally believe that she had no choice but to embrace her potential for magic. My empty hand opened and closed in a helpless fist of fear and fury as my headache returned in full force. The lights pulsed in time with my heartbeat, and I gritted my teeth against the growing pain.

"I have always loved the opera, you know," Matilda said. Her voice was weaker than it had been, and her eyes remained closed.

"The power and passion of voices that shake the building down to its very foundations. It is a rapturous experience. One I found myself seeking out regularly, though I often disguised my identity. Sometimes, I even entered rehearsals early to listen to the performance before it was fully polished."

She paused and took a few panting breaths. Mrs. Chapman gave me a meaningful look before placing her fingers gently on the pulse at the woman's wrist.

"In fact," Matilda rasped, "I planned to sneak in tomorrow, as it might be my only chance to hear them before the performance. I—I think the little blonde soprano is a particularly talented singer. I hoped to hear her one last time."

Her voice broke. I surged to my feet, but Matilda was already unconscious.

"She's alive," Mrs. Chapman said, "but she won't be waking up any time soon. If we don't let her rest and get some food into her, she likely won't live out the week."

The pronouncement of doom was easily believable. Matilda's skin was paper thin, with purple veins tracing visibly beneath, and her heart beat faintly in the hollow of her throat. She must have used the last of her strength.

God's breath, my head hurt. I would have liked to follow her lead and faint comfortably on a bed somewhere. Instead, I said, "I have faith in you, Mrs. Chapman. Under your care, I know she will recover."

Mrs. Chapman snorted, though it was one of her flattered snorts, and began bustling about with the bed clothes in an officious manner. "I can't say about that, my lady, but I'll certainly do my best. She was exhausted by the end, poor thing, going on like that about the opera. What music has to do with magic, I'll never guess."

My mind was already hard at work despite the pain, but at Mrs. Chapman's words, Matilda's meaning snapped into place. I grabbed her face and kissed her soundly on the forehead. "You, my darling woman, are a treasure. Never change."

"Lady Gwen," she groused and flailed her hands at me, "enough of that, now."

I turned to grin up at Aris, who had approached while my back was turned. "We've got an answer. Well, as much of one as we're likely to get."

"See," he said, "the pistol *did* work."

It was my turn to snort. "Not as well as the woman's conscience. If she were less noble, we'd still be in the dark. Come along. We've work to do."

"What sort of work?" he asked as he followed me into the hall where a Ratcatcher was waiting to escort us.

"We," I told them with a flourish, "must stage a reconnaissance."

15

Farmer's Markets

GWEN

*A*re you in position? I asked for the second time.

Fond exasperation tinged Alix's mental voice. *You're going to wear out these rings, Gwen. Leave me alone, and let me do my job.*

I gave an indignant huff and thought, *Excuse me!*

Was I so wrong for wanting this mission to go smoothly? Much was at stake and—"Excuse me!" I blurted aloud and drew up short. The coster gave me a dirty look through sun-squinted eyes.

I hadn't meant to jostle his produce; I was merely too distracted to pay adequate attention to where I was going. And, to be fair, his barrow was rickety. But I did catch the fat carrot before it hit the cobbles. A good thing, too, as the ground was thick with mud, manure, and every manner of undesirable filth.

"There we are." I patted the carrot as I lay it once again next to its brothers. "Not even a bruise. And these are fine onions, Mr..." A glance at the carved wheels of his barrow told me his family name. "Gardener. Of course. How apropos."

Mr. Gardener glared at me beneath his cap and leaned on the worn handle of his barrow. His wrinkles shifted to one side as he adjusted the tobacco bulge in his cheek and regarded me with a shrewd gaze. "Yer blockin' traffic. Less you're in the market for onions, kindly piss off."

Not even I had a clever response to that brazen comment, so I sidled around his cart and rejoined the flow of foot traffic, navigating the maze of stalls, carts, barrows, and stacks of boxes that comprised Covent Garden Market. Sam and I wandered this route, keeping an eye out for Sally's blonde hair while Alix and Cyrus covered the other approaches to the opera. But it was difficult to concentrate while surrounded by the madness of the market.

How is your head, darling?

I narrowly avoided another coster as he wheeled his colorfully painted barrow between two rows of boxes stacked higher than my head. *The sadistic little man has traded his knife for a sewing needle. So, better, I suppose.*

It wasn't an accurate representation of the constant throb behind my eye, but I did not feel like fighting about it. Not when concentrating on the boiling crowd of humans, elves, and dwarves made my stomach sick. But Aris did not need to know that.

No dizziness? he pressed.

None at all.

Liar.

I will not hide in the Undercroft, I thought, injecting steel into my mental voice.

Aris had spent the evening trying to convince me to wait with Mama while he, Sam, Lia, Alix, and Cyrus spied on the witches. If I gave him any indication that my concussion still bothered me, he wouldn't give me a moment of peace until I was tucked safely in bed.

And we did not have time for that.

"The King's Ratcatchers are also on the job, along with Alix and Cyrus," he'd said as we sat in our bed the night before. "And Delilah and Fleur will be waiting in that invisible auto. What did she call it?"

"It doesn't have a name yet, and stop trying to distract me. I'm going."

He had pulled me back against his chest, bunching the blankets around my hips and nuzzling the side of my neck where it met my shoulder. Shivers buzzed down my arms as he said against my skin, "How about the Wraith Wagon?"

I snorted. "Let Delilah hear you call her fancy invention a wagon, and she'll box your ears."

"Fancy? The thing looks like a closed carriage with a face."

"I'll tell her you said so. Oh! The Cloaked Carriage?"

"Too cumbersome." He trailed kisses up to my earlobe. "Arcane auto?"

I shivered and wiggled out of his grip to glare at him over my shoulder. "Is that supposed to be *less* cumbersome?"

"It has fewer letters."

"You are ridiculous."

"You mispronounced *handsome* and *charming.* A common side effect of mild head injuries, I'm told."

Resisting his playful smile would have been a trial for saints with far more self-control than I possessed, so I closed my eyes and folded my arms. "Stop trying to distract me. I'm going. You can fly above and keep me safe if it bothers you so much."

"I would have done that, anyway. You don't have a hope of spotting Sally's blonde head in the market crowd."

"And you do?"

He made a dismissive gesture with one hand. "My senses are far more acute than yours."

"Are they, indeed?"

"Indeed. We faeries feel things quite deeply."

"That sounds like a challenge."

"Take it as you will."

"Oh," I said, pushing him back onto the bed and straddling his hips, "I intend to, my dear raven."

Unfortunately, I had gotten a bit too far ahead of myself, as the little man in my head was happy to remind me. And the irritation of unfulfilled desire—combined with my general discomfort at having so many of the people I loved in danger—made me waspish.

"You are needlessly stubborn." he'd groused when I'd finally given up and lay next to him on the bed.

"It's one of my charms. Besides, if I misinterpreted Matilda's warning, I want to be in a position to do something about it."

But I doubted I was wrong. She would not have mentioned Sally's blonde hair if she meant to do anything other than give me the opportunity to find her.

More constables moving your way, Aris warned.

My mind snapped back to the present. I turned toward another cart so my back was to the main thoroughfare and began pawing through a selection of beets. The tromping boots were like drums in the background of a symphony, rising as they neared me. I handed my produce to the coster, my face turned strategically away. The boot steps faded.

Dodging the patrolling constables who searched the city for me while I sweated in the close air of the market did not improve my temper.

Nothing yet, my lady, Sam said as I headed toward the fishmongers on the river side of the market. *Just picked up a lovely little bracelet, though.*

If you get arrested for picking pockets, Samuel Dawes, I will throttle you.

You'll have to break me out first.

It will be worth it.

But you'd do it? You'd break me out of jail if the bobbies nicked me?

Of course. But I would not be happy about it. And you'd have to wait behind bars until this business is accomplished, which I can tell you from experience is wildly uncomfortable. So, if you can find it in your heart to keep your nimble fingers to yourself, it would ease my mind considerably.

Don't worry, Lady Gwen, he thought back. *I bought the bracelet; I didn't steal it.*

Liar.

His mental voice disappeared in a huff of amusement that made me smile. If he was relaxed enough to tease me, he wasn't too worried about his sister to be careful. I'd given him, and everyone else, as much information as I had: the witches were likely meeting at the opera, and Sally should be there. We were currently scattered about the landscape within walking distance of the building, all of us hoping for a glimpse that would lead us to Sally and prove Matilda right.

Donkey incoming, Aris thought.

I slipped into the cramped space between a stall and a stack of burlap bags in time to avoid the animal. It shat casually on the cobbles as it towed a vegetable cart past my hiding spot. The coster's boy hopped off the back with a shovel to scoop up the manure before it rolled beneath the feet of shoppers.

The acid and grass scent of its dung did not mix well with the aura of fresh fish, body odor, and the savory scent of street food that wafted toward us from the next block.

No sign of Sally yet, Lia's voice echoed in my mind, distracting me from the kaleidoscope of activity. Covent Garden Market was the biggest in New London and spilled out of the market building itself—an enormous structure with green iron arches and a glass ceiling—and into every side street for blocks.

"Freshly caught eel!"

"No finer turnips—"

"Meat pies!"

"Beeswax candles and clover honey!"

The shouts of costers and market gardeners, rooster crows, donkeys braying, street musicians, flower sellers, and food vendors were a veritable symphony of industry. The noise echoed inside my head until it buzzed, which disturbed the little man. He exchanged his sewing needle for a hammer and went gleefully to work.

"Best English, ma'am," said a farmer's wife. She lifted a fruit from her basket and offered it to me with a proud expression on her suntanned face. "You've never 'ad such sweet plums, I'd swear it. It's a bit of 'eaven on your tongue."

She was right. I bought three and dabbed the juice from the corner of my mouth with the hem of my apron—a scratchy affair the King's men delivered to my chamber the night before—and thought to Aris, *Any sign?*

It would help if Matilda had been a bit more specific. Sally could be anywhere, and the market is full of distractions.

And pigeons?

...I wouldn't have noticed.

An unwilling smile pulled at the corner of my mouth. *Aris, are you picking fights with pigeons again?*

Not a'tall, he thought back, offended. *Why would I waste my time on fat little birds with brains the size of peas who cannot mind their own business?*

One does wonder.

Anyway, what is one supposed to do while searching for witches no one can find near an opera house we are not guaranteed to—wait—

I froze and caught my breath.

One of the King's men signaled me. I'm going to fly over his—there! Sally. She's wearing a light blue walking skirt and vest. Leaving the Strand headed for Drury Lane. Catch her up while I see what the King's man thinks is so important.

I notified Lia, Sam, and the rest of the team and set off eastward with my heart thumping against my breastbone. *Sally is unaware that Matilda gave us information,* I reminded everyone, *so do not let yourselves be seen. If you think you are being followed, find something else to do and circle back toward Covent Garden so Delilah and Fleur can pick you up.*

Alix sent me the equivalent of a mental eye-roll, Lia said, *We've been over this,* and Delilah thought, *We are in an auto that can become invisible, Gwen.*

Of course, I knew my friends were capable. I should not doubt them. But we had the opportunity to stop the witches from interfering with the wall *and* protect Sally. It was a chance we could not fumble. I refused to allow myself, or them, to lose focus.

So I flexed my hands and left the bustling crowd behind, carrying my wicker basket full of goods as if I were a local housewife returning from the morning market. Hopefully, the disguise and kerchief over my hair would fool prying eyes.

Lia and Sam have spotted Sally, Alix told me as I turned onto Drury Lane. *We are behind them. No signs of anyone tracking her movement.*

I pulled my fabric necktie up over my nose against the dust kicked up by autos, hooves, and wagon wheels and brushed the back of my wrist over my forehead. Buying so many vegetables had been a mistake. The damned basket was heavy and the sun made rivulets of sweat run down the sides of my face. It was only ten o'clock and already the air was stifling.

I stopped to lean against a brick building and let the wave of dizziness pass.

They're a block ahead of you, Aris told me from somewhere overhead. *And the King's man thinks he has seen a member of the Covenant.*

The game had begun, then. I gritted my teeth, adjusted my kerchief, and pressed on.

She's turned into the opera, Lia told me not five minutes later. *Alix and Cyrus are circling to the back.*

What about Sam?

He went inside. I couldn't stop him.

I'll be there shortly.

I quickened my pace and tried to recall that stretch of Drury Lane. If I was right, the remnants of a burned-out tavern sat across from the opera. The cleanup crew had walked off the job after wage disagreements with the owner, who had sunk so much money into renovations he could not afford to hire another crew.

So far as I knew, the building was still empty. It was the perfect spot to keep watch over the opera while luring out any of the Covenant who might be following me.

In New London, crossing the road was a gamble with death, a fact I was reminded of as I bolted between an auto—some people truly should not be granted licenses to operate such machinery—and a carriage driven by a terrified young dwarven man.

"Watch it!" he hollered as I dodged the grinding wheels by mere inches and skidded onto the sidewalk.

I gave him an exhausted salute and stumbled into the wreck of a building. The renovations had, at least, covered the stairs, so I crept up to the second story, leaned my back against the brick next to a street-facing window, and slid to the floor.

"God's breath, it's hot," I muttered, plucking another plum from my basket. *Samuel?*

Aye, my lady?

Updates?

Sally went down to the basement through a guarded door. I couldn't even get close.

A sigh of relief escaped my lips around the mouthful of plum. With his blackened hair and inked-on freckles, no one should recognize him, so if he could not follow Sally, he should be safe. *Very well. If you cannot find something likely to be doing in there, wait outside.*

With all due respect, Lady Gwen, I know a fair bit more about sneaking than you do.

Was everyone intent on mutiny today? *Just do my nerves a favor and don't take any chances. Alright?*

Before Sam responded, I was hit with a wave of vertigo that forced me to throw my hands out to steady myself. The cool shadows of the abandoned building faded from my sight and the gaudy insides of the opera, complete with velvet ropes and fleur-de-lis wallpaper, sprang to life.

Lia? I asked as I realized what was happening. *Have you gone into the building?*

Don't bother me now, Gwen. Be quiet so I can concentrate.

Through her eyes, I watched as she passed Sam. He casually tilted his head toward the back of the room as he turned his face away. Lia followed his direction and crossed the waiting area to turn left down a narrow staircase. A dark basement sat at the bottom, filled with boxes of moth-eaten costumes, old ratty chairs, broken bits of set panels, and coils of velvet ropes. I expected to smell the must of a storage closet, but apparently, the magic of Lia's ring didn't extend to smells because I got a noseful of auto exhaust and hot manure.

A bored-looking man leaned against a wall near the basement door, picking his fingernails with a penknife. When he noticed Lia, he jerked his chin at her. "No entry down here. Go back upstairs."

Lia raised her hand. A ball of green flame sprang to life on her palm. The man presumably knew who he was guarding, but the witches of New London were never so open with their magic. And if any of them could cast as quickly or clearly as Lia summoned her fire, I would eat my hat.

He must have drawn the assumption she wanted him to because he opened the door to a dark stairway with shaking hands.

A bead of sweat trickled from my temple to my jaw and I brushed it away with my shoulder. *Be careful. If there isn't another way out and they catch you—*

I will burn them. Her mental voice was stern and precise.

A memory of kneeling before Lia as she ordered me to be whipped made me flinch, and I spread my fingers on the comfortingly real floorboards of the abandoned building. The sensation of rough woodgrain beneath my palms was at odds with the dark corridor down which Lia strode, the green flame casting her shadow on the smooth walls.

She did not so much as whimper, but her heart beat frantically through our connection.

You're safe. Lia, I'm here. You are not alone.

She gulped but nodded.

Light appeared at the end of the corridor from the right side of a T-shaped intersection. Lia glanced down the lefthand tunnel, which sloped up and into darkness, reminding me of early sewage systems long since abandoned. But a faint, warm glow lit the old bricks of the righthand corridor, and distant voices interrupted the silence.

Lia extinguished her fire and followed the sound. Another set of stairs led her further down. My heart raced. There was no knowing what was down there, and if Lia got trapped, she might be forced to fight her way out.

I'd never seen a witch in battle. Most magic required time and intent, especially as the Sisterhood was careful not to let their magic leave noticeable marks.

But a witch who did not care about passing as an average mortal might do much more. Cassandra had frozen my muscles with a word, after all. If a witch were willing to suffer the magical repercussions of channeling power, she could do terrible things. Would my sister be quick enough to protect herself?

Lia slowed, her steps smooth and silent. As she neared the bottom of the stairs, the room below her widened into almost cavernous proportions. With smoothly rounded sides and an arched ceiling, it looked like a bowl turned upside down.

Does every secret society in this city have creepy underground dwellings? I demanded.

Shut up, Gigi. It's hard enough to keep this connection open without passing out.

I snapped my metaphorical mouth shut and pressed the heels of my hands against my temples as a counterpoint to the building pressure in my head.

Lia stopped and crouched at the foot of the stair, bringing more of the space into view. A large chandelier hung from the center of the ceiling, casting light on several arched exits spaced evenly around the circle, their dark openings like mouths. Symbols were etched into the walls, but the direction of the light and the erosion of time made them difficult to distinguish. Voices echoed through the space, though none were clear enough to make out.

They must meet in the adjoining rooms, Lia thought.

She eased down another stair, and another, then crept along the edge of the room, listening. I focused on the symbols etched into the walls, though I could only catch the soft edges of them through Lia's peripheral vision. Something about them itched at my memory but I could not suss out why, and the sound of voices distracted me.

"...experiments have proven the spell will be successful."

"But we have not pushed the Eye to such lengths. If it fails while the spell is at its climax we may destroy an entire section of the city, not to mention vaporize ourselves."

"There is no indication that is likely to happen. Besides, we have a failsafe. Don't forget, we all agreed to the arrangement."

"Yes but we were not meant to start until the first harvest moon."

"That was before this fiasco of a trial. Do you truly want to wait another month while the constables search the city and Lady St. James is on the loose? That is a recipe for disaster."

"What can she do? She's been branded a traitor, no one will—"

"Do not underestimate *that woman*," a familiar voice snapped. Deborah? The witch who had saved Sam during the riots near the zoo? "She was supposed to be a tool, but a sharp knife can cut the hand that wields it as easily as it cuts the loaf. She surprised Madame Matilda, something that took me years to accomplish. The longer she is free to interfere, the more dangerous our situation becomes.

"We may have powerful contacts in the government but we do not own the entirety of it. If the constables stumble upon our circle in the search for *her*, we'll have to extricate ourselves, and that will put us badly behind schedule."

"But we have protection now."

"Is that a risk you want to take?"

Lia edged past a dark opening and closer to the source of the voices, the only lighted doorway in the row.

"It seems safer than blowing ourselves up."

"Only because you haven't seen what they do to people who fail them."

Who was *they*? The invocation of that threat silenced the speakers and I imagined them staring at one another uncertainly.

"I did not lead you into this partnership blindly," Deborah said. "When we are finished, we will never be forced to hide again. No more workings done behind closed doors, no more spending our energy on the good of others while our sisters suffer. Witches will finally receive the respect we deserve. That is the future we fight for. If it is not one you want to be part of, leave now."

Lia skipped backward a few silent steps into the nearest darkened doorway, letting shadow fall between herself and the circular room. But no one left.

I can...I could kill them now. Lia's mental voice had lost its cool edge. I imagined her chin trembling. *If they are all in one place, I could burn them to the ground and stop this spell before they have a chance to cast it.*

Sally may be in there, I thought back.

Can we prioritize her life above the lives of everyone who will die if the fae invade? Hundreds, thousands—maybe millions of people dead or displaced if not pressed into service?

I knew she was asking me a moral question, a strategic question that kings, presidents, and generals had been asking themselves for a thousand years. And the answer was always the same: one life was never worth more than ten, a hundred. Except it was.

Yes, I snarled. *Yes, we bloody well can.*

"Very well," Deborah said, sounding mollified. "Then I suggest you prepare yourselves. If you need a sister to assist you in completing the cleansing ritual, contact me. Everyone must be purified before we begin. Set your affairs in order, and ensure your wards are secure. Travel nowhere without charging your obfuscation spell. The King has eyes all over the city and one must be exposed."

There was a general murmur of agreement and the echo of retreating footsteps.

Get out, I thought to Lia, but she was already moving, backing further into the shadows. A woman passed by the open archway, walking toward the same stairway Lia had descended on her way down. Behind her stalked a creature that had no name. It was something like an enormous lynx with a stub where its tail should have been and back legs longer than its front. It followed the witch with silent, predatory grace.

Lia flattened herself against the wall and thought a word I could not translate in a rolling tongue I was unfamiliar with. Was that a faerie language?

What? I asked. *Lia, what was that?*

Mist—ah, mistcat, I think is the translation. They're fae creatures. From the Sunset Lands. None have ever gone through the wall, so someone has already opened holes. That explains the earthquakes. Dammit.

More women passed, but Lia paid their faces no mind. Her eyes were focused on the mistcats that followed. I tried to see if Sally was with them but Lia continued to back away, her gaze locked. No one passed the door for some time, and her breath leaked out in a slow, controlled release.

If mistcats are here, we must take extra precautions. They're expert hunters and can practically disappear when they're stalking, she thought as she wiped a hand across her face. *But forcing one to do as commanded is impossible for anyone less powerful than King*

Obyrron, and even he is careful in how he uses them. I could burn one if it came to that, but it would probably ignore the pain and fight until the fire incapacitated it. It's a good thing I didn't—

A mistcat padded back into the doorway, its huge frame backlit into a silhouette by the light. I couldn't make out any details, but its large square head was raised, and its tufted ears swiveled as if to detect the slightest noise. Powerful shoulders kept it perfectly still, and paws as big as my open hand flexed on the stone floor.

Lia froze. Fear like a cold hand rose to choke me. Her fingers eased ever so slowly toward her opposite wrist.

If I cannot hide from it, Lia thought, the pragmatic edge back in her voice, *I shall be forced to kill it. If I do that, the witches will know I've been here. If I cannot, it will alert the others, and they will release the mistcats to find the rest of you. Get everyone out. I'll make my way back. I love you, Gigi.*

16

Don't Take Any Chances

GWEN

"**L**ia!"

Gwen, answer me, damn you!

Get them out!

Where are you?

I crashed back into my own head, disoriented and nauseous. Words swirled around me, melting and flowing into one another in a confusing blend of sounds that made no sense. I blinked tears from the corners of my stinging eyes, watching the dark stone corridor in which Lia had been hiding fade into the gutted building across from the opera.

My surroundings wavered as if seen through heat waves, and red pulsed at the edge of my vision in time with the pounding in my head. I fought to separate the voices clattering through my mind, desperate to help my sister in whatever way I was able.

Lia is in danger! I thought to whoever might be listening and squeezed my eyes shut for a moment to recover.

I'm concentrating, Gwen, be quiet. I'll ring you when it's safe.

Lia. She was still alive. A rush of relief made me so dizzy I had to open my eyes to stop myself from tipping over. A nondescript man stood at the top of the stairs leading to the first floor, a pleased grin pulling his mouth tight. His eyes, however, were flat and dangerous.

"You must be Gwenevere St. James," he said, prowling forward a step and sliding a garrote from his waistcoat pocket. The motion pulled the collar of his shirtwaist open to reveal a bit of embroidery near the neck, just visible enough to reflect the window light with a silvery sheen.

His skin was the dull, pale color of melted wax.

It appeared the Covenant of the Silver Dawn had entered the fray. I scooted backward and flung my arms wide for balance, knocking over the basket and spilling produce onto the floor. A turnip rolled beneath the man's boot. He crushed it without slowing.

With a malicious grin, he wound the ends of the garrote around his palms and snapped the wire tight with a *ping*. Window light ran across the taut line with a dangerous shimmer. I swallowed hard, imagining the wire tightening around my throat.

Showing weakness to a predator is never a good idea, but it is exponentially more dangerous when one is at a disadvantage, so I said, "And you must be the man who is about to die."

His smile widened to reveal sharpened canines. "Charming. I've been hoping for the pleasure of meeting you."

"Have you?" I asked as my fingers scrabbled over the bottom of the wicker basket and slid across something cold and hard. I raised the pistol I'd hidden beneath the produce and sighted down the barrel. If his torso was protected by the symbol, I had to aim smaller. His eyes widened in shock before I pulled the trigger. The pistol kicked, thunder erupted, and my would-be attacker dropped like a bag of potatoes.

"The pleasure is mine," I said, barely hearing my own words through the ringing in my ears. My gallows humor, unfortunately, did not make swallowing back the nausea that always followed this kind of violence any easier.

The man intended to kill me. He wanted to unleash monsters upon the mortal world. He certainly deserved to die. So why was my hand shaking, and why couldn't I stop staring at his corpse?

He spasmed like a clubbed fish whose body did not realize its brain was dead. I'd seen people twitch after death before, and it was never a pleasant sight. Residual electrical or chemical impulses sometimes caused muscle fibers to contract. It was a normal physical response.

But since the man sat up several minutes later and wiped the blood out of his eyes so he could glare at me and grate, "That wasn't very polite, lady," it was safe to assume his spasm was nothing so mundane.

A black shape blurred through the window behind me, shimmered, and Aris hit the man in the chest with both feet and a terrific heavy crunch. They toppled back onto the stairs in a tangle of limbs and curses. A muffled grunt and a growl later, Aris regained his feet.

Only it wasn't Aris.

The creature that stood over the limp body was something out of a storybook. Enormous wings were folded tight against his heavily muscled back, the feathers inky black with an oily sheen. Black-tipped, oversized claws were curled at his side.

I must have been dizzier than I realized, or the concussion was worse than I thought because when I blinked again, the vision was gone, replaced by the Aris I knew in a well-fitted black shirt and trousers. His expression was alien, flat and hard, as if the man he killed had been a particularly irksome bug he wished he could squash twice.

The only thing my muzzy brain could think to say was, "Where is your jacket?"

When he turned toward me, his expression softened.

"For the love of the moon and stars, Gwen." He lifted me to my feet. "Can you walk?"

Shouting rose from the street outside, accompanied by the faint echo of a siren. I sighed. "I don't have much of a choice from the sound of it."

"We've got to get you out of here."

"Sam?"

"Already gone."

"What about—" My gaze drifted toward the dead body but skittered away from the blood trailing down the stairs. "If he's still alive, he might know something."

"He is not, and we don't have time. Come on."

He carried me down the stairs, but instead of heading toward the front of the building, he took the next hallway to the back. Musty air and the leftover stink of burnt wood hung in the air, but Aris ignored both the smell and the dark as he strode toward the door.

Rotted wood planks had been nailed haphazardly over the burned exit, letting only slivers of light bleed through. Aris leaned back, braced me in his arms, and kicked. Wood splintered with a crack, and chunks flew into the alley to bounce off the wall of the opposite building. Someone swore.

I pulled back my sleeve and activated my Sightscreen. A dwarven man stood brushing dust and wood splinters from his jacket and glaring at the opening. As soon as Aris stepped into the alley, the man's eyes unfocused, and he shuddered in revulsion. If he had seen my face, he likely wouldn't remember it well. The Sightscreen had seen to that.

Aris paid him no mind, only turned and ran through the twisting alleys like a rabbit in a warren. Being carried at a run is desperately uncomfortable, no matter the strength and stamina of the carrier. I bumped against Aris's chest, and my insides jostled with every impact and change of direction.

I deactivated the Sightscreen and groaned, "I think I'm going to be sick."

He took a sharp left turn and edged between a stack of crates in an alley. I slid to my feet and wobbled, breathing through clenched teeth.

Gwen, Alix said, *this place is crawling with the Covenant.*

I know. We just killed one. He recovered from a gunshot wound to the head, so be careful.

After a startled silence, she thought back, *We will. Get to safety as soon as possible. We will clear your trail. Delilah said she is circling the block to the corner of Whitebridge and Drury Lane.*

Once the worst of the nausea passed, I straightened and wiped the cold sweat from my forehead. The corner of Whitebridge and Drury Lane was several blocks southeast of our position. If we were to reach Delilah unnoticed, I needed to change my disguise. After all, the Sightscreen was only good for five minutes or so, and I did not want to regret wasting the diamond if worse came to worst.

I filled Aris in on the escape plan while trying to shrug out of my jacket. He peeled me out of the thing without much effort to reveal the worn shirtwaist beneath. Within a minute, my appearance had changed from that of a common housewife to something less respectable. One would be forgiven for making unkind speculations about my hygiene. To make the ensemble even more convincing, I wiped my fingers across the dirty cobbles and scrubbed them over my face.

Aris eyed me, and one corner of his mouth curled. "How you manage to look so enticing despite the dirt and rags is a testament to your personal charm."

"Is this really the time for flirting?"

"There is always time for flirting."

"I suppose it does make running for our lives much pleasanter," I conceded.

"Doesn't it, though?" He smiled, a full, affectionate smile, and I caught my breath. God's breath, he was beautiful. "Now, stop being so tempting and allow me a moment to change *my* disguise."

"Your—" I began and watched in a combination of fascination and horror while the lean, aristocratic features I was so used to shimmered and blurred as if a dirty piece of glass had been lowered between us. When the shimmering stopped, a nondescript man with a forgettable face stood where Aris had been.

"There," he said, giving himself a thorough once over. "That ought to do it. Did I miss anything?"

Sirens grew louder, and despite our desperate circumstances, my fuzzy mind slid toward thoughts of a much less immediate—but more entertaining—nature. "Can you do that—what I mean is, can you make yourself appear *any* way you please?"

"More or less," he said, then noticed my expression. His glamour did not hide the familiar, mischievous light in his eyes. "Are you bored with me already, darling? Looking for a little variety in your nightlife?"

"Of course not," I said as he scooped me up and crept back into the alley. "But maybe once in a while, for fun…"

Aris stifled a chuckle and started running, but not before he kissed my forehead. "Never change."

Our levity did not last long. We exited the alley and blended into the foot traffic along Drury Lane, headed toward Whitebridge. My balance returned enough that I did not appear drunk, but Aris took my arm anyway.

"We've picked up company," he murmured as he led me across the street.

His voice was tight with strain, a tone that set the hairs on my forearms standing at attention. Who, or what, would make him that nervous? I paused long enough to reach down and scratch my leg, letting my gaze drift over our back trail. A familiar figure appeared for an instant before being obscured by the crowd. Where had I seen her before?

Covenant? I thought as we wove between slower pedestrians.

No, he thought back.

What, then?

Smells like a faerie.

You can smell her from here?

Can you smell a cinnamon roll even when Monsieur is cooking lamb?

My mouth watered. *Of course.*

Then trust me. That is a faerie and fresh from the Sunset Lands. She can't have been here any longer than a week, or I wouldn't be able to smell her.

I swallowed and tried to maintain my calm. *Sìdhe?*

Impossible to tell. We're only another two blocks from Delilah, so we must lose our company before we get there. But I'm blinded down here. I cannot see far enough to suggest a route or even see if our faerie is the only one following us.

My stomach tightened at the thought of him leaving me to cover the distance alone, unprepared and weak as I was, but I made my mental voice sound airy and unconcerned. *Then guide me from above, my faithful raven. You can always squash anyone who gets too close with one of those spectacular dives.*

I'll be close.

Of course, you will.

Warn Alix and Cyrus.

Of course, I will.

Darling?

Hmm?

Don't take any chances, please.

I gave him a mental snort, hoping it sounded reassuring. *I would never do such a thing.*

We turned a corner, Aris squeezed my hand, then disappeared into the crowd.

I'm aloft, he said a moment later. *She's thirty feet behind you. And—dammit, Gwen. There are two more members of the Covenant in the crowd, following the faerie woman.*

My spine stiffened. *Alix,* I thought, *where are you?*

Trying to get away from the Covenant without endangering any civilians. I can't catch your scent.

It's crowded. Everyone is heading home after the market.

We will meet you— Alix released a flood of French cursing that would have made Monsieur proud. *There is going to be a fight. We will meet you in the Undercroft when we can. Don't wait for us.*

Speed up, Aris said, *they're closing in. I'm going to cause a scene. Be prepared to run.*

I increased my gait to the very edge of a jog, trying to look like nothing more than a woman in a hurry and not a fugitive trying to evade capture. But sweat poured down the sides of my face, and the dizziness crept back in, making the little man in my head angry enough to pull out the knife.

I winced at the first stab, then skirted a delivery crew stacking boxes and crates against the side of a building. My limbs did not want to respond, feeling heavy and sluggish as I tried to keep up my pace.

"What the—"

"Ahh!"

"Get him off me!"

The sound of crashing boxes and snapping wood made me jump. I twisted to see the delivery men flailing and batting their arms as a raven dove at them in tight, acrobatic arcs, his beak and talons flashing. The ruckus pushed pedestrians out into the street, stopping traffic and making a van pull to a screeching halt. I caught a glimpse of a familiar face I couldn't place between the shoulders of two men in the crowd. Her large, dark eyes fixed on me and burned with a hatred that made my blood run cold.

Run! Aris thought.

I bolted, trying to ignore the pain that throbbed with every heartbeat. The woman's hatred followed me like a living thing, hot and sharp as slags of iron burning into my back. Dodging every pedestrian was impossible, and I bounced off the back of a burly dwarvish man carrying a sack over his shoulder.

"Oi! Watch where you're going!"

She's coming! Aris thought. *Delilah is around the corner, Gwen, go!*

I broke free of the crowd, legs pumping as sweat trickled into my eyes and burned. Horses, barrows, and autos flew by in a blur, and all the time, I imagined the woman's eyes burning a hole in my back. I skidded around the corner, eyes searching—there! The big auto waited two buildings down, crouched near the curb and shuddering like an impatient dog straining its leash.

Fleur opened the double door on the side of the car and popped her head out, her red hair a candle in the sunlight. "Gwen!" she screamed.

I shot a glance over my shoulder. The faerie woman flew toward me in a blur of speed, her expression twisted in a fury. She moved like a hunting cat, like the Cutthroat King, smooth and preda-tory. And she gained on me with ground-eating strides.

Aris dove out of the sky like a comet, raking claws extended, and hit the woman in the side of the head. A long gash opened up in her scalp, drenching the side of her face in a curtain of blood. She stumbled to the side and screamed in frustration. The sound sliced through me in a searing cut of recognition. I heard that sound sometimes in my nightmares.

Delilah shifted the auto into gear and pulled into traffic, picking up speed. In seconds, she would be close enough. But the faerie woman had already regained her stride, and she was feet behind me. Her fingertips brushed the trailing cloth of my skirt. A gunshot cracked somewhere behind me, and a high-pitched *snap* made me jerk my head instinctively to the left.

"Look out!" someone shouted.

Delilah was thirty feet away. I bore down and pushed my legs for all they were worth.

Twenty feet.

I leaped the curb and stumbled into the street, my ankle twisting on a cobble. With a cry of pain, I lurched to the left just in time to feel the wind of the faerie's outstretched hand pass within an inch of my head. Had she made contact, she could have ripped my head off. I gritted my teeth and swerved dangerously close to the oncoming auto.

Ten feet.

Aris let out a harsh, rasping scream and struck the woman just as she reached for me. A pair of strong, slender hands gripped me by the back of the shirt, and the force of the sudden direction change hauled me off my feet. Fleur set her shoulders and pulled, and the dim interior of the auto swallowed me. I hit the wood floor of the passenger compartment on my rump and elbows, giving me a perfect view of the faerie woman as she tried to change direction in time to catch me.

Her surprised expression melted into fury, the kind of burning cold determination I felt when Sam had been in danger. Gone was the languid sensuality I'd seen in the Sunset Lands as she pressed herself against Shiverback. Hers were the eyes of someone bent on revenge, someone who would not stop until the target of her vengeance was dead. I knew that look because I had felt it in my soul more than once.

Lia had been the one to burn Shiverback, but the enmity between us had begun with me and our ill-fated dance. Clearly, Shiverback's mate blamed me for his death. If it kept Lia safe from her hatred, I was happy to be the target.

"Now!" Fleur yelled.

Delilah's palm smacked against the activation button that would render us effectively invisible, and the double doors slammed as Fleur jerked them shut. The bolts slid into place.

"Lady Gwen," Sam said and threw himself into my arms from the opposite side of the compartment. He hit me hard enough to make me grunt and wrapped his arms around me. I melted into the hug, grateful for the solid beat of his heart and the cool skin of his cheek against mine.

He was okay.

We rocked to the side as Delilah took a corner, and the engine roared. Sam steadied us against the wall, then leaned back and studied my face. "You don't look so good."

"I feel worse."

He pulled a small flask from the inside pocket of his coat and held it out to me. "Here, drink some of this."

"Samuel Dawes," I said, wincing through the stabbing pain in my head, "where under heaven did you get a flask, and what makes you think—"

"It's tea," he laughed, holding up one hand to forestall me. "Can't say where the flask came from, but Mrs. Chapman cleaned it with boiling water. She said it's the strongest willow bark tea she makes and that you ought to drink it as soon as you started feeling the least bit poorly. "

"I could have used this an hour ago, then," I said, taking several generous swallows despite the sharp, medicinal bite of the salicylic acid. "Lia?"

Sam and Fleur exchanged grim looks.

"We haven't heard from her," Delilah said over her shoulder. "Hang on. We're not out of the frying pan yet."

"You know, D," I said, leaning my head back against the wall and feeling unspeakably weary. "When you leave the frying pan, it's for the fire."

"Well, we've got two covenant members chasing us that I can see, about a hundred constables are patrolling, and the gem arrangement won't hide us forever. Those little buggers burn out faster than the ones in your Sightscreen. We're about to be visible again in a city that wants to hunt us down. What would you call it?"

I threw back the rest of Mrs. Chapman's cold tea, pulled the pistol from my pocket, and checked the barrel. Five shots were left, but bullets alone wouldn't stop the Covenant or Shiverback's mate. Aris was above, Alix and Cyrus were busy somewhere in the city, and Lia...Lia was alone in the dark, beyond aid or help.

We were on our own with no gadgets to even the odds stacked against us.

I opened the window-like hatch on the back wall of the passenger compartment, thumbed back the hammer on my pistol, and scanned the street behind us for signs of pursuit.

"I'd call it a hell of a predicament," I said and sighted down the barrel.

17

Lia, if You Don't Mind

LIA

Flattened against the stone wall, scarcely breathing, Lia was as invisible as any mortal could hope to be. The Sightscreen warmed against her wrist, but the diamond wouldn't last forever, and the mistcat crept into the corridor on silent paws. Its head was lowered and tilted to the side as if listening, large ears swiveling even as its almost delicate nose tested the air.

Mortal magic did not work properly on faeries, but the Sightscreen used a bastardized form that must have been at least mildly effective because the creature didn't pounce on her despite her thundering heart.

Lia is in danger! Gwen's voice exploded in her mind. Lia winced and locked her jaw as the mistcat froze, thinking madly, *I'm concentrating, Gwen, be quiet. I'll ring you when it's safe.*

The beast was less than fifteen feet away, close enough that she could see the breeze from the rotunda ruffle its stippled fur and catch the faint, musky scent of its pelt. The direction of the breeze was likely the only thing keeping it from scenting her. Caves breathed with changes in air pressure, and the underground may as well have been a cave. Which meant an exit was likely behind her somewhere.

If she could reach it, the mistcat might never know she was here. But the beast's lips pulled back, revealing a pair of white canines. A low growl rumbled at the edge of hearing. Mistcats were ambush predators. They did not make noise when hunting, which meant the creature believed something had violated its territory.

Two prowling steps brought those teeth within feet of Lia's throat. She knew just how it would sound: the wet pop of parting flesh, the meaty tear, the yowling as it raked her belly with its back claws. She closed her eyes and tried not to breathe.

"Have they gone?" a male voice asked.

"A moment." a feminine voice, one she'd heard speaking earlier, hissed. "Theriannon, come back."

Lia opened her eyes enough to see a feminine silhouette in the arched doorway.

"Does she scent something?" the man asked, his voice low.

"I do not think so, else she would have killed it already. But I see nothing, and these tunnels are infested with rats. Theriannon, come!"

The creature did not move for so long that Lia thought it wouldn't obey. Its yellow eyes flicked around the tunnel one last time; it snorted, then turned and slunk back toward the voices, tail lashing.

Lia's entire body shook with relief, but she didn't dare to move. Not yet.

That, she thought as a trickle of sweat trailed down her temple, *is one of the stupidest things I have ever done.*

"We are safe," the feminine voice said. "Did you hear all of it?"

"Every word. And I must admit that I mislike their doubt. How can we ensure one of them will not disrupt the spell?"

"They cannot turn back now," the woman said in a soothing voice. "Not after they failed to support Madame Matilda. And no one else is strong enough to wrest the coven from me. They cannot survive alone, and they know it."

"You've no fear of them doing something unwise? Like breaking the circle in a moment of conscience?"

Silence.

Even Lia, unschooled as she was in human magic, knew what that meant. Gwen's legs still bore the scars of the time she had broken a powerful magic circle, and only one witch channeled the power for it. With the entire coven powering the circle?

"No. Once they enter the circle, they are committed. That is why I made an example of that foolish apprentice in the first place. My sisters needed a reminder of what happens to foolish witches."

"Grotesque displays sometimes have the opposite effect of the one we intend."

"Not in this case, my love. They know this is the only course of action that will grant us the respect and protection we deserve. They just needed an object lesson in consequences. The girl would never have made a suitable witch, anyway. Dispatching her was a kindness."

"Then we are on schedule? I cannot hold the Covenant off any longer. They have already destroyed my trial by attempting to kill the St. James woman."

Footsteps echoed down the corridor, followed by the rustling of cloth and the woman's voice, low and purring. "Yes. Never fear, my darling. Obyrron has assured me he will deal with the monsters once we install him in the palace, and faeries cannot lie. Soon, we will both have the respect and power we deserve."

A chill ran down Lia's arms at the mention of Obyrron's name and the confidence with which this woman spoke of his promises. Faeries could not lie, that much was true. But it was also very easy for them to sneak into one's mind, for someone as powerful as the faerie king to subtly influence and, at last, control one entirely.

Obyrron's cruel smile flashed across Lia's memory like a lightning strike. Now and then, she still felt his hands, the strength of his fingers digging into her hips and the glint of pleasure in his eyes when she fought back a whimper of pain.

She liked to believe that she'd always been in control of herself, that she'd learned how to resist the fae and built strong enough barriers to protect her mind. But the scars she bore said otherwise.

"Very well," the man said, though his tone did not sound entirely placated.

"Any news of our escapee?"

A tired sigh. "Nothing yet. She seems to have vanished into thin air. Every constable in the city has been on a rotating 24-hour watch. I suspect the Cutthroat King, but we have never yet been successful in rooting the damned man out. Not even the faeries have caught scent of her."

"What else can be done? We cannot risk leaving Lady St. James on the loose."

"It may be too late at this point. Besides, what could she do? Even if she managed to sneak into Highgate tomorrow night, the Covenant will be there as protection. And you've said the circle is impenetrable."

"She has already destroyed one magic circle," the woman cautioned. "We cannot install you as king under the new regime if she interferes. Put more constables outside the walls if you can. Let us ensure no one enters, not even that damned woman. Not even with help."

"It will be done. And your former Madame? She is no longer a concern?"

A quiet laugh. "That one? She will always be a concern. But I have a plan for her."

A bright pinging sound interrupted the man, and he cursed under his breath. "The hour has struck. I must go. Do what you think is best. You will have my support and the support of the government, so far as I can sneak it beneath the His Majesty's nose."

Lia inched her feet backward over the stones, holding her breath. The conversation had taken no more than two minutes, but that put her dangerously close to burning out the diamond.

"After years of work, we are almost at the finish line. Just a little longer, my love."

The mistcat bounded into the tunnel like a pouncing kitten, a narrow ring of yellow circling its wide, dark pupils.

"Theriannon," the woman said with an exasperated sigh. "No, go, I will deal with the cat."

Instinct told Lia to stop retreating, and fear wanted to paralyze her muscles, but she was not yet far enough into the darkness to fool the mistcat's eyes. And the Sightscreen was minutes, perhaps seconds, from burning out.

"What do you see, you damnable beast?" the woman asked, her voice closer and louder.

Lia forced herself to move slowly, never taking her eyes from the big predator: toe-heel, toe-heel, toe-heel. It followed her down the corridor into the dark, eyes glowing like two points of gold fire. Darkness reached forward to swallow her, even as it smothered the last bit of light from the rotunda.

Ophelia Magnolia St. James

Tony.

Ophelia, where are you? Gwen said you were in danger.

She couldn't afford to answer him, to divert any of her attention from keeping out of the mistcat's reach. At some point, she would stumble, whether she caught the toe of her boot on an uneven flagstone or ran blindly into a wall. The beast would hear her and pounce.

Not now, Tony, she thought, backing up another two paces and using her hands on the wall to guide her around a corner. The corridor was so dark she would not have seen the cat if it was a foot in front of her. Her skin crawled at the imagined touch of whiskers. At any moment, sharp fangs could tear into her flesh. Darkness pressed in on all sides like a living thing, smothering and hungry. The next brush of warm air against her arm might have been the mistcat's breath. She could afford to wait no longer. Lia turned and bolted, hands stretched into the darkness.

Her footfalls echoed off the stone like a dinner bell. Having targeted its invisible prey at last, the cat screamed. Fire bloomed on Lia's palm just in time to avoid slamming face-first into a sharp righthand turn. The heels of her boots skidded against the stones, and she caught herself with her free hand only to fling her body to the right.

The mistcat had been so close behind her that the beast hadn't the time to stop. It slammed into the wall at full speed and yowled in pain. She didn't bother to look but hiked up her skirt and ran.

I'm under the city, she thought as her breath sawed in and out with little whimpers, *somewhere beneath the opera on Drury Lane. Oh, god's breath. It's going to catch me.*

What is? Ophelia, what's going to catch you?

Lia careened around another corner, and the corridor began leading upward. Was she close to an exit? A glance over her shoulder showed burning eyes reflecting green fire not ten feet behind her. With a scream, Lia threw herself down and turned to land on her back, letting a burst of fire blossom from her fingertips as the mistcat bunched and leaped, sailing overhead.

Ophelia!

The beast hit the ground, smoking from where her fire had scorched its belly. It turned, all lithe muscle and flashing eyes, arching its back like an angry tomcat and blocking the path forward. Lia rolled to her stomach, hand still outstretched between herself and the cat. It snarled, revealing jagged teeth. Singed hair filled the tunnel with a sulfurous stink that burned her nostrils and made her eyes water.

A mistcat, she thought as she climbed slowly to her feet. *Fae creature guarding the witches. I'm somewhere near the surface. I can feel the vibration of traffic.* The cat swatted at her arm, a motion so fast it blurred and made her flinch as two-inch long claws passed within a hair of her fingers. *God's breath, I can hold it off.*

There was no way to disguise the fear in her mental voice, and Lia didn't try. Every muscle trembled with the knowledge that the mistcat would attack her. It was only a matter of time. If she burned it to death, it wouldn't return to the witches, and they would know, beyond a doubt, that someone dangerous had overheard them.

Any hope of stopping the ritual would disappear. A short-term win wouldn't end the danger of a faerie invasion, only make it harder to predict. They could end everything with what they knew now if only she could get out of this tunnel alive.

Unless...*The witches plan to use Highgate Cemetery for the ritual,* she thought. *If Gwen can get inside the circle, she can stop the spell. If I don't make it out, protect my sister.*

What? Lia, no!

The mistcat sprang.

Lia raised her left forearm to protect her throat, screaming as she thrust her other hand forward. The beast hit her, wrapping both paws around her torso and bearing her to the ground. Its head twisted to the side, rucking up her coat sleeve as it turned. Her bare forearm was exposed when it bit her. Pain like knives made stars burst in her vision, but she set her jaw and grabbed a handful of fur.

Burn.

Instead of green fire, magical heat bled out of her palm and into the mistcat. This fire wasn't deadly, but it caused unspeakable pain. She hadn't tried to use it since leaving the Sunset Lands. The memory of Aris doubling over in the throne room still raked at her guts with poisoned claws. Watching him writhe in pain for keeping his word and protecting the one person she loved most in the world made using this power feel like a betrayal.

But Lia wanted to survive. She dumped power into her magic in a desperate burst.

The creature screamed. It was a human-like sound that tore at her eardrums even as its teeth ripped free of her arm and it arched away. Lia scrambled to her feet. Blood poured freely down her arm and dripped from her fingertips.

"Ophelia!"

"Tony?"

His voice sounded so close, but she could not take her eyes from the mistcat as it circled toward her weak side.

"Get down!" he shouted.

Rather than asking very valid questions like, "Why?" or "How did you find me?" Lia dropped and covered her head and neck with her arms. The wall of the corridor burst inward in a tight explosion. Force punched her in the back and made her ears ring. Bricks bounced off her shoulders and the backs of her arms, leaving throbbing pain behind.

The mistcat yowled and bolted into the darkness. Strong hands slid beneath her.

She lost a second or two of time as her body floated away from the cool stone. Screaming and shouting erupted where there was once silence. She coughed, trying to clear the mortar dust from her lungs, and squinted against the light.

A pair of worried brown eyes filled her vision. "Hello, Tony. How did you find" —another cough—"explosives?"

"I've known your sister far too long. Are you alright?"

She glanced at the arm she'd unconsciously cradled against her chest. It was soaked in blood. "I don't think so."

"Dammit, where is she?"

Lia sighed and closed her eyes, letting her head settle against his chest. Breath of god, she was tired. "Gwen?"

"Him! Over there!" someone shouted.

"'Aye, E's the one, the big bloke in the hood!"

Tony growled, and the sound vibrated against her cheek. "Hang on."

She meant to tell him that she was going to faint, but the words never came out.

Lia vaguely noticed buildings flashing by. At some point, the temperature dropped. She grunted at the bump of stairs. She cataloged all of it but had no timeline to attach to the sensations.

"For all that is holy under heaven, Miss Ophelia! What have you done to your arm? Right here, Mr. Hardwicke, if you please." That had been Mrs. Chapman, her arms full of white cloth. A bitter, syrupy taste in her mouth. At some point, Gwen had been there, and Mama. At least, she thought she remembered their faces. Was it a dream? Had she fainted or fallen asleep?

Lia tried to rub her eyes, winced, and froze at the fire in her arm. Okay, no eye rubbing. Instead, she took a slow breath and forced herself to sit up.

A large hand settled on her shoulder. Tony. "Slow down." He slid a pillow beneath her back, and she leaned against it with gritted teeth. Her ribs felt like knives.

"Moon and bloody stars that hurts."

"You bled quite a lot." He tucked a strand of hair behind her ear. "Had me worried for a moment. But you are strong."

An ember of warmth flared to light in her chest. She didn't understand why Tony's simple concern should be so gratifying, but it was.

"Then again," he continued, trying to force a bit of levity into his voice, "I don't expect anything less from a St. James woman."

The ember stuttered and died. Of course, his central concern was that she was Gwen's sister, and Gwen would be hurt should something happen to her. Stupid to let herself think that her safety mattered that much.

With a sigh, Lia glanced around the room. "Did you carry me all the way back here?"

Tony shrugged and took a teacup from the side table. "I know the Undercroft isn't exactly a desirable location, but I couldn't very well take you anywhere else. And Mrs. Chapman would have murdered me if I let a stranger doctor one of her girls. That is if your mother didn't get to me first."

She accepted the cup in her good hand and sniffed, expecting the medicinal bite of healing herbs. But the sweet bergamot of the Earl Grey tea was touched only lightly with the aromatic burn of brandy.

"Not so fast," Tony began, but she'd finished the cup before he could touch it.

"Another?"

He scowled at her but turned to pour another cup.

"What time is it?"

"After two," he admitted over the burble of pouring tea. "Mrs. Chapman gave you something to help you sleep while she dealt with all of the other injuries that poured in after we returned."

Her spine stiffened. "What other injuries? Is everyone—"

"They're alright," Tony interrupted and settled the teacup against her palm, distracting her with the warmth and bittersweet smell. "Just bruised and sore."

She sighed and let the tension fade from her muscles. "Good. That's good. But I need to tell them what I've heard."

He had pulled the tatty chair up next to the bed at some point and sank into it with a grunt. "You can tell them later."

"I'm afraid we don't have—" she began, but he interrupted with, "You have to—"

The two of them stopped and stared at one another with a mixture of amusement and frustration, but it was Tony who spoke first.

He pushed a hand through his hair, but a lock fell over his forehead anyway. "After my father was injured, I spent almost every waking moment thinking and planning. I wanted only two things: revenge against the people who hurt him, and money. I thought the revenge would heal my insides, and the money would fix everything else." He gave her a shame-faced half-smile, and she saw traces of the boy in his face, the child who must have wanted justice for his father. "I learned soon enough that I would never have my revenge. The Revenant are in France, after all, and it would take me a lifetime to track down which member of their gang attacked him. Who would care for my parents while I chased my revenge? Certainly not my brothers. We are not close like you and Gwen."

Lia bit back what she wanted to say and shook her head. She knew something about the desire for vengeance. She'd sent Aris back to protect her sister, true, and she'd tried to stop Obyrron from invading, yes. But in the end? She wanted revenge. She wanted to destroy everything Obyrron had fought hundreds, thousands of years for, and she wanted to see his face when he realized she had done it.

She would have accepted a dagger to the chest if it meant seeing the knowledge in his eyes when she died. But Tony was a better person than she was.

"So," he continued, "I threw myself into a career that would stop people like the Revenant from hurting men like my father. And I used every bit of money I could spare to make certain my parents never suffered."

"You are a good man," Lia heard herself say in a soft voice.

Tony snorted. "I'm as selfish as anyone else. But I did learn something." He met her eyes, his a warm brown with smile lines touching the corners. "I learned that if you ignore yourself, it won't matter how much good you want to do for other people because you won't be around long enough to make it happen."

Hair fell across her face as Lia shook her head. She wanted to tell him that he was wrong about her, but she couldn't bear to see the look in his eyes she knew would be there when he realized how cold she really was. How much she was willing to sacrifice if it meant hurting Obyrron. She did not even want to admit it to herself.

Tony stood and carefully tucked the hair back behind her ear. His handsome face was open, his eyes earnest. "You are quite an actress. But you aren't as guarded as you think you are. You cannot hide how much you care. Maybe you learned to do it as a way to protect yourself, to pretend things don't hurt. I know something about that. But you can't keep your guard up all the time. I see it. You've fought too long alone. And if there is one thing I learned, it's that no one can fight alone forever."

Lia closed her eyes against the intensity in his, the honesty that hammered away at her carefully erected defenses. He didn't try to force her to open them or to admit anything. He simply stayed and waited. When she opened her eyes at last, he was there.

"If you're willing to let someone fight by your side," he said, carefully taking her injured hand, "I'd be honored to be considered for duty, General."

"No," she said around an unwilling laugh and past the tears standing in her eyes. "It's Ophelia, from you, if you please. Or Lia, if you don't mind."

The corner of his lip curled in a not-quite smile, and he gave her a mocking salute. Feeling lighter than she had in a long time, Lia said, "Very well, then. Let's start our battle by exposing the witches' plans, shall we?"

18

Reasonable Revelations

GWEN

Mrs. Chapman waited with two pots of tea, a table full of medicaments, and a worried expression that pinched her already narrow face into a rather intimidating scowl. If one did not know her, they would think her furious rather than anxious. When she was, in fact, both worried we were hurt and angry at us for making her worry in the first place.

She pointed an imperious finger at the series of benches and ordered, "Sit. Now."

No one argued.

I collapsed onto the bench with the heel of my left hand pressed against my temple and accepted the cup she thrust into my right hand without complaint. It wasn't warm enough to scald my mouth, so I drank the entire cup in one swallow and leaned against Aris to watch her work.

Mrs. Chapman bullied the rest of the party, who were all dirty and sweaty, into receiving whatever level of medical care she deemed necessary. No one, not even Delilah, dared gainsay her as she fussed and scolded.

"Exactly what did you think you were doing, Miss Fleur? Just look at this blister!"

"How you managed to tear your trousers when there isn't a scrape on you is a wonder, Master Sam."

Mama wandered into the room amidst this display. She'd stayed with Lia until Tony promised to keep an eye on her if only Mama would get something to eat. Mr. Yates helped her onto a bench, holding one hand gently while she sat, then hovered patiently while she forced herself to sip tea and nibble at a scone.

Her pale lips and trembling hands made me want to toss her behind high stone walls and put a thousand guards on the battlements. But there was nowhere safer in New London than the Undercroft, and that wasn't saying much for any of us.

"What news?" the King asked as he strolled into the room.

I closed my eyes and pinched the bridge of my nose hard enough to distract myself from the stabbing in my head. "Tomorrow night at Highgate Cemetery."

He paused a moment. "That is a suitable location for such nefarious plans. I applaud their sense of melodrama."

"I'm certain they will be gratified to hear it."

The King did not respond. I opened my eyes to see him and Aris look up suddenly, like cats hearing the scratching of a mouse in the next room. A moment later, the echo of determined footfalls reached my ears as well.

One of the King's men entered with Alix and Cyrus on his heels. The poor elvin man looked as if he'd rather have a hungry tiger behind him than those two, and I could not blame him. They were both spattered with blood, their faces hard and their eyes cold.

"Three," Alix said and wiped her chin with the back of her hand.

"They put up a rather messy fight," Cyrus added. "It took us a while. But those Covenant bastards are tough, and they heal fast. If you don't catch them in a weak spot outside what is protected by the symbol, they'll brush the damage off and keep going. Who's that?"

We all turned to follow the direction of Cyrus's gaze to see Madame Matilda standing in the farthest open door, her arms wrapped around her slender frame. She looked worn out but alert, and the sight of her sharpened my senses. But the way Cyrus eyed her was frankly intimidating. Even Matilda's substantial courage failed under his gaze, though she only revealed it in a subtle shudder and tightening of her clasped hands.

"That is Madame Matilda," I said, "the former leader of the Triumphant Sisterhood. And she is here to help us stop her sisters from destroying the wall."

"I do not know how much help I can be," she admitted as she entered the room. "But you have my word that I will do what I can."

Lia's voice was clear and sharp and cut through the room like a scythe. "You can start by telling us everything you know about the ceremony in Highgate Cemetery tomorrow night." She strode into the room with Tony behind her, one hand on the center of her back.

"You should be in bed, my darling," Mama said.

But Lia shook her head, making light dance in her blonde hair. "We don't have time, Mama. We must settle this now."

We gathered once again at the King's long table, where Cyrus ate as much as two people, and everyone else sipped tea. Mrs. Chapman's miracle drink put the little man in my brain to sleep, so I leaned on Aris in relief. When his fingers dug into my shoulder, loosening the tight muscle, I had to bite back a groan of pleasure. Such noises were not suitable for polite company.

Lia told us everything she learned while spying on the Sisterhood.

"That will be Deborah and Lord Pennyfeather," I said when she described the tête-à-tête between the man and woman. "From the sound of it, they've been planning this for quite some time."

"Moon and stars," Matilda breathed. Her fingers curled around an innocent napkin as if she were trying to strangle it, but her eyes were wide and staring. "It is so much worse than I feared. And I have not done enough to protect the city. Not nearly enough."

"Then you knew in advance?" Delilah demanded, leaning on the table with both fists. "You knew, and you did nothing?"

"I did not know what they intended, only that the power of the grimoire had captured some of their minds. I wanted to put it in the safest place possible, away from my sisters. But there was no way to predict what they might want it for."

"Cassandra Monmouth was a pretty damned good indicator of what they intended. You cannot honestly say you didn't suspect what they might do. And still, you did nothing!"

"I suspected some of it, but you must understand," Matilda said, "when one creates a coven, there are oaths one swears to protect the sanctity and safety of the members. My actions were limited because Deborah acted very carefully within the confines of my oaths. But I did not do nothing." She raised her chin. "I have been protecting the city with wards for years. There are hundreds, thousands of them scattered about."

"Wards?" Delilah demanded, her face pink with incredulous anger. "That's it? What good are a few wards against the fae armies?"

"Spoken like someone who knows nothing about wards," Matilda responded tiredly. "Since I could not know exactly what might happen, I designed the wards for several possibilities."

"Then you do not know what will happen if the barrier falls?" I asked before Delilah could fire off another insult or question.

Matilda shook her head. "How can one predict something that has never happened? Entire city blocks—entire cities—may disappear."

I leaned forward with my elbows on the table. "How do we stop them?"

Matilda dropped her forehead onto the heels of her hands. Her voice shook when she said, "The only way to stop them for certain is to kill them."

"They are guarded by mistcats," Lia said. "And something called an *obfuscation* spell."

"Are mistcats monsters?" Alix asked.

"Close enough," Lia said, glancing at her bandaged arm.

Alix patted the butt of one of her pistols. "That is what guns were made for."

"How many witches are required to complete the ritual?" I asked Matilda.

She shook her head. "I cannot say. They have the eye, and that changes things. I…" But she could not finish. Whatever she intended to say must have threatened her oath because her throat worked, her jaw clenched, and she pressed the heels of her hands against her forehead.

Matilda was our best potential source of information, yet she could tell us nothing. I ground my teeth and rubbed my forehead with my fingertips.

"What about Aris?" Sam asked.

Aris raised a brow. "What about me?"

"Well," the boy began, then blanched and picked at the table with his fingernail. "Can't you—you know—use your mind powers on her? *Make* her tell us?"

Matilda raised her head, her face chalk-white. But it was Tony who spoke. "We don't want to do that, Sam. I've seen a woman tortured by a spell that didn't want her to speak. It was a horrible death. You don't want to risk that."

"Well, we can't find them!" Sam flung his arm at the world above us. "We can't just do nothing."

"We can kill them all," Alix said with a shrug. "Tell us where they live. Cyrus and I can finish the job by morning."

Several pairs of wide eyes turned in her direction, but Alix did not so much as flinch. "What? Why does this surprise you? You realize my job is to hunt monsters, correct?"

"My sisters are *not* monsters," Matilda said, and though her voice was tired, it held an edge of steel.

"They plan to destroy the wall and allow a despotic, immortal king to invade and subjugate their own people," Aris said. "If that isn't enough to earn them the title, I do not know what is."

I raised both hands to forestall them. "We are not murdering a dozen women."

"It is a good solution, Gwen," Alix said. "Anything else carries too many risks."

Matilda tossed the much tortured napkin on the table. "You underestimate them if you think they are not protected by more than obfuscation spells and fae beasts. If what you've told me is true, they are working with the Covenant of the Silver Dawn and members of our government as well. Now that they are committed, they will take dangerous measures to protect themselves."

Alix's grin was so sharp it made a shiver run down my spine. "I do enjoy a challenge."

"We. Are. Not. Murdering. Innocent. Women," I repeated.

All eyes settled on me.

Delilah muttered. "You can hardly call them innocent."

"They have not carried out the spell yet," I reminded them. "And there is clearly dissension within the ranks. Perhaps they will surprise us and take action if their consciences get the better of them. How we stop the invasion matters as much as stopping it. Besides..." I glanced at Sam, whose face had gone red with some mixture of anger and fear. The same feeling sat heavy in my chest as I said, "Sally is among them."

Alix released her pistol and folded her arms. "What other options do we have? After the carnage today, they must know we are aware of their intentions. They are taking steps to guard the location. And the circle cannot be broken from the outside. That does not leave us many options, Gwen. The safest way to stop the spell is to kill the witches who want to perform it."

"Gwen pushed through a circle before," Tony said. "We don't have to resort to murder."

Delilah shook her head. "Gwen's wool coat was felted with protective filament, then. I don't know how the artificer pulled it off, but drawing and engraving wire that small with runic sentences that maintain their integrity is the next closest thing to a miracle. Even if I had the equipment, I couldn't replicate it in time."

"Can't you use magic?" The desperation in Sam's voice squeezed at my heart, but he glowered at Matilda as if his will alone could compel her.

Madame Matilda shook her head sadly. "I'm sorry, but I cannot. My magic alone is not strong enough to counter a barrier of that magnitude."

"Then what good is it!?" He slammed both fists on the table and stood, chest heaving. "There must be some way—Aris, you flew inside last time. What if you drop in from above? What if we dig a hole underneath?"

"Sam," I began, but he turned and stabbed a finger at Alix. "And if you try to hurt my sister, I'll kill you!"

Aris stood, but Tony was already there, taking Sam by the shoulder. "No one is going to hurt Sally."

They locked eyes for a breathless moment, and then Sam's shoulders slumped. He pulled away and stalked to the other side of the room, fists clenched at his sides. I sighed and flopped in my chair, letting my forehead drop into my hands. Everything was falling apart.

"Gwen," Alix said, her voice gentle and too low for Sam to overhear. When I looked up, her eyes brimmed with tears, but her expression was resolute. "I know you love the girl. She is something special. And under any other circumstances, I would follow your lead. But we don't have many options, and I *must* protect mortal life."

Cyrus stood, his expression a mask of grief, but he put his hand on his wife's shoulder in solidarity. "You can solve this riddle. I know you can."

My heart turned over in my chest. God's breath, how could they try to force me to do this?

"I will wait as long as possible," Alix said. Then she turned to leave, taking Cyrus with her.

The King leaned on the table, his dark eyes inscrutable as they pinned me to the spot. "Your fine ideals may be putting everyone in danger. You cannot escape this trap without bloodshed. The only question is whether it will be theirs or yours."

I shoved my chair back from the table and surged to my feet, suddenly full of too much nervous energy to sit still. Evening must be near, which gave us a mere twenty-four hours to stop the ritual. I started pacing, but even that wasn't enough. My fists ached to hit something, and a scream of frustration burned in my throat.

I would *not* sacrifice Sally. If that meant stopping Alix...my stomach flipped over as if trying to escape my body. I wanted to be in my study, pacing in front of the fire. I wanted to be moving, to do something productive so I could *think*.

"Does the core of the problem stem from your inability to track the witches?" Dove emerged from the shadows where she usually hid, her long, elegant hands folded in front of her, Ripper the construct dog padding patiently at her heels.

"It goes a bit deeper than that," I said with a heavy sigh, "but yes. If we could track the witches, we might abduct a few and destroy the integrity of the circle before they can raise enough energy to power the spell. Do I have the mechanics right, Madame?"

Matilda nodded tiredly. "Every spell has a minimum threshold. A powerful witch with a magical focus may be able to handle the same spell five weaker witches can do without one. I cannot even fathom the power a spell like this requires. They will need every witch in the coven, and each will be forced to channel more than usual in addition to using the eye."

"Then we may avoid the ritual entirely if you removed one or two witches from the coven?" Dove pressed.

"Possibly," I replied, narrowing my eyes at the woman. There was something either innocent or honest about her that reminded me of Tony. Her green eyes were guileless, too sincere for hiding secrets. That, or she was just very bad at it because she wanted to say something. "Why do you ask?"

She glanced down at her hands, then turned them over to reveal a lovely gold compass that I mistook, at first, for a pocket watch. I found myself closing the distance for a closer look without realizing I was moving. But then, I have always had a weakness for clever gadgets. Especially ones as beautifully made as this one.

Instead of a single arrow pointing north, this compass was layered with several hands, very carefully engraved with runes so small they could be mistaken for filigree. The same symbols curled around the outside of the glass face.

"This is extraordinary," I murmured as she held the compass up for inspection. "What does it do?"

A chair squeaked as Delilah shoved it back to join me, her button nose almost close enough to touch Dove's outstretched hand.

"Instead of tracking magnetic north, this compass tracks magical signatures," Dove said, turning her palm. The top needle of the compass swiveled to remain, pointing to the right—exactly where the Cutthroat King stood with his arms folded and an indulgent expression on his face. "Some needles are engraved to track specific signatures, but the bottom needle, this red one, will shift to the strongest magical signature nearby."

My mouth popped open. "Are you saying magical signatures linger in the air like scent?"

Dove nodded. "Yes, something like it, so far as I can tell. At least that is how it works practically."

"How old can the signature be?" Delilah demanded, her voice hard. It wasn't frustration that sharpened her tone but fascination. "Or, how weak can the magical signature be before the compass cannot detect it?"

Color suffused Dove's cheeks, and her voice also took on an edge of excitement. "It depends upon the strength of the magic and how close one is to the magic-touched air. Magical energy seems to disperse much like the airborne particles of smoke or dust. It is most concentrated at the source and dissipates the further it gets. The stronger the source, the longer it lasts in the air. See here." She took a few slow steps toward the table, and the red needle swung across the compass face to point directly at Madame Matilda. A couple of steps to the left, and it arrowed toward Aris.

"Fascinating," I murmured, my mind spinning with possibilities. "Then this compass should also detect the obfuscation spells?"

Dove shrugged. "I don't know how the spells behave, but I cannot see why not. If the spells leak magic into the air, the compass should detect the magic, at least."

"But these runes," Delilah said slowly, letting the blunt tip of her finger graze the edge of the engravings, "they can't reveal the source of the magic, can they?"

Dove's lips screwed into an unhappy line. "No, they cannot. I am working with limited resources, unfortunately."

"Oh, don't mistake me!" Delilah flapped her hand as if waving away a fly. "This is—well, I've rarely seen work so fine or so accurate. And you without formal training! What I mean is that if Gwen takes this compass above, she might end up following a werewolf as easily as a witch. Or a fae refugee."

"And," Matilda added, joining the fray, "each of my sister's spells will have slightly different effects. I suspect that is why your Ratcatchers have failed. The compass may locate their magical signatures, but your Ratcatchers cannot visually verify what they find."

"And we do not have time to follow false leads," I mumbled, beginning to pace with my arms behind my back. I needed a way to verify the magical signature I followed, or I would waste more time than—

"My lady?" Mr. Yates asked, his tone so properly deferent it set my teeth on edge. "At Mr. Aris's request, I hid your hagstone in the usual spot with your other gadgets. Would that see through mortal magic as it does through faerie magic?"

Delight broke across my face in a smile. "Mr. Yates, will you never cease to save the day?"

He did not return my smile, but his eyes sparkled. "I will continue to do what I can, ma'am."

I gave him a quick hug, which seemed to startle him. He focused hard on setting his jacket aright once I released him.

"We have a chance, then," I said, feeling hopeful for the first time in hours. "If I can get to the townhouse quickly, that is."

"But what if someone sees you?" Mama's lips pressed into a thin, worried line. "Surely they will be guarding the place in the hope of your return?"

I held up my wrist, letting my sleeve fall away from the Sightscreen. "There are a few minutes left in my diamond. I should be able to get in and out unseen. And speaking of diamonds," I added as my mind began spitting out possible future scenarios based on my new knowledge, "Your Majesty?"

The King raised a dark brow. "Yes?"

"Have you any diamonds of this approximate size?" I held my thumb and forefinger a few centimeters apart.

"If I do?"

"I will buy them. All of them."

Fleur choked, but I ignored her, focusing all my energy on the monarch of the underground. He raised two fingers and flicked them in a *come here* motion. A guard stepped into the room from the shadows behind the throne.

"See to it," he said.

The guard bowed from the waist and disappeared.

"Lady Dove," I said in formal tones, "will you entrust me with your brilliant gadget? I promise to do my best to return it to you intact."

"Of course," she said and placed the compass gently on my palm.

I dropped the gadget into my pocket and added one last bit of advice for the King. "Send what Ratcatchers you can spare into the countryside and instruct them to look for hagstones."

"Hagstones?" One dark brow rose. "I thought faeries were the ones who spoke in riddles."

"Circle stones, ones that have a hole worn through them by some natural force, like dripping water. You cannot steal them," I clarified, "they must stumble upon them as a gift of nature otherwise they will not be able to see through glamour and magic."

For the first time, I believe I surprised the man. He blinked at me, then performed an elegant bow from the waist. "Very well, lady. I will send them out."

Aris joined me, taking my hand and squeezing it once. "Shall we?"

"I'm going, too," Sam declared, pushing forward and jutting out his lower jaw.

My mind conjured an image of Sam arrested by the constables, of the Covenant injecting him with something awful, of one of the werewolves catching him unaware, and fear I could never manage to feel for myself choked me.

"Not this time, my boy," Aris said before I could reply. "Gwen cannot sneak and protect you at the same time."

"I can protect myself. Besides, I've got to help somehow. I can't stay down here and wait; I'll go mad."

"This is not a lark or the zoo or even Chatsworth, Samuel," I snapped. "The city is overrun with people who want to hurt us. I cannot risk another member of my family."

Sam's cheeks went bright red. "You say I'm a member of this family, but whenever it's time to protect it, I'm just a kid who gets left behind."

He turned and stormed out without looking back.

"Gwen?" Mama asked. The worry in her voice raked down my back like claws. God's breath, the poor woman. I crossed the room and pulled her into my arms. She smelled of lavender and lemon, even in the musty confines of the Undercroft. She did not belong here. I had to keep her safe. To keep everyone safe.

"Go find Sam," I told her through the tightness in my throat. "He'll need someone he trusts."

The sun had not quite set when we emerged from the Undercroft, climbing up the metal ladder behind a restaurant. We left the still, cool, slightly mildewed air for a blast of residual summer heat that clung to the stone buildings. Shadows had already begun to claim the city, seeping out of corners and hollows like running ink. But the sky was still bright enough that the street lamps hadn't flickered to life. I took a deep breath, letting the familiar, complex stink of New London fill my lungs as Aris joined me.

Perhaps, for a moment, we could pretend we were not in a race against time to protect everything we loved from destruction. We could merely be Gwen and Aris, strolling through the city as any couple might do—any couple who also had to be on the lookout for assassins, monsters, and constables.

Aris dusted off his jacket and glared at the hole as the Ratcatcher beneath pulled the false cobblestone door shut and bolted it. "I feel like a cockroach. You were not smudged too badly by our climb, I hope?"

I presented myself for inspection, and he held my chin, turning my face from one side to the other. His eyes were like banked coals, the heat of his hunger barely smothered by fear and the edges of desperation. The combination turned his gaze into a physical touch that made heat pool low in my belly.

"Only a little dust," he said, sliding his thumb across my bottom lip. "But then, I rather like you dirty."

"Shall I roll about on the cobbles?" I asked.

My tone was flippant, but I was breathless with wanting him. We had no time. Everything was wrong. Danger surrounded us, and had for weeks. Small stolen moments were all that sustained us, and I wanted to lose myself in his touch like I wanted water or air.

Aris had the singular ability to save me from myself while making me feel more *like* myself. And in this quiet alley, when the two of us were at least marginally alone, I wanted that—wanted him and the forgetfulness I found in his arms—very much.

He seemed to feel my desperation because his voice was as rough as if it was dragged from the depths of his chest. "I'd like you soiled, Gwen. Tarnished." He backed me toward the building until my shoulder blades hit the brick. "I want to stain you. To sully your good name. To break you and remake you until your soul bares my fingerprints and your body is fit for no touch but mine."

His fingers dug into my hips, and he lifted me with ease, pinning me against the wall and fitting himself between my legs. When he dipped his head, lips brushing mine, my heart clawed at my breastbone. My skin felt like it was on fire. If he did not touch me, and soon, I would burst into flame.

Aris dragged his lips across mine, and I held his arms for support, feeling the muscles beneath his coat flutter with barely restrained savagery. "If we had the time, I would take you here. Let the pedestrians hear you scream my name so they know who you belong to."

He flexed his hips, and I bit my lip, though I'd much rather bite *him*. "That sounds...lovely."

I felt as much as heard the smile in his voice as he kissed my neck. "I did not know you were an exhibitionist."

My fingers threaded themselves through his hair to pull him tight against me, shivering as his teeth grazed my sensitive skin. "I doubt I would notice."

Our lips found each other, and the sweet, salty taste of him made the world spin away for a few blissful heartbeats. But he broke the kiss, pressed his forehead against mine, and sighed. "You wouldn't, but our lives may depend upon paying attention. So." He set me down and took a step back. "We shall save the savage lovemaking for next time and turn our attention toward keeping ourselves alive long enough to enjoy it."

I blew a frustrated breath through my nose and scowled. "I do not like it when you're right."

"Get used to it, darling. It is likely to happen quite often." He held out his elbow. "Shall we?"

I took his arm and let him lead me onto the street, too distracted by the ache between my legs to notice the shadow trailing us.

19

Smoke and Feathers

GWEN

Grosvenor Street was lined front-to-back with grand row houses that stood four stories high and blocked most of the sky. Traffic was beginning to dissipate, but there were still enough travelers to let us blend in with the herd, especially with Aris altering his glamour to look like an entirely different person.

My hat mostly hid my hair, but brown was not a distinctive enough color to draw the eye of anyone watching, and I had to save the diamonds in my Sightscreen for sneaking into the house. So I held his arm, walked with my head down, and tried not to notice the magic compass bump against my leg as we walked.

After we retrieved my goggles, we would see whether the little device could lead us to the witches. In the meantime, I tried to look like a tired woman, only paying attention to not tripping over her own feet, so I saw the poor bird before I smelled it.

A dead crow lay on the sidewalk with its head at the wrong angle, one wing bent beneath it. A shudder of dread ran down my spine. "Poor thing."

Birds died in New London all the time for a myriad of reasons. But seeing a dead corvid now felt somehow like a bad omen. Clenching my jaw against the mental discomfort, I tightened my grip on Aris's arm and walked faster, only to nearly step on another bird—a raven.

I skipped over its body, noting the blood pooled beneath it even in the growing dark. As we neared Grosvenor Square, more birds littered the ground. Dozens. Hundreds. Small, black-feathered bodies lay broken or trampled; some had been pushed unceremoniously out of the street, and others had been left to get trampled. With an incoherent noise, I pulled Aris with me into the shadows of a parked carriage.

Birds died in New London, but not like this.

"They're," I squeezed the words out through a throat tight with fear, "they're hunting you. Aren't they?"

Aris's voice was low and dangerous. "So it would seem." His grip on my arm tightened, and he leaned in. "Someone has been keeping pace with us for several blocks. Keep your guard up. I'm going aloft to see if I can spot them."

"But what if—" I began, my eyes straying to the closest of the dead birds, imaging Aris's glossy black feathers littering the ground.

He kissed me quickly, then thought with irritating confidence, *They will never spot me against a dark sky. Besides, darling, where is your faith in my enormous skill?* before shimmering and disappearing in a rush of wind.

I expected to see constables standing in a line outside, bouncing the handles of their truncheons against their palms. But the house looked as if I'd never left it. And given how many people were looking for me, that was deeply suspicious.

Is anyone lurking outside? I thought to Aris.

No one that I can see.

But that didn't mean there wasn't anyone. *I'm activating my Sightscreen. I'll leave a window open for you.*

It had been many, many years since I was forced to sneak in through the basement window at the back entrance, but sliding between the open pane of glass and the window frame made a nostalgic giggle bubble up in my chest. I suppressed the inappropriate urge to laugh ruthlessly, as any lady of sense would, and snuck through my own basement and into the upstairs.

Under the protection of my Sightscreen, I opened a window wide enough for Aris and turned to face the entryway. My chest constricted, crushing the air from my lungs. I pressed the button to disengage the magic and stood staring at my empty foyer. It was just as I had left it.

Mrs. Chapman might walk down the hall at any moment with an armful of linens. Sam may come pelting out of the kitchen with red cheeks and a handful of pastries, taking the stairs two at a time while Monsieur cursed him in French.

Aris shimmered into his human form next to me, and took my hand in silent comfort. When we passed the library, I half-expected to see Sally sitting in her accustomed chair by the fireplace. But the hearth was cold. And Mr. Yates did not wait by the door with a placid expression, ready to hear of my day and scold me for driving too fast.

When had my house turned into *our home*? It hadn't happened with fanfare or ceremony but in a hundred small, intimate daily moments that built on one another, one brushstroke at a time, until a picture of family life stared back at me. Would we ever sit in the study again, teasing one another as rain fell against the window?

A lump formed in my throat.

If I wanted the chance to return to this house with my little family in tow, I had to stop the ritual. There was no time for melancholy. Blinking back tears, I swiped my spare umbrella from the stand and released the safety before taking the stairs.

"Did you happen to spot our follower?" I asked.

"No," Aris said, "but I have suspicions. I want to check on something."

He turned down one side of the hall as I took the other. I retrieved a pack from my bedroom, giving the space a cursory glance to ensure I missed nothing before crossing to the servant's staircase.

The door opened without a squeak. I slid my palms along the paneled walls, feeling for the telltale divot in the wood. Lia and I hid romance novels here when we were younger. It was a small act of rebellion against Mrs. Chapman, who said such literature was *unsuitable for well-brought-up young ladies.* And though we spent most of our youth in the country, we'd found a few clever hiding spots in the townhouse while visiting.

When I began using it to hide gadgets from Mrs. Chapman and the children, it was only a matter of time until the sharp-eyed Mr. Yates learned my secret.

Of course, Aris, still masquerading in his raven form, had known of the hiding spot for years. He had ridden on my shoulder more than once when, taken by a maudlin mood and too much wine, I'd pried the board open to thumb through the last book Lia and I hid there.

My fingernails slipped between two loose planks, and I pried the board up enough to wedge my fingers beneath and pull. The nail slid out, the board slipped down, and I plunged my hand inside.

Just as Mr. Yates said, my wheels and goggles were still inside, accompanied by various small explosives, and—my fingers brushed across the unmistakable spine of a book. It was small and bound in red leather with gold embossing on the cover and spine. *Arrogance and Assumptions.*

I could still hear Lia giggle in memory as she kept watch at the corner of the stairs while I slipped the scandalous tome into its long hiding place. My fingerprints still marred the fine coating of dust on the cover from the last time I'd retrieved the book. But another, larger set of prints had joined mine. Frowning, I opened the cover. A note had been left on one of the endpapers in a fine, clean script.

*Gwen,*undefined

*I cannot say when you may find this gift, if you ever do. I write it more for myself, out of a need to express sentiments you may not be ready to hear but which I can no longer keep trapped in my heart, most especially now that I have the hands with which to write them.Y*undefined

*ou must know that loving you saved me. Allowing me into your life has been the greatest gift of mine, much of which was spent as a person I do not now recognize. I have you to thank for that as well.*undefined

*Knowing you as myself, at last, and being known by you as a man, has made me jealous of every memory of which I am not a part. I hope, then, you will forgive me for using this opportunity to insert myself retroactively into this one.Whenever the memory of hiding romance novels comes upon you, perhaps you will also think of me.*undefined

*When I dreamed of having a home as a child, I could not have known that yearning would be fulfilled in you. Your heart is now the only home I covet for myself. I hope, someday, you will find the same sanctuary in mine.*undefined

*Yours always,*undefined

Aris Blackwing undefined

Something happened in my chest, something like breaking only in reverse. I held my stomach and leaned against the wall for support, realizing with dreadful clarity that Aris deserved the love of someone far better and less selfish than I.

In the months we spent together after returning from the Sunset Lands, I had been so trapped in my own struggles that I did not bother to discover his. I'd allowed him to shoulder my burdens, relied on him, and turned to him for comfort but never offered the same in return.

He deserved more. Yet I could not—would not—give him up. The only answer, then, was to create out of the wreckage of myself someone worthy of his love. If I could do nothing else, I would do that.

I carefully pocketed the book, ensured my hagstone goggles were still in one piece, gathered the rest of my gear into the pack, and froze. Voices echoed down the hall. My heart leapt into a gallop only to plummet when I realized the voice was Sam's. I should have known. Who else would have followed us so carefully that even Aris couldn't spot them?

"I won't let her hurt Sally. I don't care who she is."

"Do you think Gwen or I would allow anyone to hurt your sister?"

"What if you can't stop her?"

"If we cannot, you certainly won't be able to."

"You're better people than I am," Sam said, his voice hard. "Maybe I'll do things you aren't willing to do."

Aris laughed, but the sound wasn't warm or amused. "Do you know what I was, *who* I was, before coming to live with Lady Gwen?"

I froze just outside Sam's room, barely daring to breathe.

"A raven?" Sam answered, his irritation colored with sarcasm.

"I was an assassin, Sam. I did things that are seared on my soul, things that leave wounds that don't heal. Do you understand me?"

I could not hear Sam's reply, so he must have nodded. A thrill of dread made goosebumps break out in a rush down my arms.

"I know you are angry and scared. Maybe more angry than scared," Aris allowed, a touch of humor coloring his tone. "But allowing that anger to control you, to make you do things that will change who you are? That is dangerous."

Sam's staccato footfalls told me he was pacing. His fists probably clenched, and his chin thrust stubbornly forward. "I have to be dangerous if I'm ever going to help anyone!"

"A double-edged sword is dangerous," Aris warned, "but it cuts both ways. When you're angry, you're as likely to hurt yourself as you are to protect someone else. Especially not with mundane bullets. Where did you get this pistol, anyway?"

"What does it matter? I can't let her hurt Sally. I won't. I don't care what it does to me."

That was quite enough of that. I strode into the room, snatched the pistol from Sam's surprised fingers without preamble, and said,

"What about what it does to me? To your grandmother?"—that last was an underhanded move, but I would use whatever leverage I had—"What would it do to your sister? Do you think your actions affect you alone, Sam?"

His expression was precisely how I imagined it: brows pinched together above his nose, chin thrust out, his cheeks red, his fists clenched. "You didn't think about that when you left us!"

The first arrow to the chest had been fired, and it hit its mark.

I raised my chin and refused to let my lips tremble. "You are only partially right. I knew exactly what would happen if I failed. I knew how it would hurt the people I cared about. And I did it anyway."

Sam's face fell. I had just disappointed him badly, but that was a wound I would have to live with. "You knew? How...how could you?"

"For the same reason you are willing to throw your soul away to keep your sister safe. For the same reason she joined the witches in the first place."

"What do you mean?"

I sat on the bed next to Aris and sighed. "She joined them so she could become strong, Sam. So neither of you would ever have to worry about food, or money, or how to protect yourselves. In short, she did it because she believed it was the best way to protect you. The same way you are considering murder to protect her. The same way I hurt you, Sally, Mama, Tony, and everyone else I love when I tried to protect my sister."

His face blanched.

"I did not intend to hurt you. I thought I could pull the spell off safely. But I knew it was a risk, and I took it anyway. Because I was selfish. I cared more about what I wanted than how you felt. It might have worked in the end. But it was still wrong, and it hurt you both in ways I will never fully understand. I will carry the guilt of that until I die. There are no guarantees, Sam, even if you are clever or strong. Even if you are prepared."

"Then what's the point in trying if I'm guaranteed to hurt you or myself no matter what?" he demanded, angry color flooding his face once more.

"If you might fail either way," Aris said, "you have to ask yourself what you can live with. What decision brings you closer to being the kind of person you can look at in the mirror? Which path makes you more deserving of the love and respect of the people around you?"

My heart squeezed until I thought I might faint. I slid my hand into Aris's.

Sam stopped pacing. His head hung on his neck, and his shoulders drooped. He clenched and unclenched his fists. "How can I live with myself if something happens to Sally, and I could have tried to stop it?"

There was no good answer to that question. I wanted to pull him into my arms and tell him everything would turn out, that we would win, and the world would go back to normal. But that would be a lie. I'd lost a sister, and I knew there was no way to put the world back together after pain like that. You only learned to live amongst the broken pieces.

I tried to think of some way to communicate that to him, but he stiffened and gasped, his face turning white.

"Sam?"

Aris stood and grabbed the boy by the shoulders. "Samuel? Are you hurt?"

Sam's eyes were wide and staring, jerking back and forth in random patterns as if watching something we could not see.

"Samuel?" I said, trying not to shout while my heart raced.

Sam flinched, then wilted. Aris held him up long enough for Sam to regain his feet. Sweat coated his forehead, but he pulled out of Aris's grip and turned to his writing desk.

"Sally," he said as he scribbled on a piece of paper. "It was Sally. She said to show you this."

He turned and held up a drawing of two circles, one inside the other, but the outside circle was drawn in dashed lines, broken in several places. Beyond the circles were black splotches scattered willy-nilly.

At the bottom were a series of dots and dashes. Morse code? I took the paper from Sam with shaking hands.

"She won't answer me," he said. "I tried to ring her back, but I think she took her ring off."

I stared at the message for a long time. Dread stiffened my muscles and made my hands feel like ice. If I could have moved, I would have thrown up.

"What does it mean?" Sam pleaded. "Lady Gwen, what does it mean?"

My lips and tongue wouldn't cooperate. How could I tell him that the message said, *Please stop me*?

"Did she say anything else?" Aris asked Sam.

His voice was small and broken. "She said she loves me, and don't be afraid."

Aris tilted his head as if listening, then stiffened. The sharp crack of breaking glass echoed up the stairs once, then twice more.

"What—" Sam began but was cut off when the upstairs window broke. Several more crashes made his face go white.

"Stay here," Aris commanded before dashing from the room. "Gwen!" he shouted a moment later. "Fire!"

Sam and I shared a startled glance before rushing into the hall.

The scent of burning alcohol stung my nose and eyes, and I had to squint against the light of the fire that had spread across the carpet at the front of the house and was climbing the drapes to lick the ceiling.

"A firebomb," I breathed, unable to comprehend the reality of what I saw.

Fire spread from the broken glass at the front wall to the door of the servants' staircase, devouring the dry wood in seconds. Aris grabbed my arm and dragged me toward the staircase.

"Sam, run!" he shouted.

Only Sam didn't run. He shot back into his room before I could reach him. "He'll follow us!" Aris shouted as he hauled me down the stairs at breakneck speed. I stumbled, but he held me upright, swinging me around the landing only to catch me before we reached the bottom stair. Heat roared toward us in a furnace blast, and the acrid scent of burning paint made me cough hard enough to start tears streaming from my eyes.

Fire engulfed the front door and was already tearing through my study, ravaging what was left of my books and jumping from window to window as if the drapes were a ladder. The other side of the hall was already wreathed in flame, open and hungry as the gullet of a dragon.

Sam hit my back, catching me about the shoulders as he skidded to a stop and said, "God's breath," before he began coughing.

Fire consumed every exit from the ground floor. No doubt whoever threw the firebombs intended it that way. Smoke rolled along the ceiling in a black river, boiling and peeling off bits of paint already cracked from the heat.

"Up!" I barked, turning and pushing Sam hard in the middle of his back.

He bounded up the stairs like a gazelle, and we rushed past the second-story landing, wincing as the heat seared our exposed skin. The third story was no better. Whoever had thrown the burning bottles of alcohol had a good arm and better aim. As we ran up floor after floor, despair sank deep into my gut. We might have jumped to safety from the second story, but the fourth? That was a death sentence as surely as the fire.

We had to find another way out.

"Come on!" Aris shouted over his shoulder and tightened his grip on my wrist. What felt like an eternity later, we stumbled onto the roof through the attic door. Sirens wailed, and smoke billowed from broken windows in oily black clouds, making it almost impossible to breathe or see.

Sam pulled the neck of his shirt over his nose and said between fits of coughing, "There's no way down!"

He was right. My house was the last in the row, and the roof next to ours was blocked by a wall of fire chewing through the roof. The firetrucks were close, but the tar was already soft beneath our feet. They would never put out the blaze before the fire reached us. And our coats, no matter how robust, would not protect us from a five-story fall.

I spun to Aris, who had come to the same conclusion judging by his horrified expression. We didn't have enough time. A thousand words pressed against my lips: apologies, promises, admissions... But I couldn't force them out, only stare at him with anguish closing my throat.

Aris took my face in his hands, his eyes searching mine as if the answer lay somewhere in my gaze. "Don't...Gwen, just trust me and don't—bloody damned everlasting hell."

He kissed me once hard, said, "Stand as close to the edge as you can," and lifted Sam into his arms. The wind dragged a trail of smoke between us, but it wasn't enough to disguise the change. Aris shimmered, as he always did when shifting between his raven form and his human appearance. But this time, instead of a large bird, a creature I did not have a name for stood in his place.

There wasn't even time to examine him. A pair of enormous black wings opened so wide they would have covered several men, and with a mighty leap, Aris and Sam sailed out of the smoke and into the sky. Sam screamed.

I may have screamed as well.

I ran through the smoke to the edge of the roof, but they were gone. All the strength left my legs, and my knees hit the hot surface. My skin stung, but I couldn't force myself to stand. An upstairs window shattered, and a gout of flame twelve feet high soared into the air. I jerked back, blocking the heat with my raised arm before rolling to the side and peering desperately through the smoke.

But Aris and Sam were gone.

The fire bathed Grosvenor Square in lurid orange light, letting me see my neighbors standing outside and staring in shock and dismay. A fire engine roared into the square, its great copper tank gleaming. But it was far too late. My home was burning, and there was no saving it.

Firefighters swarmed out of the truck and began pulling out hose, shouting for my neighbors to back up. But one figure wasn't familiar. I squinted through the smoke, glaring at the figure who stood unnaturally still.

Another gout of flame broke through the second story, and the burst of light showed me her face.

Shiverback's mate.

A satisfied smile curled her lovely mouth, and her eyes glowed orange, reflecting the light of destruction. She lost her mate to my sister's fire, and I had just lost my home to hers. Not an even trade, but one that must have satisfied at least part of her need for vengeance.

With sudden certainty, I knew that she had destroyed the safe house, as well. Who else would take such pleasure in ruining what was mine?

The roof began to buckle. It was so hot that I pushed to my feet to stop my palms from blistering, but the heat seeped through the soles of my boots. At least Sam was safe. Or, I assumed he was safe. Smoke made my eyes water until everything blurred and my lungs spasmed, desperate for clean air that didn't burn.

A black shape soared into my vision, almost invisible through my tears. Aris, in some monstrous form, shot toward me at a dizzying speed. He flared his wings and beat them backward an instant before hitting me. Clouds of smoke billowed away in a great gust of wind as he slowed just enough for a running landing.

"Gwen!" he shouted.

His voice wasn't Aris's voice. It rasped up his throat like sandpaper. I watched him dash toward me, too numb to be afraid. It was *his* face, his dark eyes, but his hands were overlarge, with black claws instead of fingernails. And the overdeveloped muscles of his torso would have shocked even Cyrus. His legs belonged on a monster, some cross between a wolf and a raven, with long feet that seemed jointed backward at the heel.

By god's breath, what was he?

The Aris creature caught me against his chest, took two more running steps, and leaped off the edge of the roof. After a stomach-clenching drop, his wings caught the air, and we shot upward and away at an incredible speed.

Sirens faded. I watched Grosvenor Square grow smaller until our home was only a distant, troublesome dot in the crowded city. No more than a pinpoint of light that would soon be snuffed out. It was once only a house. It had become a home. Now, it was a ruin. And as we soared through the smoke of my old life, I could not even weep.

20

Forgiveness and Permission

LIA

Gwen's eyes were dull and lifeless. She reminded Lia of the soldiers who returned from battle in the Wylderwood. They had been shocked beyond grief and only stared blankly into the middle distance as if seeing things only they could see. Or maybe trying not to see anything at all.

Aris brought the three of them back an hour ago, covered in soot and panting.

"They burned the house," he said as he sat Gwen on the bench. He had tried to brush the singed hair out of Gwen's face, but she'd turned away from his hand. He'd flinched as if he'd been slapped.

Now Gwen sat apart from everyone, her arms wrapped around her knees, ignoring the attempts of Mama and Mrs. Chapman to coax tea into her or words out of her. It was understandable, Lia supposed. She hadn't spent much time in the townhouse. To her, the place was still something of an exotic location, an exciting but alien place visited only during infrequent childhood vacations.

But it had been Gwen's home, one she shared with the little family she built and cared for.

Though it wasn't quite the same, Lia still missed her apartments in Obyrron's castle. They had never belonged to her, not really. But she'd had a life there and memories attached to every bit of furniture and linen. She'd learned to feel safe in that bed, comforted by the familiarity of a hundred things she saw and touched every day, a feeling she'd been missing since her return to the mortal world.

It had taken six months to drag herself out of the grief that swamped her after Gwen dragged her back. If her sister felt anything close to what she had, recovery would be long and painful. But they didn't have time to wait for Gwen to swim to the surface. The ritual was less than twenty-four hours away. Mama's gentle pats and Mrs. Chapman's less gentle encouragement were not going to force her sister out of shock.

Aris might have done it. He'd managed to keep Gwen sane when the two of them were trapped in the dungeon. But he stood alone in the shadows with his arms folded and his eyes downcast. Whatever had happened between them must have been traumatic, but recovering from that would have to wait. Something had to be done now.

Lia strode across the room and knelt next to her sister. With her free hand—the one not strapped against her chest by one of Mrs.

Chapman's ingenious slings—she slapped Gwen once across the face.

The blow wasn't hard but sharp, and Gwen flinched away. Lia ignored Mama's surprised cry and Mrs. Chapman's disapproving scowl and grabbed her sister's stubborn chin.

"Look at me, Gigi."

Gwen's eyes swam into focus and locked on hers. Those brown eyes, usually sparkling with mirth, were dull, but at least they were conscious. Her voice was small and surprised when she said, "You hit me."

"Yes, and I'll do it again if that is the only way to force you to your senses. There isn't time to grieve yet. Do you hear me? No, don't scowl at me. You can fall apart tomorrow when Sally is safe."

At Sally's name, Gwen's eyelids flinched. Hurting her sister was like stabbing herself in the chest, but she'd rather have Gwen angry with her than be unable to forgive herself if something preventable happened to the girl because she was trapped in grief.

Fire kindled in Gwen's eyes, turning them hot and hard, like burning coals. Good. She locked her uninjured hand with Gwen's and hauled them both to their feet. "There is work to do."

Gwen's jaw clenched, her chest heaved, but she nodded. "Yes. You're right. But Lia?"

"Hmm?"

"Don't hit me again. Ever."

She raised her chin, feeling defiance hot in her own eyes. "I'll do what I must. If you don't like it, I suppose you'll have to stop me, won't you?"

They stared at one another, their eyes hard, hands clasped. Not exactly the sweet relationship they'd had as children. But those tender girls hadn't survived the fire life threw them into. They'd hardened, taking shape under the blows of circumstance until the fire cooled, and they were left sharp and bright. If this was the only relationship they could have now, sword against sword, well...at least they were alive to have it.

"That will be quite enough of that." Instead of wringing her hands, Mama's expression was stony, and her voice was just as hard. "You will both comport yourselves with the decorum the situation requires. If you must lay hands on anyone in anger, let it be against those who would harm us. Am I understood?"

They said, "Yes, ma'am," as if they were still schoolgirls.

"Very well." Mama raised her chin and took her place at the head of the table. "How are we going to save my granddaughter?"

Everyone traded glances of surprised amusement, but no one argued. Mama hadn't been herself since being dragged to the Undercroft, Gwen was hanging by a thread, and the King seemed as hesitant to give orders as they were to take them.

Lia might have controlled the situation, but she did not like the person she became when she was forced to lead. Everything cold and calculating took over, forcing out the scraps of herself she'd managed to retrieve over the last few months. While she might use that persona from time to time when the situation called for it, she hated the way it froze her from the inside.

Gwen took a deep breath and said, quite calmly, "We aren't. Well, you are not, Mama. You are taking Sam and Mr. Yates back to Wainwright."

Mama's eyes and nostrils flared; Sam shouted, "No, I'm not!" and Mr. Yates looked like he had been gravely insulted. But Gwen's expression was just as stony as Mama's had been when she turned on Sam. "Do you know what might happen to your grandmother with no one to protect her if I do not come back? A Dowager Duchess surrounded by thieves and cutthroats?"

"It will not be pretty," the King said from his throne. "As much as I respect you, Your Grace, you are here only as a guest of my ally. I cannot guarantee your safety if she is removed from the equation."

That was a lie. If his influence over his people was anywhere near as strong as it appeared, he certainly could. But the King was an observant man. He knew what Gwen was trying to do and seemed willing to assist.

"I will not be disposed of like so much baggage," Mama said coldly.

"And you can't just ship me off," Sam shouted. "I have to protect Sally!"

The expression of angry resentment in the boy's eyes would have melted stone, and Lia knew it scorched her sister's insides even if Gwen did not so much as flinch. Which meant Lia needed to step in.

"You will do as you are told," she said coldly, "because you are too smart to throw your life away needlessly and because if the rest of us fail, you will be the only one left to save your sister. And," she added when uncertainty and pain softened Sam's expression, "because I will have the Ratcatchers chain you to the wall if you do not. And the King would not stop me."

"Wouldn't dream of it," the King agreed.

The fire came back to Sam's eyes, but Lia knew she'd won. He might trust Gwen's love enough to defy her, but he did not know what Lia was capable of, and it was a risk he could not take if he wanted to remain free.

"If you think you can ship me off while my girls are in danger," Mama said, her jaw tight, "you are very much mistaken."

"You have a duty to the people of Wainwright." Lia or Gwen might have uttered the same sentiment, but it was Mr. Yates who spoke. In his calm, deep voice, it sounded so much more reasonable than it would have from either of her daughters. "Your Grace, your life is not your own. You've known that from the moment you married. People rely on you. And your daughters are capable, dangerous women but they will take too many risks if they must protect you as well as themselves."

Mama was too intelligent not to know Mr. Yates was right, but she did not like it. In fact, she glared at him as if he were a traitor.

Mrs. Chapman clutched her herb bag against her chest. "You two are my only responsibility. Your mother gave you into my care as babes, and I won't be ordered away. If you want to ship me off, you'll have to tie me with chains and hope they're stronger than I am."

"I'm glad to hear it," Gwen said, a weak smile turning up one corner of her mouth. "Because if we survive, we will need your healing herbs." She pulled a folded piece of paper from her coat pocket and smoothed it on the table. "Madame Matilda, would you take a look at this, please?"

Matilda wasn't the only person to lean over the paper. They crowded around to see a circle drawn roughly in the center with several dots spaced evenly around the inside, and outside of that was another circle with dots, only this circle had been drawn of dashes. One dot, a little farther apart than the others, had been inked inside the dashed circle at the bottom. Outside the circles, random dots were scattered about the rest of the paper like stars, but the bottom strip had been torn off, leaving Lia to wonder what had been there that Gwen wanted to hide.

"Does this look familiar?" Gwen asked the former Coven leader. "Can you decipher it? It must be tied to the ceremony, but I cannot puzzle out how, not without a great deal of uncertainty, and that is one thing we cannot afford."

Matilda ran her fingers lightly over the crumpled paper, a line between her brows. "No. Not unless...if this is the ritual itself," she said slowly, tracing the inside circle with the tip of her forefinger. "It would be a very standard circle. And these"—she indicated the dots—"the position of each witch. Only twelve. That leaves five for this outer circle."

"What good are two circles?" Delilah asked.

"From a magical standpoint, it makes no sense. The magic of the outer circle cannot cross the barrier. Either the second circle is a failsafe to protect the city from an explosion of magic if the spell fails, or it serves as additional protection from outside forces."

"Meaning us," Lia said.

Matilda nodded distractedly. "Given that Lady St. James has penetrated a magical circle before, I would imagine so."

Lia pointed at the bottom dot, the one separate from the others in the outer circle. "What is this? Why is it placed apart?"

"At times, a distinctly powerful witch may take on a greater burden, channeling more of the magic for her less talented sisters. Certain spells may also require an anchor, a witch who becomes a kind of touch-point for the magic, should the spell snap."

"Like an escape rune?" Delilah asked.

Sam seemed to have forgotten his anger and glared at the diagram as if the intensity of his gaze could force the paper to give up its secrets. "What's an escape rune?"

Delilah pulled out her hammer and pointed to the engravings along the handle. "Runic sentences direct and store force. But if a rune gets damaged, the stored force must go somewhere. If there isn't an escape rune, the item will likely explode or catch fire. Sometimes, the escape rune will not work, like with Gwen's coat, because there is nowhere for the energy to escape to. But that's rare and dangerous."

"So this witch," Sam said, touching the dot, "will get set on fire if the spell breaks?"

Matilda nodded. "Yes, something like that. We do not use spells that require it for that very reason. It is too dangerous. But if a...certain witch," she said carefully, "possesses a magic artifact, it may protect her."

"And these dots?" Gwen asked, indicating the scattering of black marks outside the circle.

"Those I cannot say. I have never seen a spell diagram that resembles it. And there is no pattern."

Gwen nodded, slid the paper back into her pocket, and straightened. "Your Majesty?"

The King stood and folded his hands behind his back. "Yes, Lady Gwen?"

"Have you retrieved those diamonds?"

"Indeed I have."

An expression of resolve settled on Gwen's face, one that made Lia instantly nervous. "Good," she said. "Because I have an idea. To pull it off, we will need iron. Lots of it."

Sleeping was impossible. Not because she wasn't tired but because too many thoughts ran screaming through her mind for rest. Lia rolled over again and tried to find a comfortable position, but the bed was cold and entirely too big, and her arm hurt. Besides, how was she expected to sleep while Tony was cramped in that stupid chair?

For that matter, how could anyone sleep while worrying over what tomorrow would bring? Everyone she knew would be in mortal peril, and there wasn't a thing she could do to stop it. Their only hope lay in another of Gwen's harebrained schemes that was just as likely to kill them as the witches were.

She groaned and flopped onto her back. "This isn't going to work."

"Something wrong with the bed?" Tony's voice was raw.

He had not slept well in that ratty chair, and here she had a bed. What right did she have to complain? "No, nothing is wrong with the bed." She sat up and pushed her hair out of her eyes. "I was referring to Gwen's plan of attack. There are too many variables we cannot account for. And the consequences of failure are, quite literally, catastrophic. Yet I cannot figure a way out of it."

"If I have learned one thing in the past few years, it is not to doubt your sister. Even if her plan is so mad that it makes you want to run screaming. But none of it will work if you don't rest."

"How can I sleep while I know that I've consigned you to that blasted thing?" she demanded, flinging her good hand at the decrepit armchair.

Tony sat up. His hair was rumpled, and tired smudges marked his eyes. "What, exactly, can I do to make your sleep more comfortable, my lady?"

His sarcastic tone made her hackles rise. He was sleepless for her sake. He had blown open a wall today and carried her through town while avoiding being arrested. Twice. She should feel contrite. And yet, his vulnerable position only made her angry. Her spine stiffened.

"You can haul your tired carcass over here"—she slapped the adjacent pillow with her good hand— "and get a good night's sleep."

Even in the light of the burning candles, his scowl was dark enough to put the tunnel outside to shame. But she'd been scowled at—and worse—by much scarier creatures. And if she couldn't stop what was going to happen tomorrow, then she could at least ensure the two of them got much-needed rest.

In truth, she should have sent him away to a room of his own, but her skin began to crawl at the thought of being alone in the dark places under the ground, even with candles to keep the shadows at bay. And she didn't want him to leave.

But he said every word as if it were a sentence of its own. "I will not sleep in that bed with you."

"Why not?"

"Because it is improper."

She snorted. "According to whom?"

"According to...to the—the rules of polite society!"

His cheeks were visibly flushed even in the candlelight, and she could not stop a smile from tugging at her mouth. "Tony. You are a guest in the home of the Cutthroat King. You've been dodging constables for days and plan to thwart a coven of witches tomorrow night in a graveyard if Gwen cannot kidnap a few of them first.

Where you may be *killed*, might I add. Why under heaven are you worried about what polite society thinks?"

He clenched his jaw and thrust his chin forward until he looked like an intransigent schoolboy. "You are a lady, and I—"

"Oh god's breath, I'm not a lady. And I am no virgin. But beyond that, I have no designs on your innocence. I only want both of us to sleep comfortably and well. Nothing more."

A shade of red she did not even know existed climbed up his neck and into his cheeks. Was the damnable man going to be so stubborn about the issue that he'd deny them both rest merely to keep his misplaced sense of propriety intact? Ridiculous.

Lia flung back the covers and climbed out of bed. The move was less than graceful, thanks to her injured arm, but she was too irritated to care. She stomped across the floor—which was shockingly cold—and stood before Tony in nothing but her shift. He made a choking noise and averted his eyes.

"You truly mean to be stubborn about this?" she demanded.

He did not answer.

"Fine." She sank to the ground near his feet, sitting with her legs crossed. "Then we will both sleep uncomfortably."

"Ophelia," he warned. "This is ridiculous. Get back into bed."

"No."

"You'll catch a cold in that thin shift, and you need rest to heal your wound."

"So do you."

"I sleep fine in the chair."

"Liar."

This time, his voice came out in a growl. "Ophelia..."

"There is no point in trying to convince me, Tony, I have—ah!" She squeaked as he surged out of the chair and picked her up. This time, she was fully conscious and wearing far less than she had been when he saved her from the mistcat. And he held her just a little too tightly.

He strode across the room, and she thought he would dump her in the bed, given how fast the pulse throbbed in his neck.

But he deposited her gently on the sheet and glared directly into her eyes. "You are not to leave this bed until morning. Do you hear me?"

"I—"

"Do. You. Hear. Me?" He leaned in until his face was mere inches from hers, as if he could compel her to obey by mere force of will. She had withstood the compulsion of kings, disobeyed Mama and Mrs. Chapman, but something about Tony made her want to listen, want to know that she had put his mind at ease.

"Fine. I will. If you sleep next to me."

He let out an explosive breath and ran his hand through his hair. Twice. "You won't obey me in this, will you?"

Her voice was smaller than she thought possible and softer than she intended. "I've had enough of obeying the will of others. Besides, I am right. You know I am."

The muscle in his jaw clenched and unclenched several times before he swore and stalked to the other side of the bed. He shrugged out of his jacket, revealing a cotton shirt stretched tight over his broad shoulders. The bed sank beneath his weight, and her stomach followed, sick with the realization that she was about to sleep next to her employer. One boot plopped onto the floor, followed by the other, and Tony swung his legs up into the bed.

Lia faced forward so fast she nearly gave herself whiplash. Tony slid beneath the blankets and turned his back to her, lying on his side at the very edge of the bed as far from her as he could get.

She squirmed until the blankets reached her chin and tried to get comfortable. But she'd been out of the bed long enough for her body heat to leave the fabric. She shivered and rubbed the sole of one foot against the arch of the other.

"You're cold," he muttered.

"I'm fine."

"Ophelia—"

"I'll warm up shortly."

She pulled the covers tight around her neck, tucked them beneath her legs, and tried not to shiver. Her body would heat the blankets, and she'd be warm again in no time. It was never this cold in the Sunset Lands. Fireplaces were impractical in the Undercroft, but the King should really outfit these rooms with dwarven heaters. How did anyone remain healthy in this cold damp?

Another shudder made her clench her jaw to stop her teeth from chattering.

Tony swore, this time an impressively vile word, and rolled over. His arm shot out, wrapped around her ribcage, and pulled her against his chest. She bit back a squeak as she slid across the cool sheets.

His body was as rigid as if she were a venomous snake, and he didn't want to frighten her into biting. The poor man was terribly uncomfortable. She should be grateful for the extra heat and try not to make the situation worse for him...but he was so warm. It was impossible not to curl into him like a cat before a fire.

One big hand settled hesitantly on her back. Lia took that as permission to tuck her head beneath his chin and nuzzle into the open space between his neck and shoulder. She fit there as if the spot had been carved for her. Though she knew it was only his protective sense of honor—and that he would rather have tucked her sister against him—she could not help but release a satisfied breath.

Tony was the most selfless person she knew, the one least likely to take advantage of his strength and most likely to sacrifice his own desires for the good of others. She was safe with him. For the first time in quite a long time, a sense of comfort stole through her. And with it, a twinge of guilt for forcing this, and so much else, on him.

"I'm sorry."

His voice was colored with resigned amusement. "You have a habit of apologizing *after* you've gotten your way. Did you know that?"

She smiled. "If people would just accept that I know best from the start, I wouldn't have to."

His body shook in what she hoped was a laugh, though his voice was rueful. "As long as you mind your manners, I think we'll be alright."

Oh, how she wished he hadn't said that. The contrary need to *not* mind her manners rose inside her like a waking beast, whispering how nice it would be to kiss his neck, taste his skin, wrap her arms around that wide chest, and hold herself against him until—she stamped that vision out of her mind.

Now was not the time for defiance. She'd spent her youth rebelling against rules and expectations purely for the pleasure of charting her own course. If she was expected to behave one way, she instinctively wanted to behave the other. It was the only way she felt as if she could be who she wanted, not who others would force her to be.

That instinct had been crushed out of her in the Sunset Lands, sometimes with pain, sometimes with deprivation, and sometimes—the worst times—with pleasure. When she shivered again, it wasn't from the cold. But Tony ran his hand up and down her back in a soothing motion as if she were a spooked horse or an agitated cat, trying to warm her with friction.

Strangely enough, it worked. Her muscles relaxed, and she found herself sinking deeper into the mattress, into the scent of the clean, sharp musk of his body and the leftover bite of gunpowder that still clung to his clothes. The warmth of his body supplemented her own until she was warm and content.

His chin settled against the crown of her head, and the rhythm of his heartbeat lulled her down, down, down into the hazy, groggy land that existed between awake and asleep.

"Thank you," she mumbled against his neck. "I've been so cold for so long."

21

Of Men and Monsters

GWEN

Dread sat in the pit of my stomach like a river stone, heavy and slimy and impossible to move. My heart, on the other hand, had no intention of standing still. It threw itself against my ribcage hard enough to make my whole body shake.

My family was leaving, breaking up, and I wasn't only incapable of stopping it, but had encouraged it. The possibility that I might never see Samuel smile again or feel Mama's arms around me made me want to scream. But no matter which way I turned, this was the safest course of action. Somehow, I managed to hug Mama, comfort Sam, and prepare Mr. Yates to escort them safely out of the city.

"If they are searching for us, they'll likely have someone watching the trains," I said after pulling him aside. Everyone else was busy preparing and paying little attention to us. Aris stood in the corner, alone, watching the room with eyes that were impossible to read.

I dragged my gaze away from him. "The King is arranging for transportation that will not draw attention. I've also requested less ostentatious clothing for you and Mama. Do you need anything from me, Mr. Yates?"

The staid and confident man I had relied on as a source of practical competence for years opened his jacket to reveal a set of clean, understated pistols that appeared surprisingly well-used and cared for.

I raised a brow. "I did not know you were a marksman, sir."

A small, unwilling smile tugged one corner of his mouth upward. "I hazard to guess there are many things you do not know about me, my lady."

I took his calloused hands and squeezed. "Thank you, my friend. I would not trust their safety to anyone else. Please do not forget to protect yourself as well."

Though he tried not to meet my eyes, he squeezed back. Watching the three of them leave down a dark corridor felt like cutting out a vital organ. I'd taken for granted the sense of security Mr. Yates projected, the feeling that, if he were near, all would somehow be well. Hopefully, Mama and Sam benefited from it as much as I always had.

I busied myself with preparations of my own, trying hard not to picture the three of them trekking across the island with only

Ratcatchers to protect them, dodging constables and mistcats. It was hard to believe that those dangers were still safer than being in the city should we fail.

And we could not fail.

Only when there were no further preparations to make did I allow myself to trudge toward my room. A dull ache throbbed in the base of my skull and my bones that felt as if they wanted to sink into the earth. Whenever I blinked, I saw the face of Shiverback's mate and the fire that destroyed my home reflected in her eyes. Hopefully, I would not see the flames in my sleep.

My chamber was not far from the central complex of rooms comprising the most used parts of the Undercroft. I stumbled past the kitchens, cold for the night, and into it with as much grace as a clubbed fish, only to stop and catch my breath. Aris leaned against the far post of the bed with one shoulder, his arms folded and ankles crossed, head bowed as if in thought.

In my imagination, I saw shadowy wings stretched out behind him, though he looked as human as anyone else. "Waiting for me?" I asked, trying to keep my tone light despite the way my lungs constricted.

When he raised his head, a lock of dark hair fell over his forehead. His eyes were hard and hungry. "I've been waiting for you for years."

The lump in my throat was far too big to swallow.

"What I must know"—he straightened and stuffed his hands into his pockets—"is whether you'll still have me now that you know what I am."

I refused to be sick. Anxiety boiled in my stomach, but I clenched my jaw and closed the door behind myself. When we were safely alone, I folded my hands to keep them from trembling and asked, "What are you?"

He swallowed. "Do you want the truth, or something more palatable?"

"I always want the truth."

"Do you? Think hard before you answer, Gwen."

When I didn't respond, his jaw muscle flexed as if trying to work the words out past his teeth. "I am a killer. A monster."

"Is that...creature...is that your true form?"

"One of them. Just like the raven. And this—" He gestured to himself with both hands.

I closed the distance between us but did not crowd him. He had lied by omission more than once, and I did not want to be swayed by the power of his touch until I knew this time would be the last. Because if he held me now, I would fall apart and damn the consequences.

But making reckless decisions while we stood on the precipice of the most dangerous thing any of us had ever done was suicide. So I wrapped my arms around myself and asked, "Why didn't you tell me?"

Aris barked a hard-edged laugh, but his eyes held decades of pain. "Why? For the love of the moon and stars, Gwen, I am a *monster*. And somehow, I earned the love of the only woman in this forsaken world who —" He clenched his jaw and stalked away from me, shoulders tense. "How could I risk losing you?"

"You did not think lying to me by omission—again—was the greater risk?"

He spun. "You said you wanted the parts of me I longed to hide. That you wanted my darkness. Was that true or not? Tell me now, because if you have changed your mind, I don't think"—his fists tightened until they stood out stark against the fabric of his trousers—"I don't think I can..."

Tears ran from the corners of his eyes to spill down the high, flat planes of his cheeks. He dashed them away with an impatient brush of his hand. I had seen Aris in pain, in need, angry and passionate. But I had never seen him cry. My heart shattered. I could no more hold him accountable for keeping the truth from me than I could stop myself from wanting him even when it was foolish.

"Damn you. Damn you, Aris Blackwing!" I grabbed the ceramic pitcher from the table by the door and hurled it at him. "Damn you for making me love you"—the bowl followed—"more than I respect myself!"

Aris dodged each projectile with ease, but his face was red with anger. "Do you think self-respect has shaped any part of my love for you? I have abased myself for your sake."

"I never asked that of you!"

"No," he said, his voice quiet and dangerous. "No, you did not. But you *needed* it. You needed someone willing to meet you in the dark." His hand shot out and wrapped around my neck, exerting just enough pressure to remind me that he could snap my bones without effort. With one thumb, he tilted my chin up until our eyes met. "You needed someone who wasn't afraid of the monster lurking here." His opposite hand settled on my chest over my heart. "Does it truly surprise you, then, that I am one, too?"

A shiver of awareness ran through me. Was that why seeing his beastly form had been such a shock? Did the monster inside me call to the one in him? I could not change my shape, but if I were able to...the Cutthroat King would have been dead the day I learned what he had done to Sam. Even without a beastly form, I had destroyed the room and reputation of a boy who dared to speak the truth as he saw it, ruining his family's prospects for years.

I liked to think of myself as a mostly good person. But had I the strength or the lack of inhibitions, I likely would have done worse. Had Aris not stopped me mere days ago, Melville would be dead, and I would be guilty of cold-blooded murder.

Aris knew all of that. He saw the truth of me and loved me still. A tear slipped down my cheek and wetted his hand.

Between one heartbeat and the next, I was in his arms, the salt of his tears wet on my lips, his arms tight around my chest, holding me against him as if he could absorb me. I bit his lip and tasted blood. The backs of my thighs hit the chest of drawers, and Aris pulled away just far enough to growl against my lips, "I need you. If you do not want me, tell me now."

In answer, I wrapped my fingers around the collar of his shirt and jerked the fabric open, sending buttons bouncing off the floor. Aris needed no more encouragement. He sat me on the chest and pushed my skirts up, fingers digging into my thighs as he spread my legs.

I could not get enough of the taste of him, could not even release him long enough to let him unbutton his fly without his lips on mine. My tumultuous emotions evaporated in a cloud of heat and wanting. But if he did not take me soon, I would explode.

"Aris," I panted. "Now. Please."

He seated himself in a single thrust and swallowed my cry of pleasure with a kiss that made my head spin.

"Three gods, I will never have enough of you," he groaned.

Our bodies struck one another in a frantic rhythm that stole my breath and made stars burst at the edge of my vision. "Deeper," I panted. "Harder."

"I don't—want—to hurt you."

My fingernails dug into his shoulder muscles with bruising force. "You said you wanted to break me. You've already done it. Now put the pieces back together, damn you."

The sound he made could not properly be called a snarl, but it was something like it. He picked me up as if I weighed nothing and carried me to the bed, never breaking contact. I wanted to scream at him to hurry. He dropped me onto the coverlet, spread my legs, and pinned my knees to the bed on either side of me. When his gaze locked on my exposed flesh, his eyes narrowed. His expression was so hot, so hungry, that my skin flushed. I whimpered in need.

"You were made for me." He positioned himself, never taking his eyes from our nearly joined bodies. "I was made for you. I will not give you up." He thrust so hard and deep that I screamed and arched off the bed.

Our bodies shook with his bruising rhythm, and every impact felt as if it chipped away the shell I hid behind, one so closely fitted to my skin that I had not realized it was there. My inner muscles tightened impossibly, holding me shaking on the razor's edge of release.

Aris lifted my hips off the bed, and I wrapped my legs around his waist, locking them at the ankles.

"Touch yourself," he ordered. "I want to feel your pleasure."

Trembling, I trailed my fingers down my body and fell off the edge into pleasure that made me cry out. Aris arched against me, every muscle taut, and shook as he spent himself. He collapsed on me, breathing hard, and buried his face in the juncture of my neck and shoulder. Tears standing in my eyes, I trailed my fingertips across the shaking muscles of his back and squeezed my legs to keep him tight inside of me.

"I'm sorry," he said once he caught his breath. "I should have told you. But I couldn't—can't—bear the thought of losing you."

I wrapped my arms around his shoulders and held on tight. The idea of losing him, even now while the shock of his other form was still fresh in my mind, was inconceivable. He was mine, my Aristotle, my raven. The one person to whom I could fully surrender even my darkest parts, bits of me that would have scared or damaged anyone else.

And yet, how could we make a relationship work without trust? Would I forever fear discovering something new and dangerous about the man I loved? We rolled fully onto the bed and curled up together, still too warm for blankets. I traced the shell of his ear with my fingertip, watching the blue-black strands of his hair curl against the delicate skin of his neck.

"You should have told me. Did you trust me so little, even after all we have been through?"

"You did not exactly respond well to the truth the first time," he pointed out.

I leaned back, giving myself enough distance for a proper scowl. "Can you blame me, given the circumstances?"

"Of course I can. I blame you for all kinds of things you don't deserve." I made to slap him, but he caught my wrist easily and kissed my palm. "The real question is, *should* I blame you? And the answer is no. I should have trusted you enough to tell you but"—he sat up and rubbed the back of his neck with one hand—"it isn't easy to talk about. And when I combined that with the prospect of pushing you away, I could not bring myself to do it."

I scooted close and wrapped my arms and legs around him like a koala clinging to a tree, throwing one leg across his lap, curling the other behind his back, and resting my head on his shoulder. "I understand if the subject is too difficult to speak of, but given everything we are about to endure...I do not think I can withstand any more surprises. Is there anything else I should know that you *can* tell me?"

He swallowed and held my forearm where it lay across his chest. I squeezed in support. If he could not tell me, what would I do? I'd kept enough secrets from the people I loved to know the way they sat heavy in one's chest and slowly petrified over time, like dead trees, becoming permanent parts of one's internal landscape. The more secrets I kept, the more difficult it became to navigate without tripping over them.

After hurting myself on them too many times, I learned to avoid those places altogether. How many petrified secrets did Aris have, and how much pain had they caused him? Worse, how many would he be free of if I'd been worthier of his trust?

The book he lovingly defaced was still in my coat pocket, and my former determination to be worthier of his love came crashing back down on me. "You don't have to tell me if you cannot. But please know that, if you can, you are safe with me. I swear it."

He kissed the top of my head, and I closed my eyes, content for a moment merely to feel him against me.

"We lost our home tonight," he said a moment later, his voice so soft and full of confused pain that tears I thought long dried pricked my eyelids. "I never had a home until you made me part of yours. I did not realize losing it would hurt so much."

338

I wanted to cry. To weep for the future we lost when Shiver-back's mate burned our home. I would never again walk round the corner to see Sally in her chair by the fire or watch Sam teach Aris a new way to lose at chess. Mrs. Chapman's determined footsteps in the hall would never send the children running back to their rooms. The sound of Monsieur swearing would never echo down the corridor, and I would never again feel the comfort of the oak desk beneath my hands.

I *wanted* to cry...but I also wanted to rage. Not just to mourn the loss of my home but to make someone pay for it, to wring every stolen moment from their flesh until the pain in my chest was satisfied.

"You were right," I admitted, feeling sick. "There is a monster inside of me. And it is terrifying. How do you—how do *I* control it?"

Aris pulled me onto his lap to face him and brushed his thumbs across my cheekbones. "For a long time, I didn't. The monster is effective, after all. And feeding it feels good. But I met someone who made me want to tame it. And I learned the most important secret of all."

"What is the secret?"

"A monster lurks in every soul. Some are so small they're no more than an occasional irritation. Some are large enough, pow-erful enough, to need chains. Those of us with powerful monsters can kill them, keep them chained, let them loose, or train them.

Harness their power. Make them work for us rather than against us."

"You believe you have trained yours?"

He smiled wryly. "No, *you* have. At least in part. When you were shot..." His voice trailed off, and his hands tightened on my shoulders. "Three gods, I wanted to rip the word apart. It was only your voice that stopped me."

I'd seen Aris's monstrous form only briefly, and with such well-developed upper body muscles—and those claws—I shuddered to wonder what he was capable of. And I had proven my own abilities far exceeded what I believed possible when my monster was unleashed. That had been something worse than terrifying, and I still hadn't had time to come to terms with it.

"You're saying I need to harness and train my monster?" An unwilling laugh tickled the edges of that sentence. What a ridiculous thing to say. And yet, it was, perhaps, the most serious question I'd ever asked.

"If we're to have a hope of stopping the witches? Yes."

I rested my forehead against his and tightened my fingers in the fabric of his shirt. I did not want to admit what I had been burying since Westminster, but if Aris could trust me with his secrets, then I could do no less.

"I'm scared. Not only of what might happen, but of myself."

His arms wound around my waist, and he pulled me tight against his chest. "I'll be there," he promised.

"Do you think it will work? My plan?"

"No," he laughed, "but I always think that about your plans, and somehow they always work out anyway."

"That isn't very comforting."

His tone turned serious. "I don't have much comfort to give just now, darling. I'm sorry."

Aris was generally so charmingly arrogant that seeing him as anything less than confident made me hesitate. I didn't like it.

"Then I shall simply have to comfort the both of us," I said airily and flopped down, pulling him along with me. When we were settled, I rubbed one hand absently across his temple. "This is going to work. We will stop the ritual, rescue Sally, and save the city."

But where would we go afterward? Home was gone. And if they wanted to arrest me now, it would be several orders of magnitude worse when I ruined their plans to destroy the wall. Even if we succeeded tomorrow, nothing would ever be the same.

"Sleep," Aris said. He tucked me tightly against his body. "You are thinking so loudly I can hear the gears turning in your mind. You will not be more ready than you are now by depriving yourself of rest."

Perhaps not. But I saw flames every time I closed my eyes. And if today's events had torn open wounds that left me bleeding internally, tomorrow promised to be much, much worse.

22

Holy Places

GWEN

I checked my arsenal for the hundredth time, letting my fingers slide over the kit I had put together as I repeated the plan to myself. We'd been over it several times, with everyone gathered round the King's large table as we strapped on various forms of protection and stuffed our faces with the last food we were likely to eat for the next twenty-four hours.

If we lived.

"You are certain this will place us securely within the cemetery?" I had asked earlier as I double-checked the locking mechanism on my umbrella.

"My Ratcatchers were busy verifying entrances and exits while you slept," the King said. "We will get you inside unseen. The rest is up to you and that compass."

"And just what will you be doing?" Delilah had asked as she dropped her hammer into the holster on her leather belt.

The King raised a contemptuous eyebrow. "Covering your escape, Miss Irons. If there is any escape, that is. I have my doubts."

"I still say we should send Ratcatchers in along with you," she grumbled.

Lia straightened the line of pearl buttons on her coat and shook her head. "We may not know friend from foe. More people only complicate things."

"I need him to keep the constables out of the cemetery, in any case," I added. "I do not want more company when the fighting starts."

Alix spun the barrel of her pistol, clicked it in place, and slid the weapon into the holster on her hip. "Yes, they began patrolling the walls last night. They aren't even bothering to be inconspicuous. No doubt they will rush in at the first sounds of distress. Someone must keep them occupied and off of our backs."

Delilah gave her a suspicious glare but didn't press the matter. By then, it was too late to change things, and she knew it. If my friend weren't too guarded to show her worry openly, I would have tried to comfort her with a hug. Instead, I took her hand in both of mine and squeezed. Delilah gave me a tight-lipped nod that said, *Take care of yourself out there.*

Fleur, on the other hand, hugged me hard enough to elicit a little *mmph*. She led her wife to the garage, an abandoned warehouse in a seedier part of town, to ensure the invisible auto—which still did not have a suitable name—was ready for action.

Cyrus required far less preparation than the rest of us, as he had no weapons to clean and no armor to put on. All he required was enough food to keep his energy up, so he munched on a sausage while the rest of us waited for Percy to check our armor.

He was armed himself, with needles, thread, and scissors sharp enough to gut someone. He used them to order Tony about like a wartime general, gesturing with sharp flicks of his wrist.

"Lift your arm. Not that arm. Good, now don't move. I have to secure this seam so it doesn't twist. Don't look down; you'll tug the fabric out of line. Gwen, you're next."

He ensured everyone was as protected as his talent and skill could manage, mumbling directions around a mouthful of pins. When he finished, he took my hands—his were cold with fright—and squeezed. "I'll be waiting for you when it's over."

"I'm counting on it," I said and kissed his cheek.

Mrs. Chapman entered the room a moment later with a tray full of mismatched, steaming tea cups. They clattered as she set the tray on the table and turned a gimlet eye on each of us. "Everyone drink a cup, and I'll not hear any complaints about the taste. If you spit out, I'll hold you down and make you drink another, so help me, I will."

No one argued, and every last drop was swallowed. It tasted vile, but no one dared say so. Instead, we all looked at one another, each waiting for some signal to break the tension, but none of us was willing to be the one to do it.

"Well," Lia said, taking pity on us with a businesslike clap of her hands. "Shall we?"

We trekked through the miles of underground tunnels, following the King's Ratcatchers as they led us to our respective exits.

Alix and Cyrus took the lead, followed by Madame Matilda, Tony, Lia, and myself, with Aris bringing up the rear. We trooped silently on, alone with our thoughts despite the company. The words, *I've changed my mind*, sat sour on my tongue the entire trip.

Killing the witches would have been smarter. Asking the King to have his men assassinate every politician in the city would have been more efficient. In fact, there were several better solutions to saving the city than the one I bullied everyone into accepting—if I was willing to become a murderer.

If I was willing to ask everyone aligned with me to abandon their morals. Of course, the King likely wouldn't care and had probably done worse. Alix and Cyrus would see it as a duty.

And yet, I could not force the words past my lips.

Saving the people of New London mattered, but I could not ignore the persistent feeling that *how* we saved them mattered just as much. If we abandoned the ideals that made our goals virtuous, we may as well tear down the wall with the witches.

The result of such unremitting mental turmoil was a tightly clenched jaw and a mild headache. At least the little man in my skull had taken a nap. I wished I could join him.

After what felt like hours, we stopped at an old iron ladder bolted deep into the stone. It climbed up one side of a narrow hole that broke away from the corridor, stretching upward like the tunnel of some giant mole.

Flakes of rust peeled off the iron rungs, and the center of each was worn smooth from years of dripping water. Weakened by the oxidation, no doubt. And guaranteed to burn Aris's hands.

"Would you like a ride?" I asked in a low voice.

Aris sketched a mocking bow, said, "You are too kind, lady," and shimmered into his raven form. He hopped onto my shoulder and immediately began picking at my hair.

"I'm protecting you from this nasty metal," I said over my shoulder. "The least you can do is leave my braid intact."

The sound he made in my ear was something like an avian chuckle.

I don't like to remember that climb. With no way to measure time, the sound of heavy breathing, the clink of feet on rusted metal, and the rustling of fabric seemed to go on forever. I thought I might never get the moldy, wet-earth stink out of my nose. The bite of rust even flavored the claustrophobic air.

Unending darkness stretched above, and fathomless darkness waited below, leaving us suspended in a nowhere land where a single misstep meant a blind fall to death.

When we climbed into the belly of an ancient cistern, I wanted to weep with relief. The cavelike room was at least two stories high and stretched far beyond the reach of the light cast by Ratcatcher's dwarven lanterns. Evenly spaced pillars engraved with lines of runic sentences held up the ceiling, and an inch or two of perfectly still water reflected them like a mirror. It was practical dwarven architecture at its finest.

"Delilah would have loved to see this," I murmured.

"You can tell her all about it when this is over," Lia said and squeezed my hand.

"Alright, you lot," one of the Ratcatchers, a burly, dark-skinned man named Thatcher, said. He pointed to one end of the cistern. "Those of you patrolling, follow Blinx that way. If you're in the mausoleum, follow me."

Death and invasion were possibly hours away, and we were about to separate. We should have been hugging each other, but Alix, Cyrus, Tony, Lia, Aris, and I stared at one another for a drawn-out moment. Tony was the first to move. He kissed my cheek with brotherly affection that would have broken my heart a few months ago but now made my chest tight with love.

"Take care of yourself," he said. "We'll get Sally out of there."

I swallowed and nodded. "You, too."

Lia cleared her throat and held out her hand to Tony. He stared at it for a long moment before taking it in both of his. "If I do not get the chance to say it—thank you, Tony. For everything."

His eyes softened, but his expression tightened. It was a contrast I'd never seen on his face, one that seemed affectionate but confused.

"No thanks necessary," he said, then kissed the back of her knuckles.

Ice broken, Alix and Cyrus entered the fray, and hugs and exhortations of safety were shared all around. As I held the people I loved, it was impossible not to face the fact that this may be the last time I saw some—or all—of them. Alix and Cyrus were dangerous and capable but not infallible. Cyrus had been nearly dead the first time I met him.

And Tony? He was as competent as any human had a right to be; he even wore a coat built to protect him. But I'd seen him cut down once. And he wouldn't be safely in a tower with a rifle this time.

In a few hours, I might lose any one of them. I turned to Aris, my heart in my throat. He lifted me off the floor until our eyes met. His gaze was flat and hard, and his voice was a hair shy of threatening. "If anything happens to you, I swear to the moon and stars that I will raze this city to the ground until nothing is left but smoking ashes."

"I suppose I had better not die, then," I said.

The words were meant to be flippant but came out tremulous. Aris crushed me against his chest and kissed me hard enough for my teeth to cut the inside of my lips. I would have begged for more had we been alone, begged for the comfort of his touch and the mindlessness of losing myself in his arms.

But we were not.

"That is all rather melodramatic," Matilda said.

I imagined her rolling her eyes but could not force my gaze away from Aris to check.

"Come back to me," he said, then set me on my feet and turned to follow the retreating lamp into the dark.

Lia and I squeezed out of a rusty old grate inside a mausoleum no more than eight feet wide. First, one arm, then a shoulder, followed by our heads and a deep exhale to empty all the air from our lungs so we could fight through the tiny opening.

I scraped one side of my face against the rusted metal as I forced my way through and heard a button pop off my coat as I wiggled my hips free. The effort left us panting as we sat side-by-side on the marble floor. How the Ratcatchers had found this place was either a miracle or the King knew far more than he let on.

I leaned against the sarcophagus that dominated the center of the small building and let my head fall back. "That was rather more strenuous than I expected."

"Quite," Lia agreed. "At least it is cool in here."

"Let us hope it remains so." I glanced around the small space, dimly visible, thanks to an imperfectly fitted door that allowed sunlight to bleed through the cracks.

Lia ran the palm of her hand across the elaborately engraved sarcophagus and spoke almost to herself. "Why do mortals decorate the houses of the dead? In the Sunset Lands, faeries are given back to the earth or the sea or the sky. We celebrate their lives but do not make monuments of their bodies."

To unconsciously include herself in the generalization of faerie rituals, Lia's identity must be deeply tied to the Sunset Lands. It made sense, given that she grew into an adult there. That only made me ache more for what we had lost.

"I used to return to the fairy circle," I said, looking down at my palms. They were scraped and reddened from the climb, though not so damaged as they were the night Lia disappeared. My fingernails then had been torn and bloody from digging.

"Did you?" she asked, her voice soft.

I nodded. "First, it was to find you. I refused to believe you were gone or that you would not return. Sometimes, I slept on the spot. Mama started having me guarded after one too many nights alone in the cold. Afterward..." I closed my hands and squeezed hard enough to feel my nails dig into my palms, letting the pain remind me that we were together now. "Afterward, I brought you books and read them to you. No one else ever came. I don't think Mama could bear it. She used to sit on the floor of our room and stare at your bed."

Lia's swallow was loud in the silence.

"I suppose if we did not have those places, we might have made something like this. Some place to go where we could feel close to you."

"Did it...did it make it any easier?" Her arms were wrapped around her knees, her head down as if trying to make herself as small as possible.

"Sometimes," I said. "But you weren't dead. I knew it, despite what everyone said. In a way, it was more like sending you letters I knew you'd never read."

"I wonder if it would have been easier for me, losing you and Mama, if I'd had somewhere to go."

As a girl, Lia was radiant as a hearth fire, chasing away the shadows and filling rooms with warmth. She had the same magnetic presence as a woman, demanding attention and careful handling; only now, she was more like a sword than a fire, to be both admired and feared.

But sitting in the confined dark of the mausoleum with her arms curled around her knees, she was only...small. I scooted toward her until our hips and shoulders pressed together and took her hand. Her skin was icy.

"The cave they confined you in," I said. "It was cramped, wasn't it?"

She shuddered and nodded. "Sometimes dangling roots would tickle me in the dark, and I would wake up gasping, thinking they were bugs or fingers. At first, my fire was a comfort. I thought, as long as I have the light, I can deal with the rest. But fire burns up oxygen, even magic fire, and my cell would get too hot. And the shadows along the dirt walls looked like—"

Her teeth locked together, and the muscles of her jaw stood out sharp against her skin, even in the dim light. I squeezed her hand.

"Sometimes I dreamed about home. About you and Mama and even Mrs. Chapman. Moon and stars, I would have given anything to be scolded by her just to hear a friendly voice. A mortal voice, one not so perfect and musical. To hear one's name spoken with such beauty only to be harmed by the same voice? I've heard people speak of beauty as if it were gentle and welcoming. But beauty, at its most powerful, is a terrible thing."

In the Sunset Lands, the otherworldly perfection of the fae had weighed on me almost like a command, like wearing garments made of lead. And I had been an adult with half a lifetime of experience. Imagining Lia subjected to them, especially the Aès Sídhe in all their glory, at merely sixteen made my stomach turn over.

"At first, they played with me. I was a new toy, after all. But once they discovered my magic and realized who I was, I became the King's pet."

A thrill of anticipatory fear fluttered in my chest. "Who you were? The *Gaelethsdaughter*?"

Hazel green flashed from beneath her lashes as she glanced at me from the corner of eyes lit by the stray beams of light behind us. "Yes."

Was I ready to know? Now, of all times? I spent the last six months trying not to ask myself this question. I did not want to know whether our mother or our father had lied to us our entire lives. If it was Mama, with her commanding presence and effortless influence over others, could I forgive her? My chest grew tight with the thought.

"Do I want to know?"

"I cannot answer that question for you, Gigi. I had no choice. You deserve to decide."

"Are you glad to know, or would you take it back?"

Her mouth worked, though she was silent for a long time. "I've never known you to turn away from the truth, even when it hurt."

"Well, I haven't always felt so...so fragile." It wasn't only this moment and the truths Lia was finally telling me that turned my emotions to glass, but everything that brought us to this point and everything waiting for us outside this holy chamber. The evening hung suspended above us like a wrecking ball waiting to fall and destroy everything I loved. And shatter me in the process.

"If the past hasn't broken you," Lia said, turning fully toward me for the first time, "this will not do it, either."

"Do you truly believe that?"

"I have to."

Ah. Because if I survived the consequences of tonight, she could as well. Which meant she was relying on me the way I once relied on her. And when I thought of everything she suffered and all she had been forced to do and to become, it felt as if a light sprang to life and illuminated my sister at last.

Who could she rely on but herself? With enemies all around, there was no one to trust with her fears and her secrets. She'd been strong and brave. And alone. The man who kept her hostage with chains of silk for years, against whom she had plotted, planned, and risked her life, was hours away from invading the home she worked so hard to protect.

If I could be a bulwark for her now, when the last twelve years of her life came barreling toward her like a runaway train, I would do it. It was the very least I could do.

"God's breath, I have been selfish," I said. "That seems to be the refrain of my life."

"Only seeing it now, are you?"

I blew a little gust of air into her face that picked up the escaped strands of hair and dragged them away from her cheeks. She flinched and snorted a laugh.

"Hush, you. I am trying to be vulnerable."

The corners of her mouth twitched with the promise of a smile. "Far be it from me to interrupt such a momentous occasion."

"You sound like Aris."

"He does make good points now and then."

"Would you like me to get on with this admission, or should we just pretend I said it and move on?"

Lia bit her lips together and widened her eyes expectantly.

"I owe you an apology. You explained it to me once, but I think I was too hurt to understand it." The rest of the words stuck in my throat because the light that had finally exposed my sister was now turned on me, and I did not like what I saw. But the gulf between us, the one that hurt me for so long, needed repairing.

Perhaps what the mortar required was a bit of blood. "I went charging into the Sunset Lands to retrieve you because I needed you, not because I thought you needed saving. Even when we were there, I was determined to bring you home because I could not live with the thought of being alone again.

"I treated you like food or air. Or maybe like a cure to the poison I kept drinking. Somehow, in the years we were apart, you stopped being a person to me. You became something like this monument." I gestured with my chin at the marble surrounding us. "Something I needed for comfort. And I never once thought that you needed comfort, too. And you were too stubborn to ask for it."

Lia bit her lips together as if she did not want to release the words behind her teeth. But too many must have piled up because they forced their way out in a rush. "Needing someone is a weakness. Need makes cracks in your armor, cracks a clever opponent can exploit. I told myself everything I did was to protect you and Mama, but"—she dropped her gaze as if in shame—"part of it was to protect myself as well. And to hurt the King. I want revenge, Gigi. I want it so much it makes my stomach sick and my mouth taste like ashes.

"I want to hurt him for every time he pushed himself into me, knowing I could not say no. Knowing he could charm me into obedience, even into pleasure, and use me however he liked. I want to hurt him for every time I was sick afterward. For the people he killed. For Aris and the creature Obyrron forced him to become. And I would sacrifice so much to get it. Too much."

Somehow, we had joined hands, and our foreheads pressed together so hard it hurt, but not nearly as much as my spasming heart, which was trapped in the bars of my too-small chest.

"I'm afraid," she whispered. "I think, maybe, hating him has made me a villain, too."

I pulled her into my arms and held her tight, absorbing every sob that wracked her slender frame. Aris had seen the darkness in me. He recognized and acknowledged it. And as much as I wished it did not exist, there was a strange freedom in admitting it.

"Lia," I said, taking her face in my hands and wiping away her tears with the pads of my thumbs. "Who could be so exposed to the darkness without getting stained by it? That is no fault of yours. And look what you have done with your darkness now that you are free. You've used it to help and protect. My love, my darling, you are no villain. Look at me."

Pale lashes fluttered open and left me staring into eyes I knew as well as my own. "You are not a villain. The hero does not venture into the pit without getting dirty. But you've stood alone against the darkness long enough. I am here now. Do you hear me? You are not alone. You will never be alone again. I promise."

The force of my promise crackled in the air between us like static electricity. Her face crumpled, and this time, she pulled me to her. The vision I had after drinking the tea at Chatsworth flashed across my memory as if seeing it for the first time: two trees entwined, one silver and one gold, sharing strength.

I was wrong. The mortar needed to repair the cracks between us hadn't required blood, but tears, mine and hers mixed. They filled the gaping hole inside me and overflowed, watering the parched ground in my soul.

Alix and Cyrus, Sally and Sam, Delilah and Fleur, Mr. Yates, Mrs. Chapman, and Aris. They broke the ground, tilled and prepared it for this very moment.

Lia was right. This would not break me, not now that the cracks were healing, pulled together and held tight not by bricks but by living roots and twining vines. The bond between us was alive again.

We were going to stop the witches, protect the city, and save Sally. And we would do it together.

23
Sisters and Daughters
GWEN AND LIA

Lia

Sunlight cut across the marble floor in a knife-thin blade that trailed from the west to the eastern wall of the mausoleum as the day faded. Now, there was only a faint glow peeking between the cracks. Soon it would be dark, but she could not use her fire. Not yet.

Gwen had tested the door, and while it was heavy and old, it had been well cared for. When they were ready, the hinges wouldn't betray them. Lia rested her head on Gwen's shoulder and tried to ignore the burning muscles of her lower back. She'd been sitting far too long.

But dragging those memories, those fears, back up through the buried muck of her past and displaying them for her sister left her exhausted. Too exhausted to have much energy for anything other than keeping the panic at bay as the last evening glow faded from the cracks around the door.

Gwen said in a low voice. "Delilah rang me. She said the constables are patrolling in force outside the cemetery walls, so she and Fleur are keeping the van well away. Alix and Cyrus are in position, and Madame Matilda is ready. All we need now are the witches."

They both looked down at the open compass on Gwen's knee. The needles lay still, pointed steadfastly at Lia. Matilda's presence had made the needle swing toward her like a magnet to a loadstone, so it should do the same when the witches appeared. Hopefully. Lia gulped and fought to think of something else.

"Tony?" Lia found herself asking despite trying to keep him from her thoughts as well.

"Tony and his rifle are in position. He will not stop complaining about how cold the marble is."

Amusement took the edge off her worry. Gwen was likely exaggerating. Tony rarely complained.

"Aris is taking shelter in the trees," her sister continued. "It sounds as if they've set the mistcats to hunting, and every eye is on the sky. They've been trying to bring Aris down for days. I think they're expecting us. Or, rather, expecting us to try something."

"They would be fools not to. We've given them enough reason to believe we will."

"Keep your fingers crossed, then, that they don't expect us to show up in quite this way."

Lia made a noncommittal noise. "Unless they've got the Cutthroat King in their pocket, as well."

"He would have put an end to our shenanigans already if that were the case. He's had ample opportunity. Besides, our alliance was sealed with magic."

Lia flinched. Such a pact was a dangerous thing. "Why would you do that?"

It was impossible to see Gwen's face in the dark, but she could easily imagine her sister's patient, resolved expression. "Because we needed his help, and it was the only way to guarantee he could not hurt you."

Even magical pacts could be circumvented if one party was determined—and mad—enough. And the Cutthroat King had already proved to be both of those things. But there was no point in scolding Gwen now. It was far too late for that. And she did not want to walk into mortal danger with discord hanging over their heads, not after the pain of so much healing.

Not when the confrontation was so close.

"You asked about our...fae parentage," she said, her voice low. "Do you want to know? If something happens, this may be my only chance to tell you."

Gwen stopped breathing for a full thirty seconds before she said, at last, "Nothing will happen to you."

"Don't be stupid, Gigi. You know as well as I that you cannot guarantee that, and we don't have time to argue."

Gwen's skin flushed as hot as if it were she, not Lia, capable of wielding fire. When she squeezed, Lia's knuckles rubbed hard against each other. "You'd better tell me, then, but don't—"

The neat runes engraved around the edge of the compass needle glowed blue as it swung away from Lia to point in the opposite direction.

"God's breath," Gwen breathed. "They're here."

Though she expected them, the cold water of Gwen's words made shivers run down Lia's spine. Gwen grabbed her face and kissed her once on the forehead. "I love you. Get ready."

They had come a long way from the Battle of Trafalgar Square, where Gwen had hesitated to let Lia use her powers until it was almost too late. The two of them were walking into this fight—and the rest of their lives, if they survived—as equals.

Lia stood and positioned herself behind Gwen with her back to the wall near the door, which was cracked just enough for a person to slip through. The soft thump of footfalls joined the singing of nightbirds, and the approach of lanterns cast a wavering sliver of warm light on the wall. It was almost time.

Anthony Gawain Hardwicke, Lia thought.

I'm here. Are you alright?

Of course, his first thought would be the well-being of others. *A bit panicky,* she admitted. *The witches are coming. I just wanted to tell you*—the light grew brighter, and she nearly stopped breathing—*keep yourself safe, will you?*

If the stink of this badger scent doesn't kill me first, he thought with a tinge of forced amusement. She'd insisted everyone coat themselves with scents unlikely to draw the miscats' attention. Hiding would have been pointless otherwise. Tony had smelled rather robust. *Besides,* he continued, *Lady Evelyn said she'd have me torn limb from limb if I wasn't around to rescue you and your stubborn sister.*

The needle of the compass turned slowly, following the procession as lantern light flashed across the back wall of the mausoleum like the motion seen through the slit in a zoetrope.

Lia's heart jumped into her throat, but she held on to the moment of levity and thought, *She said no such thing.*

You cannot prove it either way.

...they're here. It's time.

The forced amusement faded from his thoughts. *Send up sparks if you need me. I will be there.*

Some of her panic ebbed away. She swallowed and watched the needle slowly turn, following what they hoped was either the most powerful witch in the coven or whoever carried the Eye of the Graeae. Other words, ones she refused to say, stuck in her throat. There was no time to say them, in any case.

As soon as the needle turned past their door, Gwen and Lia pressed the buttons on their Sightscreens and eased into the night like wraiths.

The witches strode single-file through the darkness down the dirt path between ferns as high as her hips. Tombstones of every shape and size flanked the path, row upon row, stretching into the darkness. The granite grave markers, stained with years of rain, lichen, and moss, thrust out of the ivy-covered ground like the ruined buildings of some lost civilization.

Trees closed them in, stretching their limbs out like fingers while the tombstones reached up from below, everything looking to grasp or ensnare. It felt like the place wanted to not only keep the bodies of those interred there but capture new prey as well.

It may have been beautiful during the day. Peaceful. But the single glance Lia afforded her surroundings left her with a sense of sad, brooding malevolence. Dwarven lanterns were the only light source beside the moon and cast the witches' shadows back in long streaks on the path. Gwen danced in and out of them as she crept toward the last witch in the procession.

The path angled downward toward a depression that housed a sort of amphitheater for the dead. At the bottom of a set of stone stairs, a row of joined mausoleums ringed a circular pathway that enclosed a flat-topped central structure. Turf and other wild grasses grew on its roof.

Witches trooped toward the stone staircase that bisected the circle, their loose white gowns and cowls glowing in the moon-light, hems floating behind them. They may have been druids, priestesses, or specters, and if she had not been there to stop them, Lia would have watched them ghost through the mist in awe.

The ritual would take place on that roof, above the interred bodies visited and wept over by bereaved loved ones. Power resided in such places. Lia's hands tingled with restrained magic, and the calm of the General settled on her like armor. The time for worry had passed. Action was all that mattered now.

It was time to move. Her bones ached with the breaking tension.

Lia could not see Gwen, and when she tried, revulsion and dizziness overwhelmed her. But she knew her sister would angle herself, turning the compass and watching the needle shift. When she felt confident that the needle pointed toward the most powerful member of the coven, the one Matilda said would create the anchor for the spell, Gwen would act.

Lia pulled in a breath, gathering her magic. Now. It had to happen now.

A woman's cry of surprise cut through the night, and Gwen suddenly appeared, her arm around the neck of a witch slightly taller than herself. The woman was forced to bend back against the tip of Gwen's umbrella as it pressed into her kidney.

"Enough of this, Deborah!" Gwen shouted. Her voice rang off the stones like pealing bells.

Now. Lia raised her hands and released a burst of fire that lit the area in a sickly green glow.

The witches spun with cries of alarm, half of them on the roof and the other half scattered from the staircase to the sunken path. Gwen dragged the witch back a few steps away from the sunken circle, putting them both out of arm's reach of the others. "If you do not stop this madness, I will be forced to end it for you. Please do not make me."

One of the witches laughed, a derisive sound that set Lia's teeth on edge. A woman stepped out of the procession, her hands folded and an indulgent smile plastered to her face. "Right on time. You certainly do not disappoint, Lady Gwen. But you will not kill Sally, and we both know it."

Lia's fire sputtered as dread made her stomach drop and her breath stick in her throat. Sally. The most powerful witch in the coven was *Sally*? Gwen only hesitated a heartbeat, and the note of desperation in her voice was hidden well beneath confidence, but Lia knew her sister well enough to hear it.

"She doesn't need to die to stop your ritual, merely to be absent. And I am more than willing to do that much."

Deborah shrugged. "Very well. As you will. I do not need her."

Figures appeared like ghosts out of the growing mists, stepping from behind tombstones and dropping from trees. Only their faces and hands were visible as their black frock coats disappeared into the shadows. Covenant. Deborah let her gaze drift across them before she turned back to Gwen.

"Did you think we would not prepare for this moment? In fact"—she stepped forward and pulled an orb the size of a child's skull from inside her billowing sleeve—"did you think we let you learn of our plans through foolishness or inattention when we knew Matilda wandered the city like a vagrant? Come, Lady Gwen, I thought you smarter than that."

So they *had* known. They had planted the information for the sole purpose of drawing Gwen out and surrounding her. The grim satisfaction of being right tasted sour on Lia's tongue. A fight was inevitable.

"Do give me some credit, Deborah," Gwen said.

She sounded like Mama had so many times during their childhood, calm and amused at the antics of her daughters but profoundly unimpressed. "I would not walk into an obvious trap without preparation. I need only to keep you occupied long enough to prevent the ritual."

"The ritual will take place with or without me. Without Sally, too, if need be. I have fought and planned for this moment far too long to allow it to fail."

"It is a shame you did not plan for every eventuality. You are not the only one with friends in the trees."

The Covenant closed in, hands dipped into pockets, and metal—both knives and pistols—reflected moonlight and green fire. Hunger and the promise of violence leeched into the air, sour sweet and stinking like sweat.

Deborah threw her head back and laughed, the hood falling from her short crop of blonde hair. "You mean Matilda? Lady Gwen, please. The claws have been drawn from that cat. Besides"—a malicious snarl entered her voice—"you would be a fool to think she cares about anyone enough to put herself in danger. Be assured, Lady. You are very much alone. And you will not stop this ritual."

Growing dread made Lia's stomach sick even as her limbs shook with restrained energy. They would not escape violence this night. How many Covenant were there? A dozen? More? And mistcats lurking unseen in the trees. Gwen had also mentioned Karnah, Shiverback's mate. Was she here, too, bent on revenge?

Lia's fire burned hotter, licking until the pale green turned near white at her fingertips and sucking her life energy like a babe at the breast. While she had overseen many battles, planned treason, and even killed, never had she taken the field openly against so many opponents. And she could not burn them all. Not without killing Sally and Gwen, too.

We are in trouble, Tony, she thought. Despite her sister's outward confidence, Lia knew the truth. She'd fought and won too many battles not to recognize the stakes. *It's Sally.*

Gwen

My heart slammed against my breastbone hard enough to shake my whole body, but I forced my voice to remain calm. I could not think of Sally, safe and warm in my arms, or of Lia behind me with Covenant at her back. I had to focus.

"Why?" I demanded. "Why do this? So you can turn control of mortal realms over to those who would use and subjugate you? For that is precisely what they will do. I thought *you* smart enough to know that."

"We have prepared for such an eventuality," Deborah said. She likely believed it, too. And I would not be able to talk her out of it. The light of the Eye reflected in her pupils, like madness or zealotry. Why the compass had not oriented on it instead of Sally, I could not say. Perhaps it hadn't been charged by enough magic? Whatever the cause, it had put Sally in my arms, and I needed to get her out of there. It was time for plan B.

I would never ask it of you, I thought, my stomach sick and my throat tight.

I would never do it for anyone I loved less, Aris thought back. *I'll be there as soon as I get clear of these damned cats. Distract her for another two minutes.*

I let my guard down long enough to tell Deborah the truth. "I have felt the power of the Sìdhé, Deborah. Not their magic, but their personal power. Please believe me when I tell you that you cannot prepare for that. You cannot stand against it. Let one of the lords of faerie set their will upon you, and you will give up even your desire for autonomy. You will fall on your face and grovel for the chance to do their bidding and weep for joy when they allow it."

The Sisters shared worried glances. Perhaps I did not have to convince Deborah. If enough of them believed me, if their fear made them second guess their purpose, they would never have the focus needed for such a weighty spell.

Aris would make sure of it. So long as the Covenant did not start firing.

"Lia," I said, "Please tell the Covenant to keep their distance."

Heat blossomed at my back. Green fire leaped up to create a wall between the Covenant and us, racing to cut us off and scorching the ferns and ivy to ash for several meters on either side. They flinched away from the flames—the instinctive pain of fire scared even those who did not fear death—and gave me another precious few moments of delay.

"Were I you," Deborah said, "I would lie just as prettily. But I have met the fae, remember?" She threw one hand to the side, gesturing at her sisters. "We all have."

"Perhaps you have met faeries," I allowed, "but not like this."

Aris hit the ground with a mighty crash, flaring his wings to land and sending several witches tumbling from the force of the wind. They fell like blossoms from a tree in spring. He stood in all his glory, black wings spread so wide they blocked half the cemetery from view. Feathers ran from his wing joints up to cover his shoulders and the back of his neck. His naked torso was heavy with the muscle necessary for flight, and the claws at the tips of his elongated fingers and toes gleamed like black ink.

Presence, unlike anything I'd ever felt, bloomed from him in a blast wave. The witches closest to him gasped in pleasure mixed with pain, and those still standing collapsed to their knees as if their feet had been knocked from beneath them. No wonder Obyrron had chosen to press Aris's bloodline into service as assassins.

Sally sagged, and catching her weight was the only thing that stopped my knees from giving way. Aris prowled one step forward and grabbed Deborah by the throat. She did not even try to flee.

Her neck looked small and fragile in his hands. Her eyes were fixed on his face in a combination of wonder and the beginnings of worship.

Hope burned hot in my chest. We could do this. With Aris, we would stop this damned ritual and save the city. I would get Sally out of here, find a way to break her oath to the coven, and bring her home. I had been trying not to look at her, trying to keep my mind focused on pulling off this mad plan. But I felt her body stiffen, felt her resolve coalesce around her like armor as she stood to her full height.

"Sally," I pleaded.

Her voice was contorted in pain when she said, "I'm so sorry." Her message to Sam slammed into my memory, hot as Lia's fire. *Stop me.*

But I couldn't.

She raised her arm, and the blast of force from her palm took Aris off his feet. Deborah fell in a limp heap as Aris plowed through cement memorials and tombstones with bone-breaking force. The *crack* of impact sounded like a gunshot.

The magic of Sally's spell was so intense it made the air crackle, and my muscles loosened against my will. I collapsed. I did not have time to wonder what damage the spell had done to her body or to fear for Aris. I did not even have time to scream.

Lia

Sally stepped out of Gwen's reach, pain twisting her features until she was almost unrecognizable. She joined her sisters on the path to the central rooftop as they staggered to their feet and lurched forward in a daze.

Lia could not drag her eyes from the girl's back, so she saw quite clearly when Sally dropped something small and metallic onto the path behind her. Whatever it was caught the light of Lia's fire in a moment of suspended motion, then fell to the dirt and darkness below.

The first witches to ascend the rooftop huddled in the tall grass at its center, and a low whirring sound joined the hissing snap of Lia's fire. Others began to chant, and the air turned sharp on her tongue—like the aftertaste of lightning. A chill of premonition slid down her spine. She released the ring of fire and bolted toward Gwen, sending up a shower of sparks from one raised hand in a signal to Tony.

As soon as she moved, everything slowed. Or, perhaps, her mind sped up. In either case, the results were the same; she noticed every detail, but her actions themselves felt no slower or faster. Battle clarity had come upon her.

Gunfire thundered as bullets blasted chunks from the tombstones and stairs. Rock dust and chips peppered her face and arms as she dashed headlong toward her sister. An impact, like getting kicked by a horse in the ribs, sent her careening to her left. She hit the side of the stairs, which was really just the wall of the row of mausoleums, hard enough to drive the air from her lungs.

The world spun for a dizzying instant, and Lia glanced up, trying to get her bearings. Blue energy wavered to life in the air the way a rainbow appeared, or the way she'd seen the skyfire arise in the northernmost parts of the Sunset Lands. It shifted and pulsed, creating a translucent dome around the roof of the central structure. Here and there, the energy began to solidify, turning from molten energy into something like blue glass.

The whirring grew louder, and the energy expanded from a narrow dome to encompass the entire roof, like lungs expanding on a deep breath. If it grew again, it would swallow Gwen. Lia forced herself to her feet, grabbed Gwen by the back of her coat, and pulled her to safety.

But the Covenant had wasted no time.

As soon as she'd dropped the fiery circle, they'd dashed forward with inhuman speed. A waxy-faced woman plowed into them, swinging a knife. Gwen seemed to come to herself in that instant. She spun and raised her arm in defense. The blade slashed ineffectively across the armored fabric of Gwen's coat.

The impact knocked the three of them backward, and Lia lost her footing. They tumbled down the stairs, twisting and grabbing at one another, to hit the dirt path below. Lia's head bounced off the packed earth.

Dazed for a moment, she watched as the last of the witches—all but Deborah—hurried up the wooden stairs to pass unharmed through the solidifying magic circle.

A pair of cold hands clamped around Lia's throat. She tried to gasp as a shadow loomed above her, but the pressure cut off her air supply and made tiny white sparks dance at the edge of her vision. She grabbed the woman's naked wrist and thought, *burn*. The woman screamed and flung herself away. Air rushed back into Lia's lungs, and she rolled to the side, coughing. They had to get out of here.

Aris appeared in a rush of wind and wrapped an arm around Gwen's waist. A handful of Covenant members raced down the path toward them, knives and pistols raised. He turned, putting himself between them and the oncoming rush, wings unfurled. Gunfire erupted in a roll of thunder. He grunted as he hefted Gwen beneath one arm, took two running steps toward Lia, standing unsteadily at the foot of the stairs, and sunk the claws of his other hand into the back of her coat.

She flinched away—this was the Raven she had feared since first being given command of him, an inhuman creature who made his victims enjoy their deaths—but his grip was secure. He leaped. They were too heavy for extended flight, but Aris was determined. With a mighty beat of his wings, they rose five feet, ten, picking up speed.

A dark figure leaped from the top of the outside circle of mausoleums and hit Lia, wrapping his arms around her hips. The sound of shredding fabric was the only warning that her magic coat could not withstand added weight, not when Aris's claws were the only thing keeping her aloft.

She fell.

24

Magic and Blood

GWEN AND LIA

Lia

The impact drove the air from her lungs. Luckily, she only fell a few feet and landed in the ferns rather than on one of the tombstones. Her coat heated with the force of the fall, spreading and dissipating enough of the energy to stop her from breaking bones but not enough to protect her diaphragm.

Breathing was impossible, and she struggled against the desperate need for air as gunfire cracked in a steady, precisely paced rhythm. Tony. She tried to turn onto her side but a huge, shaggy shadow sailed over her head, blotting out the sky. A crunch of impact, a howl of pain, and something hit the ground near her with a dull thump.

Was that a limb?

Lia scrambled backward, gasping as her shocked lungs finally relaxed. A dismembered arm lay twitching not a foot from where she landed. Her stomach tried to climb out of her throat, but someone snaked an arm around her neck and pulled, cutting off her air again.

Their skin was cold and waxy. Covenant.

She grabbed the forearm crushing her windpipe and willed fire through her palms. They screamed and swore, releasing her to fall backward down the stairs. Lia flung her arms wide, but the sharp edge of a stair cracked against her shoulder blade, and the side of her head bounced off something hard. She skidded to a stop halfway to the bottom, dizzy and breathless.

When she forced her eyes to focus, Lia found herself looking up at the circular structure at the center of the depression. Sally stood at the top of it. The girl's eyes were distant, already focused on the power of the growing spell. One thought raced through Lia's mind: Sally. If the girl was the most powerful witch in the coven, the spell shouldn't work without her.

Lia had to get to the circle before the witches closed it and pull the girl out. It did not matter if she was unsteady or dizzy.

She rolled to her feet and bolted down the remaining stairs, sending a gout of green flame over her shoulder toward the Covenant behind her. Almost half-a-dozen screams rose as the flames seared their flesh. Lia barely heard them. She could only think, *Get to the stairs, get to the stairs*. But the sight at the bottom of the depression froze her muscles.

Matilda had appeared at last.

Deborah and Matilda squared off on the narrow path between mausoleums, their arms raised and wreathed in undulating power that warped the air around them.

"I don't want to hurt you, sister," Matilda said as she set her feet. "I beg of you to stop this madness."

Deborah only laughed and leveled her hand at her opponent. "We are not sisters."

Get down!

Lia dropped to her knees without thinking, obeying Tony's mental voice as if it were her own. A snapping sound echoed in her left ear, followed by a thud behind her. She started to turn, but Tony said, *Don't look*.

Not imagining the sight he wanted to save her from was almost impossible, especially in this gruesome melee. But she was grateful to him for trying.

Thank you.

Tony did not reply, but three more measured shots barked from nearby. Matilda and Deborah did not seem to notice. They flung raw power at one another, eyes hard, expressions fixed. Matilda crossed her forearms. A translucent shield sprang up in front of her just in time to deflect a bolt of orange energy Deborah threw like a spear. It bounced off the shield and took a two-foot chunk out of the slab of granite behind her.

Even faeries did not fight with magic like this, wielding pure force with abandon. From everything Gwen said, the women's bodies should have been breaking down, twisting with the sheer force of magical energy. But neither woman appeared affected.

Deborah carried the Eye under one arm. It seemed to suck the energy toward itself like a dry sponge, making the jade iris glow like a small star. If she could reach Deborah and pull the eye away from her, would that stop the ritual?

Lia forced herself to her feet and sprang forward. She made it three steps before hitting a wall of power that sent an electric current buzzing through her body. Her knees gave out. With an incoherent cry, she stumbled backward and landed hard on her rear end near the wooden stairs.

Static electricity crackled over her skin, making pins and needles prickle across her scalp. Her chest hurt, and her right palm stung. Why did her palm sting? That hadn't come from the magic.

She peered at the ground where her hand rested moments before as magic billowed around and over her, pulling at her hair. The sharp edge of something shiny stuck out of the dirt. It had been squished into the softer earth at the edge of the path where moss and grass grew against granite walls.

When she peeled it out of the mud, her heart stuttered. It was the Covenant symbol but altered to include a triquetra: Covenant and Sisterhood. Sally dropped it earlier. Lydia wasn't an aunt in the true sense, but she knew enough of Sally to know the girl wouldn't have made such a blatant mistake.

Sally must have meant someone to find this. Which meant it would help somehow. Lia did not have time to wonder how because a mistcat landed on the path in front of her and bared its teeth in a snarl.

Gwen

Cyrus soared twenty feet across the path from one side of the graveyard to the other and landed within an inch of crushing a mistcat. The beast was half Cyrus's size and nearly invisible in the dark with its dappled markings, but it flashed out of his way with blinding speed.

Faster than I could blink, the beast spun and slashed, leaving a foot-long wound across Cyrus's shoulder. He snarled in pain and lunged, but the cat twisted in a sinuous motion that left Cyrus's teeth snapping closed on empty air.

Two Covenant members charged Alix from opposite sides in a coordinated attack. They were fast and deadly, but Alix had been a living weapon for three hundred years. She leaped over the head of one attacker and rolled to her feet on the other side. Her knife flashed across the throat of her closest foe before she shot him in the head with cool precision. A second shot followed the first as soon as her victim dropped, and bullet number two sent the other Covenant member stumbling to the ground.

Lia screamed. I jerked my eyes back to the center of the conflict as a dark figure threw himself at Lia. They tumbled backward down the stairs in slow motion, green fire blooming between them.

My feet pounded against the dirt, and my lungs burned, but I wasn't fast enough to stop any of it.

Light flared and sparkled from the bottom of the circle, competing with the solidifying blue light atop the grassy roof. I squinted at it as I ran. The light seemed to emanate from a glowing object at the center of the circle of witches.

What—a premonition of danger raced up my right side. My body reacted without my direction, like the instinctive jerking of a hand away from something unexpectedly hot. I dove into a roll and came up with the blade of my umbrella unsheathed.

The Covenant member who had leaped at me from behind shot me from close range. I stumbled backward from the impact, my coat flaring with heat. She adjusted aim, raising the barrel by a fraction of an inch, and her finger tightened on the trigger.

She was going to shoot me in the face.

I should have ducked, dropped, or taken a defensive stance. Instead, I lunged. In all honesty, lunge was far too generous a word, given the quality of my form. But I leaped forward, covering far more distance than I had a right to, my back leg stretched nearly parallel to the ground, my arm extended as far as my reach allowed.

The tip of my blade sunk six inches into the Covenant member's chest. Her gun fired. A blast of light blinded me. She batted away my arm, leaving the blade sticking out of her chest, and tackled me.

Years of training in martial arts kicked in. She was stronger than me and faster, but my instincts were automatic. I grabbed her by the collar and sleeve, set my hip against her waist, turned, and twisted. With her momentum against her, the Covenant member somersaulted, her feet flying over her head as I guided her toward the ground. She landed with her back toward me, leaving her neck exposed.

In training, I might have executed a choke. But it would take anywhere from six to ten seconds for her to lose consciousness. That was a long time in a fight, and would leave my back exposed. Besides, she was far too strong to trifle with. And Lia was in trouble.

So, with my newly discovered strength, I broke the woman's neck instead. After pulling my rapier from her chest, I finished the job as quickly as possible and ignored the urge to vomit. I would only have to fight through it, anyway, as the damn Covenant seemed determined to keep me from the circle.

The next thirty seconds were a whirlwind of battle. I slashed, lunged, kicked, ducked, spun, and threw one spectacular punch that took a man off his feet. When I reached the circle at last, it had been no more than a minute since I left Aris.

Many-colored lights wavered and pulsed at the bottom, nearly blinding me as I rushed down the stairs, choking on the bite of ozone and cinnamon and the smell of burnt hair. Where was my sister?

Lia

She flung a gout of flame forward like an arrow from a bow, but the miscast leaped aside, and the fire spattered against the stone wall behind it. In two bounds, it was on her. Lia hit the ground on her back with her arms raised to protect her face.

The cat's teeth sunk into her left forearm, and the jacket exploded with warmth that surged up her arm and did not dissipate till it reached her hips. Its teeth were not as sharp as Aris's claws, but the force of its bite was incredible. With a vicious twist of its body, the beast flung her to the side, and her already injured arm snapped.

At first, it felt like a blunt impact, as if someone had struck her arm with a stick. The lack of immediate pain gave her enough time to raise her opposite arm and protect her throat when the beast raked at her head. Claws traced a burning line down the right side of her face, but Lia gritted her teeth and clamped onto the cat's paw.

Burn, you bastard, she thought.

The scent of burning hair overwhelmed her, and the cat yowled in pain. But it did not release her. She willed the fire hotter, but it only shook her by the arm until her grip broke. It was going to kill her, and she wouldn't be able to save Sally, to warn Gwen, to kiss Tony, to do any of the things she had foolishly taken for granted.

A gunshot cracked, so loud in the confined space that it set her ears ringing. Then another. The mistcat spasmed and stumbled to the side to collapse, twitching. She scrambled away from it, pushing herself across the ground with one arm and her heels. Wet warmth coated the side of her face and soaked the collar of her shirt. And her forearm began to burn with pain until her heartbeat throbbed in every fingertip.

A pair of strong hands slipped beneath her armpits and hoisted her to her feet as if she weighed nothing. The motion made a bolt of heat run up her arm, and she could not stifle a groan.

Tony. It was Tony. "The cat," she said between teeth clenched in pain. "It will heal. We have to—"

"Iron bullets," Tony said, tucking her beneath his arm and turning to aim his rifle one-handed at the witches still fighting. "The ones Gwen had the King make. Handy against faeries. Cover your ears."

She pressed the side of her head against his chest and covered her right ear with her good hand. The gun barked again.

"Sally!" Lia shouted over the ringing in her ears and the constant hum of magic. "We have to get to Sally!"

"There's no getting to her now," Tony said. "She's inside the circle."

"No, she dropped...she—" Tthe amulet! Lia had dropped it when the mistcat hit her. She fell to her knees and ran her good hand across the torn-up earth. Where was it? She glanced up to see Sally standing above her at the edge of the circle just inside the wall of magic, her face raised, arms held aloft. Alone.

Sally was the anchor.

A blast of energy rolled over Lia, hot and crackling, as her fingertips brushed the cold curves of metal. She yanked it out of the dirt and fumbled it one-handed over her head. Tony hauled her to her feet.

"We've got to get you out of here!," he shouted.

But another wave of energy billowed toward them from the dueling witches, this time singing their hair and making their clothing smoke. The magic was going to kill them. Heat and crackling power thickened the air until every breath stung, and her brain felt like it would sizzle inside her skull.

Tony pulled her into the recessed doorway of the closest mausoleum and pressed her against the door with his chest, using his body once again like a shield between her and the magic.

"Hold on!"

Gwen

As I reached the center of the graveyard, the scene unfolded in sickening clarity. Two Covenant members lay on the ground, one with half of his head blown away, another burned so badly it was difficult to discern anything beyond the general shape of him. Near them lay a mistcat, both shot and burned. I scanned the scene while the fear of seeing Lia's broken body made it impossible to breathe.

There, between the carnage and the witches, Tony was crouched in a doorway, covering Lia's curled-up body with his own as magic burst in the air around them like fireworks.

Grass and ferns had begun to smoke. The granite and marble near the brawling witches were scorched black in some places and pitted in others. Without a circle or a body to contain the magic, it was twisting and warping the fabric of reality. The witches had to be stopped, or the cemetery would gain a dozen new members.

I pulled the pistol from my pocket, sighted, and fired at Deborah.

As soon as the bullet hit the undulating energy field around her, it disintegrated in a shower of red sparks. Deborah ignored the gunfire and raised the Eye of the Graeae over her head. It glowed like a small sun and threw monstrous shadows across her face. Her laughter, high and manic, echoed off the stone and seemed to come from everywhere at once.

"Thank you for donating your power, *my lady*," she crowed. Her voice was filled with triumph and spite, her eyes pinning Matilda to the spot with unrestrained glee. "I never could have charged the eye without you."

Matilda wobbled but remained standing. Sweat ran in rivulets down the sides of her face. Her cheeks were sunken, her eyes bloodshot. "You doom...an entire city..." she panted. "Deborah. Please. The Sisterhood—"

"Has no more need for you!" Deborah interrupted. With a malevolent grin, she leveled the eye at Matilda and blew her twenty feet backward with a cone of force that glowed blue at the edges.

The former leader of the Triumphant Sisterhood hit the ground and rolled bonelessly to a stop beneath a fern. She did not rise.

Deborah turned her back on the woman and stalked toward me, white gown glowing in the light of the eye. She looked like a vengeful priestess.

"Lady Gwen," she said. "It was so kind of you to bring me everything I needed to complete my life's work. You have been the most useful tool I could have hoped for. Please die knowing you helped bring about a new world."

I did not even see the magic that hit me; I only felt the impact: the insane heat of my coat pushed to its limits, my feet leaving the ground, wind tugging at my hair and clothing, and my skin burning as if Delilah had aimed another blowtorch at me. I was weightless, timeless, floating through cool air that eased the burns.

Was I dead?

Gwen? Gwen, damn you! Don't you dare die. Don't do this to me again!

The weak voice in my head...I knew that voice. *Aris?*

His sense of relief flooded through me. *By every god in heaven, woman.*

My eyes fluttered open, and the scene before me flickered into focus. Night, black as velvet, lit by undulating blue light. Bodies littering the ground. Alix spattered with gore, standing among the tombstones as a limp figure dropped from her bloodied hands. Cyrus shaking a mistcat like a dog with its favorite toy. Aris holding me upright as he shielded our back with his wings. Had he caught me before I hit the ground or just lifted me after the impact?

Waves of pain pulsed through my head in time with my heartbeat, but I fought to ignore it as I focused through my blurry vision on the brightest point of light.

Atop the roof of the central mausoleum were two circles, one within the other, just as Sam had drawn them. Nearly every member of the Triumphant Sisterhood stood in the inner circle surrounding Deborah, their arms raised, fingertips touching.

Deborah held the eye aloft, and energy burst from it in a glowing stream, released like a river in flood. The witches staggered backward, their feet digging into the turf as they fought to maintain the circle against the magical energy that rushed into the object at the exact center of the circle.

Light coalesced in the object and dulled for a moment as it absorbed the magic, making it clear for a heartbeat. It was a machine of some kind, not unlike the engine of my auto, with coils that glowed nearly incandescent.

A memory, a distant echo of a gentle voice turned defensive. *Was. I destroyed it.* What had Dove called it? The Aetheric Charger? Either she'd lied, or the Covenant had repaired it because the machine was absorbing an unthinkable amount of energy, more, I guessed, than the eye could hold. The light pulsed once, twice, then burst forth so brightly I had to squint and shield my eyes.

The dome solidified around the inner circle, blue and solid, opaque as milky glass. One figure stood alone in the narrow space between the outer and inner circle.

Sally.

Magic caught her veil and blonde hair, dragging them up and away from her head like a candle flame. Her arms were raised and straining, her eyes distant and unfocused, her face slack as if every ounce of her mind and will were turned inward. The formation became clear. It wasn't a circle at all; it was the head of an arrow.

And god's breath, Sally was the tip. She was the anchor of the spell, the single most vulnerable point of failure. Below her, Tony lay at the bottom of the stairs, his jacket blackened. Above him crouched...Lia. Her hair was loose and blew about her shoulders, her coat dirty, stained with mud and blood, and torn in several places. One of her hands was flat on Tony's back, the other arm cradled against her chest, and her bottom lip trembled as if she were about to cry.

But her eyes were hard as agates, hard as the eyes of the woman who had me whipped. Her jaw firmed. She released Tony to press her fist against her mouth, a silver chain dangling from her fingers. Expression stony, she turned to face Sally and began climbing the wooden stairs.

It was as if the world had frozen. I was standing on the moor again, facing Cassandra Monmouth with Sally's life in my right hand, Claire's life in my left, and Lia between them. No right answer, no tenable solution was open to me. All was darkness and failure, and I would bear the burden of it alone.

Whether I intended to save Lia or stop her, I cannot say. I only knew that I flew toward the circle with all the speed I could manage while carnage continued around me.

If Lia tried to breach the wall of magic, she would die. A wall like that had nearly killed Tony. It would pop her delicate body like a bug on a hot lamp.

All I could do was watch her approach a wall of deadly magic and scream as I ran.

Her body tensed as she neared the top of the stairs, and her hair blew back as if from a mighty wind. Blue light wreathed her form, and she passed *inside* the magic. I stumbled to a stop at the top of the stone stairs with Aris at my back, panting so hard his lungs sounded like a bellows.

Covenant members died at his fingertips. His growls mixed with tearing flesh and the screams that filled the air as he protected my back, giving me enough time to do something, anything to save the lives of two of the women I loved most in the world.

Lia stopped at Sally's side. Tears and blood ran down her face. She glanced once at Tony's limp form, at the ring of witches, and raised her right hand. Green fire sprang to life at her fingertips.

My blood turned to ice water and froze everything inside me. God's breath, she was going to kill Sally. How had everything gone so horribly, terribly wrong?

"Lia!" I screamed.

But she could not hear me. Grief twisted her face until she no longer looked like my sister.

"Aris, help me!" I cried as my heart broke to pieces. "Oh god, Lia, *no!*"

25

Love Lost

GWEN AND LIA

Lia

Tony lay near death in the dirt. Bodies littered the cemetery. Smoke rode the wind, dragged toward her not from the bodies she had burned or from the magic the witches threw at one another, but from the city.

Aris and Gwen were covered in dirt and blood. Alix and Cyrus had murdered dozens of Covenant members. And as bad as all of that was, it would be worse if the wall fell. If Obyrron invaded. He would subjugate mortals and use them the way he used her, like toys for his pleasure, tools to do his bidding.

"Yes," he told her once as she knelt before him with a gold chain around her throat, bruised but smiling, overwhelmed by the influence of his desire, mindless, except in her memories. "This is where you belong. Where all of you belong. On your knees before your betters, waiting for orders."

When she'd been left alone in her room at last, she'd vomited on the floor, too weak to bother finding a bowl. If she could have crawled to her window, she would have jumped out of it. By then, she had learned to separate her mind from her body. It was the subjugation of her will that made her guts writhe.

She wanted to hurt Obyrron, to kill him with her bare hands and watch him suffer and smoke. She could let Sally release the spell. Bring her enemy here and kill him. But if she failed? The people of the city did not deserve the fate they would suffer. Her revenge wasn't worth that.

Lia steeled herself and raised her hand.

No! Gwen's voice rang inside her mind with the force of a blow. *Lia, no! You cannot hurt Sally!*

Better death than subjugation, the thought back.

But if you break the spell, you'll die, too. And likely everyone in this part of the city. The magic will rebound. Innocent people will die!

Some fates are worse than death, Gigi. You don't want that for Sally. Trust me. I know.

Where there is life, there's hope. Gwen's mental voice was dripping with desperation that sliced through Lia's armor. *Lia, listen:*

you are still alive for a reason. Your suffering wasn't meaningless. And if Sally suffers, at least she will be alive to choose. To fight.

There is no fighting against the likes of Obyrron! She sent the thought flying into Gwen's mind like a thrown dagger. She'd been angry at Gwen for bringing her back to mortal lands for all the reasons she repeated to herself. But the truth cut far deeper.

She'd wanted to stay long enough to see Obyrron dead, to look down at his lifeless body and know she'd helped make it happen.

But she'd failed. *There is no fighting the likes of Obyrron,* she repeated. The hopelessness of it was crushing. Better to stop it now while she could. To put an end to it before the misery began. She swallowed and closed the distance between herself and Sally.

You did.

She froze.

You fought, and you never stopped fighting. I stole that from you, and I'm sorry. God's breath, Lia, you'll never know how sorry I am. But Sally doesn't have to suffer for our mistakes. You have new battles to fight and people to fight beside you. All I am asking is that you give Sally the same chance. Please.

The chanting behind her reached a crescendo. Deborah cried a strange word and thrust her arms heavenward. Light poured from the machine in a beam that shot straight up and faded into the sky a hundred feet in the air.

Sally gasped. Her eyes flew open. The ritual was nearly complete.

Sally had the chance to stop this, she thought back. *She didn't. I'm the only one left with a chance. Alone again. And I won't fail this time.*

Gwen

My heart thundered so hard it was difficult to hear my own thoughts, but I flung them at Lia anyway. *Sally was my responsibility. We are here because I failed her. This is my doing. I did not give her what she needed, so she searched for it in magic. My failure, not hers. She's only a child. My fault, Lia.*

And it hit me in a rush more powerful than the magic warping the air.

All of it is my fault, my doing, my mistakes and misjudgments. And if you end it now, I will have no chance to make it right. Mama will lose her daughters. Sam will lose his sister. Thousands of people will lose their loved ones. And I know I should care about that more. But...Sissy...

I hadn't called her that since we were tiny, and the word seemed to lock her in place. Our childhood came rushing back at me in flashes, a hundred, a thousand memories of us. I flung them all at her: dirty feet and broken pencils, flower crowns and the way our door squeaked when Mama opened it to see if we were sleeping or still whispering. The flowering tree we sat under to read, Lia's favorite stuffed horse, and how sometimes I would fall asleep in my bed and wake up in hers with our fingers entwined.

Words flowed out of my mind in a torrent of desperation. *I don't care about any of it the way I care about you and that damned girl. I love you both so much it's ripping me apart. Please. I can't lose you. Either of you. Stay with me. Fight with me. This doesn't have to be the end. There is hope as long as we're breathing. As long as we are together. You are not alone.*

Sally started floating. Magic wrapped around her like wind, pulling her dress tight against her body, dragging her hair into the air, and lifting her off her feet. Her head fell back, and her arms opened in a benediction or a curse.

Lia's hand shook.

Sissy. Come with me, please.

But Lia remained locked in place, indecision wrenching her features into a rictus of torment.

Magic crackled dangerously, painfully against my skin. The fibers of my coat smoked, and air burned in my lungs. But I said aloud, "I'm not leaving without you. So, if this must end, it ends here. With all of us."

Lia met my eyes, and hers were luminous with tears, hazel green as the first buds of spring.

Did you never notice, Gwen? As much as you claim to care, did you ever see?

I searched her face, taking in every familiar bit of her. *That your eye color changed? Did you think I wouldn't?*

A tear slipped down her cheek, leaving a clean trail in the drying blood. *You never said anything.*

I didn't think it was polite.

I'm...changed. Not just my eyes. I'm not the same person I was.

This was it. Our relationship had been pointed at this instant ever since I saw Lia standing next to Obyrron, glaring down at me with cold disdain. Every fight, insult, hug, tear, and longing memory had forced us down this path, pushed us to the very edge of destruction.

And it all came down to the heartbreaking question Lia could not bring herself to ask me, not even now at the end of everything. Tears spilled down my cheeks, and my chest tightened.

I'm not the same person either, I thought. *But I like this new version, too. Hazel suits you.*

Her lips trembled, her chin wobbled, and one hand reached out to me through the magic.

A single word ripped from Sally in a desperate scream. "Go!"

Lia

Idiot. Weak, sentimental fool. Lia berated herself with every insult she could think of as Gwen rushed her down the stairs. She had a chance to save the city, and she'd given it up to get her moon-be-damned sister out of harm's way. Had years of espionage taught her nothing about the danger of being controlled by emotion?

"Run!" Sally screamed again.

They did. Unfortunately, Lia was far slower than Gwen or Aris, and despite the panic strengthening her tired legs, she could not keep up. Aris might have helped, but he was dragging Tony along at breakneck speed.

Alix leaped onto the path from the ferns, her jaw set and her eyes hard as she ran next to Gwen. Matilda hung limp in her arms, unconscious and pale from exhaustion. Cyrus followed a heartbeat later. He approached from the left, saw Lia falling hopelessly behind, and slowed next to her.

She didn't know what she expected, perhaps a nudge or help if more Covenant members appeared, but Cyrus had something else in mind. He shoved his huge wolf's head between her legs and flipped her onto his back. Lia squeaked in surprise as she rolled over his shoulders and flailed for something to hang onto.

She caught a fistful of fur with her good hand, clamped her legs around his massive ribcage, and hung on with her remaining strength. Wind tore tears from her eyes and pulled her hair out behind her. Moon and stars, he was fast! In a few strides, they would be beyond view of the magic.

Lia twisted around for a last glimpse of the ritual. Sally hovered ten feet off the ground, her arms wide, head thrown back. Magic poured into her from the central circle in a constant stream of blue energy. The Sisterhood gave a final, exultant shout. Magic hit Sally in an uncontrolled rush, turning her incandescent, a white star in the night. Lia had seen faerie queens less glorious.

Without the power of the Eye to control the incredible forces they'd unleashed, Sally couldn't survive. Had she spared the girl only for her body to be torn apart by magic? Her questions died when Sally released a strangled cry, dropped her arms, and dissolved the outer circle.

Pent-up magic exploded from her in a wave that knocked the witches flat. It rushed outward like a storm wind, bending the trees in half, flattening ferns and vines against the earth. The tide of magic rushed toward them, sending fallen leaves and branches ahead of it in a tumbling crest.

Hold on! Cyrus thought.

A broken branch cracked across her shoulder blades. Cyrus stumbled mid-stride and would have righted himself, but the wall of magic struck them from behind. The impact sent Lia flying off Cyrus's back and over his head in a long arc. She hit the ground and rolled to a stop with her broken arm cradled against her chest. It throbbed with pain so acute it made the edges of her vision go dark.

"Lia!"

Gwen's blurry face hovered above her. Hands pulled at her shoulders. "Lia, get up. We can't stay here."

"I've got her."

Was that Tony? Someone lifted her, but for a few moments, she could focus on nothing but the pain in her arm and the way her lungs burned for air. And without the magic lighting up the cemetery, it was impossible to see in the shadows beneath the trees.

"Come on. I've got you."

Tony wrapped an arm around her back and beneath her arm, his hand resting carefully on her ribcage, and pulled her forward. The rest of their party had already broken into a jog. Tombstones stood as pale guardians, smudges of light against the black shadows that passed silently to their left and right. If Covenant members hid behind them, or if mistcats lurked in the shadows, they'd never see them till it was too late.

With an effort of will, Lia held her free hand aloft and, with the last of her strength, summoned fire.

Gwen

Magic crackled in the air and buzzed against my skin like a thousand mosquitoes, making it all but impossible to think. Coupled with the dark, my scrapes and bruises, and the return of the little man and his large knife, I was a perfect target for any members of the Covenant who might have escaped Alix and Cyrus.

So, when Lia's fire cast green light through the undergrowth, I was less surprised than I should have been to see several pale faces staring back at me.

"Ambush," Alix hissed and turned her back to protect Matilda as gunfire erupted.

Tony and Lia dropped to the dirt, hunching into the protective fabric of their coats. Cyrus leaped into the fray with a hair-raising snarl, and I returned fire with my small pistol.

Aris shimmered into his raven form, took two running hops, and launched himself into the darkening sky.

Six, he thought a moment later.

I relayed the information to Alix, who tucked Matilda into Tony's arms and followed her husband. Fire barked from the barrel of my pistol once, twice, as I sidestepped toward my sister.

"I'm almost out," I told Tony.

"Trade me."

Two bullets.

One.

I dropped, sliding my body in front of Matilda like a shield, and Tony stood and spun. He fired with calm professionalism as one, and then two bullets struck my back. It felt like getting kicked by an angry mule and drove the air from my lungs.

"Gwen?" Lia asked.

"I'm okay. Keep your fire burning."

Someone screamed.

Three, Aris thought. Then, a few seconds later, *Clear. I'll scout ahead.*

"Let's go," I grunted, trying to stand despite feeling like my lungs would prefer to collapse.

Alix and Cyrus rejoined us, taking Matilda and Lia, respectively, and I summoned the last vestiges of my strength to launch into a run. We wove down the curving cemetery paths with Lia's fire to guide us, taking a small, weed-choked trail toward the groundskeeper's entrance.

All the while, the magic in the air grew stronger, thickening until it was hard to breathe, and every one of my senses was alight, sensitive to the point of pain. Every footfall, every breath, the stinging light of Lia's fire, every ache and sound, and even the scratch of cloth on my skin was so acute it hurt.

The Ratcatchers have been about their business, Aris thought. *At least, we can say that much for the King. They have lured the constables to the west side of the cemetery. Your exit is clear, and Delilah is on her way. Oh, and don't look too closely at the bushes when you leave.*

A wrought iron gate in the stone wall had been locked with a thick chain that was rusted from exposure. Alix examined it, leaned back, and kicked the gate where the chain wrapped the inner and outer bars together. It snapped with a bright, metallic ping so loud to my magically sensitive ears that I winced.

Cyrus shifted to his human form, as his wolf was too big to fit through the gate, and was halfway out when the first rumble shook the ground.

"Get away from the walls," he ordered. "Looks like more earthquakes."

The rumbling grew closer, but it did not feel like the earthquakes that had shaken us days before. It reminded me of something I could not place, something I only experienced in— "Run!" I screamed before the memory fully formed.

We tumbled out the gate and into the street as a tree root thicker around than a wagon blasted out of the earth like a snake from a hole in the ground. Paving stones snapped, dirt flew in a geyser, and chunks of the great stone wall tumbled into the road.

Three gods, Gwen! Aris shouted in my mind. *Fae trees are appearing all over the city. Just popping into existence. Two buildings just fell. You've got to get out of the city.*

I brushed dirt off my coat and thought, *I'm doing my best. Delilah?*

Taking a detour. It appears New London has a new river.

Grass burst from the cobbles beneath our feet. I squeaked and leaped backward, watching the stuff sprout as if growing from the stone at a hundred times its normal rate.

"God's breath," Alix swore, her eyes locked on the skyline.

A tree quite as wide around as a building stood proudly where the ritual had taken place. Its limbs stretched out above us, as wide and curving as paths in a forest. If the witches hadn't left the spot when it appeared, the tree would have destroyed them. My chest constricted at the thought of Sally on that roof when roots and limbs tore into existence.

Could she yet live?

"Gwen, move!"

Tony jerked me to the side just as a line of vines with thorns as long as my finger curled down the length of the wall.

"Thanks for that," I said, breathless.

"What in the name of the moon is happening?" Cyrus demanded.

Lia answered in a voice so worn it was almost unrecognizable. "They broke the wall. The Sunset Lands are leaking into the mortal world."

Alix looked between the two of them. Her eyes glittered like cut glass. "Doesn't that mean—"

"Yes," Lia said. "The fae armies won't be far behind if they are not in the city already."

A white stag with antlers so broad it could have comfortably carried someone between them, bounded across the road, and easily leaped the fifteen-foot high wall to disappear into the cemetery.

Delilah, I thought, not bothering to hide the edge of desperation that sharpened my mental voice. *Where are you? Things are getting dodgy over here.*

Two minutes, she thought back. *But I've got company. I'll drop the Sightscreen when I get close. Be ready.*

Shouts and gunshots rose from the other side of Highgate. "That will be Delilah," I said. "Be ready to get the hell out of here."

"To where?" Alix demanded. Her eyes pinned me to the spot with accusations as sharp as her knives. "Where are we safe now, Gwen?"

"Out of the city," Matilda said. Her head lay weakly against Alix's shoulder, but at least she was alive. "There are wards. If we can get out, we will be safe. Mostly."

Squealing tires, gunshots, and the echo of an engine grew louder.

"Get ready," I said.

Gwen? Aris asked.

Hmm?

Will you hold the as-yet-unnamed auto for me? I think...I think I'd rather ride than fly.

The Sightscreen deactivated, and Delilah's auto, painted like a delivery van, roared into sight at the end of the street. It barreled toward us, rocking back and forth over the cobbles.

A second later, a compliment of constables burst around the corner with their rifles raised. And there were bound to be more scattered through the city. With the explosive magical growth and the constables on watch, getting out of town was going to be harder than I anticipated.

We could use a lookout, I thought as they fired the first round of volleys at the auto. Luckily, there were so many runic sentences inscribed on the damned thing it was a veritable instrument of war. But it was not invulnerable. And as soon as one of the sentences that redirected force was damaged, we would be exposed.

I'd love to, Darling, but I...I don't think I can.

Icy fingers of dread sunk into my chest, wrapped around my heart, and squeezed. I searched the sky, but it was almost impossible to see Aris on a dark night.

What do you mean? Aris?

I heard him before I saw him. A small black figure flapping weakly toward me over the treetops. He wobbled and stopped flapping altogether. His limp body plummeted toward the cobbles. I dove, barely managing to prevent him from slamming into the street. The impact knocked the air from my lungs and made the little man in my head quite angry.

But I had no attention to spare for pain. My hands were covered in blood. A chunk of flesh had been torn from his chest near his shoulder. God's breath, it was so much.

"Aris?" I turned his feathered head to the side, desperate to see consciousness in his eyes.

He blinked at me once, then shimmered. He did not even have the strength to maintain his form. I held his head off the ground and watched as a river of blood began to pool in the joints between cobbles beneath him.

Behind me, the auto screeched to a halt. Shouting and footsteps echoed from the end of the street. "Gwen! Gwen, we've got to go."

But I could do nothing but clamp my hand over the gunshot wound in Aris's chest to staunch the flow of blood and scream, "Help me!"

26

Getting Out

GWEN AND LIA

Gwen

Cyrus squeezed Aris's limp body into the back of the caravan while Tony and Alix calmly returned fire. I forced my way in behind them, ducking the dwarven lamp hanging from a ring bolted to the center of the ceiling and shouldering a shocked Mrs. Chapman out of the way.

"Great everlasting heaven," she swore as Cyrus lay Aris carefully against the bulkhead separating the passenger compartment from the driver's bench. His blood immediately pooled on the wood floor.

"We have to get it out of him," I growled as I ripped his shirt open.

Mrs. Chapman dropped to her knees on the other side of Aris as Cyrus backed out the door. I saw Tony leap in out of the corner of my eye, I heard the volley of gunfire, and I felt the van rumble to life and lurch forward, but none of it seemed to matter. My entire existence narrowed to the gaping hole in Aris's fair skin, just a few inches below his collarbone.

"What, my lady? Get what out?" she asked as she opened her leather satchel and began digging inside.

"Iron," I choked, pressing the heel of both hands hard over the wound. "An iron bullet."

It was the only thing that would have stopped his magic from healing such a wound. His lashes fluttered open, and his dark, unfocused eyes flicked back and forth until they landed on my face. Mrs. Chapman pulled a pair of forceps and a corked bottle from the bag.

"Don't bother sterilizing," I said, "just get it out. He can heal from almost anything after the iron is removed."

Misgiving made her brows pinch together above her narrow nose, but she dropped the bottle and withdrew a scalpel. "Hold him still, my lady."

I transferred my hands to his shoulders, and Mrs. Chapman made a clean, deep cut despite the uneven movement of the van. Blood welled from the incision and slid in red rivulets across his chest, but Aris didn't move. His eyes remained fixed on my face, his brows drawn together hard over the bridge of his nose. His pale lips thinned into a hard line.

Mrs. Chapman dropped the scalpel and readied the forceps. "This will hurt, my lad."

I braced his shoulders with both hands. Leaning above him that way, he filled my entire vision. Everything else receded. The rocking of the van, Delilah's cursing, the muffled gunfire, the stink of blood and sulfur. Only those dark, fathomless eyes, like a clear night sky or the depths of the ocean.

Sweat beaded on his forehead and upper lip. A droplet slid down the edge of his brow to get lost in his hairline at the temple. I did not see Mrs. Chapman begin digging, but Aris's eyes widened, his nostrils flared, and his back arched involuntarily.

"Hold him," she grunted. "I've nearly got it!"

Lia threw herself across his stomach and hips, and I leaned my torso across his shoulders. *Almost there*, I thought, my stomach knotting in pain at his white face and my memories of a surgeon tearing my flesh while searching for the ball that nearly killed me.

"Hang on!" Delilah shouted.

We rocked to one side, and I wrapped my arms around Aris, bracing my feet against the opposite wall as the van took a corner. The dwarven lamp swung on its hook, sending razor shadows dancing across his face.

"Can't you get her to slow down?" Mrs. Chapman demanded as the passenger compartment settled.

Delilah flung the words over her shoulder without looking back. "Not unless you want to argue with the constables yourself."

"Alix and Cyrus should be—" Lia began, but Delilah cut her off.

"Fighting mistcats." She wrenched the wheel to the right, and we slid across the floor until fetching up against the opposite wall. "Fleur! Use the last of the diamonds."

The delicate elf woman was pale and shaking, but she pulled open a compartment in the bulkhead to reveal a complex array of gems and runes set into the wood. The intersecting lines were too confusing to bother deciphering.

She pried out a few blackened and cracked diamonds the size of the pad of my thumb and replaced them with unmarred gems from a pouch at her hip. "Done!"

Delilah engaged a lever; blue-green energy buzzed through the etched lines and gems, and an invisible blanket of suppression fell over the van. It wasn't quite stifling, but it was uncomfortable, like the prickling pins and needles of a sleeping limb.

I pushed the sensation out of my mind and readied myself a second time as Mrs. Chapman plunged the head of the forceps back into Aris's chest. His jaw clamped shut so hard the muscle strained against his skin. I grabbed his hand and held it against my chest as he squeezed hard enough to make the bones in my hand rub together.

I'm here, I thought. *Aris, I'm here. You are going to be alright.*

He convulsed, releasing a wet, tearing cough. A trail of red spittle ran from the corner of his mouth down the side of his cheek.

"He's losing too much blood," Lia said. Her voice was weak. "Gwen, he's losing too much."

Thunder erupted from somewhere to the left. Delilah swore viciously, and we rocked to the right hard enough to hit the opposite wall on our backs as the wheels came off the road. Mrs. Chapman's head smacked against the wall. She gasped, losing grasp of the forceps.

"Grab them!" I yelled at Lia as they skittered across the wood.

Her arm shot out, but she groaned in pain at the motion even as she stopped the instrument from sliding to the back of the compartment. The left wheels hit the street again with a violent jolt, and I slid back to the floor. My side was wet with Aris's blood.

Gwen? Gwenevere?

I scrambled to my knees at Aris's side and pulled his head into my lap, smoothing the sweat-soaked curls from his forehead.

I'm here. Mrs. Chapman is going to get the iron out. Hold on. Hold on to the sound of my voice, alright? Aris? Do you hear me?

It's too late, darling. Moon and stars, I'm cold. Will you...will you hold me?

"It is not too late," I snarled aloud. "Where are those fucking forceps? Mrs. Chapman?"

She pushed herself back into a sitting position and took the tool from Lia, whose face had long ago drained of all color. With professional disinterest, she cleaned the oozing blood from the wound and resumed digging. Aris did not even flinch.

The first time I saw you, I thought you were an angel. His mental voice was dreamy, soft, and distant.

My heart wrenched hard enough to tear itself out of my chest. *That's ridiculous. I was crying; I had dirty bare feet and leaves in my hair.*

Mmm. Beautiful. I never wanted anything as much as I wanted to be loved by you. Thank you for that. Thank you for making at least part of my life worthwhile.

Mrs. Chapman's brows were drawn so low over her beaklike nose that her eyes were lost in the shadows, but her hands moved with the sure confidence of a surgeon.

You aren't dying, you melodramatic ass, I thought, not bothering to keep the anger from my mental voice. *Mrs. Chapman almost has the bullet. You're going to be embarrassed when all this is over.*

Embarrassed for finally saying that loving you was the purpose of my life? Never. Never, Gwen.

Waterdrops hit the clammy skin of his forehead with a wet splat. I glanced in surprise at the roof of the van, only to realize a moment later that the van was not leaking. I was.

"I've got it," Mrs. Chapman muttered to herself. "Just...just carefully now..."

The bullet popped free with a little sucking sound, glowing dully red in the light of the lantern swinging overhead. Relief washed over me in a dizzy wave, but it wasn't enough to drown out the explosion that rocked the back of the van. We bounced half a foot off the floor and landed with a teeth-clacking force.

Gwen! I need some help out here!

Tony? I looked around the cabin, realizing only at that moment he had never climbed inside. *Where are you?*

Glad to know you remember I exist. I'm on the—three evenly spaced gunshots—*the footman's rail. The mistcats aren't fooled by the Sightscreen spells. I think they can*—another gunshot—*I think they're following the sound and scent. Shit!*

A loud thump, followed by scratching and tearing wood, hit the right side of the van. Gunfire rolled like thunder, but Tony only had so many bullets, and he was shooting one-handed.

Lia and I locked gazes. Her pupils were dilated until no color was left, and her expression told me the same thought sunk its claws into her mind: if we couldn't lose our pursuers, none of us would escape the city.

But, Aris— I thought to her, chest too tight for spoken words.

The line of her jaw hardened. *I'll watch over him.* Her features shifted subtly, and my scared sister disappeared behind the mask of the General. *I swear it.*

With the iron removed, Aris should begin healing quickly. I had seen him heal terrible burns in mere minutes. If I wanted to give him a chance to recover safely, we had to lose our pursuers. I nodded, chin trembling, and kissed Aris once, with tears wetting our lips. His were cold, but they twitched beneath mine. Soon, his skin would be warm and flushed again. I would hear his voice and see that mischievous light in his eyes.

But not if we couldn't get out of New London.

I climbed between Mrs. Chapman, Aris, Lia, and Matilda's wilted form, opened the side door of the passenger compartment, and swung myself out and onto the railing.

Wind tore at my hair and coat as the city flew by in a blur. A mistcat crouched on the roof, its claws dug into the wood to leap or swipe. Once the creature was inside the veil, the Sightscreen's magic stopped affecting it.

It pinned its ears to its square head and pulled its lips back in a snarl, but it was the creature's unsettling yellow eyes that caught my attention. They were far too intelligent for a common animal. And they were locked on Tony with furious intensity.

The beast had only to wait until the rocking of the fleeing vehicle forced his aim to waver. Had I still been in denial of my heritage, I may not have tried such a stupid stunt. But too many lives were in danger to coddle my delicate feelings. If my parentage blessed me with greater strength and speed than the average human, I was damned well going to use them.

Using the side of a parked wagon as we passed, I kicked myself up and in a wide arc that let me plant both feet firmly against the side of the mistcat's head. The beast tumbled off the van roof with a yowl, and I landed hard on my side.

Tony's brows rose. "Nice move, Lady St. James."

"Inspector," I gasped, tilting my head sideways in lieu of a bow.

"How many bullets do you have left?"

"Four. You?"

"Two," he said. "Any other weapons?"

I drew an iron knife from a sheathe on my calf.

"That'll have to do. Give me your pistol and keep them off my back."

I climbed to a kneeling position and handed him my pistol, then flattened myself as a tree branch the size of a full-grown oak passed within inches of swiping me off the roof.

"Sorry!" Delilah called.

"Liar!" I shouted back.

She cackled madly and swung the van into a sharp turn that had me clinging to the side rail.

Wind-torn tears streamed into my hairline as I squinted into the blurred shadows of the passing city. Trees burst from buildings and curled around them, and entire alleys were filled with grass, ferns, and copses of saplings. Now and then, a surprised animal bound across our path, a doe or a fox, suddenly transported from the Sunset Lands to the city, left scrambling to find somewhere safe to hide.

People ran from buildings in their nightclothes, screaming and pointing at the unfolding madness. A faerie in shining armor appeared out of nowhere, dragged through the crumbling wall by the force of the magic. He turned, drew a slender sword, and gutted the closest man.

"Son of a—Gwen!"

At the sound of Tony's voice, I rolled onto my back and saw the mistcat hanging in the air, claws extended, a split second before it hit me. Tony's gun barked, but I barely registered the sound over the impact and the scream of pain in my ear.

My extended legs caught enough of the beast's weight to keep it from crushing me, but the impact reverberated up my legs and into my back. Inch-and-a-half-long claws swiped past my face, raking a thin line of fire across my right cheekbone. My limbs were not long enough to keep the creature outside of striking distance, so I spread my legs and let the beast fall into my guard.

It hit me full length, chest to chest. Close enough for teeth to tear into my throat if I did not move fast enough. Fortunately, the blade of my iron knife slid hilt-deep into the mistcat's neck before it had a chance to strike.

Its big body convulsed against me, thrashing while warm blood soaked my torso. I clung to it with my legs, keeping it close until it stopped twitching. When I finally rolled the creature off of me, it tumbled limp off the side of the van, and I had to clench my teeth against the urge to be sick.

"Are you alright?" Tony asked.

"I'll manage." I regained my footing with a low crouch so my tired legs could absorb the sudden changes of direction in Delilah's mad driving, then plugged my ears as Tony fired two clean shots at constables who poured out of a vine-choked alley with guns raised. God's breath, I was tired.

"So much for our invisibility," I muttered.

Gwen? Delilah's voice cut into my thoughts like a knife.

Yes?

Tell Tony to hang on.

Lia

Matilda swung the door shut after Gwen climbed out, but even that simple effort made sweat bead on her grey forehead. She sank back against the wall, panting, and closed her eyes.

"Mistress Lia," Mrs. Chapman said. The quaver in her voice made Lia's breath catch. She held the forceps up to the light and turned them. Light slid across the wet, deformed surface, highlighting a dent in one side.

"There's a piece missing," Lia breathed.

It must have come off inside Aris. And it was a small fraction of the size of the ball Mrs. Chapman held. All the blood had drained from her face because she knew what Lia knew: her chance of finding it before Aris bled to death was slim enough to be laughable.

"Matilda!" Lia reached across Aris's body and shook the shoulder of the witch. "Matilda, we need your help!" But the woman slumped to the side. She had fainted. "Bloody damn everlasting hell!"

Lia shoved her hair out of her face with her good arm, winced as her fingers scraped the cut, and tried to slow her thundering heart and churning thoughts enough to find some solution, *any* solution.

She had no skill as a surgeon, so digging for the tiny bit of iron wasn't an option. Matilda was unconscious, and while Mrs. Chapman's teas were practically miraculous, not even her most potent concoction worked fast enough to save Aris from catastrophic blood loss.

If he wasn't too far gone already.

That was the central problem. Blood loss. And, she realized with a jolt, it was a problem she was uniquely qualified to solve—if she could force what was left of her magic to do something she'd never tried before.

She pressed her palms flat against his chest on either side of the wound, ignored the sound of gunfire, and said, "I'm going to cauterize it."

"But we need the hole to remove the metal," Mrs. Chapman began.

"Just the vessels," Lia replied, though most of her mind was already focused on drawing her magic.

"Can you work so precisely?"

Could she? Honestly, Lia had no idea. But she had to try.

When doing something simple like lighting candles, it felt as if her magic reached out for things that wanted to burn. She connected those things to her magic on instinct: a wick, a bit of wood, the cotton or silk of a tunic. This was entirely different.

She forced her magic into Aris's body, tracing an imagined line along the torn flesh, the ragged edges of severed veins and shredded muscle that did not want the fire, that shrank away from the idea of burning. She had to force her magic to sear those openings and cut off—her awareness hit something. Something hard and inorganic. Foreign. Her mind slid across the shard, finding its edges, separating them from the pulsing life of Aris's flesh.

The iron fragment.

It was deep, closer to his back than his chest. Mrs. Chapman would never find the sliver, not buried so far. But maybe... Lia pushed a bit of heat, focusing on the metal, and felt her fire sink into the structure. Not just sink but be swallowed hungrily by the metal. It knew fire, remembered the heat of the forge, the pressure of the hammer, and accepted the energy almost gratefully.

She should never have been able to do something like this. Perhaps it was her exhaustion, the lowering of every concern and inhibition that let her feel the scope of her magic this way, how it interacted with the world, how it hungered to be used.

A terrible idea took root in Lia's mind.

Raven? Raven, can you hear me?

Through their rings, Aris's consciousness felt like a thread of smoke. She could not get permission for the awful thing she wanted to try. But it was the only way to save him in time for his body's innate healing magic to work. And, even then, it would be close.

So, heart squeezed with fear, Lia pushed as much fire into the little shard as possible. It bloomed with heat, and she imagined the black metal glowing red and orange as if pulled from the forge.

Aris's eyes shot open. The horrible, sweet smell of burning flesh filled the cabin. It wasn't enough to burn the metal out. Chin trembling, jaw clenched, Lia forced more fire into the fragment. Aris screamed. His back arched off the floor.

Mrs. Chapman threw her slender body across his torso, but Aris thrashed, dislodging the older woman and knocking Lia to one side.

A tiny bit of white-hot metal burned through the skin of his back, the fabric of his torn shirt, and scorched the wood floor.

Panting so hard her throat hurt, Lia snatched the shard before his body relaxed in unconsciousness. Her skin tingled with the effort to contain her wildly fluctuating magic. Still, she forced the remaining energy into his ragged veins and damaged arteries, feeling them sizzle and tighten until the blood stopped flowing.

When her magic dried up, Lia fell backward, letting the floor catch her, and fought to keep herself from passing out. Such extreme concentration had let her ignore the pain of her broken arm and the various other cuts, bumps, and bruises of the past twenty-four hours. But her broken concentration acted like a burst dam, and the pain roared back in to drown her.

Had she done enough? Had her terrible plan saved the man her sister loved, or only hastened his demise?

27

A Reckoning

GWEN

"We're not going to make it," Tony said after we'd barely avoided the last mistcat attack.

I lay on my back, sweating from the heat of my coat and all of the energy it had absorbed while I avoided getting eaten long enough for Tony to shoot the beast. There were no bullets left, and I could not keep constables away with an iron knife.

"We must be getting close to the edge of the city," I panted.

Fewer buildings stood tall enough to interfere with the dark sky and racing clouds overhead. And we had not swerved to avoid an abnormally large tree in two whole minutes.

"Close, but all it will take is one more attack."

I closed my eyes, rolled to my hands and knees, and tried to shake the dizziness out of my head. It didn't work. "We will deal with that when it arrives," I said. It was all we could do.

"When? Not *if*?"

"Tony, haven't you been around me long enough to know it is always a when?"

An unwilling smile tugged one corner of his mouth up, and despite the worry and exhaustion making deep lines in the handsome planes of his face, the sight eased my heart a bit. A smile like that, in such dire circumstances, was a beautiful thing.

I did not have long to enjoy it, though. So far we had dodged the magical explosion of flora gripping the city like a kraken curling its tentacles around an unsuspecting boat, but the tree root barring our path was too large to avoid.

There's no way over, I thought to Delilah as I stood atop the van, peering into the dark. The root curled around the main road, across an alley, and through a building. *From what I can see, the side street is our best chance.*

"I don't like this," Tony said. He'd climbed up alongside me and glared disapprovingly down the darkened street. "An ambush in here would be a problem."

He wasn't wrong. The street was narrow and crooked, with uneven paving and random porch lights. Moths had descended upon the porch lights, and some kind of lizard that should not have been in mortal lands gorged himself by clinging to a doorjamb and shooting his long pink tongue into the cloud of wings.

But, unlike the rest of the city so far, there were no other signs of unnatural vegetation.

"We haven't seen constables for a while," I muttered. But my mind was only half on our current problem. When I glanced back over my shoulder at the main road before the van turned and the street disappeared, it was as if a line had been drawn: a city forest on one side and the New London I was familiar with on the other.

What could have caused the magic to stop so abruptly? Nothing was unusual about the buildings. This part of town wasn't as affluent as the area we fled from, so now and then, a bit of Thieves' Cant appeared on a door frame or scratched into the side of stairs, but it was surreptitious. Only someone looking for it would have recognized the markings.

"That doesn't mean we won't," Tony whispered back. Speaking any louder in such a small, dark place felt dangerous. "I would feel better if we had a bit more space to work in. A few more bullets wouldn't be amiss, either."

"Wish in one hand," I said, squinting at a strange mark burned into the bricks of an older house, "and shi—"

"Don't you dare tell me what to do with the other," he warned.

I bit back the temptation to laugh, which made me feel a bit like an expanding balloon. That desire deflated when we pulled into the intersection on the other side of the block.

A squad of constables jogged toward us from the left, and two faeries stood blocking the alley on the right.

"Bloody son-of-a beetle-brained, flea-infested, scalawag! D, drive!"

Delilah must have stomped on the accelerator because Tony and I nearly tumbled off the back as the van lurched forward. The constables shouted and broke into a run, and the faeries leaped like hunting cats. We clung to the roof, ducking our heads against the tearing wind.

The constables were unable to keep up, so they set themselves and opened fire. Bullets tore chunks from the corner of the van, luckily missing the runic sentences. One hit my back and drove the air from my lungs. Delilah could not drive fast enough to save us from gunfire.

Tony flattened himself on the roof and swore. We locked eyes, the knowledge of death arcing between us like electricity.

A battle cry, loud and sharp enough to cut through the gunfire, made us both flinch and turn. Ratcatchers burst from a cross street in a controlled rush led by the Cutthroat King himself. He outpaced his minions in a long leap, twin knives flashing, and left two dead constables in his wake. They made short work of the remaining men. The King raised a bloody knife in salute as we turned a corner.

The faeries, on the other hand, were too fast for the Ratcatchers to stop. They were human-shaped in as much as they had torsos, heads, arms, and legs, but that was where the similarities ended.

Long limbs, too slender for their bodies, propelled them forward at unnatural speeds. And they ran with arms and legs, something like a bear, pulling themselves forward with their hands even as their feet pounded against the road. There was no time for relief.

"They'll be on us in seconds," I warned and adjusted my grip on the iron knife so I could hand it safely to Tony.

"Keep that, you'll need it."

"I have my coat," I said, forcing the handle against his palm. "And I'm faster than you."

He swore, took the knife, and set himself.

One of the faeries crouched and leaped, sailing through the air like a stinkbug in a strong wind, limbs extended. It landed on the back of the van with alien grace and turned its wide black eyes on me.

"You look like a damned mayfly," I snarled, aiming a kick at the faeries head to distract it so Tony could strike with the knife. My ploy worked a bit too well. The creature reached out and snatched me with one hand, wrapping long, bony fingers around my waist. So, when Tony stabbed it, and pain made it release the van, it slid off the back, taking me with it.

I scrabbled at the wood, but my legs and then my hips slipped over the edge. My fingers curled around the footman's bar, but I couldn't hold both my weight and that of the faerie.

Tony grabbed my wrist as I dangled. "Hang on!"

"I'm. *Trying*."

I did not see Cyrus but heard his spine-chilling snarl the instant before I felt him hit the faerie the way a fish must feel a fisherman pulling on the line. The faerie's fingers tightened around my waist for a moment, squeezing the air out of my lungs and snapping my body taut. Then the pressure was gone, and the air was full of snarling.

Tony yanked me forward, an effort I tried to help by kicking at the wood with my toes. As soon as we were both solidly back on the roof, I turned to see Cyrus and the fae locked in a twisting, snarling ball of limbs, moving so fast the individual movements were impossible to track.

Alix shot forward to help her husband. The fight was over in seconds. After a few heartbeats, the couple were running easily alongside us to the left and right.

Though we couldn't do much good once Alix and Cyrus were there, Tony and I stayed atop the roof until we cleared the edge of town. No more unnatural trees or streams interrupted our path. In fact, parts of the city were as silent as if the cataclysmic events of the night never happened. Though, as I climbed back into the van, the tops of the tallest trees were still visible.

Once the solid floor was again beneath my feet, I collapsed. My head was swimming, dizzy, and pounding. The adrenaline that let me focus abandoned me as quickly as it had come upon me, leaving me shaking.

"Gigi, thank the moon and stars," Lia said.

Lamplight cast dark shadows in her eye sockets, beneath her nose and cheekbones, making her look like a marble statue. But the cut on the side of her face and the other bruises were still visible. So was the exhaustion in her eyes and the thin set of her lips.

Aris's head lay on her thighs. He was as still as death. My stomach dropped, and a little whine of pain tore up my throat and past numb lips. Why wasn't he moving? He should have been sitting up and laughing at me by now.

Mrs. Chapman's arms slid around me, stopping me from crawling forward. "Hush now, my lady. Hush."

"Aris—"

"Alive," she reassured me. "Alive. It was touch and go for a bit. Mistress Lia burned out the rest of the iron. But Mr. Aris lost a lot of blood."

My throat petrified until I couldn't breathe, couldn't speak. "He—he…"

"He's alive, and I mean to keep him that way. You just let me work and don't give me any trouble, you hear? Promise now, or I'll hold you right here until you pass out."

A nod was the best I could offer.

"Go on, then," she said. Had I been a bit more aware, I might have noticed the tears in her voice. But my whole world was lying in this van, half of them beaten, bloodied, and near death. I failed everyone so profoundly, so deeply, that there were not even words to define it.

At least Mama, Sam, and Mr. Yates were safe. I had done that much.

I dragged myself alongside Aris and curled into his side with Lia behind me. Her hand settled on my head, and tears filled my eyes as she brushed my hair back the way Mama had when we were ill.

My body gave up trying to fight, and my limbs went as heavy as if they had taken root in the earth.

When I opened my eyes again, would Aris still be alive? Would I ever open my eyes again after that?

I lurched to a sitting position, gasping. "Aris? Lia?"

"Hush, my lady," Mrs. Chapman's hands, thin and calloused but warm and strong, pushed me back down. "They're alive. Hush."

My eyes fluttered closed, but my mind was fully awake and grinding through information like a flour mill. Or a coffee grinder. What I would not give for a cup of coffee. No. Tea. Warm chai with honey. I inhaled, but it wasn't the comforting scent of cinnamon and anise that assaulted my nostrils.

Instead, it was the rusted iron of dried blood that clung to Aris's clothes and the wild smell that always reminded me of night wind across the moors. I burrowed against his side, pushing close enough that the warmth of his body seeped through his torn shirt into my skin.

He was *warm*. Tears pricked my eyes, and I had to swallow a sob. I had come so close to losing him. Too close. Though his breathing was slow and even, he'd lost so much blood. He likely never had to recover from iron before, and certainly nothing so serious as a gunshot wound with severe blood loss.

But he was alive now. And I soaked up his presence like the first snowdrop to push through the frost and feel the sun on its face.

"Are you alright?" Tony asked.

I opened my mouth to reply, but Lia said, "I told you, I'm fine. Mrs. Chapman has given me enough tea to drown a horse."

"Where is she keeping the water?"

"In her bag of tricks, with the rest of her small miracles."

Tony snorted.

"The box behind the bulkhead, the one Fleur was sitting on earlier. It's full of all kinds of things. I don't know where Mrs. Chapman found a hot water tank, but there was enough inside to clean some of the blood off of my face, as well."

"I'll bet you a pound she bullied the Cutthroat King into finding one for her."

Lia's voice was warm and amused. "If anyone but Gwen could do that, it would be her."

I heard a few thumps of someone moving, and Delilah said, "Oi, be careful back there."

Creaking sounded as Tony, for no one else in the compartment was big enough to make that kind of noise, sat down.

"Don't—" Lia began, but Tony cut her off.

"Hold still. You didn't get as much of the blood off as you thought. It's crusted in your eyebrow."

A deep, long-suffering sigh. That was Lia. No one else but Mama could sigh in a thousand words like that.

"And you?" she asked a moment later. "How are you?"

"Sore. Tired. Worried. Scared. Angry. Tired."

"You said tired twice."

"Did I? Strange, that. Come here. You're knackered."

"Aris's head—"

"He'll be alright. Look, his cheeks are pink. You need rest."

Some furtive shifting made me imagine Tony situating Lia so she might lean against him to sleep. The picture was so clear in my mind, him leaning back against the wall, her head on his shoulder, their blonde heads—one bright, the other sandy—resting together, that I opened my eyes. But all I saw was the dark of Aris's side.

I was pressed so tightly against him that my nose was bent sideways.

"Sleep," Tony said.

"I promised Gwen I'd"—a yawn—"watch over Aris."

"You've fulfilled that promise and then some. I'll keep watch for a while. Sleep." The tenderness in his voice made my breath catch.

"You need sleep as much as she does," Mrs. Chapman whispered. Ha. I knew she couldn't have been asleep, not with patients to tend.

"Clearly not," Tony said wryly. "She's already asleep. Besides, someone must ensure you don't work yourself into a stupor. I can't tend all these nincompoops on my own."

"Mr. Tony," Mrs. Chapman said, sounding pleasantly scandalized.

"How much of that tea have you got left?"

Some shuffling. "Not as much as I'd like. I used quite a bit to take the edge off Mistress Lia's arm. Not a good break, that one. And quite a bit funneled down Aris's throat. He may be a faerie and all, but it can't hurt, can it?"

"I suppose not. He certainly looks better."

"That was Mistress Lia," Mrs. Chapman said, her voice proud. "She had the good sense to heat the broken fragment. I never would have found the blasted thing; it was far too small. But she burned it out and cauterized the wound. I don't think he would have made it otherwise."

A sick, slimy feeling made my guts twist. While I was outside fighting, Aris had been dying.

"Well," Tony said, "keep a bit of that tea back for yourself. You've been awake far too long."

She snorted. "Just who is doing the doctoring around here, I'd like to know?"

"It was the wards," a feminine voice said.

I blinked, then startled hard enough to send a bolt of pain across my eyes. "Oh god's damn the little man," I mumbled, squeezing my eyes shut even as I tried to push myself up.

A pair of large hands wrapped around my shoulders to steady me. "Slowly, darling."

Aris?

My eyes flew open, and I half spun—ignoring the pain—to see Aris leaning against the wall next to me. I flung myself against him with an incoherent cry, wrapping my arms around his chest and pressing my face against the flat muscle above his heart for all I was worth.

"Slowly," he said again, his deep voice tinged with pain and amusement.

I pulled away to look at his face, touching his cheeks with trembling fingers. There were dark circles beneath his eyes, and his lips were a bit pale...but he was alive and so beautiful it hurt to look at him. He went all soft and fuzzy as my eyes filled with tears.

"Don't you bloody ever do that to me again, you ungrateful, infuriating, barmy raven!"

He chuckled, coughed, and wiped my tears away by simply kissing them from my cheeks. "Come here. I'm cold."

I scooted until I could lean full against him, my heart so full that, for the moment, I happily ignored Delilah when she said, over her shoulder, "Keep such gross displays of affection on hold till we get to Wainwright. Disgusting."

"I suppose that means I shouldn't kiss you anymore while we have company?" Fleur asked.

"I didn't say that," Delilah rebutted.

"Oh, good. That's nice."

My friend's voice was tired. How long had she been driving? At least her lovely wife was keeping her awake with gentle teasing. Probably nothing else would have worked quite so well.

"You were saying," Tony said.

He sat against the same wall as Aris and I, and Lia lay curled against his chest, one arm wrapped around her shoulder to keep her steady. His other hand absently brushed her brow. She looked so small and delicate in his arms. If I hadn't already been crying, that would have done it.

Matilda sat across from us next to the sleeping Mrs. Chapman, who curled on a few wool blankets with her satchel of herbs close by. It appeared mostly empty. The poor woman had been doctoring for hours.

"You'll remember," Matilda said, "I told you the Sisters and I were protecting New London."

Her voice, usually so smooth and cultured, was raspy. Exhaustion dragged at the corners of her mouth and eyes, but her eyes, at least, were alert.

"Wards? The ones you mentioned in the Undercroft?"

"Yes. They quite literally repel fae magic of every kind. No faerie can pass them."

"Those symbols," I said against Aris's chest, "the ones I've seen burned into the sides of buildings. Those are wards?"

"Noticed them, have you? Yes. The sisters and I have been warding the city for years. We started with the most vulnerable places: the Narrows and so on."

If they had been warding the city for years but hadn't covered the entirety of the place, then either the wards only protected a small area, or they were devilishly tricky to create. Likely they also required substantial power.

"And those wards stopped the Sunset Lands from encroaching on the city fully?"

Matilda nodded tiredly. "When things began to deteriorate, I warded the palace, as well."

"Does that mean the king and queen are safe?"

"I cannot say. I wasn't aware of the Covenant at the time."

"And if the Lord True still has access to the royal family," I said, but let the thought slip away. We had no way to know anything unless Sally contacted us. God's breath, just thinking of her hurt so deeply it made my jaw clench.

"We can hope," Matilda sighed. "Though even my wards may not have been enough if Sally had not released the spell early."

I sat up, wobbled, and righted myself without taking my eyes from her face. "What do you mean?"

"Miss Irons," Matilda called instead of answering me, "have you seen proof of faerie invasion outside the city?"

Delilah sounded unsure. "Hard to say. But nothing like we saw in London."

Matilda nodded once, satisfied. "Had the spell reached its full power before being released, not an inch of this island would exist unpolluted by faeries outside my wards. After seeing the spell in action, I am sure of it. Sally either could not hold the spell any longer, or she chose to release it early."

She released it early. I knew it. I cannot say how I knew, but I was certain Sally would have done everything in her limited power to protect the innocent, even if she had to push the limits of her oath as far as possible. The memory of her blasting Aris across the cemetery was a stark, cold contrast to that certainty. It infected my belief in her like a disease, eroding my confidence.

After her oaths and under the power of the coven, could I truly be certain her heart remained that of the girl I loved? What if power and resentment twisted her the way it warped Deborah?

No. I could not allow such doubts to plague my mind. I knew Sarah Elizabeth Dawes. She was as true as the North Star, and I would not allow myself to think otherwise unless incontrovertible truth was jammed into my chest like a knife. She was still my Sally.

But I had been unable to save her this time.

Sam was never going to forgive me. Imagining the expression on his face made my heart slink away somewhere dark and small. But he was safe. I held onto that truth. No matter how I had failed, that, at least, was something I did not have to recriminate myself with.

"How long have we been on the road?" I asked.

"Six hours, give or take," Fleur said.

That long? We must be nearing York, then. And after that, Wainwright. Safety was so close I could taste it. And we were all still alive. Mama would be waiting with hot food and—

The van rocked as Delilah stomped on the brake. We slid across the compartment, ending in a tumbled pile of bodies squished against the bulkhead.

"Remind me," I groaned, pushing Tony off my leg, "to add safety straps to this damned thing."

"Gwen?" Aris said.

"Hmm?"

"Add safety straps to the InvisiVan."

"InvisiVan? That is the worst name I have ever heard."

"I kind of like it," Tony said as he pulled Lia off of Aris.

"Gwen," Delilah said, but there was no humor in her voice.

Dread condensed in my guts. "What?"

The van door flew open, letting in pink morning light bright enough to make me squint. But not so bright that I could not see the figure standing in the open door.

Shit, Gwen! Alix's voice crashed into my mind, her panic making my heart race. *There is an ambush on the road!*

Thank you. Would you mind staying back and keeping an eye on things?

I'm sorry. We were running an overlapping circle and—

Don't worry, I thought back as my companions were hauled to their feet and dragged out the door. *I have a feeling this would have happened one way or another. Keep watch, will you? And be ready.*

Of course.

When it was my turn, I tried to hop lightly down, but my body was sluggish, and I wobbled when my feet hit the packed dirt road.

The woman in front of me smiled, revealing sharp canines. "Gaelethsdottir," she said as if the word tasted like a fine vintage of wine. "It is time to settle accounts."

28
Knives Out

GWEN

Shiverback's mate smiled the way an alligator grins at a passing fish. For a moment, she stood so close that the cinnamon musk of her body filled my lungs. Unlike Aris, she did not bother hiding her magnetic presence behind a veil, likely thinking she would easily overpower my mind.

But after experiencing the full force of Aris without a glamour, and the pain of the last twenty-four hours, her beauty could not touch me. Not the flash of her large, dark eyes or the smooth curves of her lean muscles.

Her eyes narrowed, and then the smile turned into a grimace. "I tried to make it easier on you," she said, "but you are stubborn. No matter. Perhaps that will only make killing you a greater pleasure."

"You may find that task more challenging than you anticipate," I said, though my voice was tired. I had really, truly had quite enough of being manipulated.

When she smiled this time, there was so much malice in the flash of her teeth that I almost flinched. "I don't think so. I have prepared for that eventuality, you see?"

She stepped aside, and my stomach clenched so hard my knees shook. Not only had her minions taken my companions hostage—that would have been bad enough—but in the clearing next to the road stood Mr. Yates, Mama, and Sam.

And every one of them had a gun pressed to their temples.

Tony, Lia, Mrs. Chapman, Delilah, Fleur, Aris, and Matilda had been bound and dragged into the clearing and tossed into the dirt. My body reacted to the sight like a bit of artifice suddenly filled with energy or a spring loaded with force. Several avenues of attack opened up in my mind, and my muscles tensed on instinct.

"Ah, ah, ah," Shiverback's mate said, wagging a finger at me. "Be careful, Lady Gwen. Displease me, and I will have them killed, one at a time."

Nothing else would have frozen me so completely. Her long fingers clamped around my upper arm with bruising force, and she dragged me toward the clearing so I could see my loved ones up close. Several bruises bloomed on Mr. Yates's face, and his right eye had swollen shut. The scabs on his knuckles told me he'd fought to protect Mama and Sam, and that they had been captured at least twelve hours ago.

Even Mama's broken fingernails testified that the capture had not been accomplished easily. The purple bruise high on her cheekbone lit a fire in my belly, and my jaw clenched so hard I thought my back teeth might shatter.

Sam was similarly scuffed up, his expression defiant. But I knew what lay behind the fire in his eyes, and when he looked at me for confirmation, whatever was left of my heart broke into sharp little pieces. His chin trembled, but he clenched his jaw and looked away from me with his chest heaving.

I tried, I thought. *I saved her life, but I couldn't get her out.*

He did not answer me.

We stopped in the widest part of the dirt clearing, twenty feet from my captive family, and I spun toward Shiverback's mate to say between clenched teeth, "I will kill you for this."

"You will try," she said. "That will be part of the fun. Horun?"

One of her fae henchmen stepped forward and tossed a dirk at her. She caught it, drew the blade, and admired the surface. "You took everything from me."

She continued speaking, but I tuned out the sound of her voice. While she explained exactly why I must die, I forced my mind into gear and gathered as much information as possible.

She must have either tracked Mr. Yates from the city or waited along the most likely escape route from London to Wainwright. There were five faeries and two Covenant members with her, which meant there were not enough guards to adequately cover each member of my party.

Mama, Sam, and Mr. Yates were of the least use, though the faeries had not bothered to bind them. Which of them could compete with fae strength and speed, after all? But Lia and Tony were still a threat despite the knives held to their throats. Lia's magic allowed her to affect multiple targets, but would her fire work fast enough to guarantee Mama, Sam, and Mr. Yates could escape bullets? I doubted it.

They'd almost entirely ignored Delilah—which was rather stupid of them—and Matilda's involvement remained a mystery. Though the Covenant knew enough about her to keep a gun pointed at her head, too.

The only variable was Aris. One faerie guarded him with a pistol, and a Covenant member stood close with an iron knife. Shiverback's mate knew exactly who he was and took no chances. But even Aris's magic couldn't replace so much lost blood fast enough to make him the threat he would have otherwise been.

"So we will fight, you and I. And I expect you to put on a good show before I kill you. I will—"

I pulled my focus back to Shiverback's mate and interrupted by asking, "What is your name?"

She blinked, mouth open as if I had just insulted her mother, so I clarified. "I am tired of thinking of you as Shiverback's mate. It is a mental mouthful, quite honestly. Is there anything simpler I can call you?"

Her lips thinned, and her eyes narrowed. She had not liked hearing his name on my lips. "You do not deserve the honor of my name, *charietch*. If you must think of me as anything, think of me as Bás."

"Bás. Irish Gaelic for *death*. It is a bit dramatic for my taste, but—"

She slapped me. The open-handed blow rocked my head on my shoulders and made my cheek burn. Aris growled, and Mama gasped, but I did my best to ignore them. Shiverback had been easier to manipulate when he was angry. Perhaps Bás would be, too.

"I hope you enjoyed that moment of levity," she hissed, stepping in close. "Because it is the last you shall have before you die. And you will die, Lady St. James. Do not let yourself think otherwise. If you come too close to killing me, I will hurt someone you love."

One hand clamped down on the back of my neck like a vice, and she forced me to face my captive family as she whispered in my ear, "If you do manage to kill me, they will make you watch while those you love die. Slowly. One at a time. With as much pain as my love suffered before the end."

Each one of them stared back at me, some expressions worried, some frightened, but mostly their eyes were angry and defiant.

She raised her voice. "Do you see the knives my companions hold? A wound made with one of those knives will not heal. If one of you moves or speaks, my hunters will hurt the others. Starting with him." She pointed at Sam.

Aris's jaw muscle clenched, his hands fisted until his knuckles were white, and his eyes were burning coals. It wasn't only me he was worried about. This was now his family, too. And though he was less vocal than Tony, he loved the children with smoldering intensity.

I need an opening, he thought. But I did not dare respond, not yet.

"If you behave," Bás told my family but meant the words for me, "and do not interrupt our contest, I will free you. Neither I nor any under my command will do you harm. You have my word."

The force of her promise crackled in the air around us.

We will protect ourselves, Aris thought, not bothering to hide his desperation. *Do not heed her, Gwen. Kill her. We can handle the rest.*

Only I couldn't. If he knew what Bás planned for me, he would attack the closest faerie with whatever strength he had left, and I could not allow that. Even if he dismissed the glamour that had become second nature, the faeries would feel the sting of it less than our companions, and pulling a trigger took mere fractions of a second.

Aris could not, *must not*, die. Her promise was binding. She would set them free when I was dead. If my life paid for theirs, it was a small price. And Aris could avenge me when I was gone. He would take care of them. I knew it.

So I gave him the slightest nod I could manage without alerting Bás, a small lie in the grand scheme of things, and let her turn me again to face her. "Remove your coat, Lady St. James."

Dread sat heavy in the pit of my stomach as I slid each jet-black button through the fabric. Mama whimpered, and I tried not to let the sound affect me. I failed. Knowing she would be forced to watch her daughter die, to carry that burden after all she had suffered, made impotent fury go to war with grief in my chest.

Bás extended the hilt of the dirk to me and smiled, showing gleaming canines. "You will not enjoy this. But I will. And don't forget," she whispered, "make them believe you are trying."

I couldn't think my way out of this. Perhaps if there were no pistols, Cyrus and Alix could remove the threat before one of the faeries pulled the trigger and killed someone I loved. But even Alix could not perform such a miracle.

Bás had planned this well. There was no way out. Not for me. My stomach turned over with sick anticipation as I watched the muscular grace of her retreating figure. Fighting her in earnest combat was one thing. But putting on a show of desperation for my family so she could extract every last drop of revenge, hurting them to hurt me, was pure cruelty.

"Prepare yourself," she said when she reached the other side of our makeshift arena.

She did not warn me out of courtesy but to increase my anticipation, to make every second of my suffering worthwhile. My fingers reflexively tightened on the hilt. The knife was heavy, unwieldy, and unfamiliar.

If I managed to cut her with it, she would heal. I could not win this contest. It seemed the end of my life would be a series of failures. I had failed Sally. Failed to protect the people of New London. And now I would hurt everyone who loved me, loved me in a way I did not deserve.

But at least I had experienced it before it was taken from me. I had that much, and it was more than many were ever blessed to enjoy.

Stay back unless I call for you, I thought to Alix. *This is going to get messy.* Hopefully, that would stop her from charging in when I was injured.

Bás faced me, her knife catching the morning sunlight and sending a bright flash across the distance between us. I squinted to protect my eyes, and she charged, racing toward me like a hunting weasel, quick and sinuous.

We exchanged a series of exploratory attacks, strikes not meant to damage but to learn how our opponent would respond to pressure. Bás darted to one side and swiped her arm in a slashing blow I dodged by mere centimeters. I responded by leaning to one side and jamming my foot between her legs to disrupt her rhythm. She did not stumble as a human might have but stepped around me and neatly pulled the blade of her knife across the top of my thigh.

She smiled as blood drenched the fabric of my trousers.

The cut wasn't deep enough to cripple my leg, but it burned and made shooting pain flash through my muscle whenever my weight settled on it. I would manage for now, but the pain and blood loss would slowly drain me if the fight lasted long enough. In circumstances like this one, ending the fight quickly was the only way to survive.

But Bás had no intention of letting that happen. Thankfully, my instincts had taken over, dulling the pain to a manageable level and narrowing my focus. The sound of my family gasping and crying out was nothing more than muted background noise.

Bás casually licked the blade of her knife and spat in the dirt. "Not quite so impressive without your armor, are you?"

"Release the hostages," I countered. "And we will find out."

She smiled a hungry smile and changed direction, circling from the right, forcing me to mirror her and lead with my injured leg. I managed to avoid her next attack, deflecting her lunge with my forearm.

The blade of her knife flashed a few inches from my face and left her open for a quick right cross. Pain burned up my leg as my hips twisted to add power to the blow. Her head snapped to the side, and she spun outside my range, glaring furiously even as she retreated.

"You wanted it to be believable," I said lightly, trying to maintain my confidence, though blood had gotten down into my sock, making my foot slide inside my boot.

Bás snarled and darted back in, punctuating her strikes and slashes with insults that burned more than the wound in my thigh.

"You were never skilled enough to defeat my beloved," she snarled, and a line of pain blossomed down my left forearm from a shallow cut. "You survived only through sorcery and trickery." A kick to the outside of my lead knee, barely blunted by raising my leg. "In fact, you are only alive thanks to the interference of *others*."

She growled the last word as she leveled a front kick at my chest. If I allowed it to land at full force, it would shatter my ribs, so I threw myself backward at the last second. The impact still took me off my feet. I hit the dirt on my back and rolled, kicking my legs over my head to end in a three-point crouch, knife held low.

Holding myself back from using my newly accepted speed and strength was harder than I expected. The instinct to protect myself, to remove a threat, made allowing myself to be struck nearly impossible. If I just stopped fighting, she might end this, and then my family would be safe. But something in me would not allow it.

Bás must have seen the struggle in my eyes, even if she could not know what it meant. She bared her sharp canines and darted toward me nearly too fast to track. I swung my dirk fully expecting her to dodge, but she used my own trick against me and plowed forward even as I buried the knife in her side. We hit the ground. She landed on my hips and screamed as she ripped the dagger out.

Gwen! several voices shouted in my head at once.

"Without stronger people at your back, you would be nothing," she hissed and slammed the dirk into my shoulder. I jerked aside at the last second, and instead of damaging the socket, the tip of the blade skipped off the outside of my humerus to slide cleanly through the muscle, pinning me to the ground.

I screamed. I had expected the pain, but the sound ripped out of my throat anyway as stinging heat burned down my arm.

Other voices rose to join mine, but Sam's was the loudest. "Lady Gwen! No!"

I tore my gaze away from Bás's rictus grin to see Sam lunge forward, wrenching his arm to free himself from the grip of the Covenant member holding him. Bás trapped my free arm, ignoring my scrabbling to say, "Idiot boy. I warned you, did I not?" She turned her attention to her minions. "Hurt the Dowager. If anyone else moves, cut the boy's throat."

The faerie holding Mama backhanded her with the butt of the pistol. He moved so fast that no one had a chance to interfere. She crumpled to the dirt, one hand pressed to the side of her head as she wobbled. I could not even be grateful he did not use the knife because fire bloomed behind my eyelids, exploding in my brain and dropping a red haze over my vision.

I hadn't desired violence when Bás had us dragged out of the InvisiVan. I wanted to live and protect the people I loved. But seeing blood trickle down the side of Mama's face made me hungry for pain, for hot, slippery blood between my fingers. *Fucking hell*, I had to stop myself before I made a mistake that would damn my family.

If Mama walked away from this with no more than a cut and a bruise, I should be grateful. My companions did not seem to have my self-control and lurched to protect her.

"Stop!" Lia screamed. "They will kill him!"

The Covenant member holding Sam pressed the blade of the knife hard against Sam's throat, forcing his head to the side. The skin dimpled but, thankfully, did not break. My companions froze, their faces twisted and red with impotent anger as the faerie hauled Mama to her feet. Blood ran down the side of her face.

Tony's muscles strained against his clothing, and Delilah's features were set in lines of fury.

Sam looked sick. His chin trembled.

I tried not to look at Aris, but his thoughts drew my eyes to his face with inexorable force. He was still too pale, but his expression was dangerously calm, and he was so still that a chill ran down my spine. *End this, Gwen. Or I will.*

You can't. They will kill all of you.

I know what you are doing. You cannot escape your guilt by becoming a martyr. I will not allow it.

Tears threatened my eyes. *My love, you cannot stop me.*

Bás jerked the blade free of my arm in a blinding burst of pain and held the wet edge against my throat. She leaned down like a lover, her dark eyes soft and excited. "If you would have died the first time, like a normal person, we wouldn't be here. The bullet should have stopped you. The fire should have stopped you. But fate intervened again and again. What could I conclude, except fate wanted to give me the full gift of enjoying your pain? I thought making you watch your loved ones die would be suitable justice, but seeing the agony in their eyes as you suffer is so much more fulfilling."

Her lips brushed my ear, and the blade slid against my throat, parting the first few layers of skin in what was almost a caress.

"Do they know what you are? That you are a liar? A murderer? The Gaelethsdottir? Do they know how unworthy you are of their love? Shall I tell them?"

A smile came unbidden to my lips in contrast to the tears leaking from the sides of my eyes. "Yes," I said. "They know. And they choose to love me, anyway."

She leaned back enough to let me see the furious trembling of her lips and feel the hatred burning from her eyes like twin fires. "Then your death will hurt that much more!" she screamed and plunged the knife down.

29

You Are Worth It

GWEN AND LIA

Lia

Despite the magic Lia had instinctively gathered tingling beneath her skin, her stomach had taken up residence in her throat. Every time Gwen dodged a blow by a fraction of an inch, the breath lodged in her chest. She could not even blink for fear of opening her eyes and seeing Gwen dead on the dirt.

Why wasn't her sister fighting back? She had seen Gwen fight, and this was not how her sister moved. It was as if she was holding herself back. A duel like this one, which was common enough in the Sunset Lands, required every ounce of speed and power. Gwen knew this, yet her responses were sluggish. She never properly attacked.

Raven, what is she doing? Lia thought desperately. *She's taking too many chances!*

She thinks she is protecting us, Aris thought back, his mental voice coldly furious. *She's planning to die to keep us safe. We've got to stop this ourselves.*

Bile rose up the back of Lia's throat. Of course, she was. The fool. *How? None of us are fast enough to stop bullets. Not even you.*

There must be something. I've spoken to Alix and Delilah. They're ready. I can take another bullet if I must. But I can only reach one person at a time.

What can I do? I am not as fast or powerful as Gwen.

This is no time for self-deprecation. I have seen you in action, and your brain is more dangerous than your magic. Think!

Shiverback's mate leaned over her sister. If it had not been for the hatred that made the air around them crackle like an oncoming storm, they would have looked like lovers. But Gwen was on her back, and she wasn't fighting. Breath of god, what could she do? Her magic was useful, yes, but she could not stop bullets!

Bullets. They were the problem. Perhaps if Lia had time to plan she could do something, but fire did not have much effect on— The blade above Gwen's throat flashed down and everything seemed to explode at once.

Power rushed out of Lia in a reflexive torrent. Heating the metal inside Aris's body had given her an insight into her magic she never had reason to use before, and she aimed every bit of energy she'd been gathering for the past few minutes at the nearby bullets and magical knives.

Metal superheated, hammers clicked and gunfire erupted. The knives turned red hot and were dropped with cries of pain. Pistols burst as the bullets adhered to the inside of the barrels and the pressure backfired in small explosions. Mama cried out and collapsed. Mr. Yates dove toward her with a shout, throwing himself between the dowager and the explosions.

Sam spun, though his eyes were dazed, pulled his concealed knife and attacked his captor in one fluid motion. The fae man clutched his damaged hand, staring at his mangled fingers even as Sam bore him to the ground with a scream.

Delilah swung her hammer in vicious arcs, and Fleur darted to the side as the Covenant member nearest them attacked despite his burned hands. Tony tackled the closest enemy target, his fists already flying, and Aris surged upward with a roar that sent a chill up Lia's spine. Wings exploded from his back, hitting the Covenant operative and the faerie closest to him with stunning force. The wind of his leap blew the hair back from Lia's face.

She prayed none of the magical knives had found their targets and squinted against the blast of air. Gwen and Shiverback's mate were locked in a battle for the dagger. The tip of the blade was gone, and the shattered end was only inches from Gwen's throat.

Fight, Gigi! she ordered. *We're safe and we'll cover you.*

With a scream of fury, Gwen bucked her hips, raising her attacker off the ground, and twisted like a snake. Shiverback's mate toppled to one side with a surprised shout. Gwen rose above her opponent, expression cold, almost disgusted, and her dark eyes were intent. Gone were the sluggish responses and too-slow attacks.

Gwen fought like a woman possessed. Shiverback and his mate were well-known in the Sunset Lands as warriors, and the only reason Gwen survived her first encounter with the fae man was because of her coat. But the woman who fought for her life now, bloodied and with no protection, was a very different person.

Gwen was confident and furious. She had finally accepted the truth of who and what she was. Her sister picked the other woman apart one strike at a time, moving faster than Lia had ever seen her, so fast it was hard to see the individual movements.

Of course, concentrating on anything was hard when a faerie curled their fingers into one's hair and dragged one off the ground. Lia's body wrenched backward, muscles screaming at being twisted the wrong way. She reached behind herself, wrapped her fingers around the wrist of her attacker, and thought, *Burn*.

She did not have much energy left, but it was enough to force the woman to release her. Tony barreled in, his fists flying. He was larger than the fae woman, but he wasn't as fast or strong as she. Without a gun, he wouldn't survive the fight. The faerie ducked a right hook, shot toward Tony's midsection, and buried her fist in his stomach.

His coat stopped the worst of the impact, which would have sunk deep into his guts otherwise, but the blow still drove the air from his lungs. He crumpled, mouth locked in an O as he tried, and failed, to regain his breath. The faerie leapt upon him but was thrown backward by a hammer to the face.

Delilah swung the heavy tool like a golf club, and the sharp impact took the other woman square in the nose. She lurched off of Tony in a spray of blood.

Sam flew through the air and hit the ground, rolling to a stop against Mrs. Chapman's knees. One side of his face was wet with blood. He pushed himself up dizzily as Alix and Cyrus roared into the clearing.

The giant tawny wolf sailed over Matilda's prone body and landed on the Covenant member attacking Aris with a meaty *thump*. Everything was madness and confusion, a scene of boiling energy captured in millisecond frames as Lia tried to take it all in.

"Kill him!" the scream was loud and strangled.

Lia flinched as the rawness of it drew her eyes back to Gwen. Her sister was locked around Shiverback's mate, the two of them grappling for dominance, but the faerie woman was covered in blood and slid out of Gwen's grasp too often for her sister to end the fight.

Lia pushed herself to her feet and staggered toward them, ignoring the battle raging behind her.

"Kill him!" Shiverback's mate screeched again.

Gwen curled around the other woman's body like a spider, her legs locked around the faerie's ribcage, arms wound about her throat. But Gwen's hold was not tight enough to strangle the other woman. She'd been exhausted by everything that had happened and hadn't the strength left to finish the fight that way.

Lia was tired, too. Moon and stars, she was so. Bloody. Tired. But she advanced on the writhing bodies until she stood over them, staring down at the woman whose life she had destroyed with fire.

Bàs had risked her life to push through the wall and hunt Gwen for months. She'd arranged for assassination attempts, burned Gwen's home, and tried to torture her into suicide.

Lia understood the woman's hunger for revenge, even sympathized with it. But sympathy would not save the faerie. It would have been easy to call on the General in that moment. It would have been comforting to let the detached, pragmatic part of her carry out the execution. Comforting, but cowardly.

Lia did not need the General to decide how to respond.

She told the struggling woman, "I killed him, you know." Her voice was flat and emotionless. "I burned him to death. Gwen only wanted to escape. You should have come after me."

A pair of maddened eyes locked on Lia's face, wide with recognition and fury.

Lia bent and cupped the woman's cheeks. Whatever magic she had left drained out of her chest, down her arms, and sank through the palms of her hands into the woman's head.

Blood vessels burst in the faerie's eyes, coloring the sclera pink, then red. She spasmed as the heat entered her brain. Her back arched, mouth open in shock and pain too deep for sound. A second later, she fell limp in Gwen's arms.

Even a faerie could not recover from being boiled inside her skin.

Lia wavered, then wobbled to the ground as her knees gave out, twisting as she collapsed. A wave of dizziness washed over her, and she caught herself by one hand. The fight was winding down, and she watched it in detachment while her mind hung to consciousness by threads.

Gwen crawled to her side, leaving the body behind them.

What Aris did to his last opponent was too gruesome to describe, and Lia dragged her eyes away from the slaughter. Mr. Yates sat on the ground with Mama cradled against his chest. Delilah and Fleur pulled Tony away from the dead body and crushed the face of the faerie who had attacked him.

Sam struggled to his feet and helped Mrs. Chapman to hers. The two of them clung to one another as Aris, Cyrus, and Alix finished the last Covenant member. Lia should have cried or laughed or felt something. Everyone she cared for was still alive. They were together. That was enough for some emotion, any kind, to overwhelm her.

But she was blank, inside and outside, entirely drained. Even the throb of her broken arm was distant and blunt. Her gaze settled on Tony and stayed there. He was scruffy and bruised, and he looked so tired. But he was still the handsomest man she'd ever seen.

The honest goodness in him, the consideration for the welfare of others, and the profound gentleness so uncommon in powerful men made her heart ache. That was an emotion, at least. One she hung onto. One she feared she would never be able to have after suffering under King Obyrron.

His eyes, such a soft brown, flicked across the carnage and landed on Gwen. The affectionate relief in them would have been painful to see if she'd been capable of feeling more than heartache. Then they slid to the side and landed on Lia.

Are you alright? His voice in her mind was soft.

I'll live. Are you?

Sore. And I could sleep for a week. I think I've had enough of faeries and magic.

Shall we run away into the woods?

He smiled, and little needles of pain pierced her heart. *I can't think of anything I would like better.*

She was about to respond when movement caught her eye. One of the Covenant members, the one Cyrus had killed, wavered to his feet. Half of his neck was gone, and one arm hung by a few strings of flesh at his side. He should have been dead, but he raised the knife calmly and leveled it at Sam.

Lia tried to scream. To fling power across the field in an arrow of fire that would have burned the man to the ground. But her body had ceased responding. She watched, horrified, as the man reared back and threw.

The knife tumbled through the air. Sunlight caressed the engravings that ran along the length of the blade. The world slowed again.

"NO!" Mrs. Chapman held her hand up, palm toward the weapon, her brows pinned together above her hawklike nose, a look of absolute command on her thin face. The knife slowed. With speed she should not have been able to manage, Mrs. Chapman yanked Sam aside. Her black boots dug into the dirt as she was shoved backward by the forces she tried to control.

The knife seemed to hang in midair, catching the light of the risen sun for the space of a heartbeat as it completed a slow rotation. It lasted fractions of a second. Long enough to save the boy.

But physics would not be ignored. Mrs. Chapman gasped, her hand fell, and the knife leaped into motion. It spun through the breathless air and plunged into the housekeeper's chest.

She did not fall. She wavered as she stood, panting and sweating, one hand gripping the fabric of Sam's coat, the other hanging limp at her side. Beside Lia, Gwen made a noise like someone had reached down her throat and pulled her heart out by the roots.

Mrs. Chapman gasped; her knees wobbled, and she fell.

Gwen

There wasn't enough room in the passenger compartment for everyone. Alix and Cyrus ran alongside the van, Tony and Aris clung to the roof, and Sam and I crouched over Mrs. Chapman's thin frame while Mama dug through the older woman's satchel with Mr. Yates hovering behind her.

"Tell us what you need," I said, holding her hand tight against my chest with my uninjured arm. "Tell us how to mix up the right tea."

"Don't...worry over me," she grouched, but her voice was weak, and her lips were turning blue. The hilt of the knife rose and fell with her labored breathing.

"As your employer," I told my stubborn housekeeper, "I shall worry about whomever I please, thank you. Now, walk me through the steps. Sam can mix up the herbs."

Mrs. Chapman coughed, a wet tearing sound that stained her lips red. "There's nothing to be done, my girl. The knife is in deep. If you pull it out, I shall die within seconds. And I don't have enough herbs left to stop the bleeding."

Claws of pain raked my insides. "Lia, can you cauterize the wound like you did for Aris?"

"Matilda!" Lia growled, pulling the witch upright by her collar with one hand. "We need your help."

But Matilda was still too far gone to be dragged back to full consciousness. Lia stared at me with eyes like raindrops on leaves in the summer.

"I have nothing left," she choked. She rubbed her fingertips together and tried to create a spark. Nothing. She tried again. And again. Helpless tears rolled down her cheeks.

"She's spent," Mrs. Chapman said. "Magic requires will. Mistress Lia is...is exhausted."

"That's another thing, you lying old goat," I growled. "You hid your witchcraft from me for years!"

She chuckled, but the sound was breathless. "Thought you were cleverer than that, my lady. How you did not see the signs, I will never know." She coughed, brow furrowed at the pain the motion caused.

"Can't we go any faster?" I threw the words over my shoulder, not caring how sharp they sounded.

"My foot is on the floorboards," Delilah said between clenched teeth.

"There's nothing," Mama said as she crouched over Mrs. Chapman's medical box pulling out tin after tin, little leather pouches and crumpled paper envelopes. "There are no herbs, no poultices"—she threw the satchel against the wall—"nothing!"

Mrs. Chapman coughed again, her head falling back against floorboards already stained with Aris's blood.

I flung a thought at him, and the depth of sadness in his voice made my stomach drop as if I was falling into an endless pit of grief.

My magic doesn't work that way, darling.

"Then what good is it?!" I cried.

"My lady." Mrs. Chapman patted my hand. Her skin had gone grey, and there were deep purple smudges beneath her eyes. My shoulder throbbed with every heartbeat, my arm was slick with blood, my leg burned, and my head pounded, but none of it hurt as much as hearing Mrs. Chapman rasp out, "My lady, don't. It wasn't your fault."

"It was mine," Sam said. His voice was thick with the tears that left clean tracks down the dried blood on the side of his face. "Oh god's breath, Mrs. Chapman, I'm sorry. I'm so sorry."

"Shh." She touched his arm with the hand I wasn't holding, but she didn't seem to have the strength to do more than that. "Not your fault, Master Sam. It was my choice. And I would make it again—a hundred times. You are worth it. Do you hear me?"

He shook his head, making dirty, light brown hair fall into his eyes.

Mama cleared her throat. The emotion that showed itself in her outburst must have been exorcised because my mother was gone, and the Dowager had taken her place. "Mrs. Chapman must rest and keep her strength. We cannot be more than an hour or two from Wainwright. She still has stores there, I am certain of it. Send Alix ahead and have her alert the doctor. We will have everything ready for emergency surgery."

The frigid, self-contained sound of her voice was a rasp over my exposed nerves. I cannot say why the dispassionate authority in her tone lit me like a spark on gasoline, but I found myself growling, "How can you speak so coldly, madame?"

Mama drew herself up and glared down at me with such intensity that I would have quailed beneath her gaze at any other time.

"Someone must remain calm and direct matters," she said in the dictatorial voice I had always hated.

"You can't control everything!"

"If I could, do you think I would have allowed you to put yourself in such continuous danger?"

"No, you would have made me your little doll, your perfect puppet, so I could follow in your perfect footsteps and never have a life worth living!"

Red flamed in her cheeks as if I had slapped her, and her nostrils flared. Good. She did have feelings.

"Gwenevere Violet St. James, you will not speak to your mother in such a tone." The familiar voice, always so calm and proper, took me off guard. Mr. Yates glared at me, his usually placid expression transformed into something hard and disapproving. "This woman loves you beyond your ability to comprehend, and she is as afraid for Mrs. Chapman as you are. Don't take your grief out on her. It is cruel, and it is beneath you. I will not allow it."

A little sob crept up my throat. I dropped my eyes, unable to look at either him or Mama. My emotions were gladiators using my chest as an arena, and I was powerless to either stop them or predict the winner.

Mrs. Chapman's hand, a competent hand that had scolded, healed, and brought order to my chaotic life, was so cold. Her chest barely rose and fell. I wanted her to wake up and tell me how foolish I was being, but Mama was right. If we had any hope of saving her, she needed her rest.

I can't lose her, I thought.

We aren't going to lose her, Aris replied. *I'm flying ahead. If there is any medicine to be had, I shall return with it.*

Are you...can you fly?

Nothing could stop me.

And then he was gone.

The next miles passed slowly, taking hundreds of years as we listened to the soft, labored breathing of the woman who had become the bedrock of our lives. Every one of us had suffered the sharp edge of her tongue and been on the receiving end of an autocratic demand. The possibility that I would never again hear her order me to bed or threaten to box my ears seemed ludicrous.

And the fact that she had used all of her magic, magic she'd hidden from me for years, to infuse the herbs that healed us while leaving none for herself made me furious. The damned woman would die of selflessness! No. It could not happen. How could a world exist where Mrs. Chapman wasn't angrily tidying something and telling other people how best to live their own lives?

I slid in and out of sleep while clutching her hand to my chest.

Her gasp dragged me out of the half-doze where I'd been hiding from the pain. How long had I been semi-conscious? I blinked and focused on Mrs. Chapman. Her skin had gone waxy and seemed to hug her skeleton, letting every bone show in sharp relief.

Her lips were pale grey, and her open eyes weren't focused on anything, but her expression was worried and searching. "You save my girl. Save my girl. You promise, now. Save my girl."

She must mean Sally. The old woman had gone from suspecting the girl of stealing all the fine silver to loving her like a granddaughter. I leaned down to be certain she could hear me. "I will. I promise. I will save her."

"My girl," she repeated, sounding more concerned as her voice grew weaker. "My girl. Save her. My Gwen."

"I will. Mrs. Chapman, I am here."

"Promise. She promised."

"I promise."

She sighed as if finally convinced, and the strength drained out of her. Her breaths came farther and farther apart. Sometimes, several seconds passed before she gasped another shallow gulp of air.

"Here!" Delilah called.

She did not slam the van to a stop, but we all had to catch ourselves to keep from sliding as she rolled into the gravel drive. Sam leaped from the van and bolted toward the house, shouting for someone to help.

We piled out, carrying Mrs. Chapman on a litter made from my coat. The red brick manor house loomed over us like a forbidding castle beneath a stormy sky. Was it day or night? The storm was so dark that I could not tell.

I held Mrs. Chapman's head as we hauled her into the foyer, and Mama bolted for Mrs. Chapman's rooms. A fire was high in the hearth, and we lowered my housekeeper onto the chaise near the flames.

"Gwen?"

"She's barely alive," I answered as I heard Aris's voice. "Have you found the medicine? The doctor? We must hurry."

"Gwenevere."

I pulled open Mrs. Chapman's shirt, revealing her bony chest above the plain corset and chemise. Seeing the metal buried near her heart nearly made me vomit. Thrown knives did not land with such precision, or penetrate so deeply. Unless one were as strong as Alix, a thrown knife was more of an irritation than a true danger. For it to land like this, between her ribs, was a hundred, a thousand to one chance. It could not be real.

A large, warm hand settled on my shoulder.

I turned, impatient, but it wasn't Aris I saw. Instead, I saw past him to the woman standing regally where Sam, Sally, Mama, and Mrs. Hardwicke had played badminton over the winter. Her beauty was the stuff of legend, of gods and goddesses, and it stopped every thought in my head.

She was graceful even in stillness, soft like late spring rain, skin rich and deep as fertile earth, eyes the green of living things. Her belly might as well have been the earth itself, round with life and potential. Flowering vines were braided into her black hair, and a crown of buds graced her brow.

Lips, red as berries, curled in a smile that was sad, welcoming, comforting, and consoling all at once. I knew her, though I had never seen her face. My heart swelled in my chest, and I found myself on my knees at her feet, weeping openly.

"Queen Titania," Aris said, "may I present Lady Gwenevere St. James?"

30
Royals and Realizations

GWEN

G rief and fear were the only things that kept me from losing touch with my consciousness in the presence of such concentrated power. King Obyrron had a similarly powerful aura, but he pushed his out like a thunderstorm sending lightning before it.

Queen Titiana's presence was self-contained. It drew one towards her like the scent of a rose, only to capture them by the impossibly delicate swirl of perfect petals.

"My lady," Lia said and fell to her knees next to me. "Our faithful nurse has been injured unto death. Please can you—" Her voice broke.

"So I see," Queen Titania said. Her voice was a cool breeze in spring and made a ripple of pleasure run across my body. "Take me to her."

I nearly collapsed when the weight of her attention slid off me, and Lia guided her toward the barely breathing body of Mrs. Chapman. The Queen knelt at her side and touched one gentle finger to the hilt of the knife that rose and fell with every shallow breath.

I focused on my friend and tried not to notice the way the firelight limned the Queen and made her glow like the otherworldly creature she was. Her fingers rested lightly on Mrs. Chapman's brow. She closed her eyes and hummed a soft refrain that sounded like rain on a still pond.

When she opened her eyes, the regret in those golden green depths pulled me down into a well of pain that stole my breath and made my stomach knot. "I am sorry, Gaelethsdottir. There is nothing to be done."

"But there must be something," I heard myself say in a voice raw with emotion. "You must be able to do *some*thing!"

The pain gave me some defense against her influence, so when she faced me, I did not lose touch with my mind. "Even had I poured my magic into this woman at the moment of impact, I could not have saved her. The knife is endowed with power. I cannot be certain without examining it, but my instinct tells me that any wound made by this blade will not heal."

"No," I said, shaking my head and shouldering past the Queen to take Mrs. Chapman's hand. "No. We can do a transfusion, we can cauterize the arteries. She is a witch; she has bespelled herbs and—"

"The magic of the living world is in my veins," the Queen said gently. "I tell you that even with all the skill of every healer in the land, you could not save this good woman. She clings to life now to save you from pain. But it hurts her very much. Best for you and her that you let her go."

"No!" The sound tore out of my chest and ripped up my throat, flying at her like an attack. "She will not die! I will not allow it!"

"I am afraid the outcome is beyond even your indomitable will, little changeling. Let her go. Let her leave this world bathed in love, not in fear."

She did not level the power of her influence at me to force my compliance, but I felt the weight of truth in her words, nonetheless. A beam of sun that melted the stubborn frost and left everything soft and tender.

Mrs. Chapman was the best of us. The judgmental old shrew loved with a fierceness that even her foul temper could not touch, and losing her made me feel as if I was being unraveled from the inside out.

My head rested gently on the uninjured side of her chest, and I heard the uneven but stubborn beat of her heart. The Queen was right. She refused to let go.

"It is alright, Mrs. Chapman," I whispered, smoothing the escaped strands of iron-grey hair from her forehead. "We will be alright. You've prepared us well."

Hands settled on her arms, shoulders, head, and chest. I had not realized the others silently joined us, but they knelt, too, tears running freely down their cheeks. My housekeeper, my loyal friend, rested cocooned in the warmth of their love.

"We are here." I squeezed her hand and swallowed the lump in my throat. "You kept us all alive. It is okay to let go."

Her chest rose and fell.

Rose.

Fell.

Rose once more.

And when it fell, the sound rattled like a door closing for the last time. It did not rise again.

A profound stillness settled on the room, one where every breath caught and every heartbeat paused in expectation. Only the crackling of the fire broke the silence for a long time.

When the Queen began to sing, I was not aware at first that it was a voice I heard. It may as well have been wind through the branches of a bare tree or a wolf crying on the moors. But the sound of grief and longing—and hope—that rose from her throat turned into a melody at once timeless and familiar.

Other voices joined hers, and my grief rose to meet them in a keen that pulled my soul from my chest and displayed it to the waking world, high and cold and forlorn.

When the singing ended at last, the Queen stood and shook out her gauzy sleeves. The scent of honeysuckle and rain filled the air and lightened my heart.

"Grieve this night," she said. "What we must discuss will withstand the rightful mourning of a good woman. But first, you who are wounded, come to me."

Queen Titania laid her hands on my family one at a time. Bruises faded. Wounds closed, leaving bright scars behind. When her fingertips settled gently on my shoulder, the warmth that uncurled from her touch was sunlight after rain, a cup of cocoa on a winter night, and all of the tension I held melted under the comforting heat of it. I did not bother looking to see whether my injuries had healed, only turned to see Mrs. Chapman lying still and cold, unable to benefit from such warmth.

"Do not fret, Your Grace," Mr. Yates told Mama, putting one comforting hand on her shoulder. His eyes were soft, though he did not cry. "I will see to it she is rightly cared for. We will say our goodbyes properly tomorrow. You can rest."

"Thank you, Mr. Yates."

What more was there to say? Nothing, not even healed bodies, could make the loss of Mrs. Chapman more bearable. I wanted to hug Mama, to cry with Lia, to break every delicate object within reach, but my mind and body were too heavy and numb to agree on any course of action.

How did both of those truths manage to exist in the same person? I turned and dragged myself up the stairs, feeling as if everything good about me had been drained from my eyes and left in the tear stains on Mrs. Chapman's blouse.

We stumbled down the stairs in ones and twos and gathered in the hall by the fireplace. I huddled against Aris, feeling like a rain-soaked squirrel using a mighty tree as shelter against a storm. Lia and Mama were both pale-faced and frail-looking, and Mr. Yates hovered behind them with a tired, concerned expression.

Delilah and Fleur held hands, their eyes grave. Tony stood with a hand on Sam's shoulder, though the boy seemed not to notice. His arms were wrapped around his torso, shoulders raised as if to protect himself, and his eyes were downcast. I wanted to comfort him, but the betrayal I saw in his eyes when he realized I hadn't been able to save Sally made me doubt how welcome my comfort would be.

Matilda stood apart, watching all of us with large, haunted eyes. Alix and Cyrus stayed out of doors and were waiting for us when we trooped silently into the soggy morning. Silvery mist hung about the landscape, softening every line and cloaking the world in a dreamlike haze.

We entered the family cemetery one by one and gathered in a loose circle about the freshly churned dirt of Mrs. Chapman's grave. Dew clung to the clumps of earth like little gems.

I wanted to speak, to honor her, but what could be said about the woman who had shepherded and guarded us all without ever expecting a thank you?

"We loved her too little," Aris said. His arm tightened around me—less, I thought, for my comfort than for his. "And showed it far less than she deserved. Any good we do for this world is only because she kept us all alive long enough to accomplish it."

Who would keep us alive now? Who else had so little fear and so much confidence that she would bully even Mama? No one could ever replace the unique position she had carved for herself in our lives.

And she was gone.

Had I allowed Lia to stop Sally, Mrs. Chapman might still be alive. And how many other lives were lost—were currently being lost—due to my inability to make the hard choice?

This isn't your fault.

Aris's mental voice made me stiffen. *Stop reading my mind.*

I'm not. I'm reading your body—a book I am well-versed in.

Now is not the time for that sort of irreverence.

Times like this are the only time irreverence exists. Besides, self-pity is a terrible color on you, my darling. And I would rather have you angry with me than flagellating yourself.

I took a deep breath and exhaled slowly through my nose, letting my head tip back. The sky was a solid wall of endless grey, like a cloudy mirror arching above us.

Is that what I'm doing?

You think I do not know you well enough to see it? Punishing yourself will not bring her back. And it won't stop other people you love from following her.

He was right, of course. Action was the only remedy. And no one could stop me from blaming myself while I got down to business. I turned and left the cemetery, leaving my loved ones standing like stones in the mist.

"I expected you earlier," Queen Titania said as I strode into the hall. She sat on the couch near the fireplace with a cup of cider between her elegant hands. Several other faeries, utterly devoid of glamour, stood about her as if waiting for a command. But neither their unique forms nor the beauty of the Queen touched me. The grief was far too heavy.

"I'm sorry to disappoint you, Your Majesty."

Her smile was gentle. "I doubt that very much. I suspect you quite enjoy disappointing people merely to make a point."

She wasn't wrong, but I had no intention of letting her know that. "Why are you here, at Wainwright?"

She placed the cider on the side table and stood. "To share with you everything I know. And to make an offer. But I will do so once the rest of your party has returned."

My nostrils flared as I dragged in a calming breath. The woman was a queen, after all. And judging by the way both Lia and Aris treated her, she was trustworthy.

But I needed to know one crucial detail before I considered anything else she had to say. "Do you intend to fight the invasion?"

"You certainly have no fear of authority or power, do you?"

"It is one of my greatest failings." I sighed and tried to banish the growing anger from my chest. This situation, this pain, was not her fault. It was mine. But seeing her standing there, alive and so beautiful it made my heart ache, while the most worthy woman in the world was cold in the ground, made me irrationally angry.

Her eyes pinned me to the spot, seeming to sink into my body and soul like spring rain upon freshly tilled earth. Like she could feel and test the very depths of me. I squirmed and dropped my gaze.

"Yes," she said at last. "I plan to oppose Obyrron."

"That is not the same as fighting the invasion."

"I think you will find my aim accomplishes the same goals."

The front door swung open, and footsteps echoed through the hall. "We will see." I nodded my respect and took up position near the window.

Mama ordered refreshments. Trays of food and drink were carried to the table while we gathered and waited to hear the Queen. Either she had purposefully dimmed her influence through a glamour, or the grief protected us all at least a little.

"Your Grace," the Queen said once she deemed the moment ripe. "Before we continue, I humbly ask for guestright."

Mama cut a glance at Aris and me, but the look was brief. "You are most welcome as a guest in my home," she said.

The Queen gave a slight nod to respectfully acknowledge and accept the offer without implying thanks were owed. "In repayment of your kindness, I shall take the members of your household under my protection."

Lia and Aris both stiffened in shock, but neither made so much as a peep. I knew enough to recognize the significance of the statement but not the full implications.

Mama mirrored the Queen's nod.

"I have crossed the breach where the wall once stood to gain information and to find a staging ground through which to lay siege to the stronghold of my estranged husband. And to kill him if it can be done."

We stood for a long time in shock. Could Obyrron *be* killed? During our escape from his palace, he'd called everyone to his cause with merely the force of his will, and we followed him like hunting hounds.

"I would recruit all of you to the service of that goal," she said, "if you are willing."

A snort of disbelief escaped, and it took me a moment to realize I was the one scoffing. "I do not know if you are aware, Your Majesty, but we are the reason the wall fell."

"No," Alix said, speaking for the first time since escaping New London. "You are the reason it fell, Gwen."

"Minx," Cyrus warned, putting a hand on Alix's shoulder, but she ignored him.

"I love her as much as you do, but this needs to be said. We could have stopped the spell. I wanted to stop it. You made me believe we could. And when the opportunity presented itself, you pulled back."

"Sally would have been killed," I snarled.

Alix shook off Cyrus's hand and flung an arm toward the south. "And how many people died to save her life? How many people suffer now for the life of one girl? One," she said, holding up a single finger. "If it were you alone, I would not argue. If it were one of us, even then, I would have been willing. But you chose for all of *them*, too."

My stomach twisted into slimy knots of anger and grief, and Sam climbed to his feet, his fists curled tight at his side. Aris released a slow breath and left my side to stand near enough to Sam to stop him from doing anything he would regret later.

She is being unfair, he thought.

She isn't saying anything I haven't said to myself. And she is right. You know it.

His jaw worked, but he did not answer.

"You are right, Alix. I chose. And I would do it again. Of all the people trapped in New London, Sally is the only one I promised to protect."

She opened her mouth, but I cut her off. "Tell me you would not have sacrificed me and everyone else in that city to save Cyrus's life. To save Mercedes. Tell me truthfully, and I will concede your point."

Her golden eyes narrowed, her lips thinned, and her fingers curled tightly around the butts of her pistols. Alix was dangerous. Maybe one of the most dangerous creatures on the planet when all was said and done. But she was also smart and honest enough to admit to herself I was right.

She did not have to like it, though. She turned and stalked out of the house, snarling beneath her breath.

I lurched to follow, but Cyrus held out a hand. "Give her time. Let her temper cool. She'll return when she's ready."

The front door slammed, and I flinched. Would she come back? Had I pushed her too far past the bounds of our friendship? Our relationship hadn't always been easy, but it had always been honest. And now, more than ever, the people around me deserved the truth.

After a moment of silence, Queen Titania said, "My husband thinks honesty is a weakness. He enjoys taking our compulsion to be truthful and twisting it, turning it into a weapon of obfuscation and deceit. I do not share that opinion. He believes vulnerability is a weakness. I do not share that opinion, either. And I do not believe you are responsible for the collapse of the wall."

I rolled my shoulders to loosen the tension growing in my muscles. "Unfortunately, my friend was correct. We were in a position to end the spell. I choose to flee instead."

"To save the life of your ward?"

My jaw clenched, and I nodded.

Her green eyes softened. "But you did not create the spell, speak it, or power it."

"No. But my inaction allowed it to—"

"If anyone must be blamed," Lia said, standing and stepping away from Tony, "it is I. I was within the protection of the outer circle. If I chose, I could have destroyed the spell from the inside. Had I followed my training, I could have stopped the entire affair days beforehand. I chose not to. The burden of the decision is mine and mine alone."

"You are both so eager to bear the responsibility for this failure. But I must tell you that I have no intention of punishing either of you, even if I had the authority to do so."

We exchanged a surprised glance.

"No," the Queen continued. "Unfortunately, you will not assuage your consciences so easily. All must bear the burden of the power they were born with and live with the consequences of the decisions only they can make. And our intentions, for good or ill, cannot guarantee the wished-for outcomes, or protect us from the guilt of poor choices. Even summary punishment will not alleviate the sting of it, I am sorry to say.

"To be in command is to abide with guilt. I know of no relief, of no other path but one that leads to the destruction of your soul."

She said the words with such profound, timeless sadness that she could not be thinking of anyone but King Obyrron. Her estranged husband must have taken that point at some time in the distant path. Given what he had become, the warning made sense. But the good sense of her words did not make the truth any easier to accept.

Perhaps she and Aris were right. I was looking for punishment, retribution for allowing such a terrible thing to happen. But did I not deserve it? Didn't a failure of this magnitude deserve some recompense? Why should I be spared pain when so many people suffered for my choices?

I wrung my hands until they hurt, wishing I could argue with her but knowing instinctively she would not hear me. She seemed to sense the direction of my thoughts, and her attitude shifted, the welcoming posture and kind eyes melting into something far more businesslike. It reminded me of Mama.

"You carry guilt for your inaction, but you made the decision you knew without a doubt would save one life."

"But so many—"

"You do not know how many have been lost. How could you? Those are possibilities outside your knowledge or control. But you did what was in your power to save *one*. I think that makes us allies in the war to come." Then her gaze shifted from Lia and me to Mama. "You have done well by them, Gaeleth."

Every eye locked on Mama, some with confusion, others with apprehension. My stomach fluttered as it sometimes did before I was sick. Lia took my hand and squeezed. Her palm was damp with sweat.

This was it. The truth I'd been ignoring since the vampire first called me *changeling child*. The truth I wondered, even at this moment, whether I could forgive her for hiding from me.

Mama's blonde brows drew together. "Excuse me?"

Mr. Yates stepped from behind Mama to shield her with his body, squaring his shoulders. He flicked a quick, worried glance at me and Lia, then focused on the Queen, his chin high. He bowed with one hand on his chest. "Your praise is much appreciated, my queen."

All the air disappeared from the room.

"What?" Was that my voice? Had I spoken?

I thought I heard several voices ask the same question, but I could not place any of them through the dull ringing in my ears and the dizziness that made my stomach sick.

Mr. Yates fixed his eyes on Queen Titania and *shimmered*. His salt-and-pepper hair grew, deepened to the color of bitter chocolate, and curled around his ears. The lines of care on his face disappeared, filled and rounded. Eyes a familiar shade of brown stared from an unfamiliar face. A handsome, masculine version of *my* face.

Lia's grip tightened until my knuckles rubbed together beneath the pressure of her fingers, and my heart thumped painfully against my breastbone. *Holy bloody everlasting hell*, I was going to faint.

Mr. Yates hesitated, then turned as if a firing squad were behind him and faced Mama.

She took a shuddering breath, her beautiful face locked in horrified comprehension even as she shook her head. "No. No, it cannot be."

When he responded, it was not the professional, disinterested voice of Mr. Yates. It was raw and cracked, too desperate to be hopeful. "Hello, Evie."

Mama's eyes rolled back in her head, and she fainted.

31

Making Calf Eyes

LIA

G wen wasn't in the library. She wasn't in their old room or the tree they'd climbed so often as children. So Lia put on a sturdy pair of boots and snuck out of the house to find her sister.

She strode into Wainwright forest, letting the foliage close behind her, cutting her off from the red manor and the grieving hearts inside. With every step away from the oppressive atmosphere of the house, the heaviness in the pit of her stomach lightened.

Sweat trailed down her lower back despite the shade from the pines and broad-leafed maples and oaks. She pushed aside a low-hanging branch and ducked beneath the trailing vines of a blackberry bush, tucking her skirt tight against her leg to prevent it from catching on thorns.

Sunlight poured through breaks in the canopy in golden pillars and lit up the figure of Gwen sitting beneath a tree. Her sister leaned against the rough bark and let her head fall back as if staring at the sky, but her eyes were closed. In the bright sunlight, her brown hair was the color of melted dark chocolate.

"Before you come any further," Gwen said without opening her eyes, "tell me this. Did you know?"

"That our father was fae? Yes. That he was Mr. Yates? No."

Gwen sighed and opened her eyes. She plucked a stick from the ground and began peeling the bark away from the vulnerable green flesh beneath. "I supposed that from your reaction, but..."

"You had to know?"

She nodded. "I can only stomach so many people lying to me at once."

Lia picked her way into the small clearing where their lives had changed so many years ago. The place was frozen forever in her mind, a photograph that neither changed nor dulled. Looking at it now, as an adult, she saw how much of the place had been colored by the mind of her sixteen-year-old self.

The trees seemed smaller, less noble, and the boulder wasn't the last remnant of some mighty fortress that stood here long ago. It was merely a large stone. Magic and romance did not hide in the moss or the wild roses. She had brought those with her and imposed them on the place.

Now, it only appeared to be a break in the canopy where a few living things took advantage of the sunshine. Even the pixies who flitted now and then from under the leaves seemed no more remarkable than dragonflies. She should be grateful to have the fantasy stripped away from a place that saw the death of her girl-hood, so why did her heart hurt so much?

"I destroyed the circle," Gwen said.

Lia blinked and dragged her eyes away from the mossy bit of forest floor where, once upon a time, a faerie circle stood.

"When I couldn't find you," her sister continued. "I crushed every mushroom. I dug in the dirt until I broke my fingernails."

Lia lowered herself onto the forest floor next to her sister, tuck-ing her skirt beneath her. When she thought about that time in her life, her mind dragged her back to the pit, to the pain and her loneliness. Despite knowing better, there had always been a sense of resentment attached to those memories. Her family was safe and happy in the mortal realm while she suffered alone and far away.

But the mental image of Gwen on her hands and knees, scrab-bling in the dirt with tear tracks on her cheeks, broke the hold of those memories. Maybe they had all suffered in different ways. There should not have been a sense of peace or unity in that feeling. After all, who wants their loved ones to suffer?

But the knowledge still chipped away at the self-sufficient lone-liness that had become her shield, and little raw bits of the girl who once stood in this clearing peeked through the cracks, still too afraid—or too damaged—to venture forth.

She scooted toward Gwen until their shoulders and hips touched and cleared her throat. "Those mushrooms often grow where the wall is thin. Bits of magic seep through and infect the land around it. I don't know why mushrooms are so sensitive to it, but—" She shrugged. "Looks like there is truth in all those old wives' tales you loved to batter me with."

Gwen forced her thumbnail beneath a bit of bark and peeled it from the twig in a long strip. An unwilling smile teased one corner of her mouth. "I did warn you."

Lia laughed. "Now? You are going to rub it in *now*?"

"Can you think of a better time?"

"I suppose not. It's remarkable how one small thing can alter the course of a whole life. If I had listened to you then, none of this would have happened. Of course, you'd never have met Sam and Sally. Or Aris."

Her sister's face sobered. "Perhaps. Perhaps Sam and Sally would have been better off never having met me."

"That is foolishness, and you know it."

"Is it?"

"If you can't see that it is—"

Gwen peeled off a long strip of bark with a vicious tug, leaving a pale green scar on the wood. "The very fabric of reality has changed because of what I did, Lia. People are dead who would be alive, otherwise. And Sally and Sam are separated. Just like we were."

Lia clasped her hands in her lap and stared down at her joined fingers. She couldn't argue that point. Sam hadn't left his room in days, and he'd barely eaten. He refused to speak. She hadn't realized just how much life his presence brought to those around him until it was taken from them.

The smiling mischief of confident youth was gone. Lia remembered what it felt like to lose that. To realize the danger and uncertainty of the world were real and that, when all was said and done, one had to face it alone.

"We are going to get her back," Lia heard herself say and was surprised to find that she meant it. Gwen had never given up finding her, despite the years that passed in fruitless searching. True, their situation would be entirely different if she had not, but then again, who could predict the future?

"Percy said New London is inaccessible from the outside," Gwen said. "The city is a patchwork of building and forest, thanks to Matilda's wards. Trains are locked in place, and the few roads that were not damaged beyond repair are now controlled either by the occupying fae or the mortal resistance. Did you know they are already calling those areas Wards?"

Lia decided to follow Gwen's lead and find a dead bit of foliage to destroy. "New Londoners are nothing if not adaptable. Does Percy know how far the damage extends?"

"No. He knows no one who has ventured outside the city. Aris is planning a reconnaissance with Alix and Cyrus to see if they can map the extent of the intrusion."

They'd seen no sign of the broken wall this far north, but a telegram from York said that several major cities on the island had been completely overrun. Stretches of forest long since destroyed in favor of farming had, according to the report, reappeared overnight. Which meant starvation for hundreds, if not thousands, of people over the coming winter. How many acres of farmland had been destroyed?

Luckily, the sheep herds and boars could forage, farmland or not. And Queen Titania promised to influence the growth of wild edibles. But they would still have to start hunting and drying meat. Alix, Cyrus, and Aris would be indispensable for that. The idea of the three of them putting themselves in danger again made her stomach sick.

"Why not wait for the army to send dirigibles up?" she asked. "Surely, we will hear the reports once they do."

"Imagine how badly communication was damaged when forests popped up where telegraph lines used to be. Besides, Aris is faster than they are, and Alix is still feeling rather violent."

A shiver of fear made goosebumps rise on Lia's arm despite the warm sun. If the three of them left, the security of Wainwright would fall upon weaker shoulders. Lia was afraid hers were not up to the challenge. "They haven't spotted more monsters, have they?"

"Not since the last one," Gwen said and snapped the naked stick in half.

It had taken Aris, Alix, and Cyrus to bring down the crone after she killed one of the village children. Her burned flesh made the charhouse smell like sulphur. The putrid stink still had not dissipated from the walls, and the servants refused to enter the building or burn any more refuse there until it did.

Lia could not blame them. Burning the remains of monsters had stopped being part of the daily life of rural British citizens a hundred years ago. They had no stomach for it.

But more monsters would appear, and they both knew it. The island was in a state of shock, unable to respond to their current situation with anything approximating a unified effort, and that made it a perfect hunting ground for monsters. The Covenant was undoubtedly to blame for that.

Unfortunately, there was no hope of a quick solution, not from the Army or the more specialized elements of underground society, according to the Cutthroat King. After all, how does one remove an occupying force who quite literally controls the center of one's government?

"When are they leaving?" Lia asked.

"Soon."

She tugged the broken stick from Gwen's hand, threaded her fingers through her sister's, and squeezed. It was such a simple, familiar embrace to impart so much comfort, one they'd been practicing since the womb. That thought made the sick feeling return to her stomach.

"What are we going to do about Mama?" she asked.

Gwen tensed, her grip tightening for a moment. "What are we going to do about Mr—" She bit the words off and shook her head. "About our *father*?"

"I don't know. I don't know how to do any of this. I thought you might have dreamed up a plan."

"I'm done with making plans, I'm afraid. They never seem to work out the way I want them to. Aside from supper plans. And plans to sit alone in the woods and drown in self-pity. Those have been going rather swimmingly."

"To be fair," Lia said, laying her head on Gwen's shoulder. "Your non-plans haven't done much better."

Her sister snorted. "What about you, master strategist? Isn't all this what you do?"

Lia closed her eyes and sighed, humor fleeing. She rubbed the fingertips of her free hand together and watched little green flames dance along the edges of her skin. The magic had taken days to come back, and it was still weak. "I suppose so. I just...I haven't wanted to become *her* again."

The flames sputtered and died.

"You know," Gwen said, her voice soft. "As much as you do not like it, the General is part of you. I've seen you call on her in moments of need. She answers to you, Lia. Not the other way round."

A lump formed in her throat. "She's stronger than me. I don't want her to take over. Not when I finally feel as if becoming human again is a possibility."

Gwen scooted until they faced one another and tucked an escaped strand of blonde hair behind Lia's ear. The gesture held the casual intimacy of familiarity, as if the last painful years had never separated them, and they'd never become two new people who had to learn how to love one another again.

"Well," Gwen said, letting a small smile curl the corner of her mouth, though her eyes were serious. "We *aren't* humans. Are we?"\

Tony stood near the window the two of them had shared after her return from the Sunset Lands. He rested one heavy shoulder on the windowsill, and the evening light cut across his features, making the sturdy planes of his face stark, even under the softening influence of a short beard.

"Haven't had time to shave?" she asked, joining him by the window.

He tossed back the last swallow of whisky—his knuckles were still scabbed—and set the crystal glass on the table behind himself. "There doesn't seem much point now. Who am I trying to appear professional for? I shall have no more clients for the foreseeable future."

That was true. She hadn't had time to think about how their flight from New London would affect SPI. "I'm sorry. About your business, I mean. I know how hard you have fought for it."

He waved that off and turned back to staring out the window. "My mother and father are safe here, at least. I cannot ask for more than that."

Sunset light glowed off the tops of the trees of Wainwright forest and touched the hair of one large man with molten gold. Cyrus stood just outside the shadow of the trees with his arms folded, staring at Alix and Gwen. The women faced one another, their figures tense as they gestured sharply. Cyrus didn't intervene, though he sent sympathetic glances at Aris now and then.

"How long have they been fighting?" Lia asked.

"As long as it took me to finish my drink."

She shook her head. "Stubborn."

"Alix or Gwen?"

She snorted.

Their eyes met, and a little thrill skittered down Lia's spine. She'd never seen eyes like Tony's, a warm brown not quite as dark as Gwen's, flecked with gold and filled with honesty. He gave her a rueful smile that conceded her point.

"They'd better work it out," she said as Alix turned and strode into the forest. Cyrus kissed Gwen's cheek and followed his wife.

"They will. Gwen may be stubborn, but she's not stupid. Most of the time."

"She was stupid enough to walk away from you," Lia said, then bit her lips shut so hard she tasted blood. Oh god's breath, why had she said *that*?

Tony blinked at her. She would have called his expression bewildered, but Tony did not get bewildered.

"I'm sorry," she said and turned to the cabinet to pour herself a few fingers of whisky. "I should not have said that. Your relationship is none of my business."

A stream of amber liquid sloshed into the glass, and Tony cleared his throat. The noise was so uncomfortable it made her want to find a dark corner to hide in. She tossed back the first glass and poured herself another.

"I'll take one more if you're pouring," he said.

She accepted his glass without looking at him, poured three fingers, and handed it back. He raised a brow at the amount, shrugged, and took a healthy swallow.

Stupid, stupid, stupid.

"No need to apologize," he said in a voice raw from the liquor. "To be honest, it was for the best, though I would have disagreed a few months ago."

The statement piqued her interest and squashed a few of her misgivings far enough that she asked, "Why do you say that?"

Tony resumed his post at the window and stared down at the tree line. Aris and Gwen stood alone, deep in conversation. There was a bubble around them, and whenever they moved, it was like watching two magnets pushing and pulling one another.

"Those two just...fit," Tony said wistfully. "And if I am honest, though I care for Gwen with all my heart, it may be nice to love someone who did not constantly scare the very devil out of me."

Lia snorted and allowed herself a mouthful of the peaty scotch. It burned smoothly down her throat to sit warm in her chest, and the fumes climbed the back of her throat to tingle in her sinuses. Smoke and earth, it tasted like, and went straight to her head, loosening the bands of self-control she kept bolted around her emotions.

"Loving Gwen is something of an adventure," she admitted. "Unfortunately, she is infinitely lovable."

He gestured to the view out the window, where Aris was kissing her sister as if he wanted to pull her very essence into himself, his body curled around hers as she arched up to meet him. "I think Aris agrees with you."

"When I see the Raven with her," Lia said softly, "or even with the children, it makes me wonder what magic transformed him. He was terrifying."

Tony glanced at her from the corner of his eye. "Not magic. I think it may have been a bit more mundane than that."

"Love," she whispered.

Suppose love was capable of turning the Raven into Aris. Was it also capable of turning the General, with all of her coldness and cunning and cruelty, into regular, plain old Ophelia? Gwen had already worked a bit of her magic in that regard, but she was an unusual person, one who continued to push long after others would have given up.

"It is a great misfortune"—she swirled the liquid and swallowed a mouthful—"that we are not all as perfectly lovable as my sister."

Tony turned away from the window and stared at her in disbelief. "Perfectly lovable? Forgive me, but have you met your sister? She is stubborn, autocratic, and reckless; prone to drinking, swearing, and constantly involved in drama of the deadly sort. No one who knows her loves because she is perfect. We love her because of how much she cares. And, forgive me, but that is a quality the two of you share."

Lia swallowed another mouthful and closed her eyes, letting the liquor burn. "But she is charming, and I am...cold."

Tony set the heavy crystal glass on the side table with a *thunk*. When she opened her eyes, he stood before her, his eyes more gold than brown as he took her glass and held her hands between his. His skin was very warm, and his calluses were rough as he dragged his thumbs across the backs of her knuckles.

"Cold, Ophelia? God's breath, you have fire in your blood. Who could ever think you cold?"

She stifled a sound that may have been a laugh or a sob. From the first time she met this man, she'd felt safe speaking her mind to him, safer even than she felt with Gwen. And with liquor loosening up her tongue, words she'd kept inside for months came crashing through her lips.

"Everyone. Everyone does, Tony. I do not blame them. Haven't I made certain of it the past few months? I walk into a room, and people look at me as if I am about to start issuing orders. Moon and stars, you have seen how Delilah looks at me."

To her surprise, Tony smiled. "They are intimidated by you. I won't lie and say they do not have reasons. You are clever and confident, and you inherited Evelyn's—your mama's—presence. But their being intimidated isn't the same as you being intimidating. Or cold."

"It amounts to the same thing. At least, it feels the same way. And I do not know how to change it. I didn't used to be this way, this person. I was open and friendly and...but that girl is lost, and I do not know the way back to her."

A hot tear slipped down her cheek, but she did not want to pull her hands from Tony's to wipe it away, not while he held them and looked down on her with such warm compassion in his eyes.

"And it is worse now. The people I love need a general more than they need a sister or an aunt. But the more I embrace her, the farther I feel from the person I want to be. And I—" Her voice broke. "I don't want the violence anymore. The lies and...I don't want it."

Tony released one of her hands and cupped her cheek, running his calloused thumb across her cheekbone, wiping away the next tear that fell. "Sometimes the world needs us to be someone we do not like. And I will grant you, the world is an uncertain place right now. But that doesn't mean we must cut away the rest of ourselves.

The person you want to be isn't lost, Ophelia. I have seen the traces of her in you for months. From the very first time you came to New London because your sister said she needed you."

She shook her head. Gwen would lie to her and had. She did not believe Tony would, but for some reason, that did not make it easier to trust his words.

"If you don't believe me," he said, holding her face gingerly in both hands and forcing her to meet his eyes, "or if you're having trouble finding her, I am happy to help. I'm rather good at finding lost things."

The smile that pulled at her lips was a trembling, uncertain thing, but moon and stars, it felt good.

"Are you two going to kiss or just stand there making calf eyes at each other?"

Tony flinched and backed away as if he'd been burned. Color that had nothing to do with surprise heated Lia's cheeks.

Gwen stood in the doorway, her arms folded, that damned eyebrow raised as she surveyed them, her lips pursed. "No? Well, that is disappointing."

Without thinking, Lia snatched a throw pillow from the closest chair and hurled it at her sister's face. Gwen sidestepped. The pillow hit the doorjamb with a fluffy *pop*, and her sister glanced down at the unoffending cushion, then back up at Lia.

"Hmm." One corner of her mouth curled, and her brown eyes twinkled with mirth. "Very interesting. Please"—she held up both hands and backed out of the doorway—"go about your business. Do not let me interrupt."

Lia and Tony stared at the door, then at one another.

"I had better, ah—I'll just—" He jerked his thumb at the door. "Go check on Sam."

He retreated without looking back, and Lia snatched her half-empty whisky glass from the table, draining it in a single gulp.

32

Empty Chairs

GWEN AND LIA

Lia

They met for supper later that night. Lia let her eyes roam from one side of the formal table to the other, cataloging each member of their household as if counting which assets could be added to the list of potential weapons.

Sam, Matilda—who appeared to have regained her health—Delilah, Fleur, Queen Titania (whom no one could look at for long without having their brains scrambled), Alix, Cyrus, Mr. Ya—no, her *father*—Gwen, Aris, Mama, Tony, Mr. and Mrs. Hardwicke—who must be considered non-combatants—and one empty chair where Mrs. Chapman should have been.

Everyone glanced at the chair at least once before looking resolutely away. Whatever they decided tonight, her memory would weigh on them.

"We have all had time to grieve," Mama said from the head of the table. She stood straight, her chin raised and proud, and she carefully kept her gaze away from where their father sat at Queen Titania's side. "But now it is time to gather and form a council of war."

They'd known it was coming. As it related to faeries, their small, strange family was likely the most experienced and informed people on the island—those most able to affect the fae occupation. And still, hearing those words in Mama's voice made the situation feel more surreal even than watching trees burst from the cobblestones a week ago.

As they discussed sending a telegram to the army in Catterick, how to mobilize Wainwright village and the surrounding farms to keep everyone safe and fed, how best to put Delilah to work, and how the smithy might be altered to create a suitable workshop, Lia watched the faces of her companions.

Fear was there, certainly. But they were all resolute. And perhaps none more than Sam, who listened to every word with the intensity of a cat at a mouse hole.

"Can we count on the faeries who fought with us at the Second Trafalgar?" Delilah asked.

"It is hard to say," Tony answered. "They were all rather traumatized. All except Hilder, who is tough as old leather."

"I can ask Percy to reach out to her," Gwen said. "He is safe in the Undercroft under the King's protection. I'm certain the King will take in any faeries who need sanctuary."

"What about witches?" Matilda asked. "The Sisterhood may be the only coven, but there are hedge-witches and wise women and other practitioners in the city."

"I will ask him," Gwen replied, "but given what the Sisterhood has done, I cannot make any promises."

"Lean on him, then," Matilda said, raising her chin. "Those women will be indispensable in the coming months."

"How?" Delilah asked. "Human magic does not work on faeries."

Matilda glared at the dwarven woman, but Gwen jumped to her feet and burst out, "Oh, stone the crows!"

"I take exception to that," Aris muttered, but Gwen ignored him.

"Will the lies never end?" Gwen demanded of no one in particular. "Matilda, you...you...*damnation*! Is this your doing as well?" She glared at Queen Titania while gesturing at the chagrined witch.

Queen Titania smiled, but everyone else looked baffled.

"In fact," Titania glanced at their father, "Gaeleth is the one who suggested it."

Gwen's eyes narrowed as she stared at him. Neither of them had dared speak to him yet. In fact, no one had spoken to him, as far as Lia knew. However, her sister appeared to be on the verge of exploding.

"Would anyone mind explaining?" Delilah growled.

Gwen dragged her attention away from their father, who looked as if he wanted to speak but did not dare, and said, "Apparently, *he* sent a faerie to New London to start training witches. Witches who could ward the city effectively against faeries. Is that right, Matilda?"

Neither Matilda nor her father spoke. Gwen turned to Queen Titania, her cheeks red with anger, and spat, "That little plan backfired spectacularly, didn't it? All this time, I felt I bore the burden of this disaster while you were the one who created the scenario that allowed it to happen!"

The Queen ignored the acid in Gwen's tone, but their father did not. "Gwenevere," he warned, but Gwen spun on him like a striking snake.

"Do not speak so familiarly to me, *sir*. I do not associate with those who spend years lying to my face."

He stood and put his hands flat on the table. His voice was low and harsh. "I spent years watching over you. Keeping you safe. Lying for you. Shadowing you when you strode through the city at night. I will not apologize for making choices I believed would keep you and your mother safe. And yes, that includes ordering a faerie to teach New London's witches how to ward your home against faeries. I certainly will not be scolded by a child no more than—"

"You will watch your tone, Gael."

Mama's voice cut through the room, a sickle through dry wheat. Every eye turned toward her, their father's, most of all. Lia's heart hiccuped, then sped. Tony took her hand under the table.

"Evie—" Gael, her father, began, but Mama held up one hand, palm out, to cut him off.

"You have not earned the right to chastise our daughters. You abandoned them."

"I did not—"

"You abandoned *me*!"

Mama's cheeks were bright, her eyes hard as cut glass. "You left me alone with *him*. I had two girls to raise and no one in the world to turn to. Do you have any idea what it was like? To lie beneath him while he sweated and grunted, only to turn and suckle *your* babes? To see your eyes, your curls, your smile in their faces as they grew?"

There was no air in the room. For Mama to have broken the rules of propriety and spoken like that, of such a delicate and private matter and in front of others, she must have been more angry than Lia had ever seen her.

Their father's face went pale, the lines around his mouth deep. When he spoke, his voice was ragged. "You ask me if I know what it was like to be alone? To watch my daughters grow and never be able to speak to them, to touch them, or hold them when they cried? To watch another man raise them? Another man touch you? What sort of monster do you take me for?"

Whatever pity entered Mama's eyes as he spoke melted away at his last words. Her voice was cold and unforgiving as midwinter ice as she bit off each word. "The kind who made a lonely young woman fall in love with him before abandoning her. Do not speak to me. And stay away from *my* daughters. Or I will kill you."

She turned and left them all sitting in silence.

Gwen

When I found Sam, he was sitting on the lowest branch of the tree Lia and I used to climb as girls, one leg dangling as he kicked his foot.

"Eventful morning, wasn't it?" I asked, keeping my voice light though my guts were tied in knots.

He grunted and continued chewing the tender end of a blade of grass, staring into the distance as if I were not there. Perhaps there was nothing for it, then, but to say what I came to say and hope for the best.

"I know you are disappointed in me, Sam. I wish I could tell you this will be the only time and that I will never let you down again." I leaned against the tree and folded my arms across my chest. "But it won't. No matter how hard I try or how pure my intentions are, I will let you down. And, I hate to tell you this, but you will let people down, too. You'll do everything within your power, and sometimes you will still fail."

Sam stopped swinging his leg.

"I am sorry I couldn't bring Sally home. More sorry than I could ever express. You may not believe me now, and I understand that, but I love the two of you more than..." I had to stop and regain my composure. I never intended to be a mother, but I had become something like one by accident. These children, these young adults, had wormed their way into my life and heart, burrowing deeper than I could ever have anticipated. And I bore their pain, their anger and frustration, alongside my own.

"You cannot be more disappointed in me than I am."

Sam turned and swung down. He landed softly, facing me with his jaw clenched. How had the snub-nosed boy with jam on his cheeks become a young man so quickly?

"This isn't about you," he said, his tone angry, even defiant.

But Sam's anger often served as a mask for other emotions. And something in his eyes told me he was in pain far deeper than he was willing to show.

"Do you want to talk about it?" I offered.

"What good will that do? It won't bring them back."

"Sally—"

"Sally *left*! She left us all. She joined those damned witches, and do you know why? Do you?"

I flinched at the fury in his voice. I did know, but Sam clearly needed to say it.

"She did it for me. To protect *me*. She thinks power will let her save me any time something goes wrong. For some godforsaken reason, she thinks I'm worth sacrificing herself to that bloody coven. But I'll tell you a secret." He took a step toward me, his chest heaving. God's breath, when had he gotten so tall? "I'm not. Not for Sally. Not for Mrs. Chapman"—his voice broke over her name—"not for the old woman in the woods. God's breath, I can't even think about the way she died without feeling sick. I keep trying to stop people, but no one listens! And then they get to leave, and I'm stuck here without them. But you don't abandon people to protect them! You don't leave the people you love!"

My chest tightened until my ribcage crushed my heart. It slagging *hurt*. What did you say to someone who was discovering for the first time that nothing was more painful than being loved too much? Loved more than one believes they deserve?

"That's why my dad left," he said, his voice scarcely more than a whisper.

For a moment, I hesitated. I wanted to pull him into my arms, but he was taller than me now and fiercely independent. If I tried, he might find the gesture insulting and pull away. But the tremble in his voice and the unshed tears in his eyes called out to me with a force too powerful to ignore.

I grabbed his arms and shook him once. "You listen to me, Samuel Dawes. Sally did not abandon you. I have rarely seen anyone love someone else as much as your sister loves you. No, *listen to me*. I've had a few days to think over what happened, and I believe Sally planned the whole thing."

He stiffened.

"No, not like that. I think she knew there was no way for her to stop the spell. She knew Deborah would try to use her against us. So, she planned for us to discover as much as we could without breaking her oath. I think she's done everything in her power to help us as much as she can."

His chin trembled, and he spun the silver ring on his finger. "Then why won't she speak to me? Lady Gwen, why won't she talk to me?"

I refused to say, even to think, my greatest fear: that Sally hadn't survived the release of the power behind the spell. No. My girl was smarter than that. She would have planned for it.

Instead, I said, "We have to trust her. If she doesn't ring us, it likely means she cannot, or she thinks doing so will put us in danger. She'll reach out when she can. I know it. In the meantime, we simply have to trust her."

There was nothing simple about it. Mine was an insufficient answer, but I did not have a better one to give. His Adam's apple bobbed, and the vulnerability on his face hardened. He stepped out of my grasp and said, "I'm done trusting people."

I watched as he walked away, striding toward the house with his hands clenched at his sides.

Aris's hand swept slowly from my shoulder to my elbow and back again. My head rested on his chest, just above the jagged white scar the iron bullet left. Beneath my ear, his heart beat slow and steady.

"I don't know what to do," I admitted.

He sighed. "There may not be anything you can do, darling. Some lessons must be learned alone. And some people are more stubborn than others. Even if you had all the answers, do you think he would listen to them now?"

"No," I said and closed my eyes. "No, I doubt he would. So many, so very many things have gone wrong, and it feels as if there is nothing I can do to fix them. New London is in shambles. Crops have disappeared, and people may starve. Sam is hurting in ways I am completely unequipped to solve. Lia is adrift. Mama and my—my father are...I do not have words for that debacle, and no, before you ask"—I held up one hand—"I am not prepared to talk about it. The point is, everything is wrong, and I have no plan. No way to fix it."

Aris sat up, dislodging me, and scooted backward to rest his back against the headboard. The blanket fell to his hips, leaving the carved muscles of his torso on display, but my eyes locked on the scar. The sick feeling that always invaded my gut when I thought about how close I'd come to losing him made my jaw clench.

Aris brushed the curls off my forehead and asked, "Who appointed you the fixer of every problem?"

I rolled my eyes. "If I don't, who will?"

"Despite what your ego may claim, you are not god, Gwen. You cannot, in fact, solve everyone's problems."

"Oh, so I'm arrogant now, am I?"

He grinned. "That is one of the things I love about you, just so we're clear."

"How charming," I said, but the words dripped with acid.

"You are as clever as anyone I've ever known. But, did you ever think that by trying to fix everyone's problems, you're robbing them of the chance to become the hero of their own stories?"

I shut my mouth and glared at him. "What, exactly, are you saying?"

"I'm saying that you attack every problem as if it is your personal responsibility. It is quite endearing in a way. You care so damned much. But you've also surrounded yourself with an incredible group of highly talented and capable people."

"I know that. Do you think anyone appreciates them more than I?"

"Then why do you assume they are not as capable as you are of solving their own problems? Of coming up with solutions to problems you cannot, maybe should not, solve?"

I opened my mouth, then closed it and exhaled hard through my nose.

One black brow rose, and the corner of his mouth curled in a mocking grin. "Afraid to share the spotlight, darling?"

No, I wanted to say. *I'm afraid of how helpless I will feel when I have to watch them hurt, watch them struggle, and know that I cannot fix it. I want to be doing something, anything, to make it better, even if I fail.*

His expression softened as if he was able to read my thoughts, those dark eyes shining in the dim candlelight. He settled me astride his hips and brushed his fingers over my features, tracing my cheekbones, nose, the ridges of my brows, and my jawline as if he were memorizing my features or molding them.

"Some problems are too big for one person, my love. Your head is smart enough to know that. Now, we must convince your heart."

I held his forearms and pressed my cheek against his palm, closing my eyes. For so long, I had been the one in control, the one guiding the metaphorical ship. It certainly hadn't done us any favors. Perhaps it was time to do more than love my friends and family.

Maybe it was time to take the advice I'd tried to give to Sam and trust them, too. Aris traced the pad of his thumb across my lips in a tender caress that stole my breath.

I felt him stir beneath me and didn't bother trying to conceal a smile. "Already?"

"You can hardly be surprised. Not with every luscious bit of you on display."

I snorted. "Something is wrong with your eyes."

"My eyes are far better than yours, and that makes them more trustworthy. But you know that, so I must assume you are merely fishing for compliments." His hands outlined my shoulders and down my back, curved around my waist, and slid up my ribcage. His thumbs met on my breastbone, long fingers wrapping around my chest as he considered me. "I suppose it is possible you do not know how delectable you are." He placed a shudder-inducing kiss between my collarbones. "But I doubt it."

"I am as bruised and scabbed as an apple that hit every branch when it fell from the tree," I said but slid my fingers through his hair to hold him close.

He trailed kisses across my chest, making my skin tingle and my heart leap as his grip tightened. The whole world, every problem and worry, faded when I was in his arms.

"You," I breathed as he bent to my breast, "are the most powerful drug I have ever had the pleasure of trying."

His laughter against my skin sent a rush of goosebumps down my arms. And when he flexed his hips, I gasped, my hands flying to his shoulders to steady myself.

"Fucking hell, Gwen," he growled as he slid into me. "Making love to you is like coming home."

I watched his pupils dilate, watched sweat bead on his upper lip, felt the pressure of his fingers digging into my hips, the sharp pain as he bit the tender spot where my neck met my shoulder, and the slick, sliding glory of him inside me.

For a while, only we two existed. There was no invasion, no lost loved ones or surprise fathers, no hurting sister, or aching pain I could not fix or solve; nothing but Aris and pleasure that filled my entire world.

The escape of his touch was like a fine wine, and I drank every drop of euphoria until I was drunk enough to pass out.

Lady Gwen?

I jolted at the sound of Sally's voice and sat up so fast my head spun.

"Gwen?" Aris asked. His voice was sleep-roughed, one hand resting on my knee as he turned to light the dwarven lamp near the bed.

Sally? I thought, my heart racing half from being wakened so unexpectedly and half from the fear I'd only dreamed her voice.

I can't say much. I'm so sorry. I love you. Tell Sam. Tell him I'm going to fix this. I'm going to fix everything.

Where are you? Are you alright?

No answer.

Sally!?

"Gwen, are you well? Did you have a nightmare?"

I swallowed back tears and pressed my palms against my chest as if pressure could stop my heart from breaking. "Something like that."

THE END

33

Acknowledgments

The unsung heroes who helped this book come to life and kept me sane during the writing process:

Abbie, you will never know how much I appreciate you every time I open a book you've edited. The way you know (and forgive) my bad habits and polish my imperfections will never cease to amaze me.

Jamie and Jen, my lovely Legendary Subscribers whose support has been absolutely incredible: thank you doesn't cover it, but it still needs to be said. So, thank you.

Elizabeth and Monique, if you don't know how much I appreciate you and all of your help and support, then I deserve to be dragged over hot coals. You're amazing.

Ella, thank you for taking time out of your schedule to help me. It helped so damn much. I appreciate you.

Elena, your iconic book covers have done more for promoting my books than anything I could have done. They are incredible. Thank you for your artistry.

34

Also By

Other titles by this author include

SERIES: The Gwen St. James Affair

- Vanished

- Moonstruck

- Spellbound

- Bedeviled

- Forsaken

Companion novels in The Gwen St. James Affair

- Blood and Silver

- The Cutthroat King

SERIES: The Eververse Chronicles

The Founding Trilogy

- **The Laws of Founding**

- **The Founding Lie**

- **The Founding War**